I0590100

EVERLY CLAIRE

Never Lost: The Unchained Book Three

Cover Designer: Qamber Designs
Editor: Emily A. Lawrence
Proofreader: Brianne Matheny

Copyright © 2025 by Everly Claire
All rights reserved.
No part of this book may be reproduced, distributed, or transmitted in any form, including photocopying, recording, or other electronic or mechanical methods — except in the case of brief quotations in critical articles or reviews — without the written permission of the publisher. For permission requests, contact info@everlyclaire.com.
All names, characters, and incidents portrayed in this book are fictional. No identification with actual persons living or deceased, places, or things is intended.
All brand and product names used in this book are trademarks of their respective holders.
Published by: Hudson & Hawk Group
New York | Miami | Road Town | Hamilton
EverlyClaire.com

For Nigel. I'll be home soon.

WARNING

This series is set in a dark fictional world and contains potentially disturbing and triggering themes. For a list of potential triggers in this and future books in the series, scan the QR code below or visit everlyclaire.com/triggers.

Please look after your mental health.

PREVIOUSLY

This book is a continuation of *Never Broken (The Unchained #1)* and *Never Bound, (The Unchained #2)*. They must be read first and are available on Kindle Unlimited. Scan the QR code or visit books2read.com/u/3yJBwV.

At the end of *Never Bound,* our two main characters were ripped apart after our MMC kills(?) Louisa's jealous classmate and suitor, Corey, in defense of Louisa. Our MMC was almost sold to a mine, but billionaire Max Langer, impressed with his genius, offered to "borrow" him from Louisa's father as a technical consultant in exchange for paying off Corey's family to avoid a public scandal. Langer was also suspected of holding our MMC's sister, Maeve, captive, but when asked, claimed to know nothing about her.

Langer seemed to have an unusually close relationship with Resi, his head researcher for Project White Cedar, the code name for his top secret project to "disrupt" slavery. She had originally claimed to be leading a slave rebellion, but was revealed to be a sexual predator. When our MMC started asking questions about Maeve, Resi assaulted and threatened him.

He also met Lemaya, a "research assistant" and abandoned slave who was Maeve's friend, who gave him a tour of Resi's lab. There, he overheard Max anxiously questioning Resi about the state of the research. Resi angrily told him about a prowler near the lab, and said she planned to "take care of the problem." Our MMC feared she was referring to Louisa, whom he knew continued to investigate Resi with the help of her professor, Erica Muller, and Erica's network of anti-slavery activists.

Louisa, meanwhile, was forbidden from searching for our MMC, and and had only his cryptic last message, "When You Are Old," for comfort. When Erica suddenly went silent, Louisa went to check on her at her house near campus. There, she was stunned to find an injured Maeve herself waiting there instead ...

1

This should have been his moment. Not mine.

It should have been *him*, not me, standing here while Maeve—*his* Maeve—curled up in a hammock, looking at me with eyes just like his, asking for him. I wanted to grab my phone, to call him, to fix the fact that *he* was now the one missing. But I couldn't. Because I had no idea where he was.

And I had no idea how to tell her.

So I didn't. For now, I just let her talk. I think she needed it.

"*After they said they would free us, we all stopped working,*" Maeve said in French. "*The riding school closed; they'd gone bankrupt. But none of us had the official papers, so we also couldn't leave. And yet they wouldn't feed us. One woman had an infected wound from where she'd been bitten by a horse, and they wouldn't take her to a doctor. They said they didn't have to. We were all terrified, thinking they'd lied and couldn't afford to buy our freedom; that we'd either be stuck there, starving, or have to leave and risk being caught and enslaved again. That's when I met her.*"

"*Resi,*" I prompted.

Maeve nodded, still curled fetally in the hammock in a pair of tiny shorts and a tank top, looking impossibly young with her short, baby-fine blond haircut. But as skinny and battered as her body was, she was the furthest thing from broken. She spoke calmly, without stammering. And even when she averted her fiery eyes, it only took seconds for her to flick them back boldly in a way that was so familiar it made me shake.

It had become clear, after Maeve had appeared in the doorway of their house like a ghost, that she knew no further English other than the few phrases she'd clearly practiced ahead of time—what she'd already said, plus "yes," "no," "I don't know," and, of course, "I don't speak English."

Not to mention, she kept asking about her brother, and I hadn't been able to respond—and wouldn't even if I could. The last thing I wanted to be responsible for was telling Maeve that *he* was now as missing as she herself had just been.

And where the hell was Erica? Not to mention, where was *he*? Not just so he could help me communicate, but so the siblings could have the reunion they deserved after seven fucking years apart. Instead, this poor, exhausted, injured, bewildered girl—who longed only to see the brother who'd promised to come for her—was stuck with me. Useless, hopeless, helpless me, who didn't even know how to speak—

"*Français?*"

I hadn't looked too closely into Maeve's all-too-familiar amber-gold eyes right away, for fear I'd be crushed under the weight, unable to continue the conversation. But as they'd lit up like a sunburst—and a smile had crept over the pale face with its sprinkling of freckles—I couldn't help but admire them. In joy, they were beautiful—every bit as beautiful as I remembered.

"*Ouais!*"

Of course. Maeve's brother didn't speak three languages

because he was gifted. He spoke *four* languages because he was gifted. But Maeve spoke three languages because she was from Luxembourg, as I knew thanks to him that almost everyone there did.

I pulled over one of the lounge chairs up close to the hammock and leaned in. My own French was proper, evenly paced, schoolgirlish. Maeve's French, however, was rapid and spoken in what I soon realized was a heavy Luxembourgish accent, which meant I still missed about two-thirds of what she was saying.

"*Répètes-toi, s'il te plaît? Lentement*[1]." I gave her an apologetic smile, and this way, we haltingly continued. I hadn't wanted to push her too far or too much, nor insist she explain what exactly she'd been through.

But now, as she continued, Maeve didn't hold back—much.

"*A friend, another slave I knew who lived in town, introduced us. It happens all the time, Resi said. Owners lie. They say they're going to free you and then they don't. But they don't want you anymore, so they just let you starve.*"

"*She wasn't wrong.*" Thanks to Erica, I knew this happened. I knew slaves had *died* because of it. "*But wait. Then that meant—*"

The realization made my stomach flip.

"*You went with her. By choice.*"

Maeve nodded, shame clouding her eyes. "*I didn't tell my brother that. I was embarrassed.*

It was... okay, at first," she continued in French. "*The house was beautiful, and we had nice clothes and food. For the first time in my life, I didn't even have any real work to do. I didn't even know what to do with myself. Most of us didn't go outside—we were afraid to, anyway, because we might be caught and sent back. Eventually,*

---

1. "Repeat yourself, please. Slowly."

she took some of them to the lab. She said she needed our help to free us all."

"Did they come back?"

She shook her head.

"She told us she was experimenting with something that would make it so we would never have to worry about being enslaved again. That it would only take another month or so and then we'd all be free to go, without worrying about being caught, and that we'd have money, too, and education. A brand-new life. Most of them believed her and went with her willingly to the lab. But some didn't come back, and it was taking longer than she said it would—and then we who were left started asking more and more questions that she wouldn't answer—and then she started getting scared—and locked the doors—and started making us—and then finally, finally, she took me to the lab." She closed her eyes delicately.

Shit. I'd pushed her too far.

"Lie down, Maeve," I said. "Relax. You don't have to tell me anything before you're ready." I got up to refill the glass of water she had been drinking from and rummaged around for some food—cheese, crackers, granola bars. I didn't even know if Maeve was hungry, but it felt useful, for some reason. On the way in, I noticed the blood soaking through her bandage. I was no doctor yet, not even close, but I knew enough to know she'd need that changed soon.

Maeve closed her eyes, and her tiny form curled in on itself. *"I just—I made up stories."* She closed her eyes as if this were the one nice memory she'd kept—as if she'd maybe even substituted stories for reality, as she'd done long ago, much to the annoyance of her brother. *"And I told them I had a brother who was coming for me. That he'd help us. That he'd help them."*

"The other girls, you mean?"

"No," she said, glancing down at her bandage.

And for the first time, I looked, too, at the thick gauze

wrapped around Maeve's arm and hand, so tightly that from a distance it would have been almost impossible to tell what was there—and what was missing.

I recoiled in horror, turning my head away and covering my mouth.

Maeve looked, tears rolling down from her beautiful eyes. *"Not all of them needed help. Just the ones like me. The ones who found out the truth."*

—•—

When the door finally opened around four, Maeve had passed out in the hammock again, under a furry white blanket I had draped over her to keep her from the desert's evening chill. Soon after, I had fallen asleep too on the lounge chair, a book of Irish poetry over my face. I was grateful that Maeve had drifted off first because trying to explain that tears were streaming down my cheeks because I *thought* I'd just discovered a love message from her older brother would be too embarrassing for words.

I bolted upright at the noise but collapsed back down in relief a second later. It was Erica and Milagros.

I watched from the doorway as my professor dragged herself through the door, more of a disheveled whirlwind than usual, and collapsed on the densely pillowed sofa. Millie the cat bounded over, meowing, and Erica stroked her tail absently. Milagros, meanwhile, her aquamarine hair spiked up high and wearing a black tank top with a rather rude message printed on it, went to the kitchen to feed the cat and open a bottle of Txakoli. She noticed me standing in the doorway of the kitchen and didn't even flinch, as if she'd somehow expected me to be there.

"How is she?"

"Asleep. Where—"

"An eight-hour meeting with the Board of Regents," called Milagros, with predictable vitriol in her voice. "That's the answer to the question you were about to ask."

"But why did you cancel your office hours? Don't they know that you—"

"Louisa, I don't have access to my office or my email." She sighed. "I've been suspended from teaching."

"What?" I exclaimed, clapping a hand over my mouth so as not to wake Maeve.

"Somehow, someone found out what my associates were doing to help get Maeve out of the house, traced it back to me, and reported it to the board."

"What did they do?"

"They used one of our med students' credentials to schedule an ambulance," she said. "Claimed Maeve had a specialist appointment off-site on orders from Max Langer, which Resi didn't contest. The driver was one of ours. Unfortunately, doing that for three other girls proved unfeasible, and we didn't have time to come up with a different plan for them. And now," she added forlornly, "if I get caught doing anything else like this"—she gestured around the room—"I'll be fired. And Milagros will be expelled. I have it all in writing." She whipped a piece of paper out of her leather satchel and tossed it limply on the coffee table. "And my other associates can't, either, because that will be linked back to me, too."

"What? Why now?" My head spun with the implications. "I thought they already knew you—"

"Some of them did. One of the most powerful guys on the board was anti-slavery, and he was my biggest advocate—defended me through countless complaints and threats. But he resigned this month—abruptly." She sank further into the pillows in uncharacteristic despair. "I've been thrown to the wolves."

I winced. "So what do we do now?"

"I didn't get that far with Maeve—you probably did better communicating with her than I did—but from the sound of it, Resi's given up on mere psychological manipulation and has moved on to false imprisonment. It sounds like there is at least one, maybe two other girls locked up in there. And before we move any further, deal with Maeve's legal situation, or anything else, we've got to do something about that." She nodded toward the mutilated girl in the hammock. "Maeve was circumspect about it, but that's not the worst I'm afraid they might be facing from Resi."

I gasped. "But why now? Why is she locking them up now, when she wasn't before?"

"Something spooked Resi. Spooked her a lot, I'd say."

"What?"

"Two theories. One, I suspect Langer has a deadline looming with his investors. He's worried that Resi isn't delivering. He's putting her in a squeeze, and she's desperate. Two, she might have found out one of the girls was freeborn—or Langer might have. I don't know how, or how or why the girl ended up there, but it means she's now committed a crime that the police might actually care about. The good news is, if we can get to that girl, Alma, whoever she is, she can testify in court about what she witnessed."

Another theory was brewing inside my head. "Do you think Langer even knows? Maeve never met him, from the sound of it."

Erica looked at me critically. "Anything's possible, I suppose."

"So... then can we call the police?"

Erica shook her head. "The police will help the freeborn girl. For the others, they'll do the exact opposite."

"Then I'll do it," I said immediately. I didn't even have to think. "I'll go. Maeve can show me where."

I hadn't realized Maeve was awake until she spoke in Luxembourgish. She must have been listening, curled up in the hammock, silent as a shadow while still taking in every single thing we were saying.

She'd had plenty of practice at that.

Now I whipped out the translation app on my phone, but she repeated what she'd said in French before I had the chance.

"I know exactly where to go in the house."

"But how?" I asked, also in French, as Erica and Milagros watched us with concern, not daring to interrupt to ask for a translation. *"I thought you weren't allowed to leave the room."*

"My friend told me all about it," she replied. *"She went everywhere. Resi liked her best. She told her everything. She let her go everywhere."*

"Friend?" I asked warily. *"What friend?"*

This time, Maeve smiled. "Lemaya."

HIM

That evening, I got a call from one of the assistants, telling me to go down to the parking lot. I did, just as a silver Porsche convertible—gleaming so bright in the evening sunlight that it hurt my eyes—sped from around the corner and up the circular drive. The arrival of the car surprised me. The identity of the driver did not.

I just stood there, staring at the model, blinking. My mouth was probably hanging open, but I didn't care.

"Is that—"

Langer raised his dark sunglasses and nodded. "It's a nice

day and I've had my eye on this one for a while, so I got it for a twenty-four-hour test drive," he explained. "Get in."

I had no specific reason to object other than spite, and my feelings of spite toward Langer, at this point, weren't nearly as strong as the almost supernatural draw I was feeling toward this car. My hands were practically shaking as I removed my suit jacket and shoved it in the minimal space behind the two black leather seats, rolling up the sleeves of my shirt. I wasn't exactly nostalgic for my old castoff clothes, but one thing was certain: in the desert heat, keeping cool in jackets and dress shirts—no matter how awesome they looked—was a lost cause.

Of course it also occurred to me right away that this might be an opportunity to get answers. I had used the rest of my time at work that week to look for them, firing up the tablet I'd left charging, and experimenting to see which of the passwords worked where. Some of them didn't work, which I'd expected. Some of them revealed files behind additional security that I'd need to try to hack into. And some unlocked some files so huge that it would take days to make any sense of them. Many appeared to be financial. Resi had wanted access to the books and been shut down, so it wouldn't surprise me if she—and Corey—had been working on finding another way in. Unfortunately—though calculus had come easily—finance, for someone who had never had any money, had been easy not to waste time on trying to understand. So before I got much further, I had to go to school.

Good thing I'd always wanted to go to school.

As for Lemaya, by the time I got back from my spying expedition, she was gone, and I hadn't seen her all week. Of course Resi ordering her to be imprisoned, tortured, and/or killed because she'd allowed me to sneak away from the tour wasn't the only possibility, but it was definitely a possibility.

Fucking hell, was there any woman I'd ever interacted with whose life I didn't end up ruining?

I sank into the seat, hoping Langer couldn't tell that I'd never been in a convertible before. Langer didn't say anything as he slammed on the gas pedal and I savored the sound that beautiful German engineering made as it roared to life. Another thing I could get used to but shouldn't. And then, as suddenly as a pair of screeching tires, I stopped. I wasn't going on any joyrides. Not today. "Max, wait. I—" I bit my lip.

"She's fine."

"What?"

"Keith's daughter. Curly Sue. Loulou. That's what he calls her, anyway. I forgot what the hell her real name is." He glanced over.

"Louisa," I said faintly, burying my head in my hand and sinking into the soft leather seat as he pulled out onto the highway at top speed. I kept my eyes on the pavement melting away beneath the tires as saguaros flew by against the backdrop of the ever-distant mountains. "How do you know?"

"I talked to him this afternoon. I know you think I'm lying because you always do, but I'll even show you the message he sent me. He mentions her by name."

"No," I said weakly. "I don't need to see it."

So Resi's claws hadn't reached Louisa. Yet. I felt the tight knot of dread in my chest that had been my companion since that afternoon fade by a few degrees. Maybe for a few hours, I could have only two people to worry about instead of three.

"And I'll ask about her again tomorrow."

"He'll get suspicious," I muttered, hating to admit that Langer was again offering the worst thing in the world he could possibly offer to someone who had long ago vowed to kill him: kindness.

"No, he won't. Besides, I see you pining over her every damn day like the lovesick teenager you are while failing to offer any better ideas. And, anyway, I'm good at this shit."

"What, deception and subterfuge? Yeah. I noticed."

Langer smirked. "I'd tell you to look in the mirror, but you wouldn't recognize yourself in those clothes."

Funny guy.

"Anyway, a less self-aware man would expect a thank you." Before I could scoff in outrage at this prospect, Langer continued, "But I don't. Because as much as I've tried to create the illusion that you're here by choice, you're not, and to expect you to be grateful for that would make me as delusional as Keith. But I will take this opportunity to point out that you've yet to successfully catch me in a single actual lie. To you, anyway."

"You're wrong."

Langer whipped his head around so fast I was surprised the convertible didn't go flying off the road.

"You keep telling me my sister was never here, but you're wrong."

Eyes on the road again, Langer paused before answering. "I know."

Now it was my turn to whip my head around. "What the fuck, Max? You knew and you didn't tell me?"

"I didn't know until today, and I'm telling you now," he said irritably. "Anyway, it doesn't matter anymore because she's gone. She left. Okay?"

Even the roar of the engine seemed to quiet as I sat silently suspended in a wind tunnel of horror. "Gone? When? Where?"

"I don't know."

"You don't know? Do you know what this means? What I had to go through to get—" I groaned and ran both hands through my hair in frustration, unable to even form sentences. I was back to square one. Below square one.

"I fucked up, okay? I'm sorry. Resi lied."

"No shit, she lied, and thanks to you, now my sister could be anywhere." For the first time, I twisted in the seat, turning my entire body toward Langer. "Fucking hell, Max, how tightly does this woman have you by the balls? Why do you believe everything she tells you unquestioningly? You're fucking her, aren't you? Because that's the only explanation I can think of that makes the least bit of sense."

"I'm not fucking her."

"Then what? What is this all-important, all-consuming history between the two of you that nothing, not even the truth, can come between?"

Wordlessly, Langer swung a hard right down a dirt side road, one that seemed to lead clear out into the middle of the desert, and I had a feeling, not for the first time recently, that I'd just made a huge mistake.

"She's my sister."

2

I almost choked, or maybe it was the road dust. "You mean, the one your father—"

Langer nodded.

I had thought—even at the time—that it was one of the few things Max had said during his impromptu visit that couldn't easily be dismissed as utter bullshit. And that's why it had stuck. "But you said—"

"When I told you I didn't know about her," Langer clarified, "I meant I didn't know she was my sister. I did know *her*. But I thought she was just another slave girl, the daughter of one of our housemaids. I had no clue we were half-siblings, and neither did she. Not until years later."

As the mountains drew closer, my pulse sped up. Even more so when Langer skidded the Porsche into the driveway of a house—a sprawling, ultramodern specimen of desert architecture, one so well-suited to the land that I hadn't even noticed it was there until just before we pulled into the drive. And when I slid out of the car and reluctantly followed Langer up to the door, I saw why—mirrors, set into the roof so as to reflect the nearby mountains. Actually, they were more than *nearby*. After a month in the desert, I'd finally made it close enough to actually touch them.

"Where are we?" I asked warily, trying not to look too awestruck as I craned my head around at the landscape.

"My *house*," Langer said witheringly. "Where the fuck else would we be?"

"But—oh." Of course he owned two homes. It would be weirder if he *didn't*.

"You should see the one in Sedona. The ex-wife got that, though. Anyway, don't get comfortable. We're going on a little walk."

I stood rooted to the spot, just looking at him.

"And don't worry. If I were planning to murder you, do you think I'd do it in my own goddamn backyard, of all places?"

"I guess not." With no choice, I followed Langer as he started down a well-worn path winding through the extensive landscaping—complete with javelina fence—and up a well-groomed, stone-lined path into the mountains, one lined with mesquite, barrel cactus, and ocotillo.

"Anyway, starting when I was ten and she was maybe eight, we got close. Not in *that* way," he clarified as we went, noticing the look that must have been on my face. "I told you the kind of shit I had to take from my father growing up. But what I didn't mention is that he gave it to *her* ten times worse. And so we bonded over that, but as soon as he *realized* we'd gotten close, the bastard started using *that* against us. He started making me watch, and vice versa. And he let his friends—and some of the other slaves—give her some shit he *didn't* give me. And he made me watch that, too. He was the most possessive man I've ever known. He couldn't stand that anyone, in any way—even his own legitimate son—would dare to get between him and his property. And he was trying to tear us apart. But ironically, the more he hurt us, the more we needed each other."

"And did he—with her?" I asked, my voice faint.

"If he did, I didn't see it. And she would never tell me."

I left that alone. Look, it wasn't as if I hadn't heard of—and seen—some of the most depraved and horrifying shit imaginable, from a very young age. As a slave, you did. And you took it for granted. But.

"Anyway, what happened must be an old story to you. In our spare time, I taught her everything I learned in school, starting with the ABCs. In a matter of months, that evolved into reading entire novels, then algebra, then chemistry, then calculus. Fuck, I had to stop her from trying to do my homework for me on top of her other chores. That was one thing she inherited from my father, who could have done so much fucking good in the world had he not chosen the opposite. Most of all, just knowing I'd see her smile made coming home almost bearable. And it didn't take long before I was promising her that I'd have my own money someday. If I didn't get any of my dad's, I'd make my own. And I'd get her out of there and away from *him*. But my mother didn't feel the same about her as I did, for obvious reasons, and I was young enough that when my mother left, I had no choice but to go. We found ways to keep in touch, but every time we spoke, I saw how all of her messages grew more and more bitter, more spiteful, more twisted, as my father continued to hurt her. And I got angry because I was worse than useless. And as soon as I could, I came back, and you know the story after that, but it couldn't make up for what she went through. Nothing could. And I blamed myself, of course."

Sounded familiar. "And you've been trying to atone for it ever since."

Langer nodded, clearly glad I had said it instead of him. All the while, the elevation was rising as we climbed. The path wasn't particularly steep, and the sun was already low in the sky, so it wasn't as taxing a walk as I had been expecting, especially because my physical condition was still far from ideal, even with the hourly ibuprofen I'd been popping.

Langer took an abrupt turn down a side path. I squinted ahead, and a huge sandstone butte loomed in the distance, jutting from the otherwise flat landscape. As we cautiously emerged from the shadows of the mesquite trees, I noticed an intricate mosaic of windows and a wide doorway, intricately carved into the rock face.

"In the old days, they used to call this a folly," he explained.

"What do you call it?"

"The place I built to hide from my wife."

Langer opened the door. Through the doors to the wrap-around balcony, I could see the sand stretching for miles and the horizon already pink from the sun. Inside, there was a surprising amount of living space—and a full bar, which was of course where Langer went first, opening a massive, state-of-the-art wine refrigerator.

"I don't have anything from Luxembourg this time. How about Germany?"

He got out glasses and a bottle of dry Riesling and poured two glasses, prompting more than a little déjà vu of our impromptu meeting weeks ago.

"Prost," he said and led me out to the verandah, decorated with massive potted cactuses and rustic terracotta furniture, faced due west, and already enveloped in the longest, most crimson sunset I had ever seen.

Was every night like this out here?

We both leaned on the stone railing.

"Long story short, I made up for lost time. I put her through school and got her her first job. I did everything I could to give her everything she deserved. But despite what you think, I was never under any illusions about her. I've known for a long time that she's... off. Sexually, sometimes it seems like she doesn't have any boundaries. Like something's broken in her. And I understand why, obviously. But keeping her out of trouble has been... a challenge over the years."

He took a thoughtful sip of wine, staring at the deep-red sky. "My wife left me over it. Well, officially, it was Resi's fault. But unofficially, it was because I was an arrogant, selfish, workaholic rat-bastard of a husband."

"Really? You?" I remarked, swirling my wine, prompting a chuckle from Langer. "I know about the bailout in Belgium," I added.

"Yeah, well, the media over here doesn't, but you don't even want to know what I had to do—how many corrupt bureau-cratic pockets I had to line—to get her out of there and keep it quiet. And that was far from the only incident. And I suspect that's where she met your sister, too. Right?"

"Met?" I laughed derisively, staring into the wine. "That's one way of putting it."

"Your sister never said she was kidnapped, did she?"

"Well, no," I said slowly. "But she didn't go willingly."

Langer looked at me critically. "Are you sure?"

I froze. Fuck. We'd never talked about that, and if Maeve for any reason *had* gone willingly, she had probably been too ashamed to say it.

"She said she was scared," I said stubbornly.

"I didn't mean for that to happen. There was obviously a breakdown. Resi's foreign language skills are shit, and she didn't interpret things well enough for her. But it's also my fault for not insisting she try."

"Maeve stayed because she had nowhere else to go," I said. "And the police wouldn't help. They'd just auction them all off and be done with it."

"I know. *We* know." Langer's voice was steady. "Let me try to explain something. Resi's like me," he said carefully. "And like you. She starts feeling restless and bored if she doesn't have anything to occupy her mind. And then she starts getting in trouble."

"Sounds about right."

"So I gave her something to occupy her mind. Something we'd talked about doing since we were kids."

"White Cedar."

He nodded. "And I know—I'm convinced—that after we do this, after I *give* her the chance to do this, she'll settle down. Be the person I know she is and would have been before life fucked her a thousand times over. The person I've *seen* in her, with my own eyes, and I know is still in there. So I can see that smile again. The one I came home to every day. The one that made life worth living."

"But what if she... isn't being honest about what she's doing?" I asked diplomatically. "I mean, she's obviously feeling the pressure to deliver. Anyone would. And how long have you been working on this?" A while, from what I'd overheard.

"It's science. You know it takes time," he said quickly. "Anyway, like I said, I'm under no illusions about her. I *know* she's capable of dishonesty. You've seen that. But not about this."

To my shock, there was actual, genuine determination on his face. Determination for atonement and for winning back some of what they'd lost before slavery fucked them over as it fucked over absolutely everyone and everything associated with it.

And that was a powerful thing. Powerful enough to be worth deluding yourself for, certainly.

"It's the microchips, isn't it?" I asked. "That's what you're doing."

He nodded. "She didn't think we should tell you. I told her you'd probably already figured it out. I was overruled."

"Look, you know as well as I do that removing someone's chip doesn't make them not a slave. It just makes them a slave who's breaking the law."

"If it means they can't be tracked down by their owners or the government—at least long enough for them to disappear and forge a new identity—then for all intents and purposes, it *does* make them not a slave. And that's the point."

"So you're figuring out how to remove the chips, using the girls as guinea pigs. That's the research."

"Essentially, yes," he said. "You know the trick is locating them, so the goal is to find a chemical formula that can be injected, react with the chip, and bring it quickly and painlessly to the surface from wherever it is in the body."

Now he was speaking my language. My mind started turning immediately. "Are they performed humanely? The experiments, I mean?"

Langer paused. "Resi sees to that. I trust her. And in exchange, they're not only going to get freedom, but a new life," he went on. "And a better life than most free people, at that. Help with housing, transportation, tuition, capital to start a business, whatever they need. I have the resources to do it. I can't free every slave, not yet. But this is a start."

"Wait," I said in wonder. "You really are anti-slavery, aren't you?"

He turned. He looked incredulous. "Wait. Did you think I was lying about that?"

"I thought you were lying about *everything*. I still do, mostly."

"So it's only 'mostly' now? Wow. All right, I'll take it."

Under the terracotta bowl of this desert sky, the world had toppled. Max Langer—a good person? Okay, a not-evil person?

And what it meant for my sister, or Lemaya, or myself, or the whole enterprise, I still wasn't sure.

"So... what if a miracle happens and this works? Do you actually think you can make money off this?"

"Maybe, but believe it or not, it's about more than just *my* making money. To me, disrupting slavery is about making it economically unfeasible to enslave people and forcing the development of other business models. And that, in time, will transform how we *all* make money. That's the idea, anyway."

Economics. Along with finance, another field of study I was somewhat deficient in. But it made sense to me.

"How many girls have you worked with?"

"I'd have to ask Resi, but five, maybe? Six?"

"All accounted for?"

"As far as I know."

Or maybe they were dead and their bodies were dumped out in the desert. Or maybe Langer had no way of knowing either way.

"If you care so much, why don't you just buy slaves and then buy their freedom?"

"I have. Quite a few, over the years. But that's just working within the system. It's fueling the machine, not disrupting it. I had to find another way."

"What about the hot tub?" I suddenly remembered. "The champagne? What about Lemaya? Who disappeared mysteriously after the tour today, by the way."

"Disappeared?" he asked, somewhat alarmed. "I don't know anything about that."

Probably true but not reassuring.

"She's completely infatuated with you, you know." I paused. "And she's not the first, is she?"

Langer rolled his eyes, confirming what I needed to know. "She's an adult, like the others I've had over, and she came there willingly. And you can't argue that I don't treat them like royalty when they're with me, which is something they deserve after everything they've been through."

"Must be nice," I remarked. "A bunch of willing young fuck-toys you can call up day or night."

"Hey, let's put it this way: I haven't had any complaints."

"You're a real knight in shining armor, Max."

He smirked. "I've always thought so."

"I don't know how all this works, but you'd think at the very least you could get them to sign, like, a release agreement or something."

"They can't. They're slaves."

"Fuck, you're right." I sighed. "But wasn't one of them born free?"

He raised his eyebrows—alarmed, but only slightly. "What gave you that idea?"

Maeve. Maeve gave me that idea. But then again, Maeve also didn't speak English, and as he said, there was a chance that the language barrier had caused her to misconstrue the situation, or even misconstrue several situations.

"And no one else has access to the girls? It's just you and Resi?" I asked, thinking of the note in Corey's desk drawer with the two passcodes, which seemed to give him access to the house at any hour.

"I don't control who has access to them. Resi does. You can always ask her."

"Oh, right. Except that, as any idiot should have noticed—except for you, apparently—she doesn't like me. Or maybe she likes me too much. Either way, it hasn't exactly been conducive to a collegial work environment."

"Believe me, I noticed," he said dryly. "And I talked to her about it."

"*Talked* to her about it?!" I exclaimed. "Come on, man. Are you *trying* to make the situation worse?"

He thought for a second. "Okay, point taken. But you know, you *can* tell her to get fucked. She's supposed to be mine to deal with, not yours."

"Noted," I said, though I'd already tried that. But now that I knew she didn't have Maeve anymore... but what about Lemaya? My head was frankly tired of swimming in all the possibilities. Actually, I realized I'd been holding my breath, and I was the one always telling people not to do that. I knocked back the rest of the wine in my glass and turned to my drinking companion. "This atmosphere is better than our first 'date,' I'll give you that."

Langer smirked. "Yeah, you're not covered in pig shit."

"Fuck you."

But we both laughed as we started back down the hill. Outside the Porsche, Langer hit the button to unlock the doors, but when he approached the car, he didn't head immediately for the driver's side. My heart immediately sped up, responding to some elemental male connection with steel, rubber, and octane.

"Anyway, here's what I know you really don't want to hear," Langer said, "which is why I'm yet again going for the extremely responsible technique of plying you with alcohol and a fast car. But I need you to please, for the love of God, stop all the poking around you've been doing."

I ran my hand rapturously over the console. "I don't know what you're talking about."

Langer opened the passenger side door. "Bullshit. At least give me a *little* credit."

Actually, I had done so much poking around I wasn't exactly sure which particular poking around he was referring to, but I decided not to ask for clarification. "Is that an order?"

"No, it's not an order. I can't *order* you to do anything. I'm not your master. But I will say that if you think Resi has a problem with you now, you don't want to see her when you've really pissed her off. And now that I've told you what White Cedar is—what we're working on—I trust that you can appreciate the gravity of what we're doing here. *Everything* is wrapped up in it. I've put my shares in Orbital Dynamics—and my other companies—up as collateral on that lab."

I swallowed.

"And if something fucks this up—if *you* fuck it up—all of this"—he gestured to the sprawling mansion, the grounds, and the folly in the mountains beyond—"goes with it. Including you. Back to Keith. And wherever he sends you, you know it won't be back to Curly Sue's chemistry homework."

I bent my head and closed my eyes against the thought. "You're threatening me."

"No. I'm not threatening you any more than I'm threatening myself, although unlike me, you have more to lose than money. And let me be clear: I'll help you find your sister. And I'll figure out what the deal is with Lemaya, too. Maybe Resi sent her to a meditation retreat for a week. I don't fucking know. Either way, just let me handle it, okay?"

"I'm not promising anything," I said, breathlessly opening the driver's side door and sliding into the buttery-smooth leather seat with its intoxicating smell, knowing that I was being shamelessly bribed. But couldn't I have a minute—okay, a few minutes—in which I didn't have to care? I looked up into the icy blue eyes staring down at me. "You'll get a chance. And my personal guarantee that if you're still up to something, I *will* find out."

"God, you're fucking impossible."

"Hey, *you* wanted me. Remember, I'm just a poor, innocent,

oppressed slave, dragged here against my will. Keys." I
beckoned for them with exaggerated boredom.

"Ever driven a manual?" Langer asked, raising an eyebrow.

"All the time." Well, twice. Four years ago. For ten minutes.
Illicitly. But hell, I would have lied and said I knew how to fly a
helicopter if I'd been offered the chance to fly one like *this*.

"I'm buying it for you, you know. I mean, if you like it."

"Yeah. I figured that out." Only about three seconds ago, but
still.

Langer shook his head and tossed the keys into my waiting
hand. "You know, in another life, you would have made a damn
good rich kid."

I laughed as I started the engine.

"Happy early birthday. It's next week, right?"

Startled, I asked, "How did you—never mind." I'd forgotten
about it myself, as I did most years. I slammed the clutch to the
floor and shifted into first gear with every scrap of muscle
memory I could conjure up. I tore out of the driveway, guiding
the convertible along the dirt road, down the highway, into the
twilight, and toward the lights of the city, awash in such adrenaline that I almost didn't mind when Max gave me a few well-
curated tips about when to release the clutch.

"By the way, if the girls can't go out, why did Lemaya get to
go shopping with me?" I shouted over the wind and engine
noise.

"Because we're pretty sure her owner's dead," Langer
shouted back.

"How do you know?"

But I couldn't hear the response.

That night, "the girls" came over to the penthouse again.
Only in place of Lemaya, a willowy redhead calling herself
Sloane was the one sitting out on the terrace, eating panko-
crusted swordfish courtesy of Langer's personal chef, guzzling

champagne and raspberry liqueur, and climbing all over her "boss" in the hot tub as I stood on the other side, staring past the city lights at the distant mountains with a heating pad on my shoulder, sucking down bourbon like water and trying not to be sick.

And for once, Resi made no threats, no insults, no constant reminders of what I—and Langer—were trying to pretend I wasn't. From the other side of the marble bar, glass in hand, she just smiled sweetly.

3

HIM

I had Lemaya's number—or what she'd said was her number, anyway—programmed into my new phone, and I tried messaging her over the next few days, with no reply. Max informed me he'd seen her yesterday and that she said she wasn't feeling well, which only partially reassured me. I tried my sister again, too—if she was away from Resi, maybe she'd have access to a phone again and would be able to respond to me over the same network. No luck there, either.

Langer gave me daily updates, having put out Maeve's name and picture to his network of contacts in the high-level abolitionist community, of which he apparently had quite a few —even sending me screenshots of their baffled replies. For the first time, I had no reason to think Langer was lying. I still wasn't sure it mattered, though.

Langer also had daily video calls with Wainwright-Phillips, calls that he even let me listen in on if I wanted. Normal-sounding calls that Wainwright-Phillips definitely wouldn't be doing if his daughter were missing, hurt, or dead, and it was all I had for now, so much so that—as stupid and sad as it was—I imagined Louisa catching snatches of them from the hallway outside her father's study, completely unaware of who else was on the other side.

Finally, I worked. Mostly on Orbital Dynamics and its (numerous) engineering problems. Rocket shit. The kind of thing that as a kid I'd only dreamed about being allowed to do all day, let alone get paid for. If only I could have fired all the engineers and, in particular, the middle manager who had hired them, since from what I'd gathered, he seemed to be cut from the same cloth as Corey and had made it a point to hire a bunch of miniature Coreys. But I couldn't do that. All I had was a smartboard, a computer, the choice between sitting at a desk or a beanbag chair, a stress ball to throw up in the air and catch while staring at the ceiling, and what seemed like infinite hours in the day to think up solutions to the problems they handed me, since I never went anywhere except back and forth between the office and the condo. And, of course, the opportunity to look sharp while doing it. Frankly, I was shocked at how much Langer had allowed me to spend on flashy clothes, considering I had virtually nowhere to wear them. I didn't go to meetings or power lunches; didn't deal with marketing or sales or IT or legal. Hell, there wasn't a single employee of the company I was helping to make millions who even knew who or what I was. All of my ideas were filtered through Langer—I passed him ideas, and he showed me what and how he planned to present them to the team, incorporating my suggestions and changes. It was an odd, if efficient, system, I had to admit. But when the time came to go live, my presence was erased. I was a shadow; a ghost.

"I'd take you out on the town, but you'd have to brush up on your manners and lose *that*. It's nonnegotiable," Langer said, pointing to the bracelet half-hidden under my sleeve. Before I could get indignant about this attack on my manners, Langer continued, "I can't be seen in public with a slave, or anyone who slips up and *acts* like a slave, even inadvertently. For your own good and mine, it's just too risky."

For your own good. I'd heard that phrase plenty in my life, and it was pretty much always bullshit, but in this case, I knew it wasn't. I didn't want my cover blown any more than Langer did.

"I'll think about it," I said, which was true. "By the way, is there anything more to Project White Cedar than what I saw on the tour?" I asked. "Another location maybe? Another lab?"

"Nothing but what you saw, except for maybe the house where the girls live, which isn't far away from the warehouse. There's not much to see, obviously, but I can arrange a tour of that if you want," he said. "I know you don't believe me, but I'm actually trying to be transparent here."

"I appreciate that," I replied, even though the claim was a total joke—well, not a total joke, given what I now knew about Max and Resi. "But you don't have to do that."

The standard tour wouldn't help, anyway. I needed the VIP tour. The Corey special. Because it wasn't just about *getting* to the house, or even seeing it—it was about proving what Resi was doing with the girls in it. Not only for myself, though. I was starting to think that maybe, if the proof I found was strong enough, I could convince Langer, too. My boss would hate to hear it—he might not even believe it at first—but maybe I, being who I was, was the only one who could open his eyes. It was worth a try, right? The problem was, some vague notes between Corey and Resi and reams of dense financial spread-sheets didn't prove anything, even if they were slowly coming into focus the more I combed through them. If anything, they just made it *more* confusing—and easier to plausibly deny.

If only every other plan I could think of didn't risk blowing up the entire company and sending me to a mine.

So for a few days, I lay low and played the good employee. And for my efforts, I saw and held the crisp new bills; inhaled their intoxicating aroma and locked them in the safe myself with a combination I set, then just kind of stood there, staring at it all in a daze, because money, if you'd never had any, was a full sensory experience.

The problem was, it wasn't actually mine.

I had never been under any illusions that learning to live like a free man—were I ever to get the chance—would be easy. But I had also never thought I would need *to* do it while still being a slave. I could take a two-hour lunch, leave early, or stay late to play arcade games and guzzle bourbon. I could eat all the chocolate from the jar on one of Langer's assistants' desks, which I had first tried to earn by teasing her about the source of her unconscious smirk as she stared at her computer screen. But I soon realized that I could have gotten it *without* flirting with her, or even asking nicely. Hell, I could have just opened the jar, scooped out all of it, and walked away, with no consequences whatsoever.

And that, for some reason, was mind-blowing.

It hit me: free people didn't *have* to charm and manipulate to get even the most basic kindnesses and courtesies. They didn't have to spend every spare moment racking their brains to exhaustion, figuring out ways to be smarter and better than everybody around them, for the mere privilege of not being kicked in the teeth. They just... expected it. Because they were free, and they were people.

In the meantime, I followed Langer's directive and told Resi several times to get fucked. And to my surprise?

She did.

But something told me that it—like, let's face it, everything else around me—was a lie.

Look, fuck yes, I would have made a good rich kid. But I wasn't. I'd never been a kid at all. Not the way free people got to be kids, anyway. And I could delude myself all I liked, but the fact was that Resi was right that I was never going to outrun what I was with sports cars and suits and bourbons and beanbag chairs, or even removing the outward symbol of servitude.

And while I was stuck pondering all of that, the next day, Resi did the most terrifying thing she could have possibly done —disappeared. Which, needless to say, had been nowhere on my bingo card.

"She's taking the week off," Max explained that morning. "She does this sometimes. Just disappears somewhere and fucks her way through a new city. It's her version of a wellness retreat."

It sounded like bullshit, but before I could add investigating *that* to my long list of other things to investigate, my phone buzzed. An unknown number, but I caught on pretty fast as to who it was from.

UNKNOWN NUMBER

> you were right

"Excuse me," I told Max and dashed into my office and locked the door.

LANGER ENTERPRISES TECHNICAL CONSULTANT

> Lemaya?? Holy shit. Where have you been?
> Are you okay?

UNKNOWN NUMBER

No

LANGER ENTERPRISES TECHNICAL CONSULTANT

Where are you? What happened?

UNKNOWN NUMBER

I can't talk long. I shouldn't even have this
phone

LANGER ENTERPRISES TECHNICAL CONSULTANT

Tell me where you are. I'll get you out

UNKNOWN NUMBER

You can't. Not yet. Listen, I know you're looking
for Maeve. I knew all along. And I know how to
find her

My fingers tightened around the phone.

LANGER ENTERPRISES TECHNICAL CONSULTANT

What?? How??

UNKNOWN NUMBER

I think I know where she is. But you have to
come here. The house. I'll tell you everything

LANGER ENTERPRISES TECHNICAL CONSULTANT

When?

UNKNOWN NUMBER

Friday. Resi won't be here and I can distract her
security goons. I can still move around the
house a little. I'll give you everything you need
to get in

LANGER ENTERPRISES TECHNICAL CONSULTANT

How do I know this isn't a setup?

Yes, I felt like an asshole, but come on.

UNKNOWN NUMBER

I swear it's not. I wouldn't have messaged you
if I had any other choice. I thought I could
handle this, but I can't. I'm so sorry

LANGER ENTERPRISES TECHNICAL CONSULTANT

Fuck. No, I am. I never should've gone off the
tour. I got you in trouble

UNKNOWN NUMBER

No. That wasn't your fault. You were right to
look for Maeve. And now she needs you. We all
need you

And just like that, I had what I needed. Or at least, I thought
I did. Because if I was wrong, if this was a trap—well, it
wouldn't be the first time I'd walked straight into one. I stared
at the screen, my pulse hammering.

*If your opponent offers you a free piece, boy, ask yourself why
they want you to take it,* the old professor used to say.

Then again, he also used to say, *sometimes the only way to
know if it's a trap is to step right into it—and hope you see a way out
in time.*

LANGER ENTERPRISES TECHNICAL CONSULTANT

Okay. Send me everything

A pause. Then:

UNKNOWN NUMBER

I will but I have to go

I needed a plan. I also needed an insurance policy.

———

It came to me the next day.

"By the way," said Langer, over a catered sushi lunch from a place he'd described as "the best," and which I didn't like nearly as much as tacos, though I liked it much better than I'd expected from the description. "I found out this morning that Corey invited two guys from the Orbital Dynamics marketing team to fly in from San Francisco. They were supposed to meet, have dinner, and tour the office and the labs, but apparently, no one got around to telling them he was, uh, indisposed. They can still do the tour, I guess, but I'm busy and won't be around, so they aren't going to be happy. But frankly, that's not my problem."

"Wait, Corey invited them?" I asked, pausing with a roll awkwardly impaled on the end of a chopstick, only to have the roll fall apart before it got to my mouth. Fuck this. I gave up and tossed the plate on the table. "To tour the labs? The White Cedar labs?"

These codes should help you next time. Feel free to bring some friends.

"Yeah, but you don't have to do anything," Langer replied. "I'm just giving you a heads-up to make yourself scarce, too. The assistants will get the dubious honor of trying to explain what happened to Corey, which I figured was better done in person. They'll hate me for it, but what can you do?"

My brain was going about as fast as I had driven the Porsche down Interstate 10 the other day, despite having nowhere to go. I didn't have a full strategy yet, but I could see the opening moves. *Pawn to e4, set the trap, force a reaction.*

"Has Corey ever met with them before? The marketing team?" I asked, hoping the question didn't sound as urgent as I was afraid it did.

"Not as far as I know. Both of the guys are kind of new, from what I understand." He flicked a glance over at me curiously. Not suspiciously. Not yet. "Why?"

Damn. "Just trying to figure out how many different areas of the business he managed to fuck up before you got rid of him," I answered quickly. "Well, *we* got rid of him."

Max laughed and clapped me on the arm. I laughed, too, for a second. And not *only* about Corey's severe brain trauma.

And that's when I realized that Max thought I had stopped snooping. He thought I had made peace with Resi. He thought I was on his side.

He thought I—his reluctant, stubborn, rude, insolent protégé—had made him *proud*.

And even though I'd rather die than admit it, there was the tiniest part of me, now, that *wanted* to have made him proud.

Stunned and horrified by this realization, I stuffed one last piece of spicy eel roll in my mouth and slipped down the corridor and back to my office. Closed the door and rested my head against the thick, cool glass for a second, closed my eyes, and just breathed.

A good player controls the board. A great player controls his opponent.

Well, shit.

⸺ ◆ ⸺

HER

The sunset outside 211 Cholla was a witchy purple streak behind the massive cottonwood trees that lined the avenue. I crouched, only breathing, outside the basement stairs behind a sprawling mid-century rambler in one of the city's oldest, most expensive neighborhoods, wearing my favorite jeans and black hoodie, but my mind hadn't moved on with me. It was still dwelling in the adobe house near the university a week earlier.

But I didn't pause before punching in each number Maeve had given me. Because if I paused for even a second to think about how girls like me didn't do things like this, then I would no longer be a girl who *could* do something like this. And right now, that was the only thing in the world I wanted to be.

The box beeped, bright blue light flashing rapidly, and like an idiot, I jumped back about three inches, my heart racing. *Stupid, scared baby.*

Girls like me didn't do things like this for a *reason*.

But I didn't run.

Instead, I closed my eyes and thought of Irish poetry.

One second, two seconds, three seconds passed. I waited for something to happen. Nothing did. So I pushed open the door.

I was in. So why was I *still* standing here paralyzed?

Maybe because, when the door swung open and I started creeping down the dim corridor, I realized this didn't look anything like how Maeve had described it.

Especially not the second door on the left, which was supposed to be my escape route.

I'd volunteered to buy them twenty minutes. *Them*, meaning Maeve and the girls. We'd all been horrified at the idea of letting Maeve go back, but with Erica and Milagros and their network shut down, there was no one else to do it. And Maeve, despite only being familiar with one area of the house, had assured us, thanks to her friend Lemaya, that twenty minutes was all she would need to slip the trapped girls out through a different door while I created a distraction for the security guards and escaped via *this* door. We'd diagrammed it all out. We'd *planned* it.

But instead, standing there like some demented host waving me inside with a flourish, was the pockmarked, tooth-less face of the old gardener, grinning as if the moment he'd waited ten years for had finally arrived.

And this was *not* part of the plan.

"Oh, don't look so worried." He chortled. "You're right where you belong."

—◆—

Obadiah.

That was the name embossed on the shiny, elegant name badge pinned to the front of his crisp, brand-new security guard's uniform. Not that it mattered. I knew who and what he was, and a new name didn't change that.

And I couldn't say I was pleased to (re)make his acquaintance.

He'd been standing right there behind the door when I opened it, no warning, no time to react. Just the instant, stomach-dropping knowledge that I'd walked straight into a trap. Especially when he grabbed my wrist with all the glee of a pervert's wet dream and cackled with that gaping idiot's rictus that had always made me queasy. If Langer or whoever had freed this bastard and bought him that fancy uniform, wouldn't you think they could have at least paid for him to get his fucking teeth fixed, too?

The house itself was enormous, far bigger than it had appeared from outside. At least three stories, with wide hallways, tall ceilings, and an eerie, expensive, tomblike quiet that managed to feel both empty and claustrophobic. A musty mothball aroma like half a century of decrepitude.

Ten minutes. It had to have been ten minutes by now at least, I thought. Enough time for me to still accomplish my mission if I didn't freak out or die first. After all, I had come here to create a distraction—and running, screaming, or fighting back might save me, but it wouldn't necessarily help Maeve or the girls. After all, I didn't even know where I was going. There was nowhere *to* go.

I could do this.

In all the years this guy had terrorized me, he'd never actually touched me—he'd valued his life, even though it was shit. But now, I had to face the disgusting fact that his greasy paws were all over me as he dragged me stumbling behind him, one hand locked around my wrist, leading me down a long hallway lined with sleek gray molding, walls bare except for one huge, baroque mirror that made the space feel endless. We passed two closed doors before he turned and shoved me through the third: a room decorated with Greek columns, carved like bleached bone. About the size of a master bedroom but colder. The floors were polished stone overlaid with plush carpet. A light odor of incense and eucalyptus wafted through it, a potpourri to mask fear. A bed in the middle, like a white leviathan. The whole thing was clean, sterile, eerie, like a temple intended for human sacrifice.

Guess what I was about to be?

He unzipped a black bag on the dresser and pulled out a sheer chemise trimmed with lace and red satin ribbon. New. Expensive. "You've been requested to wear this."

"By who?" A stupid question. I knew he would just laugh. I was right.

"People know where I am, you know," I said. "Not to mention that when Daddy finds out about this, he's gonna cut your dick off."

He laughed again. "Is that so? Remember, you're not the princess here, princess. And Daddy isn't the king."

Choking in the stuffy, airless room, I slowly, clumsily pulled the soft fabric of the hoodie I'd had since I was twelve over my head, a security blanket being ripped away. I let it slip off my shoulders and glide down my body to slump helplessly at my feet. There had to be some way to do this with dignity, but I couldn't kid myself. I was about to be forced to undress in front of the most disgusting pervert I knew, and nobody was going to burst in and stop it.

My fingers trembled against the fabric of my T-shirt. I slowly slid it off my shoulders and stepped out of my shoes, my jeans and panties now the only barrier between me and pure exposure. I didn't meet Obadiah's jaundiced eyes as they followed my every move, reveling in his own refusal to hide his lust. He stood at an angle by the dresser, close enough to block the door, not touching me, just watching. Smiling. My pale, vulnerable body screamed for me to protect it, to not let this happen. As if it sensed something that, if violated, could never be put right.

And that was only being forced to undress. Not whatever might happen after.

Don't think. Don't panic. They'd realize something was wrong. They'd come for me. *Someone* would come for me. If not Maeve, then Erica. Or Milagros. Yes, they had their futures to think about, but this was my *life*.

The alternative was unthinkable.

My finger slid down to my jeans, then stopped. I physically couldn't do it. Tears, as usual, ran down my face and dripped onto the carpet.

"Take your time, princess," he said, looming closer. "I like it slow."

I wouldn't give him *that satisfaction*. Growling, I yanked down the zipper on my jeans, ripped off my pink lace panties, angrily kicked them off my legs, and pulled the stupid, lacy, embarrassing piece of shit over my head as fast as I could, the gardener cackling at me all the while.

I squeezed my eyes shut, but they might as well have been open for how aware I was of his eyes drinking me in as if through a straw, like some suction force, pressing down on my exposed body and prying into every inch of me, divesting me of everything good and holy.

"Good girl," he said with a chuckle, pulling two pairs of shiny handcuffs from his pocket. "On the bed." He pointed.

No. My eyes darted like a trapped animal in a cave. *Idiot.* I should have run while I had the chance. Why hadn't I *run*? I'd agreed to create a distraction. I hadn't agreed to *die*. My body stiffened as if to flee, but I only backed up in a daze. The truth was, there hadn't been anywhere to run to then, and there wasn't now, and I guess that reassured me somehow.

That I'd been doomed no matter what.

My breath hitched as the unforgiving steel dug in, cold and alien against my flesh, and didn't release. He'd cuffed my wrists to the carved, decorative headboard, one on each side. I was trapped upright against the pillows, knees trembling beneath me. My body clenched as he pulled the cuffs tighter—*as tight as they would go?* Not like I would know—trapping each wrist in place and immobilizing me. My breath did not release, however. I just lay there, as choked as if his hand had been clutching my throat.

And there I stayed, shivering against the rich, silken comforter. The air seemed to congeal as raw, unfiltered horror washed over me and my throat closed in panic. My senses sharpened, the dread I'd held back when I'd been convinced rescue would come now pumping unbidden through my veins.

For him, after ten years, the tables had turned. Here I was, and here he was. The only thing standing between us was every depraved thought he'd ever had about me.

"Why would you do this?" I gasped. "You're risking your freedom. They'll catch you. You'll be a slave again. "

He laughed. "You're one to talk, in that position."

My face burned. "You'll get thrown in a mine."

"Is that right? For doing what?"

"For kidnapping, dumbass," I said. "For, um"—I swallowed, gulping to get enough air in my lungs to at least finish my sentence—"for rape."

He laughed. "Rape? You wish. No, princess," he said. "Not me."

I squeezed my eyes shut and turned my face into the pillow as he leaned in close enough to choke on a cloud of his fetid, alcoholic breath, see the coarse gray stubble lining his heavy jowls, shudder as he ran his finger, permanently yellowed by dirt and decay, up and down the soft, unbroken skin of my arm.

"Well, not yet."

HIM

"On behalf of Langer Enterprises," I muttered, leaning back in my chair, squeezing my stress ball, and concentrating on forcing out my rounded European vowels and hard consonants for flat, nasal, elided American ones. *Again.* "On behalf of Langer Enterprises."

I had spent all Friday afternoon hunched over the files from Corey's tablet, squinting at the spreadsheet that I'd now transferred onto three different drives. Scanning the columns and lines for anomalies, I recited what I'd learned from the free online accounting course I'd sped through, a quiet dread building in my chest. Corey and Resi had been plotting something financially, of course. That didn't surprise me. The file prominently labeled *Wainwright-Phillips*—and what it contained—did.

So much so that I thought there had to be a mistake. I went back through the files, backward and forward, looking for some other explanation, but found none. And worst of all, I still couldn't prove the theory I did have. That would probably take days, and I didn't have days. I didn't even have hours. Eventually, I collapsed back onto my beanbag chair, my mind on one and only one member of the Wainwright-Phillips family.

Louisa would suffer. I'd known that. From the goddamn day I arrived at her house, I'd known that. And I'd tried. I'd tried so fucking hard not to love her. Because I didn't want her to have to end up *here*, face-to-face with what I'd found in that file. But here she was anyway, and a maudlin love message out of a dusty old poetry book by some dead fucking Irish guy was not going to make up for it.

And even though I was doing it for her—had convinced myself I was doing it for her, even if she couldn't see it, even if she *never* saw it, which seemed likely—neither was what I was about to do tonight.

Because right now, I had two different pieces of the puzzle. One was the finances, which I *still* couldn't prove. The second was whatever was going on at the house itself. Lemaya—in the single message she'd been able to get out to me—had all but confirmed my suspicions about the spreadsheets, implying that nothing was okay over at 211 Cholla. But I needed to get there to prove *that*. And that was why I needed to convince Felix Sorrentino and Arlo Callwood, arriving at 5:15 p.m. from San Francisco and who I was 99 percent convinced were headed there—to let me take them there. Lemaya had given me all the details about the security goons' movements, and assured me that Resi would "set up" the girls for Felix and Arlo before she left. Which was disgusting, but it was also key, because it meant that I could first, prove to Langer what Resi was doing to the girls, and second, get them out of it.

Assuming I did every single thing right with no slip-ups, of course. And assuming Lemaya was telling the truth.

And nobody could know anything. If the marketing guys found out, it would implode the company. If Resi found out, she'd implode *me*.

In other words, I'd need to deliver the performance of a life-time. At least until I got to the house. After that, I could only improvise.

I checked the display on my phone. It was almost four. It was thirty minutes to the airport, and the rest of what had been on my to-do list for that day—like rehearsing how not to get myself killed—was shot.

"On behalf of Langer Enterprises," I said one last time, slowly. This time, I tried to emphasize the laconic West Coast cadences Louisa had always told me she heard in my voice, to my amused disbelief.

Right. Now I not only sounded like a foreigner but a foreigner with brain damage.

Fuck it. It was time to get out of here. My heart beat faster as I opened my top desk drawer and pulled out a small, exquisite emerald-green box. I'd brought it from my bedroom at Langer's condo this morning but hadn't dared open it since. The more I did, the more nerve I'd lose.

I didn't open it now, either. Instead, I slipped it in the pocket of my gray pinstriped suit jacket, turned off the computer, stepped out, and locked my office.

If only someone had informed Lizette, the assistant with the candy jar, that I had a very important con job planned and couldn't be interrupted for a blow-by-blow account of her daughter's piano recital last night. But the way I figured it, I had exactly ten minutes to rummage through one of the downstairs storage rooms for the very specific tool that Langer had told me was sitting on the third shelf up, do what I had to do, and be behind the wheel of the Porsche en route to the arrivals terminal.

So I nodded and smiled and silently watched the floor numbers tick down as we descended, reminding myself that even in the close confines of the elevator, there was no way she could hear how hard my heart was pounding or see that my hair was damp despite the air conditioning.

"The nerve of some of these parents. Walking out after their own kid finished," Lizette was saying. "I suspect they're just jealous that Hallie is progressing so fast. Why—"

"I'm sure she'll be playing *La Campanella* before you know it. Have a good one," I said like a tool, ducking out the second the doors opened and reminding myself for the millionth time that here, turning my back on a free person was not going to earn me a beating. And that I had a very important date with a pair of very illegal industrial-strength bolt cutters.

Or so I thought until I actually checked the shelf.

Fuck. I set the green box down and rummaged frantically through the junk cramming the closet, feeling along every crevice, cursing myself for waiting this long to check. Meanwhile, the chain on my wrist, which most of the time felt like just another part of my body, suddenly seemed to weigh a hundred pounds, chafing my skin like the day they'd first welded it on me at fifteen, replacing the one intended for the wrist of a smaller, skinnier kid. As if it had sensed what was coming and was crying out for release.

In the corner, a glint of silver caught my eye. Heart pounding, I reached in and dragged out a vacuum-sealed canister of liquid nitrogen with a spray nozzle—and a ten-pound sledgehammer.

I took back everything I'd decided about Langer and his trickery. Deliberate or not, it seemed the guy had just made me a victim of the world's sickest chemistry joke.

Whatever. I could get revenge later if needed. My minutes were ticking down to zero. The original plan had been for Arlo and Felix to take Langer's car service straight here to the office, and I needed to head them off before they did. Thanks to the internet, I knew what they looked like, and though the assistants might be curious as to why they didn't arrive, I was counting on them not being curious enough to call Langer. Or if they were, that Langer wouldn't be curious enough to care. But first, I needed to even get *there*, and there was rush hour traffic to account for.

I took several deep breaths and, hands already shaking, grasped the cold canister, moving to the center of the room and spreading my fingers flat on the steel table. Palm up? Palm down? Down, I decided. It took me a couple of pumps of the nozzle before I succeeded in sweeping a heavy fog of the liquid over the entire chain. I only needed to break one link, really, but best to be thorough.

Then I turned to the hammer.

I noticed two problems immediately. One, there was very little give between my skin and the chain, I only had two hands, and one of them was obviously useless. Two, my free hand was attached to my bad shoulder, giving me less force and less chance of a clean strike. I'd have to aim precisely, with just enough force to break the link—the steel alloy's chemical bonds weakened by the nitrogen—without shattering my wrist into a million pieces if I missed. Easy, right? Well, that wrist was already scarred to hell, anyway, reminding me that I'd endured worse, for worse reasons.

I blew some stray strands of hair out of my eyes, spread my fingers wider, and choked up on the wooden handle, fingers trembling as I lifted the sledgehammer: a tool designed for no higher purpose than to destroy things. Should I close my eyes? Yes? No? I half-closed them, and before I could waste another second talking myself out of it, I struck, unleashing a clang that must have echoed through the entire building, loud enough to stifle a scream as the block of dead solid iron collided with the side of my wrist.

I took a second before opening my eyes, almost afraid to see the violet-colored bruise blooming and swelling where the hammer had landed. The pain was right on cue, and I hunched over against the throbbing, gasping for breath, fiercely blinking back tears before they could dare to fall. I'd known this was coming. But, like always, knowing pain was coming made it no easier to take.

I managed to weakly move my wrist back and forth. So it wasn't fractured—at least not entirely. Brilliant.

What wasn't brilliant was that the blow had only partially hit its mark. One of the links was not so much smashed as severely dented, which was no surprise. This thing had *not* been made to come off.

Again, then. If I got lucky, it would only take one more to shatter it, assuming I didn't pass out from the pain first.

My hands, weaker and shakier now, gripped the hammer as tightly as I could and took aim. An even louder clang and an even better hit had the entire table vibrating.

And the link *still* held. I resisted the urge to pound the table and scream something in Luxembourgish. The storage room had very little air circulation, and sweat was already dampening my hair and forehead. I angrily reached up to swipe it all away with my good hand. Retook my grip with quivering wrists. Brought it down.

Last one. Please.

I opened my eyes.

—◆—

If I had been either of the two guys waiting impatiently on the curb outside the domestic arrivals terminal, I'd like to think I would have looked up from my phone to see an all-American golden boy in a pair of shiny aviators and sliding confidently out of a blindingly shiny silver Porsche convertible, only a minute off schedule and impeccably styled in a gray pinstriped suit, gold and lapis necklace, and a casual mauve shirt printed with a weird duck-feather pattern that still somehow worked— thank you very much, Lemaya. On the wrist of a hand adorned with thick gold signet rings on the middle fingers, a stunning Rolex watch peeked out from under the cuff of a tailored jacket. But it was the other hand I extended.

"On behalf of Langer Enterprises, welcome to Phoenix," I said, with a steady gaze and a luminous smile as confident as my grip. "I'm Corey Killeen."

4

I screamed. I didn't care who heard.

The bedposts were carved with women and griffins, the women's hands held up in surrender as the griffins' teeth sank into their flesh. Over my head, an ornate gold mirror was mounted, in which was reflected a beautiful girl, hair tumbling down her back, head bent as if in prayer, eyes cast down. A perfect submissive posture.

This wasn't part of the plan.

I jerked my left arm away from its cuff, then the right one, testing how tight it held, only succeeding in painfully scraping the inside of my wrist. The metal pinched something awful, a constant irritation that grated no matter which way I twisted. I stopped. I lay back, gulping for air, panting from panic and exertion.

Breathe, dammit, said another, blessedly familiar voice. *Don't die before you're killed.*

But he wasn't here, and neither was anyone else. It was just me, alone, fucking up as usual. I wasn't sure I *wanted* him here to see that. He'd seen it.

"This wasn't part of the plan," I whispered to the hot, silent, stifling room.

Of course, if I were smart—if I were *him*—I'd come up with a new plan. But I wasn't, and I couldn't, so all I could do was cry, the injury of rivulets running down my cheeks. The insult of being unable to swipe them away. Helplessness and humiliation. A slave's insult.

I'd seen the scars on *his* wrists, but I never fully understood them until now. I'd never understood a thing.

HIM

"What the fuck, bruh?" Felix exclaimed, prompting me to practically jump out of the driver's seat, nearly lose my grip on the steering wheel, and narrowly miss crashing the Porsche head-on into a light pole. Well, so far so good. "Arlo says Langer isn't even here?"

I looked over at Corey's—the real Corey's—doppelganger. Felix didn't look much like Corey—he was shorter, fairer-skinned, and lighter-haired—but he had the exact same supercilious sneer that privilege seemed to beget. His colleague Arlo —taller, more flashily suited and accessorized, with dark brown skin and black hair—seemed slightly less odious, though since he'd arrived, he hadn't taken his eyes and/or ears off his phone for more than a few seconds.

"Max sends his regards," I said, once again shouting over the noise of the wind and the engine as I guided the Porsche away from the airport and onto the freeway, toward downtown, grateful to be putting distance between us and Langer's head-quarters. "But he had this big meeting with a couple of legislators he helped get elected. After all," I added in a conspiratorial tone, "how else are they going to know which laws need to be changed in our favor?"

Arlo and Felix just looked at each other blankly.

Nice going, dumbfuck.

They burst out laughing.

"This guy." Arlo nodded, jabbing at me with his thumb.

I exhaled. Perverting the course of democracy, huh? I'd have to remember that topic the next time I ran out of quips.

However, Felix still didn't look happy about Langer's absence, and I noted it as yet another thing I'd have to keep an eye on. In the meantime, I was dying to pry them for more, but I couldn't. And here, if anything, was the plan's fatal flaw: How was I supposed to find out anything when the real Corey already knew everything?

Somehow, I helpfully reminded myself.

"So what did you guys have in mind for tonight?" I said. "You know, besides…" *Doing unspeakable things to innocent girls?*

The two visitors looked at each other again.

"I thought we were headed to your headquarters," said Arlo. "It's brand-new. I figured Langer would want to show it off."

I shook my head vehemently. "Trust me, I spend all day there. There's nothing worth seeing." Except for a bunch of people who, nice as they were, would rat me out instantly.

"Well, if Langer isn't even there, I guess it doesn't matter much," said Felix.

I sighed in relief.

"That's not why we're here anyway," Felix added, looking at Arlo, who nodded.

"Oh, one hundred percent," I agreed, noting that nothing they'd said so far had disabused me of my suspicions of what they had planned, which was great, since the other thing I'd been afraid of was that they would show up and actually want to talk about marketing.

"Anyway, I'm starving," said Felix. "I had to rush out to the airport after a meeting and haven't had a bite all day."

"Don't you want to check into your hotel?" I asked. I'd been hoping for at least a little downtime to research just what the fuck to do with these guys.

He looked at his colleague.

"Nah," said Arlo. "We can leave the bags in your trunk, right, Corey? What do you think?"

What I *thought* was that I'd never eaten in a restaurant in my entire life, and I couldn't think of a worse possible time to start. But what I *said* was, "Sure. Where?"

Felix gave me a funny look. "How should I know? It's my first time in this town. You're supposed to know all the hotspots."

Fuuuuuck. Thank God I now had instant access to all the same information free people did. If only I'd spent more time in the past week poring over restaurant listings instead of reading three different research papers about the new subatomic particles they'd discovered at the Large Hadron Collider. And if only I weren't driving, and if only one of my hands wasn't mostly useless and radiating searing pain to every other part of my body. I was already driving mostly one-handed, which in a manual was no small feat.

"Oh, yeah, no, sure, of course. There's this fantastic place downtown," I bullshitted. "You'll love it. Best fish tacos I've ever had."

"Fine, just as long as I can get them gluten-free," Felix said boredly.

"Since when are you gluten-free, man?" asked Arlo. "Is it some kind of medical thing?"

"Nah," Felix replied. "I just don't like the way it bloats me. I won't have any energy for the gym all week. But I say it's a medical condition. It's the only way you can get these idiot slaves at these places to get your order right."

I groaned inwardly. I'd fully expected to end up praying for death at some point during this excursion, but I didn't expect it to be quite this early. "Let me check if they're open tonight."

I fumbled in my pocket for my phone, one-handedly punched in "fish tacos," "gluten-free" and—for good measure —"hotspot" into the search field and frantically clicked the first thing that popped up: the brand-new top-floor restaurant of a high-rise building downtown, not far from Langer's condo. I'd probably even passed it once or twice.

"Hey, bruh, is your hand okay?" asked Arlo curiously. "It looks like—"

"It's fine," I cut him off, a little too quickly. "I just kind of busted it up, uh, lifting weights. Doctor says I just need to rest it."

Arlo raised his eyebrows and turned to survey the view on the other side of the car. "If you say so."

It took us another fifteen minutes to pull into the building's circular drive, and only an additional ten seconds for me to realize that the guy in the vest standing in the circle with his hand outstretched wanted to park my car for me. I glanced at Arlo and Felix, who made no sign that they'd noticed anything amiss. Yet.

At sunset, the rooftop restaurant was at both its most stunning and its most crowded, with hanging lanterns and low tables draped in gauzy curtains to cordon off lounge spaces for the chicest patrons. Who were no less chic than I was, thanks to Lemaya, though they were a hell of a lot more relaxed.

Who were decidedly *not* relaxed were the slaves, whom I spotted immediately in dark heavy-looking uniforms—as usual, running food, washing dishes, cleaning toilets, and doing whatever other unpleasant kitchen chores none of the paid staff wanted to do.

With a start, I realized that Felix—who'd been making bored observations about the desert scenery on the drive over—was now following my gaze suspiciously.

Shit. By noticing the slaves at all, I'd made my first mistake. To Corey and his ilk, slaves were beneath notice. Until they dared open their mouths, anyway.

The hostess—a free girl, as per usual for a front-facing role—approached.

"Table for three," I said. "Your *best* table," I corrected myself, eyes flitting to Felix, who—while Arlo tapped his phone—just stood there with his arms folded, waiting for me to fuck up again.

Yeah? I'll fuck you *up, asshole.* It made me feel a little better, at least. Good enough to pull out my brand-new Italian leather wallet and hand the hostess a one-hundred-dollar bill, and I could almost feel the girl's—and Felix's—eyes widen. "Immediately."

HER

Well, twenty minutes had come and gone. Ten times over.

There was only one high window, with nothing outside, but enough to know that the sun was gone. The room, the entire house, was silent.

The girls must be free by now. I had to believe they were, anyway. That this would be worth something. That my *life* would be worth something.

You're not the princess here, princess, and Daddy's not the king.

For Obadiah, this was Mecca. His old master's daughter lay chained on the bed, at his mercy. Payback, not only for himself, but for all the slaves. For years of pain, humiliation, and cruelty.

And who's to say I didn't owe it to them? If not for anything I'd done personally, then for all the wrong I'd seen and done nothing about; for being a daughter of privilege and plenty in a cruel, broken world built on their backs.

You didn't have a choice, any more than I did.

Well. There was one, at least, who thought my soul unblemished. My boy had had every chance to condemn me, and had not. Had weighed me in the balance and found me unwanting.

You have your whole life to do good in the world. You've already started.

I made a promise, then and there. If I ever got out of this room, I would do nothing *but* good for the rest of my life. Wherever I found to do it, whether I owed it or not.

And if I didn't get out? Well, that was just doing penance in a different way.

He hadn't told me he loved me. As terrified as he was, he'd chosen a poem—*When You Are Old*, the one I'd caught him reading at Erica's—to do it for him. If I ever saw him again—even if it was only on the other side, the one he didn't believe in—I'd recite that verse back to him from memory. I recited it now, over and over again, under my breath, like a prayer. Something else he didn't believe in.

But I did.

> How many loved your moments of glad grace,
> And loved your beauty with love false or true,
> But one man loved the pilgrim soul in you,
> And loved the sorrows of your changing face.

I closed my eyes, my eyelashes sticking to my sodden cheeks. If he were here now, he'd see those sorrows rain down. If he were here now, he'd see how proud I would make him.

HIM

"IDs, please?" the server asked right after we put in our drink orders at the low table by the rail, the one with the most incredible panorama of city lights.

Arlo and Felix immediately reached for their wallets.

"Forgot mine at home," I said apologetically, my heart already hammering in my ears. Idiot. I could have just asked for water.

As soon as the server left, Arlo and Felix just stared at me, and time seemed to stand still. "Don't lie to us," said Felix after a second. "You didn't forget your ID, did you?"

I swallowed thickly. "No, I really—"

"Bruh," Arlo cut me off. "Relax. You think we care if you're underage? We'll order for you. I do it for my brother all the time. They never catch on."

I nodded, breathing again, though even after I had a cocktail in my non-half-shattered hand, it didn't prevent me from being consumed by the terror that every time I moved, someone would start wondering why I had so many calluses on my palm, or spot the cattle prod scars just below my shirt collar—a world away from the toned, moisturized, tea-tree-oil-infused skin of the two men across the table—and instantly know that my only role in a place like this should be scouring pots and pans.

The thing was, I *shouldn't* be nervous. Not really. Like any born actor—or con artist—I was a natural observer. I knew people: their habits, their desires, their weaknesses. I knew how they would react in just about every situation, enabling me to think three, four, five moves ahead, always. It was how I'd survived this long, and no one I knew was better at it.

But I'd only ever done it as a slave. When the time came to act, I acted—and reacted—as a slave would. As a good slave, or more often a bad one, but either way, as a slave, always. And now those survival skills I'd spent twenty years perfecting were exactly what—if relied on—were going to get me killed.

I swallowed, stuffing down the urge to run out of the room, down the stairs, and back to Langer's condo, where I'd promise to be an exemplary employee and never question anything ever again. So what if Resi was defrauding the company and leaving Lemaya and the other girls to be raped, violated, and God knew what else? They could handle themselves, and—

Suddenly, my attention was drawn to someone—not to a slave this time, though. To a girl in a cream-colored lace minidress—backless, like one lodged in my memory from what now felt like very long ago—and wedge sandals, sitting cozily in the corner, leaning on her elbows, twisting a glass stem between her manicured fingers. Endless, bouncy curls just a shade lighter than brown, whose texture I could still feel flowing like soft ribbons between my rough hands. It wasn't her, of course. I could see enough of her face to know she was ten years older than Louisa, at least, with a narrower, more angular face. But her moonstone eyes still swirled under the hanging lanterns, and she sat across from a tall, equally well-dressed man, his features in shadow. The two spoke intimately but not secretively. And not in sweet nothings, either. About something that mattered, clearly, both to them and to the world. Something important.

Sometimes it works out.

From where I sat, though—so deep in pain and danger and deception I couldn't see any way out—I couldn't fathom how.

But she was happy, this girl, this angelic messenger from a kinder universe. And though I couldn't see the man's face, I figured he must be, too. How could he not be, with a girl like that?

"You know that chick?" asked Felix, glugging his second

cilantro-lime-and-something-stupid-infused tequila cocktail, demanding my attention back.

I shook my head. "Wish I did," I said, hoping it sounded suggestive instead of wistful.

"Eh, not my type. I don't need that much to grab onto," he said, setting his glass down to pornographically mime the soft curves of her body. "I like them tiny. Fragile. Like they might break if you drop them."

Fucking hell. If I got through tonight without jamming a broken martini glass up this son of a bitch's nostril, I should officially be declared a saint. "And what if they do break?"

Felix grinned. "I like that even better."

"Remind me again," I said, seizing the opportunity. "Have you met Tresa Hahn? Max's head of R&D?"

"Never," he said. "But from what you've told me, she seems to prefer playing with her own kind."

Actually, I was pretty sure Resi preferred playing with *every* kind. "Fuck if I care, anyway," I replied with a knowing laugh. "Just as long as she's willing to share, right?" I laughed along with him. *That's right. Keep chuckling, dickhead. I've got you where I want you.* "And what about Keith Wainwright-Phillips? His new partner? What do you think of him?" On a roll, I thought back to the spreadsheets. Likely these guys were too low-level to know anything about what Corey and Resi had been up to on the financial fraud front, but it was worth a try.

Felix chuckled tipsily. "I *don't* think of him. Dude was a CEO like a million years ago, wasn't he? Kind of went nuts and lost it all, from what I heard. Langer tells him to jump and he asks how high. But hey, who am I to question it?"

"Pretty sure Max knows what he's doing," I said with an air of confidence and a large swallow of alcohol.

But I'd been too confident. Felix paused. My words hung in the air. We'd both heard it. The alcohol, all the toxic masculine talk, had lowered my guard. My vowels had become too long, my consonants too sharp. My accent was lying right out on the table, naked.

"Where did you say you grew up, again?" Felix asked, eyeing me from behind his martini glass.

"Right here."

"Funny," he said, tipping back the rest of his drink and snapping his fingers at the server for another. "You don't sound it."

Fresh beads of sweat had broken out on my face, and since the lights were dim and the temperature had dropped twenty degrees since sundown, there was no blaming it on the heat. "Well, you know, I studied abroad," I said, groping for an explanation that *probably* couldn't be debunked by a quick internet search. "Backpacked around Europe. I'm a sponge like that. I pick things up."

The food arrived, thank fucking God, and we all turned our attention to our plates. I'd already cursed myself for not better observing the eating habits of free people—fuck if there hadn't always been a million more interesting things to pretend not to be looking at during my masters' dinner parties. Gingerly, I picked up a fork.

"What the hell is this?"

I dropped the utensil with a start, but the outburst had nothing to do with my table manners. Felix was addressing the kid who'd delivered the food—who, given Felix's all-too-familiar tone, had to be a slave.

Yep.

I was almost starting to *regret* beating the real Corey into a coma, if only because it was cruel to prevent the guy from being united with his platonic soulmate.

"I said gluten-free, you little shit."

The kid, freckled and strawberry blond, looked about fifteen and had that gawky, underfed look we all had at that age. And a death wish, apparently. "With all due respect, sir, this is pea flour. There's no gluten in it," he said, glancing up from under his hair with what I could swear was a glimmer of *what-a-dumbass*-style amusement, one that Felix would never—*could* never—pick up on.

But I did. Instantly.

"Pea flour? What the fuck is that and what do I care?" Felix demanded. "Bring it back and get me another one."

"But—"

"Go, before I get the manager." Whether by accident or design, he shoved the plate—actually a wooden plank with a stylish little metal stand where the tacos were arranged—toward the slave a little too forcefully, and it flipped and landed face-down on the floor, quiet enough to humiliate the kid without attracting additional attention. Wouldn't want to ruin the evening, after all.

But as I looked closer, that defiant glimmer wasn't just *there*, hiding under that hair. It was directed at someone—at *me*.

I wasn't sure how or why, but this kid *knew*.

"What are you waiting for, boy?" Felix said. "Pick it up."

If he was as smart as he seemed, the boy would clean the mess up quickly, disappear back into the kitchen, and end this for all of us. But he didn't get the chance.

"Is there a problem over here, sir?"

Everyone's heads turned. The manager—huge, well-muscled, and red-faced, with a name badge reading "Bryan"—had arrived. But I barely listened to Felix's angry, mostly inaccurate explanation. I just watched the boy, who had frozen and lowered his eyes, growing paler by the second as he listened. He wasn't afraid of Felix, and good on him. But he *was* afraid of this man. The day-old bruise around his left eye probably explained it.

Shut up. Keep your head down. Get out alive. That was the voice whispering to me as if I were just another slave standing there, observing, trying to go unnoticed. Except—for all they knew, anyway—I wasn't. I could *do* something.

Bryan's lips curled in a smirk toward the boy, who had made himself as small as possible, having kneeled down to frantically scrape whatever he could of the mess on the floor into some napkins. "Rest assured, it'll be taken care of." The glare Felix sent in the boy's direction was enough for the manager to know what he expected.

Shit.

"Excuse me," I said.

The boy's head shot up for a second before he forced it back down to the floor.

"Yes?" Bryan asked coldly. He looked from the boy at me— the sophisticated, impeccably stylish, obviously privileged young man who had just spoken.

And so did Felix. As if all the evidence piling up had just collapsed under its own weight and fallen right on top of his head. As if he were now X-raying my expensive ensemble to all that lay beneath—to every bruise, to every scar, to the thin white line hiding beneath the luxurious watch. The thin line between one life and another: between *this* life and the life that was destined to be mine, again, forever, if I couldn't get all of us the fuck out of here without doing something as idiotic as what I'd been about to do.

"He—" I swallowed, turned away from the kid—and the hope in his eyes—and faced the manager's scowl. *It's for Maeve. It's for Lemaya. It's for the girls. It's for all of us. I'm so sorry, kid.* "Nothing." I waved my hand, glancing contemptuously at the kid. But not in his eyes. "Clean it up and get lost, boy. We're trying to have dinner here."

I turned away as the disgusted manager sharply grabbed the crestfallen, now-visibly-shaking boy by the back of his shirt and shoved him back in the direction of the kitchen.

"I'm terribly sorry for all of that, sir," the man said obsequiously. "We'll have a new plate out for you in no time."

Felix waved off the manager almost as easily as he'd waved off the boy. "Good," he said, turning his attention back to whatever Arlo—who'd lost interest in all of it five minutes ago—was sniggering at on his phone.

I collapsed in my luxuriously upholstered seat, close to shaking now myself. *Nothing* was worth this. Well, almost nothing.

I would have been relieved when the bill finally arrived a half hour and another round of dumb, pretentious cocktails later—if only it hadn't been the biggest minefield all night. But at least I was prepared for this one. I grabbed it, whipping out my thick, crisp wad of one-hundred-dollar banknotes like it was the most natural thing in the world.

"Lost my company card at the gym this morning," I said with an exasperated shake of my head. "Spent an hour and a half on the phone with that fucking bank, but they told me seven to ten days for a replacement. Can you believe that?"

Arlo and Felix just stared. Fuck it. I sorted out the cash, threw it on the table, and excused myself, wandering back through the maze of glittering lanterns, gauzy curtains, and sprawling banquettes to the back of the restaurant, with the vague idea that I could find the boy and hand him one of the C-notes, of which I still had plenty. Because if I'd learned nothing else recently, it was that money made bad things go away.

At least, if you were free, it did. At best, though, if the manager found the boy with it, he'd confiscate it; at worst, he'd accuse him of having stolen it and beat him double for that. Besides, he'd have nowhere to spend it. The best he could do would be to find a good hiding spot under the floorboards. And then hope to get another one hundred dollars from another equally generous or guilt-ridden person every day for the next five years, at which point he might have saved up about half the price of his freedom, assuming his owner ever let him buy it.

I spotted the boy on the floor of the pantry, chained by one wrist to the bottom shelf, a short length of cuff and steel looped through the slats like he was part of the inventory. Looked familiar.

He'd stripped off his stiff uniform, down to a thin T-shirt that left the bruises in plain view — black and blue stripes across his shoulders and neck, fading to sickly yellow at the edges. His face was swollen, eyes nearly shut. No food in reach, just dry goods stacked neatly around him like a joke.

He flinched when he saw me, then looked away.

Helplessly, I came closer, hastily undoing the watchband, revealing my half-limp wrist, which was really becoming a work of art—the pale line the chain had concealed; the purple, swollen bruise from the hammer; the reddish indentations from the links.

He didn't turn. He barely moved his eyes. But he was looking.

I knew that trick.

"Yeah?" the boy muttered. "So?"

"So? I'm—" I glanced behind me. "I'm sorry." I held out a cold can of ginger ale I'd palmed from behind the bar, and grabbed a bag of melba toasts from the top shelf, but he shook his head. He couldn't eat or drink it fast enough to conceal the evidence, and they'd still probably find out no matter what.

Then I held out the one hundred dollars. As if he could eat *that*.

"Fuck your sorries and fuck your money," he said. "I'd rather be a slave forever than whatever you're pretending to be." He looked away.

I left the food, drink, and money next to him. He'd have to make the choice. Because while it may not make the bad thing go away, at least it might make my *guilt* go away.

Right. As if anything could ever do that.

The restroom was luxurious, dimly lit, and paneled with burgundy leather. I swallowed four ibuprofen from the bottle in my pocket and splashed cold water on my face. The night wasn't even half-over, the second part was going to be worse, and the beat-heavy, melody-free music was boring into my brain like a drill, competing for space with the alcoholic fuzziness of the two cocktails I'd downed without tasting.

I shouldn't have even had *one* cocktail. Maeve and Lemaya needed my help *now*. They *all* needed my help. The slave boy was right to be disgusted with me. And the girl in the lace dress, and Louisa herself, who'd risked everything she had to help Maeve, to help *me*—would be appalled that I'd wasted two weeks on expensive booze, ridiculous outfits, and sucking up to my boss while tooling around town in a Porsche. Emphasis on *tool*.

I blinked at my dim reflection in the mirror. Max Langer had been only half right. It wasn't the clothes. It was my face I didn't recognize anymore.

But the guy who threw open the door sure did.

I spun around. "Hey, bruh, I—"

"Don't 'bruh' me," said Felix. "I want to know what the fuck's going on here."

5

"How dumb do you think we are?" Felix's face and neck muscles bulged inelegantly in the garish purple mood lighting of the porte-cochere as he and Arlo cornered me between two potted palms where I'd instantly fled after pushing past Felix and out the door of the restroom.

Muscles taut, throat dry, legs weak, I instantly recognized it as the kind of question where no possible answer I could give would improve the situation. Over Felix's shoulder, I scanned the drive, but there was still no sign of the Porsche pulling up. Fuck valet parking, I decided. Sure, it was cool and all, but what good was it for a quick getaway?

Meanwhile, Felix was looking me up and down with contempt. "It's so fucking obvious. Avoiding the office. The cash. That shirt."

Well, that was uncalled for.

I wasn't sure which was preferable—that they call the police and report me as a runaway, or just beat me into a pulp and leave me there. Arlo, at least, had some serious muscle on him, and it wasn't like I could do much to defend myself in my present physical condition. And either way, I'd be fucked the second Langer—never mind my master—found out about it.

"Langer doesn't know you're here, does he?" Felix demanded.

"Wait. What?"

"Do you seriously not speak English, dumbfuck? I said Langer doesn't know you're here. He doesn't know anything about this entire trip, does he?"

I could have kissed Felix's sneering, well-moisturized face. I'd been caught in the wrong lie. Again. "No," I admitted, trying to sound filled with remorse instead of glee. "He doesn't."

Felix turned to Arlo and jabbed his thumb at me disgustedly. "Figures. This whole trip was a fucking joke. I should have known better than to trust a guy dressed like *that*."

If I ever saw Lemaya again, we would have to have a talk.

Felix turned back to face me. "You've got two seconds to explain yourself before I kick your ass across the goddamn street."

"Relax, okay?" My heart rate slowed. This I could handle. Sort of. "You think I haven't taken every precaution? He won't find out."

"Yeah, he will." Felix pulled out his phone and waved it wildly in my face. "Because I'm going to call and tell him everything."

I would have bet all of my remaining money that Felix didn't have Langer's direct number, but I still didn't want to test him.

"And, with any luck, it'll only be you who gets fired for this. I'll get Employee of the Year."

I swallowed hard and took a deep breath. "Listen," I said slowly. "If you don't tell Max about any of this, I swear it'll be worth your while."

Felix raised an eyebrow and crossed his arms over his chest.

Arlo, meanwhile, had finally put his phone away and had just been standing there looking vaguely intimidating. But now his interest was clearly piqued. "Why should we believe anything you say?" he asked.

"You know Max has millions upon millions. You already know he has access to the best shit in the world, whenever he wants it. The best food, the best booze, the best everything. All at his beck and call. Day or night."

"Yeah, but—" Arlo began.

"Well, why should it be any different with girls?"

They were listening, so I went on.

"The only problem is, like most rich guys, he's fucking selfish and doesn't want to share. Well, tonight, thanks to me, that changes. Do you know how fucking lucky you are that I'm even letting you be here for this?" Felix didn't move, but I continued, my confidence buoyed. "You pick up that phone, you'll regret it for the rest of your life."

Neither of the other guys moved.

I barreled onward with the sales pitch of a lifetime. "What's the dirtiest, kinkiest, most insane thing you've ever seen a girl do in a porno? Name it."

"But—"

"Hey, shut up, man," broke in Arlo, leaning closer. "Let him finish."

"Name. It."

Felix rolled his eyes. Leaned in. Mumbled something.

Look, I prided myself on having a mind as filthy as anyone's. But even I blushed a little at that answer. "Well then, get ready to have something to brag about at every party for the next thirty years."

Felix put his phone away, his perversion and greed winning

out, as I had known it would. "The second I think you're bull-shitting me again, this comes out."

The Porsche pulled up. And the whole right side of my body shuddered in one long column of pain and exhaustion as I took the keys, settled into the driver's seat again, swiped more damp hair out of my face, and forced myself to shift into gear rather than collapsing in a heap on the wheel.

Well, the easy part of the night was over.

—•—

I trudged up the walkway to 211 Cholla, with Felix and Arlo trailing silently behind me like vultures circling their next meal. Langer's old neighborhood—lined with cottonwoods and midcentury homes that nevertheless seemed ancient—was silent as I zeroed in on the entry keypad at the back door. I'd memorized the code Lemaya had given me—34562—in an effort to look cool and confident. Unfortunately, my chances of looking either cool *or* confident had been dwindling for the past few hours, and the fact that nothing happened when I put in the code—not even a blinking light—quickly finished them off.

Luckily, here was where it came in: my insurance policy. I'd also memorized the code from Corey's tablet, in the off-chance Lemaya's code didn't work. In fact, I was pretty damn pleased with myself as I punched it in.

Until that didn't work, either.

Okay. Proceed to Plan B. I must just have it wrong. Ignoring the fact that Felix was clearly seconds away from reaching out and bashing my head into the doorframe, I reached into my pocket, fumbling for a sticky note that was very clearly no longer there.

Given the various near-catastrophes tonight, I wasn't

surprised I hadn't noticed a piece of paper fluttering out of my pocket.

Okay. Proceed to Plan C. I started hitting every possible combination of buttons. 62534. 25643, and the like, wildly, again and again, all to no avail. A single drop of sweat raced down my face. The young men standing behind me were an almost physical pressure, their eyes boring into me like drills.

Okay. Proceed to Plan D. A window and a brick?

I squeezed my eyes shut for a second and turned around. "Uh, guys, we—"

The door opened. Automatically. Which was odd because there was no one on the other side of it. I felt the sudden, ridiculous urge to hop back in the Porsche and leave the other two in a cloud of very expensive dust. But fuck if I had just gone through the dinner from hell for nothing, and if I thought I couldn't face the accusing eyes of that poor slave boy before, how much would I loathe looking at my own face if I bailed out now? After all, these girls were just slaves, too. The police sure weren't going to help them. *Nobody* was going to help them if I didn't help my own.

That's why we were going inside if it killed me, and at this point, the chances felt like roughly 50-50.

I took a deep breath and led them into a hallway with plush carpeting and ornate wallpaper, doors concealed in the shadows of alcoves, each one a dark rectangle. The decor was about what I'd expected from the outside—1950s architecture updated to look contemporary, and nothing immediately nefarious. The staircase looked like gray marble, the steps winding up and out of sight, the rail adorned with detailed carvings that were unreadable in the dim light filtering in from some invisible source. I spotted an elaborate bar cart, which Felix made a beeline for, pouring a generous helping of tequila into a glass.

"Well?" he asked as he drank.

In my brief exchange with Lemaya, in which I'd explained the bare bones of my plan, she had directed me toward three specific rooms upstairs. That, at least, still seemed valid. But I couldn't just let them in there, could I? The ultimate goal, after all, was to *help* these poor girls, which meant keeping them as far away from these clowns as possible. With a sigh, I started up the stairs. In the upstairs hallway, I paused, swearing I heard a noise from *somewhere*, though I couldn't tell which room it might be coming from.

Felix's eyes glinted sharply in the moonlight when he pointed out the three doors. "What, only one each? If anyone's down for a trade after, let me know."

Fucking hell. The first thing I would do if I ever got out of this was take a long, thorough shower.

I turned to Door One. If there was someone in that room— and I miraculously managed to both convince her that I wasn't some depraved sicko *and* get her to play along—maybe she'd be able to give me the insider's guide to finding my way—and hers —the hell out of here.

No such luck. The screaming started before I even opened the door.

6

HER

"Get it anywhere near me and I'll bite it off!"

Yeah, I'd rehearsed that line, but how the fuck else was I supposed to have occupied myself for the past hour?

My arms were numb and stiff, almost frozen, and I was certain my wrists were rubbed raw by now, probably bleeding. I'd adjusted them hundreds of times until every possible position stung more than the last. Still, I strained against them, gritting my teeth and praying, somehow, for the sheer force of will to get myself out of this. There *had* to be a way out of this.

My heart picked up again as, in the gloom, the form neared. Tall, broad-shouldered. Well, shit. Whoever this perv was, he wasn't, as I'd hoped, some scrawny weakling.

"I'm here to—"

I screamed, loud enough to drown him out.

At once, a hand clapped over my mouth. A rough palm and metal that clanked on my teeth. Rings. Thick, ornate ones. Oh, a fancy boy, was it?

"Would you stop—"

I started thrashing *and* screaming. It shot shafts of agony through my poor arms, but thank God my legs still worked and he hadn't tied them down. I kicked wildly, aiming for the money spot.

"What the hell? Would you please *stop*? I told you, I'm not going to—ow, *fuck*." My kick must have landed somewhere good because his hand fell away from my mouth as he hissed in pain.

"Oh, you don't like that?" I taunted. "Well, that's too bad, you sick fuck. You'll have to gag me, or this is what you're going to get, all the way through. Is that what you want?"

When I'd had my wisdom teeth removed last year, I'd come out of anesthesia in tears, not knowing why I was crying, just knowing I had to cry. But no. *No.* I wouldn't open my eyes, crying or any other way. Because not this man. This man wore a suit more expensive than anything my father owned. This man had a gold watch on his wrist in place of—

With nothing but the weak shaft of moonlight cutting through the high window, I saw his beautiful face, blinking at me, every bit as shocked as I was. And before I could even take in *that*, my senses were already full: full of that familiar calloused thumb wiping away the tears now flowing from my cheeks; the incredulous sun-chapped lips landing lightly on my mouth as if testing to see that I wouldn't melt away.

And then, to my surprise, he just collapsed there. His moonlit hair spilled across my breast, the tension in his impossibly strong shoulders slowly crumbling as if he'd been bearing the weight of something far too heavy for far too long.

My only regret was that I couldn't hold him. Not the way I was.

Instead, all I finally whispered was, "I got your message."

"I'm so sorry, Lou," he said, raising his head as if he'd just remembered where we were.

"Shh. You have nothing to apologize for."

"No, you don't understand, *mäi léift*."

"*Mäi léift*," I whispered. "What does it mean? You wouldn't tell me before. What does it——"

His hand clamped down on my mouth again before I could get the rest out. He paused as he ran his good hand through his hair, then glanced at the door, then moved away from the bed, still keeping one hand pressed over my mouth, and my heart seized. In the moonlight, his tailored silk-lined jacket slid off his shoulders and onto the floor. One hand moved to the front of his shirt—expensive and perfectly fitted to his body but printed in some bizarre pattern; where had *that* come from?—undoing the buttons. Then he stopped. Again. In the darkness and the silence, I only heard him breathing, and when I dared to open my eyes again, saw only the outline of his broad, bare shoulders moving up and down minutely. He leaned in closer, and his breath, both hot and somehow icy, made my skin quiver like a struck musical note.

"Remember how you told me you were in that school musical, and you used improv to warm up before rehearsal?" he whispered.

"Yeah, and I hated it," I tried to tell him, though his hand was still muffling my words.

And I was starting to get scared.

"*Remember what they told you?* To keep the scene moving, you never say *no*. You always say *yes, and*."

"But why——"

"Because you're to wrap those perfect, pink princess lips around my cock. The ones I knew the second I saw them that they'd never sucked off anyone, ever."

He closed his eyes briefly and settled himself on his knees on either side of my torso, straddling my waist. I was lying flat, back pressed into the mattress, arms stretched up and cuffed to the headboard, the chain taut enough that I couldn't shift much. Suddenly, his body jerked upward, his breaths coming out in sharp gasps, biting down on his lip, gritting his teeth. With one hand, he crudely fisted a hunk of my curls and jerked my head forward, forcing my chin up off the pillows, and pushed his cock past my lips and farther in. I couldn't see much in the dim moonlight, but I could feel every bit of the swelled, solid mass of him filling every cavern of my mouth, forcing me to loosen my jaw as I bit back a scream.

He fucked it in and out as slowly and precisely and perfectly as he'd moved it once before, in a room full of breathing plants. But there was nothing alive in this room, this mausoleum of white marble, except for us. And the classical Greek pillars on either side of me may as well have crumbled, the menacing carved griffins cowered and retreated, at the sight of that magnificent sculpted body, towering powerfully over me, his head bent, forelock of golden hair tumbling loosely over half his face. His chest, the scars etched into his skin like blood scrawled onto parchment and dried, spilling out a history of anguish and bravery alike—was bare, except for the glint of a thin gold necklace with a blue pendant, *where on earth*—and the watch—and the thick gold rings on his two middle fingers that curled tightly around mine. Accouterments for an aristocrat; a prince.

And I was his slave.

Twisting forward, I widened my eyes in the dim moonlight just enough to see the veins in his beautiful, scar-covered, muscled arms swell tautly as he launched into a new, violent pace. If only I could meet his eyes in the darkness. If only I could look.

There must be a reason. He never does anything without a reason.

But he wasn't telling, and he wasn't stopping. His hands weren't his hands. The dark, unknowable pits of his eyes were strange. And despite myself, despite the shame of being tethered there like an animal, I could already feel the sopping sheets beneath me, a sick heat curling low in my stomach as my body responded to what I feared, to what I wanted, to what I deserved.

Because I was terrified. Terrified that he wouldn't stop. And terrified that he *would*.

I stiffened and gurgled, squeezing my hands where they were trapped and pushing helplessly against the metal as he took no quarter, merciless in his expertise: his speed, his roughness, his control.

And I couldn't catch my breath.

Stop.

Keep going.

He shifted slightly, one arm slipping down, fingers brushing against my wrist, probing, lingering on the cuffs as my skin raked against them.

I squirmed and shook, rattling against the cuffs and as he groaned, coming undone around my slick, helpless tongue, foam and saliva and hot tears flowing over my chin and cheeks, my pussy practically gushed over the sheets and down my legs, ready to come from the wanting alone.

"No," he growled, plunging even deeper into me with a hiss as I took him down to the root and held him there. Suddenly, he pulled up sharply as if to tear himself away. As if he *wanted* to tear himself away, but didn't.

Why?

It didn't matter. I was screaming now.

Stop. I can't breathe.

But he didn't stop.

He didn't stop.

And I didn't want him to.

"I've been taking orders my whole life, princess. From now on, we'll only stop when *I* say."

What? Could he really mean—

But before I could decide, before I could *think*, he dove in again, his teeth and jaw clenched, jerking my head forward by one curl.

Please. I can't breathe. Please.

But he was right not to listen, after all I'd done. And just as his hips had begun to snap with each thrust, he slowed them down, forcing himself back into the confines of my mouth, watching me gag.

His rough hand was still at my wrist.

Not moving. No, not quite.

A flicker of something deliberate, something pressing, something moving—*just barely*.

"You deserve this, you know," he whispered. "To choke on my cum. To gag on my cock. To just once feel like I feel. To scream and have no one hear you. To be voiceless. To be helpless. To submit to your master. So," he added, "do you? Submit?"

My tongue lolled uselessly as I stared up at him, managing a helpless, shaky nod, agreeing to whatever he said.

Yes. *Yes.*

Because he was right. I deserved it.

He laughed softly and plunged deeper still, swelling and throbbing as he braced himself over me, his chest heaving with violent effort, one large hand curled painfully in my hair at the nape, even while the fingertips of his other hand still grazed the binding edge of metal. His teeth clenched so hard I expected to hear them shatter any moment. And then he came, and I shuddered at the eruption of all, that I'd become a vessel for the guilt and humiliation and shame, the chains and the muzzles and the whips and locks and the oppressed desire, all those untouchable basement nights, all of it spilling into me.

The object of his hate. Because what else could I be?

I'd realized it hours earlier, lying there chained to the bed.

I was the monster. Not him.

And I couldn't look. So I looked up, at the mirror in the ceiling, at the infinite reflections and refractions of us, all the twisted-up faces of his power and my lack, as I tasted every drop of his climax, salty and sweet and exquisite and awful as my tears, raining down my throat and over my lips and down my chin.

And then he shifted again—just barely—but it was enough. The rough drag of his body against mine, the rhythmic snap of his hips, the sharpness of his breath above me. No hands, no mercy, just his presence, overwhelming and undeniable, pressing me down into the heat I couldn't escape. My back arched as much as the cuffs would allow, the pressure cresting with nowhere to go, and when he growled low in his throat— *mine*—it broke something open inside me. I came with a silent, shuddering cry, everything tightening and splintering as the release tore through me, wave after wave, brutal and bright and unstoppable.

And I didn't fight because I was giving him this. Doing penance. As if it could ever be enough for what I'd done. For what I *hadn't* done. For having been weighed in the balance and found—

Wait.

Yes, and.

He caressed my throat as the warm cum kept cascading down my esophagus with a finality that was chilling despite its heat. He pulled out of my mouth, marking me with a single, delicate rope across my face, one that fell hotly across my cheeks where the tears had been. With horrific fascination, I watched him, his flanks aglow with slickness, shoulders moving up and down as he gazed down at me as we both heaved. For a moment, we were silent.

His other hand, still lingering by my wrist, made one final movement. The softest, lightest *click*.

"Good girl," he whispered, a phrase that, when I'd heard it mere hours ago, had filled me with unfathomable disgust.

Now?

"Now—"

But before he could get out another word, someone else's clammy, meaty paw clamped over my mouth before I could respond or even think. I screamed and sank my teeth into the palm, but I doubted the bastard could even feel it through the doughy, leathered skin.

Next to the bed, another, even bigger man had ripped my boy off me before he had time to react, flattening him loudly and violently against the wall, pulling his hands behind his back, no doubt destined for the same cold metal as my own.

Rendered helpless, I rattled my restraints against the bedpost, determined to give a struggle. But the palm only pressed harder into my face, shoving the remaining fluid into my nose and mouth, cutting off my breath, and I was already exhausted.

"Oh my God. You're good, Rocket Boy. You're really good."

Over the hand crushing my face, I could barely see the female form silhouetted in the weak moonlight, her hands clasped together near her mouth like a rhapsodic schoolgirl. But the woman came closer, and then all of her came into focus: the blond hair floating in a wispy halo around her face, the body-skimming white crop top and leggings she wore and the stylish matching ivory-handled knife sheathed at her waist; the little bounce she did on the balls of her feet as she giggled with glee. "But you're gonna have to do a *little* bit more to make me believe you hate her as much as all that."

7

M *y love.*
That's what it meant. Why didn't I fucking tell her? Instead, I subtly flicked my eyes up from the floor where they'd been forced to look. Over to the bed, where, in the helpful glow of a lamp someone had switched on, Louisa had gone quiet. Understandably, since the former gardener—Obadiah, apparently, now, though the repulsive creep scarcely deserved such a grandiose moniker—had strapped a muzzle on over her mouth and nose after Resi had decided she'd heard enough of her screaming and cursing.

What a girl. Too bad she'd never speak to me again, which I deserved.

Though the former gardener's grip forced my neck down toward the floor, I could just make out her body, still clad in the white lacy thing they'd put her in, chest rising in and out, quivering ever so faintly. It was those tiny movements, only, that kept *me* calm. Kept me able to think. Unfortunately, what I thought was that everything I wanted to say—*let her go; it's me you hate; it's okay, Lou, I love you, and I'm sorry*—were the last liabilities either of us could afford if I had any chance of figuring out a plan to get us out of this while staying alive long enough to actually enact it.

Love. It's just another thing they use against you.

Even a dumbass like Corey had known that; it was what had landed me with Langer and subsequently here; and if there was one thing *that* had taught me, it was not to give Resi the same advantage.

Because my life was the kind where protecting the people I loved, more often than not, came down to breaking their hearts. It had started when Resi, at the precise moment Arlo and Felix had disappeared into their respective bedrooms, informing me that Louisa—my Louisa—was chained to the bed upstairs.

Good, I'd responded without thinking, hating *myself* for not hitting her right in her blindingly white, artificially aligned incisors. Of course the two gigantic men on either side of her pointing pistols at me probably had something to do with that.

And Resi had laughed. *Good boy,* she'd said. *I've got to see this.*

So I'd done it. I'd finally stopped *calling* myself a good actor and actually performed. Acted like I hated Louisa, terrorizing and violating her and no doubt making her hate *me.* I knew Resi could be lying, but if I'd refused, she would have slapped the cuffs on me as soon as I'd walked in the house.

And given that we were now *both* in chains, it looked like I'd failed anyway.

Still, part of my plan had worked: I'd been able to get one of Louisa's cuffs loose in the process of face-fucking her, and as far as I could tell, Obadiah hadn't noticed. Of course I wasn't sure Louisa had noticed, either, even though I'd tried to give her a fairly idiotic hint with that *yes, and* shit.

Anyway, until I figured out something else, I had to stay compliant as Resi, practically quivering herself, trailed one of her long, vanilla-sugar nails—as sharp as a knife's edge—along my jaw, then tilted it. Not much else I could do, given I'd been kicked to my knees, still naked though half-covered in a sheet she'd thrown me, my stiff arms and wrecked shoulder silently screaming that they'd had enough. Meanwhile, my scarred and bruised wrists had been cuffed stiffly behind my back, with Obadiah latched onto one arm and an even bigger, balder guy named Noam on the other, preventing me from doing anything about any of it.

Better they held me, though. Because it meant neither of them was near *her*.

"Did you say something?" Resi asked lightly, tapping my nose like a naughty puppy. "Please don't make me muzzle *your* pretty mouth, too. I like looking at it too much."

I lowered my eyes, a show of submissiveness that I hoped would draw her attention away from Louisa and her loose cuff, at least for a second.

Buoyed by this, she removed her hand from my jaw and stood back to inspect me, bowed head to bent knees. "Now," she said, "doesn't it feel so much better not to be living a lie anymore? To be back where you belong? And," she added, "and to have *her* finally see where you belong?"

My heart clenched. The angle was wrong, so I couldn't see what I wanted to see most: where Louisa's eyes were fixed, whether she was staring at me in disgust, chained and kicked into submission. Hating me as much as I'd assured Resi I hated her.

Because Resi was right. Louisa had *still* never seen me like this. She hadn't seen me at the dealership the day her father had collected me. She hadn't seen me chained to the fence being whipped. And she hadn't seen me curled up helplessly in the storage closet, straining to reach her hand.

As if it would make any difference. As if she'd care either way. Right?

Resi moved behind me, crouched down, and stroked the underside of my wrist where I still wore the Rolex, next to where the metal cuff dug in. She let out a girlish gasp at what she found.

"Oh! So you finally did it," she whispered. "But you must have known you were just going to exchange one piece of metal for another." She smiled as she glanced back toward Louisa, raising her voice. "Sweet, sad boy. Just wanted to pretend to be free for a while. But tell me, did *she* think you were free? Did you lie and *tell* her you were, just before you slipped your cock down her throat?"

From Louisa, more thrashing; more desperate, indecipherable noise.

Resi giggled, a cloud of sweet poison mist that seemed to curl through the air and cling to every surface. She glanced up at the ceiling. "Ah, you managed to convince your girl that that mirror was just a tasteful design element. Nice going. Too bad you didn't convince *me* of anything." She shrugged innocently. "Oh, cheer up. You both got a lot more action tonight than your buddies did."

I raised my eyes. Had the two other girls escaped somehow? Fought them off?

"Your bros are gone, likely to the airport and from there to San Francisco," Resi explained. "A threat to report them to the feds for being accessories to human trafficking means they won't be back for a while."

Thank you.

"You must be crushed," Resi remarked. "I could tell how much you all bonded. Because you have so much in common and everything," she added.

My face burned, but she only laughed as she gently

smoothed my limp hair back from my face. Her lips parted to reveal her catlike tongue, which flicked around the perimeter of her mouth delicately, her breath soft and delicate and sweet, like all of her edges. A stinging sea anemone tossed in the current. Beautiful, alluring, and pure artifice.

In a flash, she dropped her hand lower.

I squeezed my eyes shut, the memory of what had happened the last time it had ventured down there still ringing in my pain receptors.

"I know, I know. God, you are *so* much easier to condition than you think you are. But you know," she breathed into my ear, "I can make it good, too. For boys *and* girls. For Alma. For Sloane. Your sister wasn't as playful, I'm afraid."

I bit back my growl.

"But I made it *really* good for Lemaya." There was something different in the way she spoke this last name. Something in the way her light blue eyes flashed.

I raised my head without thinking, only to have it forced back down toward the floor with a harsh chop to the back of the neck from Noam. "She led me here. It was a trap."

Resi didn't seem to notice. "It was a *double* trap," she clarified, glancing back at Louisa, forgetting she didn't want to hear my voice.

Yes. That's it. Keep the villain talking. Classic stratagem. Let's go.

Subtly, I tested the cuffs. Obadiah had fucked up the double lock on one of Louisa's; chances were decent he'd done the same thing with mine. Maybe I could feel for it without either of the goons catching on.

"Your sister and Lemaya became such good friends," said Resi. "Teaching each other and everything. It was super cute, actually."

Well, fuck. It seemed that whatever Louisa and Maeve and

Erica's plan had been, it had been doomed from the start the same as mine because we had all been going off the same wrong information—the layout, the locations of the girls, the timing and habits of Resi and the security guards—from Lemaya. But they had had no reason to disbelieve Maeve, while I had had *every* reason to disbelieve Lemaya. Hell, I *had* disbelieved her, but I'd done it anyway. She—like the new suits and gold watches and aged bourbon—had been just another accouterment, another accessory, sent in to distract me, to play both me *and* my sister.

"Where's Maeve?" I asked.

Resi's eyes flashed again, but she didn't answer. I swallowed. What did that mean? Resi hadn't spoken much about her whereabouts, or those of the other girls, either, except to hint that they'd been mercifully spared the attentions of Arlo and Felix.

"Before Lemaya was either your friend or your sister's, she was mine," Resi was explaining, gazing out the narrow window almost nostalgically. "And no wonder. When you're the only slave in a crumbling mansion with a filthy, senile owner on death's door, it doesn't take much convincing to let someone finish him off for you. Someone who's promised you a job, followed by freedom. And especially someone who's pulled it off once before."

Before?

Suddenly, some puzzle pieces fell into place. "With Max's—with *your* father," I said. "After Max came back. And wrote himself into the will."

Resi laughed lightly. "Yup. Nothing like murder—if you can really call it that when the person *so* deserves to die—to bring long-lost siblings together again." She gazed around the cave of a room, with its pillars and vicious griffins like sacred carvings; its massive bed like a white marble slab. "Huh. Come to think of it, it happened right here in this room. *Everything* happened in this room. Master, or should I say, Daddy, used to let his friends go at me right over there, in that bed, while Max was tied up in the corner and forced to watch, poor guy. All he ever wanted to do was help me, but he couldn't. Explains a lot."

There might actually have been something genuine behind her voice, but it was hard to tell, concealed behind layers upon layers of trauma and sociopathy.

"Until a few years later, when he stood right over there *by choice*, watching me press a pillow over dear Daddy's face." She looked around fondly. "Probably why I haven't changed up the decor much. Too many happy memories."

I could almost see Louisa's skin turn a shade of green, her body seeming to squeeze in on itself. Fucking hell, how long had she been lying on that bed of horror, waiting for more? The *more* I'd given her? I had to end this. I had to make it right. My wrist wriggled in the cuff, trying to expand its circumference without drawing attention to it.

"You see, Lemaya and I had a lot in common, obviously," Resi was saying. "We both loved my brother, for instance. And that's when I put the idea in her head," she continued. "Why be a vet tech when you can be a billionaire's trophy wife instead?" She giggled. "Promising her I could make it happen was one of my best bedtime stories. Good enough to get her to do anything I asked, anyway."

Lemaya had betrayed me, and Maeve, *and* Louisa. I *should* hate her. But she'd been through as much hell as any of us, maybe more, and I couldn't blame her—or any of the girls, really—for cashing in everything for a free ticket to a life she'd never before dared to dream of. She'd been a victim twice over —once of slavery and again of Resi's false promises of freedom.

"You put ideas in all their heads, from the sounds of it," I said. "Ideas that didn't exactly pan out, did they?"

She tossed her head back. "Well, see, my brother and I—I gather he told you about this, right?—had this dream. One from a long, long time ago. And we agreed that it would be my job to figure out how to remove the tracking chips from the girls we chose, ones we could be confident their owners weren't looking for," Resi said. "And that we would save them; and in time, all slaves. That was our dream."

"It was *his* dream," I muttered, too low for Resi to hear. However, it prompted the former gardener, who must be getting paid a shitload of money to continue to act like a good slave, to punch me in the ear, leaving the echo of pain ringing through my frontal cortex. Despite this, it was enough of a distraction to give me a chance to expand the one cuff that hadn't been applied properly, nearly enough to slip it off. Assuming neither thug noticed, it was a start.

"No one was better qualified to do it," Resi was saying. "Max made sure of it. He sent me to California, to the best research universities there, while he made the money, all in preparation for our one big chance. But sadly, even though we quickly found a formula we thought would work." She shrugged.

A formula? The science nerd in me couldn't help but perk up at that.

"My experiments failed, one after another. And we only had finite capital, you see. Naturally, I started getting desperate. If I had to go back to Max and beg him for more money, he'd start asking questions. He'd be like *you*. And then he'd find out I started cutting corners. And that the results of the failed experiments weren't exactly as humane as I assured him they were. One of the girls, sadly, we couldn't save."

She spoke about the dead girl in the desert like a flower she'd forgotten to water.

"But at least she died knowing she was advancing the noble cause of freedom. Or something."

Louisa jerked on the bed at that. I closed my eyes; opened them again. If only I could see her face. See whether she was still with me. Whether she trusted me to have a plan to get us out of this. Whether she trusted me at all, which was doubtful at this point.

"And my sister? Was she one of the failed experiments?"

Resi just laughed. "Even worse, our main financial backer— I think you both know him quite well—would spook. And that would be the end of our dream." A strange, faraway look in her eyes. "And everything that happened in this room would be for nothing."

"So the girls were tools." I forced myself to keep my voice measured, even. Any emotion I showed, anything I purported to care about—up to and including the girl on the bed—would immediately become a weapon Resi could exploit. I had to approach this like the businessman I'd just been trying to fool everyone into thinking I was. "To fuck your dad. To fuck the system."

She came closer and kneeled, pressing a hand lightly on the side of my face. "Oh, sweetie, we both know someone's *always* going to get fucked," she said sadly. "All I cared about was that it was never again going to be me."

I swallowed and looked down, ashamed that what Resi had just said made sense to me—or had, too many times in my past.

"Meanwhile, I promised them more and more, anything to help me. But some of the girls knew I was lying; *I* knew I was lying. They were asking about the missing one. Especially your sweet sister. She threatened to run; to tell someone; or to find her brother, the one who was going to come save all of them."

Maeve *had* always had a talent for getting under people's

skin. And it sounded like her language barrier hadn't been as big as I'd feared.

"And the free one, too?" I asked.

"Alma was crazy anyway," Resi scoffed. "She'd have to be, to pretend to be a runaway slave just to get food and shelter. By the time I realized she didn't have a chip, it was too late. Luckily, I had all the resources I needed for a *very* successful—and fun—side hustle," she said, looking around the room, nodding at Louisa's prone, shadowy form on the bed as if she were just another part of the decor. "Sadly, I couldn't tell my brother, who, God only knows why, still upholds *some* morals and principles and stuff, though I've frequently begged him to stop. Anyway, he wouldn't touch any of the girls, or let anyone else touch them, unless I could convince him they were there by choice." She tittered. "Luckily, they thought they *were* there by choice."

"Were? Past tense?" My heart began to thrash against my ribcage at the implications.

"Little sis may be a pest, but she's a star. She still figured out where the girls were *despite* Lemaya's best efforts. So yes, they're gone. Almost certainly on their way to the police with Alma and those two cute little sapphic snowflakes I got suspended, if they're not already there. And it may be too late, but don't think for a second I'm going to let them get away *that* easily."

She could be bluffing, but I didn't think so. "What happened to them?"

She looked at her watch, raised her head, and smiled. "I'll find out soon. And once I do, all that remains is to figure out how to wrap up our little gathering here before the cops break down my door. And Max's. And Keith's."

I watched a shiver wrack Louisa's body, and an ice-cold fear rose in my chest. I could almost feel her heart thumping with terror as Resi spoke, my eyes, for the millionth time, trying to find an escape route from the room she'd been trapped in for hours already. Fuck.

Because though Resi would torture me, chances were she wouldn't kill me. Not yet, anyway. Not while Max was still around. But Louisa would never be anything more than a loose end.

And I forged ahead with the assumption that Louisa knew that. Because if she didn't, what I was about to do would kill her.

"No," I said. "Only Keith's."

"What?" A crack in Resi's shell, for the first time since she'd arrived. For the first time since I'd met her, almost.

I sped ahead, knowing if I paused to think, I'd trip on my words and it would be over. "You already had his name on the warehouse deed, but you wanted to go further. You were trying to steal as much of his money as you could while framing him for it. For the sex trafficking. For all of it." I paused, but only for a second, to take a gulp of air. "You *knew* the police would find the girls. That's why you wanted into Max's books. It was going to be your Plan B. Corey was helping you. But you didn't finish the job."

Louisa had grown silent. *Everyone* was silent, an audience watching the soliloquy of a lifetime.

"And? Well?" Resi crossed her arms, a posture that revealed more than she probably thought.

"Well, I can make it happen," I continued. "I found the files. I've already doctored most of them. I just need to finish a few more. We drop it in the cops' laps, and you and Max are free."

More silence. Resi barely moved.

"He'll be ruined," I swallowed. "At the very least. The whole family will."

"And at most?"

"Well, I'm pretty sure people's families still got sold into slavery for major debt, don't they? They'll get a taste of what it's like to be you. To be me."

"And you?" Resi pressed.

"With Keith out of the picture, I'll be free, too. Max will make sure of it."

Lou, don't believe me. Please don't believe me.

I knew how hard she'd worked. I knew how much she loved her family, despite it all. I'd seen it all. I understood. I wasn't supposed to, but I did.

An enticing smile flowed over Resi's face. Her gaze shifted between me and Louisa.

Then she burst into laughter. She even tipped her head back.

"Girl, it wasn't a lie after all. He fucking *hates* you." She kept laughing as she crossed the floor in a few strides of her toned legs, opened one of the bureau drawers, and removed something from a velvet bag.

No. Not that. That wasn't what I meant.

"Tell me more, baby," she implored me. "Tell how much you loved watching her choke." Resi unsheathed the sleek, brand-new electric cattle prod, slowly, reverently, and tossed it to Obadiah. "And to think," she said with a glance back at me. "I was going to use this on *you*."

The former gardener moved the prod over Louisa's chin, and my eyes narrowed as I watched it glow like a blue halo in the dim light, the low hum of a thousand other moments. The sound of helplessness; of being owned.

"Your master's spoiled brat. Helpless. Restrained for your pleasure." Resi's eyes flicked to Louisa's cuffs, which by now must have cut off all circulation in her arms, which might be a blessing. "I should have known. You're just like me." Her tone was slow, rich, feline, her mouth parted again, tongue showing, blue eyes swirling. "You want to see them all burn."

She nodded, and Obadiah's hand shot out. Louisa's scream tore through the muzzle, split through the walls and into the night air beyond. She bucked and kicked and thrashed, but that wouldn't last long, I knew. The prod shot out steam, cauterizing the flawless virgin skin of her neck, filling the air with the smell of her burning tissue—*hers*, the girl who had never known slavery, who had no reason to be here at all, who had only wanted to find a way to do good in the world. And I couldn't see her face, but picturing it—and the tears I knew were streaming down her cheeks—was enough. She began kicking and thrashing anew as Obadiah dug into her flesh, moving from her neck to her shoulder to her legs, where, from my angle, I could see massive blisters begin to sprout like mushrooms everywhere the electric prongs dug in.

And I watched it all, blinking back a different searing heat behind my eyes—of guilt, of shame, of tears that no matter what, I couldn't let fall. Not here.

And I said nothing. Because if I said something, she'd use the prod on me. And then I'd never be able to get these cuffs off and save Louisa.

Hell of a choice, as usual.

After an eternity, Obadiah stopped. And I couldn't look at what was left of my princess.

"You see, Louisa, no one ever really bothers teaching slaves right from wrong," explained Resi, nodding at me as if in approval of my performance. "They assume our minds are too simple to handle such weighty matters; that our masters will always be there to decide for us. So when we finally do get a chance to make a choice... Well, sometimes we get a little carried away." She laughed. "Come to think of it, he isn't even *here* under honest pretenses. You know he had to con his way in by pretending to be your ex-BF-turned-vegetable, right?"

On the bed, Louisa's body curled up into itself like a dying spider. Watching it, I felt like dying myself. Her mind must already have my greatest-hits album of deception on repeat, starting from the moment I'd walked into her bedroom and ending with the moment I'd walked into *this* bedroom. I was starting to wish I'd *told* her the long story, at least so she didn't have to hear it *this* way.

"You knew it was too good to be true. Slave crosses an ocean, meets master's daughter, stars cross. Guess while he was fucking you, he was also fucking you over." She sighed. "But hey, it's all he knows *how* to do." She shook her head, blond, wispy hair bouncing. "Anyway," she said, her face turning serious again before promptly pasting on another grin. "Let's make sure."

Oh, fuck no.

Noam's meaty fist released his grip on my arm, and he stepped back. Resi's face wore a mask of concentration as she plunged a hand under the sheet and between her own legs.

And in the former gardener's hand, the prod hissed to life again.

Gingerly, she took my hand, the tips of her fingers beneath her nails petting it with a delicacy that surprised me. Her hands, of course, deceptive as the rest of her, weren't quite as smooth as a woman who had been born free. Like me, she'd spent her childhood—her miserable, broken, ruined childhood—toiling for her masters, in more ways than one. Her movements, though, were calculated but gentle, carefully, rhythmically petting me, almost in time to Louisa's choked-off screams as Obadiah continued his trail of terror over her soft flesh.

I twitched, struggling to breathe in and out without gasping. Our only chance was for me to hold the line. To buy us time. To convince Resi I still had something she wanted.

And, most importantly, that I wanted to watch Louisa burn. Because I had to keep *myself* from burning to keep her alive instead of tossed in a shallow grave out behind the Langer family cottonwood tree.

So I closed my eyes and focused on breathing as Louisa's muffled screams continued, as Resi's wicked hands looped around mine with the barest brush of her barbed-wire nails. She was behind me now, her chest pressed to my back, her body curled against mine like a lover's, one of my arms pinned between us at an angle I couldn't quite register. She rested her face gently on my shoulder, her other hand snaking around my neck, then carding through my hair. I couldn't see exactly where she guided my hand, but I could feel her—the slick heat of her, the rhythm of her breath hitching—as she used it for her own pleasure.

"This is for both of you, you know," she whispered to me. "So you don't forget who and what you both are. Now come on, sweet thing. Touch me. Touch me like you mean it."

I clenched my jaw against the way her body buckled under my touch, while Louisa's tortured scream collapsed into a thousand others—the women whose hands I'd had to let go of, whose bodies I couldn't pull back from the edge.

If there was one thing the world seemed intent on teaching me, it was that nothing I could ever do, no tools I could ever acquire, would be enough to save the ones I loved.

"You're right."

Yes, and.

"What's that?" Resi gave me a smirk before finally glancing back at Louisa, who lay still, limbs at funny angles, a broken doll a bored child had flung aside.

The same heat that radiated up from her limbs seemed to

sear behind my eyes. Bubbling out of her muzzled mouth came maybe a whimper, maybe a "fuck you," maybe both.

Obadiah dropped the prod and leered his graying, wrinkled, toothless face down at her, practically licking his lips at the idea of seeing his former master's daughter helpless and whimpering.

That sick fuck better not get comfortable. When I got out of here, he'd be at the top of my fucking list.

Resi wasn't having it, either. "Don't get any ideas, pal," she told the former gardener without looking. "I'm sorry, but this hot little scenario does *not* include you."

Obadiah's shoulders sagged with disappointment for a second before he opened his toothless maw again and fired up the prod, the steam from the tip billowing up in a white cloud. Louisa's body twitched again, and she squeaked helplessly, her muscles tense against the pain. She knew what was coming now. It didn't take long.

Yes, and. Yes, and.

"You're right. It's true," I said louder, shoving down the desperation in my voice, or any cadence that would reveal that my heart was being ripped apart piece by piece. "I wanted to see her fucked. I wanted to fuck them all."

"Yeah?" Resi rasped as she stroked herself harder, eyes dilating, cheeks flushed. *She* was getting off on this. At fucking the fuckers. That's the only thing she loved; the only thing she *could* love, after what had been done to her. And she thought I was the same, because why wouldn't I be?

"Again," she said. "Say it." My pulse raced, and she grew breathless as she rubbed herself. Almost involuntarily, her teeth tapped my neck, murmuring something as her other hand tugged harshly on a clump of my hair. But I couldn't hear her now, or myself. I only heard Louisa. Louisa's face was lost to me, and thank fuck it was because I'd never be able to look at her again after this.

"Say. It," Resi gurgled. "Or you get the prod instead."

I love you. I'm not going anywhere. Never, ever give up on me.

"I hate her," I said, mind racing faster than my mouth. "I hate that she gets under my skin," I blurted out.

"I hate that when I close my eyes, it's always, always, always her face I see. I hate the way she reminds me of the freedom I can't get, of the person I can't be, of the name I don't have. But most of all, I hate the way she's the only one who's ever looked at me like I'm someone worth saving," I finished breathlessly. "Someone worth loving. Someone *able* to love. When I know I'm not."

Breathe. Please breathe.

Resi's blue eyes rolled back in her head, lost in some beautiful or horrible place only she would ever know. She raised her hand, triumphant, and pressed one nail to my lips, as if sealing my mouth shut with some twisted promise. She was so caught up in her own sick victory that she didn't feel my fingers working at the already loose latch of my cuffs, the one Obadiah had now fucked up twice—once on Louisa's, once on mine. It figured that Keith had never given him training in proper use of restraints, and Max had apparently overlooked it, too.

Still, I could feel his leering presence behind me, the prod still buzzing, still hot.

I breathed through the nausea as Resi shifted against me, the scent of sweat and something sharper curling in the air. My stomach churned at her touch, at the damp heat of her breath near my ear, at the way her hands still clung like she owned me.

Almost there. Almost—

The cuff gave.

My wrist slipped free just as Resi leaned more heavily into

me, her attention focused entirely on what Obadiah was about to do.

I didn't hesitate. With a sharp twist, I wrenched my hand free and grabbed the ivory knife from Resi's belt, using her body as cover just as Obadiah stepped forward, salivating for his turn to do *something*.

Not tonight.

I whirled, slashing upward, blade catching the soft, stubbly flesh of his throat. The electric prod clattered to the floor as he staggered back, fingers clawing at the blood spilling between them.

Resi barely had time to register the shift before I drove my elbow into her ribs, hard enough to send her stumbling backward. It was more than enough, and I lunged for Louisa, unbuckling and yanking the muzzle from her mouth as her limp body tumbled off the bed and onto the carpet, whorls of beautiful hair strewn like so much litter across the floor. For a second, sheer terror washed over me when her chest wasn't rising.

The bed—wide, too wide—sat in the center of the room like a stage. Resi hit the far edge, crumpling, while Obadiah bled out at the footboard. I was kneeling on the floor, Louisa in my arms, one cuff still clamped around her wrist and the other still binding her to the bedpost.

Breathe. Please breathe.

Behind me, Resi gasped, then snarled. I ducked as a bullet from Noam's pistol shattered the glass windowpane, sending shards of glittering rain down on the plush carpet and bed. But I was already moving. I grabbed the fallen prod, flipped it in my grip, and swung.

Resi crumpled, twitching, the air crackling with the sharp scent of burned ozone and the sound of her breath hitching in a raw, ugly gasp. She was already getting back up, I knew, but I didn't wait to see it. It didn't matter. "The handcuff key," I ordered.

She didn't hesitate to flip it toward me.

Louisa's lashes fluttered. Her lips parted. A breath, shaky but real. I crushed her against me, against my chest, pressing my forehead to hers, as I undid her remaining cuff and the one on my other hand. I knew I had seconds only before the other goon's gun went off again, and this time he wouldn't miss.

"I got you, *mäi léift*," I whispered. "I got you."

"Back off," Resi rasped from the carpet. But she was talking to her goons, not to me. "Leave him alone."

"But—" Noam began.

"You heard me. Put the gun away," Resi said and I realized —they didn't have to shoot us. They didn't have to do anything. They just had to watch us immolate ourselves.

Because Louisa was drawing in another choking gasp of air and half-raised her head, her limp hair matted and formless and damp, half-hiding the red, pus-filled blisters on her face that glistened, intermixed with bloody abrasions from the muzzle and rainy streaks of tears. For a second, we regarded each other unblinkingly. Her mouth wavered at the corner, marred by the shininess of the burn. I couldn't even bring myself to look at the rest of her body, afraid I'd be sick. She moaned again, a weak, rattling, helpless sound. I knew how it felt, exactly how it continued to burn, the receptors burrowing like insects underneath the skin even after the initial heat was gone. Insult to injury; humiliation to hurt.

They owned you, after all.

How the fuck was there any fixing this? "I'm—"

"Don't touch me," Louisa shrieked suddenly, ear-piercingly, leaping up from the floor and pawing half-blindly at her remaining clothing scattered across the room. Her hands and arms were stiff as claws, and she was unsteady on her feet, the lamplight just enough to reveal the blisters all over her body had begun to glisten and ooze.

"Where are you going?"

I dove for my own clothes and started throwing them on. Whatever shit options I had to fix this situation, I wasn't going to accomplish any of them naked. From the pocket of my suit jacket, I felt the vibration of my phone. Without looking, I knew who was calling. I ignored it, just as I ignored the rapt, blood-sprayed peanut gallery staring at the drama unfolding before them.

"Where do you think?" Louisa hissed back, tripping drunkenly down the stairs two at a time before unlocking the door, across the lawn next door, into the vast, dry suburban sandscape that sprawled around us in every direction. "To find Maeve and the rest. Maybe it's not too late. No thanks to you."

"I know, but you're burned. They almost *killed* you. You can't just—"

She swung her knee and landed a blow with an amount of force I was, somehow, not at all surprised to find she still had in her, knocking the breath out of me and sending me reeling backward. Away from her.

She turned back, only once. Raised her eyebrows. "Yes. And?" Flat, bitter. No improv this time. Not a callback.

Just a goodbye.

And she ran, blazing her erratic path out into the street, still clutching her clothes to her chest. Her skin was awash in the orange-gold glow of the identical lampposts planted in every yard, while the remains of the torn white chemise and her wild, tangled hair swirled around her like ghosts. She dashed blindly, right in front of an oncoming van.

I shouted at her again, but the van slammed on the brakes inches away from her face, honking furiously. She paused in a daze but only for a second, then kept running in a zigzag pattern, her bare feet crunching across the neighbors' land-scaping rocks, over a low fence and into another yard and behind another house, where she disappeared from sight.

And then I was alone forever. Again.

"The boss says you got three hours to deliver those files," Noam said suddenly, casually, from behind me.

"I was lying about that, you idiot," I said without turning around.

"She knows it was a lie," he said as he lumbered away, and when I turned my head, I caught him lovingly petting the pistol concealed in his jacket. "But now ya gotta make it true."

Oh, right. Now I could frame and defraud Keith all I liked because Louisa would never speak to me again either way, and Resi and her goons would kill me if I didn't.

I guessed that explained why they weren't killing me now. Because they'd have plenty of chances to kill me later—and everyone I cared about, too.

My phone was still vibrating. Slowly, numbly, I swiped and raised it to my ear.

"Hey. Kid."

From a cottonwood across the street came the lonely, croaky chirp of a nightjar, followed by the soft, leathery wing flaps as it took flight, its body ablaze with orange light from the identikit globes lining each yard, bathing this serene residential neighborhood that, for years, had hidden the evilest depravity humans could devise.

Speaking of that, the list of recriminations I should be screaming into Max Langer's ear—starting with the fact that the man was indirectly the reason why the girl I loved had once more turned tail and disappeared out of my life—was almost infinite at this point. But it was all those very same things that made me want to hold off.

So instead, I just stood there and waited for what he had to say.

And like many things that had come out of my boss's mouth over the short time I'd known him, it was a surprise.

"Ever seen the sunrise from the window of a private jet over the Gulf of Mexico?" he asked.

"No."

"In a few hours, you will."

8

HER

It wasn't until I finally collapsed in exhaustion in a patch of short, soft grass on the edge of what I assumed was someone's fussy rock garden—maybe three, maybe five, maybe seven blocks away in what I could only pray was the right direction. Only then, curled up there, helpless, barely conscious, nearly nauseous, taking rattling gasps of air, harpooned by searing pain that at times seemed to almost be strengthening, did I allow myself to confirm that he was smart enough not to have followed me.

Not that some stupid, delusional, self-destructive part of me didn't still hope he *had*.

But if it came down to a choice between him holding my hand while I breathed through this and watching him get thrown on the ground by the police and dragged away because Daddy had triggered his tracking chip, the choice was clear.

It was funny that *that*—that every second I remained in his presence, I was putting him in danger, and that I had to get away from him—was the thought running through my head as my skin was being melted off my body, minutes after he'd fucked my mouth to oblivion. But it was.

That and the fact that he so *clearly* had a plan.

Clearly.

At this point, I hadn't a clue what time of night it was. But I did know that as the minutes ticked by, my standard studying-in-the-library lie—knowing how my father's mind worked— was going to get flimsier and flimsier. It was basic math. Daughter missing for hours with no phone + forbidden to see boy + boy instantly trackable by implanted chip = jackpot for Daddy.

Of course I had to consider the possibility that my boy didn't know why I'd run, or thought I hadn't figured out what he'd been doing. That I hadn't figured out why he'd said what he said, or done what he did. That he didn't realize that what he'd been trying to accomplish—saving my life—was a damn sight more important than protecting me from hearing him say he'd plotted to destroy my entire family. And that he hated me.

When he still hadn't even fucking said he loved me.

Yes, and.

Eyes closed, my mind replayed a supercut: the marble walls, the clink of the cuffs, the terrifying way his body moved like he *owned* mine. Like he owned me. He'd even said it:

Mine.

And I'd been shaking and soaked and confused out of my mind, like my body couldn't decide if it wanted to escape or collapse into him. But what if that was the point? What if he was playing a role so dark it scared *him* just to wear it because that was the only way to undo the cuffs, to keep Resi fooled, to keep me alive? What if he already knew me well enough to know exactly where I could take pain, and where I couldn't? And if that was his way of keeping me from breaking, then maybe it wasn't hate at all. Maybe it was love, in the only language we were allowed to speak.

I hate the way she's the only one who's ever looked at me like I'm someone worth saving.

He did hate it. I believed that. Because for him, that meant being a person, and he didn't fully know how to do that yet.

But that didn't mean he didn't believe I was worth saving, too.

But my burned throat and scream-weary mouth were as parched as the sand, and stray gravel from the rock garden was digging into the open pustules of my burns alongside the dirty, sticky, gauzy, torn fabric of the stupid fucking lacy thing I was wearing. When I'd been running, the pain hadn't mattered, but now that I'd collapsed, it was back, and even raising my head off the grass seemed impossible.

And anyway, the burner phone Erica had given me was dead. Even if it hadn't been, I had no real means to stop the wheels Resi had put in motion. I didn't even know what the wheels *were*, really.

But I had to *try*. I had to do what I'd hoped I'd conveyed to him that I *would* do—find and look after Maeve so he had time to do whatever he needed to do to hatch his plan. The plan that he so clearly had. The plan pretty much *had* to be to stop Resi and save us all because at this point anything less would be failure.

But I wasn't seeing to anything. I wasn't even moving. I was lying in some grass, curled up like some red-and-purple pus-covered worm. I *should* be dead. The only reason I wasn't was that Resi *thought* she had neutralized me as a threat. That I wouldn't, and couldn't, help anyone, let alone *him*.

And right now, I sure didn't feel much like a threat.

I was grateful for the cool night air on my skin, at least. Even though I didn't deserve it.

A brief hissing noise hit my ear, and to my surprise, tiny drops of rain began to pelt me.

No. Not rain. Not *here*.

A scrabbling in the rocks by my head told me someone, or something, was approaching. *Fuck.* Raising myself partially off the now-damp grass, I managed to partially roll my body over with a groan, heart rate quickening, knowing that even if I could get up, there'd be no chance of escape.

But there was no need. Through my blurred vision, in the partial moonlight, I could spot a dog, a mottled blue-gray border collie with one pale eye, panting and jumping around me in excitement, not quite getting the picture. She turned her wet nose under my arm, sniffing furiously, and I could just make out a name on the collar: *Thalia.*

The Greek muse of comedy. How appropriate, because this exercise in improv was all becoming a brilliant farce. Might as well send in the clowns.

As much as I knew I needed help—and water, and rest, and aloe, *so* much aloe—I prayed that by some miracle this dog, collared and well-fed and well-groomed, was unattached to a person. I didn't want to be found by a person. I *hated* people. People enslaved and tortured and killed others for no reason at all and turned their victims into people who enslaved and tortured and killed others in turn, fueling an endless water wheel of pain and grief no one seemed to know how to stop.

Plus, a person would call an ambulance, and an ambulance meant police. It meant giving statements. It meant contacting my parents and being forced to confess everything I had seen. And worst of all, *who* I had seen. I had no reason to think that my dad, once he heard that one of them was *him*, would give a fuck about the rest of it, even if it meant his own downfall. And I had no reason to think that whoever owned that dog, especially in a neighborhood like this, would give one, either.

"Miss?" A cell phone light cast the vaguest heat on my face. It was accompanied by the voice of a young person of indeterminate gender. "Miss?" They turned to someone in the distance.

"What." My attempt to reply came out as a groan.

Shoes crunched on rocks as the person kneeled, though they didn't touch me. "Shhh. It's okay. My—my mistress is a nurse. Well, sort of."

I'd been found by a slave. Well, fantastic. One thing was for sure: Whoever this mistress was, nurse or not, I'd rather wither and die out here than interact with her.

"Ivy! Ivy! Come quick!"

Before I could remark that it was an odd way to address a mistress, Thalia, the collie, whimpered, her warm, furry body pressed against me protectively. *That* I was okay with. This person might own slaves, but at least she had a nice dog.

Another pair of footsteps joined the first, then more crunching.

"Shit. Oh, shit. What happened to—" A cool hand pressed to my forehead, my throat, feeling for breath, a pulse. Smoothed back my hair. Startled by the gentle touch, I wasn't sure whether to recoil or lean into it.

"Wait." A second light shone closer to my pupils. "Louisa? Little Loulou? Is that you?"

"Huh?"

"I-I'm Ivy. Ethan's friend. Oh, you remember me, don't you? No, of course you don't."

But I did, and she'd once been more than Ethan's friend. They used to date, and I remembered her as tall and thin and stylish and enviably gorgeous, like all of his girlfriends. But *unlike* most of them, also smart and nice. After they'd broken up, she had stayed friends with my brother—partying and drinking and using, of course, but I'd still enjoyed seeing her every once in a while. When Ethan disappeared, I lost touch with Ivy, too, and it seemed safe to assume that her life had gone much the way of his.

But what if it hadn't?

What if she'd married some rich jerk and lived in this neighborhood and owned a gaggle of slaves and—

"P-please." I jerked my body away from her touch.

"Oh, no, no, no," Ivy interrupted. "Don't try to talk. Just lie still. God only knows what injuries you have. I'm going to touch you to check, okay?"

I felt a light pressure on my crusted-over eyelid, which refused to open. The chemise was bunched up and thrown aside again. A smooth hand slid into mine.

"Can you squeeze? Okay, not really. I'll call for help. Can you tell me—no, shit, scratch that. I told you not to talk." She seemed to be digging deep for some nursing training that she hadn't paid much attention to the first time around.

I groaned more insistently, trying to choke out the one thing I needed to say before I gave up on trying to talk altogether. "Please," I spat. "Please don't call the police."

"But—"

"No!" I said, as frustrated as a barely verbal toddler.

She sighed. "Louisa, listen. I was an addict. I OD'd twice. The only reason I'm alive is because both times, my friends drove me to the hospital, dumped me off at the entrance, and drove away. Believe me. I get it. I won't call the police. I won't even ask you what happened if you don't want me to. But you *do* need help. Luckily, I *can* help, but the problem is, we're a mile away from my house, and we're in the middle of a golf course."

Well, shit. That explained the "rain." It was a sprinkler. Figures I'd end up on a golf course of all places. The way my luck was going, Daddy probably had an early morning round scheduled.

"Hold on. I've got an idea."

Problem was, I didn't want any part of this girl's ideas. She might be sort of a nurse, she might be Ethan's old friend, she might be nice, but none of it mattered. If she owned a slave, she couldn't be trusted, period. There was no telling how she'd take it when the first person I asked her to call was known abolitionist radical Erica Muller.

But what choice did I have?

Ivy wasn't waiting, anyway. She turned to murmur something to her apparent slave, and a second later, I heard their footsteps pounding away.

In the meantime, Ivy's hands gently examined my body, careful not to put pressure on the burns.

"Shit. These look like second-degree. Which I know doesn't sound like good news, but it is. Here, do you think you can drink this?"

The sound of a plastic water bottle uncapping, then a hand holding my head up. My lips felt too weak to close around the bottle to ingest much, but even the sensation of cool, fresh water reminded me that dehydration was probably closer to killing me than the burns. I was still trying to gulp the water when a whirring noise approached, and before I could struggle or protest, Ivy and the slave kid each took an arm and laid me down awkwardly across the back seat of an electric golf cart—the same kind my father seemed to spend half his life zooming around in.

But the breeze on my face felt oddly nice as we sputtered off the grass and over the pavement at all of five miles an hour, the engine humming and jouncing gently beneath me. Ivy and the slave talked to each other, but I couldn't make out what they were saying. As if they didn't want me to.

But that was nothing I had the energy to worry about.

For now, it was enough to feel Thalia's wet, cold nose on me from where she panted and snuffled from the floor of the cart, and to smell her faint canine musk.

"Thalia's being so good back there," Ivy remarked.

"She hardly ever tries to jump out of the cart anymore!" the kid spoke up excitedly, clearly for my benefit.

The remark received a gentle shush from Ivy, but I got the sense that it was entirely for *my* benefit. In any case, it sounded cautious, not angry. Odd.

I wished I could see where and how Ivy lived, and who else lived with her. But I could only be dragged along blindly as the two others managed to haul me out of the cart and into a house.

"I'm putting you in a cool bath now, okay?" Ivy explained, her voice echoing as we entered what must be a high-ceilinged bathroom, already ringing with the sound of flowing water scented with herbs.

With no further warning, Ivy plunged me into it, and it was a revelation. The cool evaporated the heat, erasing the pain on contact, at least temporarily. The musk of grit and sand and charred flesh that had filled my nostrils for the past hour was at last replaced by lilies and hyacinths, and the echoes of rushing water filled my ears and drowned out all my other senses. I inhaled deeply as Ivy's hands stroked my hair and soaped the detritus off my body; the bubbles indistinguishable from the tears I knew were falling again for reasons I couldn't even explain.

And then, for a few minutes, Ivy left me alone.

The swelling and pain near my eyes lessened. I blinked away the soapy water and opened them, revealing a typically cavernous bathroom tiled in blue-and-white swirls. Droplets glistened like diamonds as they fell from my eyelashes, catching the light of the candle resting on the ledge of the claw-foot tub I floated in.

And in the corner, setting a pile of fluffy towels on a chair, was the slave.

They couldn't have been more than thirteen, with creamy, unmarred skin, freckles, and dark, wavy hair falling across their face. They were dressed in a T-shirt with a brand logo and shorts—clean, well-fitting, even expensive-looking. Except for the bracelet—a chain that looked too tight, as if they were growing out of it—they looked... normal. Healthy. Nourished. Not quaking in fear or covered in bruises.

They startled when they saw my eyes open. They gently stroked Thalia, who'd come to them after lying protectively at the foot of the tub.

"Oh, I'm sorry, miss, I thought you were—"

"Call me Lou," I managed to get out. And then, ridiculously: "Are you okay?"

They didn't have time to answer. A second later, Ivy—long, straight, auburn hair, peachy skin, full lips, and thin eyebrows penciled in high—entered the bathroom.

The kid looked from one to the other. And I didn't know how or if I could explain that they needn't be afraid. I wasn't one of *them*.

Not like I was doing all that well at proving it.

After all, what about Maeve? What about Erica? What about my father?

"Why are you helping me?" I finally blurted out. "I don't even deserve it."

"In a world as shit as this one, I can say almost definitely that that's not true," Ivy said. "Now who do you need me to call? There's obviously someone."

I tried to shake my head, but it probably came off as a twitch of pain. I couldn't say the name. What if it resulted in me being thrown out wet and naked on the lawn, or worse?

"I know you don't trust me, and it's not surprising if

someone did *that* to you," Ivy said, hands on her hips. "But I know there's a story here, even if you won't tell me what it is. And I know there must be someone who can do something about it."

I took the deepest breath I could muster. "Erica Muller."

Ivy didn't even hesitate. She took out her phone but first turned to the kid.

"You're awesome for helping me, as usual, kiddo. It's way past your bedtime, though."

Then, to my surprise, Ivy leaned down and kissed the kid's forehead tenderly. It was as if the name *Erica Muller* had been the secret password that allowed her to demonstrate her true feelings.

"Can I play video games first?" they asked.

"I'd rather you read a book," she replied. "And I need you to let Thalia out one more time. But sure. Only for ten minutes, though. And I will be up to check."

In a daze, I watched the dog eagerly follow the kid out of the room, and Ivy nonchalantly crossed her legs, settled herself on the throw rug, and made the call. And one to Milagros, too, which was the only other number, besides my dad's, that I had memorized. No answer at either. No surprise there.

Ivy set down the phone. "Do you trust me to send a friend to go to their house?"

I nodded. Based on what I'd just seen, I'd trust Ivy to do anything. Now that I realized the only reason that mistress and slave had been acting oddly was because, given my background, they weren't sure if they could trust *me*.

Ivy seemed to follow my thoughts. "They've got a little brother, too," she said. "He's asleep upstairs. We have to be careful, and they know that, especially in my parents' social set. Sometimes someone will see me treating them like people, and it's just like this rage bomb goes off for some reason. It's awful. It's why I don't have anyone over anymore, and we don't really go out during the day. And it's safer for me, too. I'm less likely to relapse. In the meantime, I'm homeschooling them and doing this correspondence course for nursing, which I'm shit at, but thankfully, with the trust my dad set up for me and my mom, I don't need a job for now, and we've got each other." She gazed back at the door, shaking her head in awe. "I got clean for them. They're the one and only reason. If it weren't for them, I'd be dead. No doubt in my mind. They saved me."

I laid my head back on the porcelain and stared at the vaulted ceiling, speechless. "But why—"

"They aren't technically mine," Ivy explained. "They're my mom's. She owned their mom, who died years ago. And my mom has dementia, a really virulent kind. She's probably only got a few years left, and then they're both free according to the will, and I'll get the house, too. Nothing I can do until then." Her expression changed to one of determination. "But no one has ever hurt them, and as long as I'm around, no one ever will."

"I-I understand." I should just say it. Just tell her story, *our* story—mine and his. But I didn't have ten hours, or a voice, or a way to keep from crying through it all. "Someone saved me, too."

Ivy's serene smile at that was enough for me to believe, just for a second, that if I had been saved, maybe we *all* could be saved.

"It's not my place to give them names, by the way. The younger one wants a different one every day, and the older one, well, they're still thinking it over."

I smiled.

"There's a bed waiting for you upstairs when you're ready. But we're going to have to put something on these burns," she said. "Do you think you can—"

The cold water had turned warmer and formed a blissful

cocoon around my body. The body whose wounds, for now, I didn't have to think about or look at or remember.

"Okay. Take as long as you need," she said, getting the picture. "By the way," Ivy said tentatively, trailing her finger in the water, "I was so sorry to hear about Ethan."

"Thanks. Me too." I'd heard that before. People meant well, but...

"Have you seen him?" Ivy continued. "I mean, do they let you see him? I don't really know how it works."

From the other side of the door came a tentative knock. Ivy tilted her ear slightly, but she turned back when I sat straight up in the tub, water streaming off my shoulders.

"What's the matter?"

"Does *who* let us see him?"

Ivy still looked confused as the knock grew more insistent. And from somewhere else in the house came Thalia's alarm bark.

What was going on?

"Whoever bought him."

"What?"

"Ivy! Ivy!"

"You're supposed to be in bed, kiddo!" Ivy called back.

"I know, but you have to hear this!"

"Hear what?"

Though I didn't know why, my heart began to pound as the kid threw open the door, waving a phone wildly. They clicked "play" on a news video and turned up the volume.

"...An apparent road rage incident this afternoon has left two dead and one in critical condition after a car was run off I-10 and Ventana and into a wash by a vehicle that then fled the scene."

The newsreader continued, but a second later, even that

voice had been drowned out by Thalia's frantic barking, which was thundering ever closer to the bathroom.

Then the door flung open wider, revealing not only the collie but Erica Muller herself, holding the hand of a saucer-eyed teen girl with glossy dark brown skin and a jumble of skinny black braids dangling over a bloody bandage on her back in desperate need of changing.

"Louisa, what happened to you?" Erica demanded.

"What do you mean, *what happened to me*?" I exploded back through my parched throat. "Are you listening to this?"

"The two dead were later identified as recently suspended social sciences professor Erica Muller and Alma Mensah, a nine-teen-year-old woman from San Diego who was reported missing last year."

Though my eyelids were open, I could barely see. My fight-or-flight had taken over, my heart beating out of my chest, my throat closing up.

Dead.

"Breathe, Louisa," said my very-not-dead professor. "You can see with your own eyes that the report is wrong. It's all wrong."

But I couldn't breathe. It was just that word, *dead*, ringing in my ears. *Dead, dead, dead.*

"But what about Maeve, and Milagros, and——" I gasped.

"Louisa."

Erica's face barely changed, but it did change. Still, she spoke with a miraculous level of calm as she settled who had to be the also very-not-dead Alma on the chair with the towels.

Meanwhile, Ivy leaped up and grabbed the medical kit she had taken out earlier, rapidly unrolling a spool of gauze.

"I'll explain everything," Erica said. "But you need to get your anxiety under control first. Because it would be dangerous for me to tell you anything else until you do."

9

"I didn't know about the dead girl," Langer said before I had the heavy door to the roof all the way open.

He turned away from the edge, where he'd been standing in a semicircle of whatever fluorescent light source existed there. The glow reflected off the bare cement, casting a bright yellow ring around him. Beyond it, the city grid unfurled in a sprawl of light, swallowed by desert on three sides.

My boss was stripped down to a light blue dress shirt and suit pants, his usually sculpted, gravity-defying hair hanging in dark, loose strands around the faint lines of his face. He looked simultaneously older and younger—human, instead of the levitating forcefield of pure neodymium I'd first perceived him to be.

I hadn't known there was a helicopter landing pad up here. Then again, I'd never asked.

Suddenly unsure where to stand, what to do with my hands, I walked to the edge and gazed down at the mostly empty parking lot below. Mostly empty except for a dark, nondescript Japanese-made sedan. I'd watched it in the rearview mirror the entire still-one-handed drive here. I knew who was inside: Noam.

If Resi thought I was stupid enough to let my guard down, she was even stupider. But I wasn't. And she wasn't.

"Holy shit, kid, what did they do to you?" Langer asked, apparently finally getting a good look at me.

I hadn't checked a mirror, but I knew. The flashy, peacocking tech bro I'd pretended to be when I left? Gone. In his place: a throbbing, bruised, bedraggled, abraded, barely upright disaster—though probably still, for once, in better shape than Louisa, wherever she was.

The roof hadn't been my first stop when I got back. I'd made a few others, the last to the break room fridge for an ice pack, which I'd ripped off my hideous-looking wrist in frustration after less than a minute. I hadn't even attempted to deal with my shoulder. No time for comfort. Not for me.

I'd closed my eyes and pressed my forehead against my glass office door, trying for the millionth time *not* to conjure up her skin burning, her screams muffled, her—

I'd shut the door angrily. *Stop ruminating and do something, you idiot. Fix this. She thinks you fucked her mouth without her consent. She thinks you hate her. She thinks you plotted to destroy her. She thinks—*

She thinks you have a plan.

Fuck.

Standing in the middle of my dim, silent office, it hit me. How could I have been so stupid as to think Louisa *wouldn't* assume I was being smart?

It hadn't been all acting, of course.

Fuck, the way she'd looked up at me, chained, helpless, laid out the way someone like her was never supposed to be in front of someone like me. That moment when she went still—first out of fear, then, I hoped, out of trust. And the weight of what it meant for *me* to choose what happened next.

Part of me had wanted it all. Not because I wanted to hurt her—but because some raw, buried part of me finally wanted to know what it felt like to hold someone down and not be the one begging. After a lifetime of being chained, ordered, punished, having everything taken from me... to take. And it was *her*. Of course it had to be her. To protect the one person who had ever treated *me* like a person, I had to pretend to break her.

I just prayed it wouldn't, couldn't break her. Or break us.

And of course she thought I had a plan. She was giving me the benefit of the doubt, because she *always* did, even when I didn't deserve it. I'd once gotten in trouble for not giving her the same. It had almost wrecked us.

So it was time to atone, once and for all.

The only problem was that I *didn't* have a plan. I had the barest seed of an idea based on a tossed-off remark from Resi and one file among thousands I thought I'd seen earlier, but that didn't amount to a plan.

So I'd have to make one.

Both shaken and reassured, I had soon covered both of my LCD monitors with files—mostly lab reports about Resi's experiments and folders of related financial data that Corey had lamely attempted to hide inside puzzles of poorly written code. My heart thundered with each click of the mouse, jumping at even the tiniest movement outside. If Noam wasn't in here murdering me now, it only meant he thought I was doing exactly what I'd said I'd do. And that he'd be all the angrier when he found out that I wasn't.

I had only the tiniest seed of an idea of what I was looking for, but my hands still trembled when I spotted *The Law of Sympathy* at the top of one file. A file I'd skipped over earlier because I'd been certain—knowing Corey and Resi—that it couldn't possibly contain anything of actual scientific value. But Resi, in the midst of her other evil gloating, had mentioned a formula.

She shouldn't have.

But as it turned out, they'd made a good team: Resi had been smart enough to produce at least one breakthrough, and Corey had been dumb enough to slip up and reveal it.

So after I'd scoured each line, reading it over and over until the letters and numbers were burned into my neurons, I'd written it out on a sticky note. It hadn't taken long.

And then, with two clicks, I'd deleted it forever and gone upstairs, for better or worse, to face my boss.

"By 'they,' you mean your sister, right?" I bit back in response to Langer's question. "And don't fucking lie and tell me you didn't know all along what she was capable of."

Langer paused, clearly realizing the time for prevaricating had long passed. "Yeah. I knew."

"Then why—"

"I didn't believe it."

I spun around. "Max, she fucking raped and murdered other people, too. She tortured Louisa. She killed Lemaya's owner and your—"

"You don't think I fucking know that?" he exploded. "I watched her do it. I *let* her do it. And I justified all of it to myself because all I saw when I looked at her—all I *ever* saw—were those eyes. Those blue eyes. That innocent, helpless creature, crying and begging me to help her. And me, fucking failing to, over and over again. And I figured, what are a few old, worthless lives in the face of everything she endured, of everything we all endured, if it means we can finally fucking make it right? I couldn't hurt my sister any easier than you could hurt yours."

"But you could have stopped her."

"No." He sighed. "I couldn't have. Not without hurting her."

"But you could have helped her," I insisted. "Got her therapy. Got her—"

"I tried, kid. For years. She got thrown out of two different therapists' offices for trying to grope *them*."

I didn't want to understand it. But I did.

"You know it was only by pure chance that she didn't kill *Maeve* and dump her out there," I said, thrusting my good arm toward the vast, sand-covered waste out somewhere behind the mountains. "Would you have justified that, too?"

"Not after I learned she was your sister," Langer replied quietly.

"Oh, like that's supposed to make me feel better?" I stepped farther away from the edge. "They were *all* someone's sister, or daughter, or friend. But I guess that doesn't matter if it serves the greater good."

"Look, kid, I don't mean to sound callous or uncaring here, but what we were trying to do was *beyond* the greater good. It was beyond her, or me, or you. It was beyond any of us."

I crossed my arms, suddenly realizing the desert night breeze was cold. "And you thought I'd be okay with that."

"Hell, you *were* okay with that. You and I both *know* you were. That's the whole reason I brought you here. Remember the guy who wanted to play by his own rules? Remember the guy who aimed to serve only science, only logic, only truth, with none of those messy emotional and spiritual ties to fuck it all up? What happened to him?"

I stared down at the cement as I listened to my own stupid, arrogant, childish philosophies get shot back at me like bullets. Of course I remembered.

But things had changed.

Hell, they'd changed just *tonight*.

"You know, Max, I'd take this opportunity to say you're just as bad as Resi, but I won't because you're not." I raised my head, blinking evenly at him. "You're worse because she *can't* care. You *can*, and you choose not to."

To my surprise, Langer's response came immediately. "I don't choose not to."

"What?" I was afraid I'd heard wrong. And if I hadn't, well, this was new.

In fact, as I peered at him closer, I thought the look on his face indicated *he* couldn't believe what he'd just said.

"I don't," he repeated, swallowing. "Choose not to."

"Are you saying—"

"Fuck me, kid, you know what I'm saying."

Another look into Max's eyes—at those icy blue irises that maybe weren't as cold as I'd always assumed—and I knew. Though he was talking about me, he was also talking about himself. Max Langer. The man who had scars. Who knew pain. Who'd endured suffering and been forced to watch others suffer in turn. Who understood what his sister didn't, and who knew that when you were lucky enough to have the brains and the charisma and the money and the power to afford it, how much fucking easier it always was to just stop caring.

Hell, he and I had both *tried* to stop caring. And we'd both failed because despite it all, no matter what we told ourselves, we still cared so goddamn much.

Langer coughed, embarrassed enough not to demand to know what revelation had just crash-landed into my brain. "Anyway, it should be pretty fucking self-evident," he continued, regaining a bit of his poise. "Given that I'm standing here waiting for you when I could already be eight miles high over the Gulf, on my way to Rio Dulce."

"Rio Dulce?"

"River town in the jungle. Nice hotels, cheap tacos, good tequila. You get everywhere on a boat or a motorbike. Mayan temples. Monkeys. Toucans. Manatees. It's where the Central

American elite go on holiday. More importantly, the officials there don't ask questions of rich gringos with offshore bank accounts who happen to want to stay indefinitely."

"But they still have slavery."

"Yeah, and so does everywhere else that's even remotely livable. But it's not as ubiquitous there. And anyway, it won't matter to you because you're not a slave. You're the son of said rich gringo." He looked pointedly at me.

This, of course, would be as good a time as any to accuse Langer of lying. But those days were over. What he'd told me over the phone was as real as the two of us standing here. It hadn't—as I'd half-convinced myself on the drive over—been my exhausted, throbbing, contused head conjuring up surreal shit out of nothing just to taunt me.

And even though my very body vibrated with the thought of what it meant, I couldn't let Max know that.

As if there were any way he *couldn't* know.

"Sorry, *Dad*," I said once I regained my voice. "But I already have a family member waiting for me."

"I know."

"Then—"

"I'm getting to that, okay? So I put my lawyers on it, and as it turns out, one of those fucking goons ran the car your sister was in off the road shortly after their getaway and—"

I turned away, reeling, already barely hearing him. Heart pounding, blood rushing through my head, I didn't wait for the rest of the story, or ask who she'd been with or who'd been driving. Did it matter?

"Fuck, *that's* what Resi was talking about. When she said she wasn't going to let them get away that easily. What happened to her, Max?"

"I'll tell you, but you have to promise not to freak the fuck out."

"I *don't* promise that, and you're gonna fucking tell me anyway," I snapped, trying to focus my eyes on something, though I could no longer see much. None of what Max had said earlier seemed to matter now.

What if—All this way, and—

"Where is she?"

"She's fine," Langer assured me. "She wasn't hurt. Okay?"

"But then—"

"She's been detained."

"Detained?" The word mowed me down like a rogue wave. "You're telling me my sister's in *jail?*"

"Fucking hell, kid, will you let me finish?" Langer cut in. "It's the safest place for her to be right now because it's the one place Resi can't get to her. Yeah, it's not exactly Tivoli Gardens in there, but she's alive. And like I said, my lawyers are getting her released as we speak."

"So what are you saying?" I demanded.

"What I'm saying is that they're presenting evidence that her last owners abandoned her, and then I'm buying her. Legally. If all goes well, she'll be there to meet us at the airport."

What had started as a rogue wave had become a storm, waves hitting me one after another, each with a new and astonishing revelation.

After seven years, I was about to see my sister again?

Right now?

My heart kept racing.

Because as much as I'd wheeled and pushed and plotted and planned for the past seven years, her face and her fear a constant fluttering presence in the back of my mind, never, not even once, had I let myself speculate on the details of our reunion when and if it came.

Like freedom, it was something I had, in the interests of

keeping my wits sharp from day to day, honed the ability to think about with only half my mind.

Fuck, would I even recognize her? What would I *say*? "Then you mean—"

"That's right," Langer said. "Looks like I'm getting a daughter, too."

I just stood there, mouth open.

How could I possibly not go? Well, let's start with the obvious. "Speaking of Resi's goons, there's one parked right down there." I pointed.

Langer cleared his throat and motioned to the sky. "You. Me. Helicopter. Jet. Rio Dulce. Now. Unless he's got anti-aircraft artillery mounted on that shitty little Datsun, I like your chances for a clean getaway." He placed his hands on his hips.

"Well, that takes care of me, but what about Resi? And the other girls? They aren't safe."

"Maybe not, but there's nothing you can do about it dead, and she's going to go for *you* first."

Langer gave me another pointed look and turned, his eyes drinking in the long line of a hundred miles of desert lights twinkling in a semicircle around us.

Lights I could choose, right this second, to never see again.

And if I did, why would I care?

I hated this place.

Mostly.

I took a deep breath. "Look, I never thought I'd be saying this any more than you thought you'd be hearing it, but what about Keith? You're planning to just leave him here to take the fall for you?"

He shrugged.

"He was your partner!" I exclaimed. "You were a guest in his fucking house. You played *golf* together."

"I played golf with him because I needed him to help me free slaves."

"It sounds like you played golf with him because you wanted to fuck him over."

"Fucking him over was Resi's idea, not mine. But despite everything, I'm not going to stand here and say it wasn't a good one. And what's more, I dare *you* to stand here and say that, and that he doesn't deserve every goddamn thing that's coming to him and more."

No, I wasn't going to say that because it wouldn't be true. Not really.

I didn't hate Keith Wainwright-Phillips, but my master certainly deserved to be hated, and normally, that would be enough for me to happily throw anybody under the bus.

Except.

"What about Louisa? Does she deserve whatever she gets?" My eyes flicked down below. Maybe it was my imagination, but the Datsun appeared to have moved from its earlier spot.

"Well," Langer said matter-of-factly, "she could have been here now, and she's not."

"That's just because I told her I hated her and plotted to destroy her and her entire family."

"Well, fuck, kid." He chuckled. "What the hell did you expect?"

"But I didn't *mean* it," I insisted, like a goddamn child. "And she doesn't believe it," I added, with even less assurance.

"Look, only you know whether you think she believes it or not," Langer said. "What *I* know is that either that goon or the police or both are going to be breaking down my fucking door very shortly, and I, for one, don't plan to be here when they do. Neither will my staff. And needless to say, if *you* are, you're on your own."

"But I need more time, Max."

Time.

Why was I always asking people for time they didn't have and that I didn't deserve?

Still, I wrapped my hand once more around the formula in my pocket. I hadn't intended to show it to Max. Then again, I hadn't intended *not* to show him.

"There's something down there, on the computer. Something I missed." I glanced warily down at the parking lot again, thinking of Noam and his muscles and his weapons. His muscles that *were* weapons. And then back up at Langer.

"Shit, kid, we don't *have* any more time. I've already spent way too fucking long waiting for you and your sister, and—"

He was cut off by a sound like a buzzing wasp, tiny enough for me to want to bat it away. But it wasn't a wasp. Wasps didn't make entire rooftops vibrate, or quickly grow from tiny black dots on the horizon to something the size of a horse, then an elephant.

Before our eyes emerged the massive helicopter, the city lights reflecting off its whirring, hypnotic metal exoskeleton, its own lights a circus kaleidoscope of swirling pastels that illuminated its sides, bringing it alive as it soared closer and closer until it stopped and simply hovered, hundreds of feet above us, its blades echoing through the night air like a giant mechanical insect with a menacing roar that overpowered the sound of the traffic below.

Langer ran to the edge of the roof, cupping his hands around his mouth and shouting something inaudible above the gigantic rotor blades, so strong they were kicking up miniature tornadoes of dust and sand. I could barely see or hear, the wind whipping almost painfully at my face and clothes. The copter was close enough now that I could make out the pilot behind its window—a black-clad man in sunglasses, pointing and shouting. Langer gestured, and the copter rose by a few dozen feet, enough to give us some breathing space.

Langer turned back, and my eyes darted frantically from the helicopter to the roof to Langer.

"Listen," I said, fingers curling weakly around the sticky note in my pocket. "Maybe we can—"

"There's no 'maybe' here anymore, kid. It was my money, my lab, my resources." Langer raised his voice over the chilly wind whipping at us from every direction. In a second, he was going to have to start shouting. "There's no weaseling out of this for me, kid. Even if somehow I can beat trafficking charges for the free girl, I'm still on the hook for theft and damage of the other slaves and defrauding my other investors of millions. They'll make sure we go down hard. Believe me, these rich fuckers do *not* like being taken for a ride. And I don't blame them. What would you even *do*, anyway?"

"Well, Keith *is* innocent, you know." I raised my voice to be heard. "At best, he'll be ruined. At worst..."

"*He* gets thrown in a mine? Oh, the irony." Langer rolled his eyes. "What? Don't look at me like that."

But I kept looking, and I knew roughly what the look had to be because my boss groaned and ran his hands through his windswept hair.

"Oh, come the fuck on. Do I seriously have to spell out that the bastard fucking *owned* you? And he wasn't even a good owner! He *knew* how brilliant you are and he *still* treated you worse than his goddamn dog. Not only did he have you whipped and chained and forced you to work in the dirt, he ripped you away from the girl you love after you *saved* her. Someone who does that is irredeemable. You know it. I know it. So for the love of all that's holy, why are you still wasting even a single ounce of sympathy on him?"

"Because it's *not about him*!" I exploded.

Langer groaned. He'd known this was coming, too, clearly. "Kid, she left you. She *ran away*. What does that tell you?"

"It tells me there's more to the story," I insisted, wishing I had a better answer. "It tells me I need to think more critically. It tells me she thinks I have a plan." I didn't, but that was beside the point, right?

"Okay. Let's be real. Say you decide to play the role of the hopeless romantic idiot, ignore my sage advice, and go after her," Langer shouted. "What then? You're still chipped. You'll get maybe an hour together before the police show up, drag you away, and lock you up, probably for good. Call me crazy, but there doesn't seem to be a whole lot of critical thinking involved in *that* decision."

"No," I replied, turning away for a second. "But there is another option. One that might work if I could get more time." I swiped some of my own hopelessly windblown hair out of my eyes and raised my eyes to the massive rotor blades still chopping up the atmosphere.

Langer didn't miss a beat. "Kid, you know I'd take her with us in a second. But to do that, you'd have to find her. And right now, finding her is the dumbest, most dangerous thing you could possibly do."

"Then I'll go straight to Keith," I countered. "I'll figure out what to say. I have a plan." A plan I was making up on the spot, but I figured Max probably knew that.

"Right," he replied. "Except Resi's goons are still on your tail, so assuming you don't get killed, which you will, and assuming you do figure out some kind of plan, which you won't, what the fuck do you think Keith is going to say? 'Oh, yeah, no, sorry, my bad, I guess you're a person after all? Here's my blessing to date my daughter?' Are we even talking about the same fucking guy?"

I gritted my teeth, fingers weakly digging into the crumpled piece of paper in my pocket, the echoes of every conversation I'd ever had with Langer burying me all at once. Conversations where the guy had proven that he always knew the exact spot to thrust in the spear to make all of my armor fall off.

Langer continued patiently, waving off the pilot yet again, talking loudly over the noise. "Okay, for a trial balloon, let's say a miracle happens. What are you envisioning with this girl? Dating? A real relationship? Marriage? The white picket fence? Garden parties, family reunions, Christmas? You'll have no money, no home, no degree, no job, no credit rating, in a world that's fucking hostile to all of that. And even if you find a way around it, what about *her* career? Do you think she's going to take you to med school with her? To her residency? To bougie cocktail parties with her surgical colleagues? If you think Corey was bad, you haven't seen shit. Medicine is a conservative field, and it's absolutely infested with guys like him. Sure, you're a good actor, so you might be able to blend in for a while, and she'll have your back, but sooner or later, it's going to come out, and she'll be a pariah. Her career will suffer. *She'll* suffer. And if *she* suffers, you'll suffer. But the relationship will suffer the most."

"Louisa's different." I knew how naive I sounded. The kind of naivety that just a few months ago, I would have laughed at because of course I was smarter and savvier and more cynical than that. Hell, I'd been more like Max *then* than I was now.

"I agree."

I looked back at him with shock.

Max clarified. "I mean, I don't know her at all, but from what I've gathered, she *is* different. So I'll give you that. But she's still her father's daughter, and she's just a kid, and so are you, and neither one of you has a goddamn clue what you're up against. And I'd say don't ask me how I know this, but I *know* how I know. The legacy of slavery, even once you're free, is like a virus that hides in your cells long after the disease has passed. And it keeps making you sick, and it always will. At least as long as I stay in the fucking toxic miasma that gave it to me. And if I stay here, I'll always be in it. Choking on it. Dying.

I didn't even attempt to argue with that, and anyway, I knew Langer wasn't finished.

"Kid, I'll tell you something else. You already know it, but hear me out anyway. Hardly anyone, slave or free, has your gifts. Hell, *I* certainly don't, and I'd give anything to have them, but the next best thing is to have *you*. And I know you've always known, on some level, that you were destined for so much more than what you were given. Since before that pompous lush of a professor plucked you out of that cage, since before you could even add or recite the alphabet, you knew it. You *knew* it."

Of course I had. I was just too polite to ever say it.

"But what you might not realize is, not only do you deserve more than slavery, you deserve more than the stigma of having *been* a slave. I don't know what's in store for us down there, but I do know that it's the best place I can think of to get not only real freedom but a real *life*. Or at least, I'll try my damnedest to make sure you get a shot at one. Maeve, too. Because as much as I fucked up with Resi and with White Cedar, I'm going to make it up to you and your sister."

"I—" I spun around just in time to see the locked metal door to the roof bounce on its hinges, very much like a heavy boot slamming into it. "That door is reinforced, right?" I asked warily.

"It better be. I sure paid enough for it. Anyway, I told you this before, but I don't think it quite sank in. And it's that in this world when you break the rules, they'll put you back in your place every time. Breaking the rules isn't enough. You have to *make* the rules."

I stood frozen, almost literally caught between heaven and earth.

Langer tried one last stratagem. "If you could somehow ask her, right now, what do you think she would say?"

Well. She'd tell me she loved me. She'd tell me to take my chances while I had chances to take. She'd tell me I needed to be with Maeve, and that she, Louisa, could take care of herself, even if it meant suffering, the kind of suffering she in no way deserved and that her life hadn't prepared her for. And she'd tell me I was brave. And all of it would be true.

But then, there were things that *I* had told *her*, too.

But all I finally said was: "She'd tell me to go."

Langer just nodded. It was *the* nod, I realized with a swallow. The one that signaled he knew my choice had been made. And it *had* to be made. Because that door wouldn't hold much longer, and the giant metal insect was descending, right in front of our eyes, and the wind and the swirling pastel kaleidoscope of lights were coming to a gentle, precise stop on the yellow circle.

And with one Italian leather shoe perched on one of the thick metal skids, the multimillionaire tech mogul held out his hand. And at once, everything slowed—the shouting and waving of the pilot, the whirring of the rotors, the bright dots making up the city below breaking into a million drunken, swirling pieces of light. Making me forget, almost, the pain, the joy, and everything in between.

"The jet's already waiting at the municipal airport," Langer shouted. "We've gotta leave before sunrise to give ourselves the best chance. And the sunrise over the gulf, well, like I said, it's not to be missed. And not to put too fine a point on it—" He paused as if searching for the right words to say to me. Like anybody—except for one person—had *ever* worried about the right words to say to me. "I know you didn't get much of a view from the last plane you were on. And," he added, "you deserve that, too." And then he mounted the helicopter. The impatient pilot reached down to hand him a headset, but he paused again, and the other man huffed a sigh.

I raised my good hand, but the rest of me still stood frozen on the spot.

"Come on, kid. Let's go."

Slaves hardly ever got to make decisions, and when they did, they were agonizing. You chose something horrible so you wouldn't be forced to accept something even worse, for either your loved ones or yourself. And I wasn't so naive as to think that freedom would put an end to those decisions.

But I had thought, nonetheless, back when Langer had first proposed his deal all those weeks ago, how remarkable it felt to be treated, for once, like a free man. Like a man at *all*. Yet I hadn't understood what that meant. Not really. Not until now did I understand that freedom didn't *ever* come free.

Well, shit. I really should have figured that out already.

The damp, crumpled paper weighed in my hand, the total extent of my brilliant plan. The *last* of my brilliant plans.

"Max?" I shouted over the roar.

"Yeah?"

"That day you came to see me, you asked me if I thought I was going to get lucky again."

He glanced up and nodded. "I guess we know the answer now."

It all still felt like slow motion as the door to the roof burst open, revealing Noam's bald, massive, sweaty frame silhouetted in the harsh light of the staircase. As he thundered toward us, drawing a nine-millimeter pistol from inside his jacket, I gritted my teeth and grabbed hold of the metal frame of the copter with my one good arm, hoisting myself up on the skid, ducking, and swinging into the seat behind Langer, who was already setting himself beside the pilot, headset over his ears.

Well. Time to run away for the last time. Except—except I'd been running away my entire life. From love, from attachments, from guilt, from failure, from shame. Other than Maeve, I'd never had anything or anyone to run toward.

And for once, that might be nice.

"Yeah." Noam's aim was just good enough to put one bullet hole in the fuselage, but it must not have been anywhere critical, since the pilot barely noticed as Langer signaled to him to take hold of the collective lever and lift us up and to the left, the copter already well off on its solo trajectory over the city.

And maybe it was the hum of the engine, or maybe my hand really was shaking as, just before closing the door, I took the paper out of my pocket and let it fly, letting the rotor blades—so I didn't have to—shred it to ribbons.

"I guess we do."

10

HER

In the end, what calmed me was watching Ivy. My brother's old friend may not have been at the top of her class, but she had the unconscious grace of someone who had spent her childhood diligently attending her dance lessons, instead of—like *some* people—bursting into tears halfway through her first one and demanding her mother take her home. Ivy's long fingers nimbly bunched up one of the fluffy towels from the wicker chair and guided me to the edge of the bathtub. She lifted me out, still dripping, before my burns could meet the dry, unforgiving desert air. But as those burns and the memory of what had made them came back into painful relief, my knees buckled. Ivy caught me, valiantly keeping me upright and spreading a beautiful rose-scented aloe gently over my arms, turning around to slide her willowy fingers down my chest and back.

Alma had been settled in the other room and the child had finally been coaxed to bed, but Erica still stood in the bathroom doorway, arms crossed stonily, waiting for me to calm myself.

But as soon as she started talking again, that calmness melted down.

"Maeve and Sloane are *where*?"

"Milagros convinced me to go," Erica said, starting at the beginning, still keeping tight control of her voice. "Because of course she did. She felt so useless sitting there, letting you and Maeve put yourselves in danger, when *we* were the ones with all the experience. She figured if we borrowed a friend's van, no one at the university would know it was us. And then we found Maeve, and she'd found the other girls despite the bad info, and we helped get them away. Thanks to you and your distraction."

I tried to smile. So it hadn't been useless, after all, even though it had felt that way.

"But Resi sent one of her goons to give chase, and they ran us off the road."

"So there really *was* a car accident. But—"

"Once we realized everyone had survived, before the EMTs could show up, we made a plan to make lemonade out of lemons. We'd trick Resi into thinking her plan to kill us had worked. Since it almost did."

"But how? How did you get that item in the news, and—"

"It's a bitter irony that in a society where the mainstream media cannot be trusted to tell the truth, for the sake of the greater good, I had to enlist one of the few trustworthy reporters I know to put out a lie."

"Okay," I said. "But what about the police, and the hospital, and—ouch. Fuck. Ivy, I don't mean to seem like an ungrateful bitch, but what *is* that?"

Even under the balm, my entire body still burned as if the electric fingers had left embers that still popped and smoldered angrily underneath my skin. I hissed when she started dabbing on something from a much smaller tube.

"Antiseptic cream. Burns can get infected, you know," said

Ivy. "And no worries. I'm glad you're bitchy. It shows you're healing."

Erica hadn't answered my question. Did she have friends in the police, too? Frankly, that seemed even less likely than having friends in the media. "So they rescued you," I said. "And took Maeve and Sloane to jail."

She nodded. "After they looked them over for injuries."

I gave her a look.

"They're alive, Louisa, and I guarantee they're safer than we are right now. And before they took them away, I made sure they both knew we were working on a plan to get them out."

I squeezed my eyes shut, uncomforted. "I was supposed to *protect* Maeve. God, just when I thought I couldn't fuck this up any worse. Not to mention I've been sending messages to Ethan for three years and all the while he was..." I shrank, keen to bury my head like a turtle into the robe Ivy was draping around me. To disappear altogether. Out of my very body, if I could. Right now, being in it was doing me more harm than good. "And for that matter, what about Milagros? We haven't even—"

"She's fine," Erica cut in quickly. "Alma is who we have to worry about right now."

Blankly, I let Ivy lead me out of the bathroom, Erica following, our footsteps light but deliberate on the marble tile as we ventured through the vaulted, Art Nouveau house with its domed living room and filigree brasswork stretching along the walls and windows, like something out of the turn of the last century. Our destination was the curved veranda that overlooked the rest of the gardens, filled with plants in brass urns, more delicate, inlaid Edwardian-style furniture and glass everything. Ivy clearly had other things to occupy her time than redecorating from her grandmother's day. The breeze carried a chorus of crickets, and the stars, at last, shone as bright as ever the clear desert sky could make them.

Too late, I couldn't help but think.

On one of the sofas, Alma sat utterly still, in a pink robe even fluffier than mine, clutching a mug, her legs curled under her and her gaze fixed on some distant point. Besides the older, deeper, massive chunk taken out of her shoulder, now bandaged, she had an ice pack pressed to her right wrist and a bandaged cut below her eye, a slash of blood mixed with tears, and her skin was marred with purplish bruises. The "accident" —if one could call it that—had clearly been real, even if the news report was not.

Ivy led me to the other sofa, her touch patient and gentle as she settled me there, though we both knew there was no position that wouldn't cause me pain. I closed my eyes again, and for a second, tried to see if I could pretend that everything was the way it was supposed to be. *Maybe if Ivy and Ethan had stayed together. Maybe if he had, like I had, found something, or someone, to save him. Maybe then he—*

Well, I was crying again. That had worked well.

Ivy, as if she could read my thoughts somehow, brushed a lock of wet hair away from my face. "Hey, maybe I should just open my own no-questions-asked hospital here," she remarked, glancing around her. "I mean, I've got the space."

Erica, seemingly unbreakable, had no intention of sitting down. "You know, that's not a bad idea," she said. "We could really—"

Noticing my quivering lip, she uncharacteristically cut herself off. It could wait.

And then, at last, Alma turned. When she caught my eye, I spotted the faintest trace of a smile. *I won't make you talk if you won't make me.*

I sank bodily into the sofa, happy to oblige.

"Alma's already given an initial statement to the police," Erica explained. "She's exhausted, as you can see." She looked with concern at the other girl. "She was really brave, and I'm proud of her, but unfortunately, Resi seems to have drugged her before and after her experiments, and she doesn't remember as much as I'd hoped. We're going to try again tomorrow when she's better rested."

I nodded uncertainly. "But if you went to the police, then everyone will know that you're not—"

"No. They won't," Erica said. "There's a specific agent at the federal investigation bureau that I trust, believe it or not," she added, recognizing my incredulous look. "In fact, he helped arrange to send out the false news releases to put Resi off our trail. He even got in touch with Alma's mother in San Diego first so she wouldn't see it and think the worst. We've agreed that Alma will speak to him and only him, and he's ensured absolute discretion until it's safe for us."

"But does he know about Maeve and Sloane?"

"Yes. And he's promised to do his best to keep them safe until we can get them out."

"*He* could get them out," I grumbled.

"Maybe. But they still wouldn't be free. And then we'd just have to find somewhere else to hide them in the meantime. Somewhere no doubt a lot less secure than where they are."

I crossed my arms stubbornly, though it aggravated the burns on my arms. Every position did, really. "You seriously think hiding them in *jail* is the best thing for them?"

"Right now?" Erica sighed. "Yes." She said no more, blinking at me from behind the wire-rimmed frames of her glasses.

The silence lingered.

Shit. It was *my* turn to talk, and I didn't want to, any more than Alma did. Erica probably already knew who had been responsible for the burns. She knew where I'd been, after all. What she didn't know was how—and why—it all went wrong, and what we—but mostly he—had said and done to turn it a little bit right again. And recounting that was about as appealing as lying in a charred, smoking heap in a golf course bunker, but Erica deserved to know it.

So I gathered up every part of my brain except the one needed to tell the story and left my body. When the words started pouring out, I was hovering roughly somewhere over my own right shoulder, weightless, watching my mouth move without moving it, hearing sound without making it. Feeling nothing until Erica's hand—smooth and cold, with its prominent veins and short, businesslike nails—found its way over to mine.

When the story was over, safely settled back into my body again, I watched her face.

"I want you to talk to this agent, too."

"Oh, fuck no." I was fully returned now. "The whole reason I'm here instead of the hospital is that I wanted to *avoid* the police. So why would I go to them now?"

"If they are trying to defraud your father, this is your best chance to help him."

"But he's a suspect."

"Yes, and one of the prime suspects, I'd say. His name was on the lease and he was a primary shareholder. And if—" Erica cut herself off.

For a second, I peered at her, unable to figure out why. "Oh, no."

"Louisa, I didn't mean to suggest—"

"No, no, NO." I felt the blood drain from my face, struggling for any words that conveyed both "you're wrong" and "fuck you for suggesting that" to someone I cared about as much as Erica. "You don't understand. What he told Resi that he was trying to do to Daddy was a *lie*. To get us out of there safely. He didn't *mean* it."

"But how can you be sure he didn't lead you right into that trap?"

"Because he *didn't*," I shrieked. Automatically, we both glanced over at Alma, who had collapsed into the deep cushions and drifted off to sleep at some point in the last few minutes, her hand partially over her face. "He. Didn't." My heart was pounding as hard as if I myself were on trial. Reels of the past night flew by in a daze. What we'd said. What we'd done. What Resi had said about what we'd done. *Tell me how much you loved watching her—*

"Lemaya did," I burst out. "The same girl who gave Maeve the shit info that got you all almost caught."

Erica stayed silent.

If I'd had the strength, I would have gotten up and hurled an antique glass swan across the room. "I can't believe what I'm hearing. Not from you, of all people. You know him, Erica. We stayed in your—you let us—you *trust* him," I finished helplessly. "You wouldn't be helping him otherwise. Right?"

"My primary concern was Maeve and the other girls," Erica said quietly, staring out into the distance as if there were anything—except for the stars—to be seen beyond the monotonous patchwork quilt of suburban lawns that pressed in on us.

I tried one more time. "Erica, he was conned. The same as we were. It was Lemaya. *That's* why they caught up with you. That's why they chased you down, that's why Maeve and Sloane were detained! To try to pin this on him is—is—what about Maeve? You said she was your primary concern. Are you going to look her in the face and say that about the brother that she's spent *years* trying to fight her way back to?"

Erica continued in an even quieter voice. "Louisa, please calm down. I want to believe you. I *do* believe you. But not all slaves turn out to be heroes. Some of them have spent so long being oppressed and beaten down by the system that when they get a little power or freedom, they don't know what to do with it." She softened her voice further. "And then they make the wrong choice."

And all at once, I felt myself spiraling back to that stifling mausoleum of a room; felt that lurch of panic deep in my chest, while all of my blisters cried out with the memory of what had made them, of the blue lightning zapping the very thoughts from my head, of being unable to scream, of being unable to—I desperately reminded myself to concentrate on my breathing, or I *knew* Erica would make good on her threat to cut short the conversation. And then I wouldn't get the chance to prove her wrong.

"That's exactly what *she* said. And that's what she did."

"Look, listen to me. It's just another part of the terrible legacy of slavery, one all of us who've taken part in it, even involuntarily, have to eventually come to grips with. It's not personal. It says nothing about him, or about you, or your relationship, or your judgment. It's the system. But I would be remiss if I didn't at least try to warn you that maybe he's—"

"*No*," I cut in, and the fierceness in my voice seemed to hit Erica now, all at once. "He's not her."

"Louisa—"

"*He's not her.*" I swallowed the lump in my throat, my voice ragged and raw. "I'm sorry about what happened. I am. I mean, *look* at me." I burst into tears again, gesturing down at my own body, unable to look at it myself. Honestly, I couldn't contemplate looking at it fully ever again. "But he did not do this, and he did not say that. Resi did."

The moment was cut short by a crash from beyond the circle of light on the veranda, followed immediately by crazed barking from Thalia, somewhere far away upstairs. I froze, then scrambled up from the sofa so quickly I almost knocked over the delicately inlaid coffee table as it scraped against the aged floor tile. Fear rose in my throat and in my chest. The house was well-hidden from the road, but that didn't mean Resi's guys hadn't found us; they knew far too much to be sure any hiding place would remain secure for long.

Erica followed my lead, the two of us flanking each other as we scanned the darkness outside. The crash had come from the direction of the garage, but it was impossible to be sure.

"Do you have a weapon?" Erica whispered, and her hand reached for something tucked into her waistband. *Erica? Armed?* Then again, she wasn't some flower child. She was a former militant radical and had spent years as a fugitive. No telling what she'd had to teach herself during that time.

I shook my head.

Erica exhaled hard and drew something from under her sweater—a slim, fixed-blade knife in a black micarta sheath, clipped discreetly inside her waistband. Clearly used. She held it out to me. "Take it," she said when I opened my mouth. "Don't argue. Just keep it on you." Her voice trembled slightly. "It's not for show. If someone grabs you, you aim for soft spots and don't stop."

I took it, stunned, my fingers curling around the solid weight of it. This wasn't Professor Muller. This was someone who'd learned exactly what the world could do to a girl without a weapon.

And so had I.

"Meanwhile," she said, "I'm calling Agent Wheatley. Now."

I must have looked skeptical because she gave a little bless-your-heart smile as she took out her phone. "Louisa, do not even *attempt* to out-ACAB me because mark my words, you will lose. Anyway, this isn't just any cop I'm calling. I told you, I trust this one."

Still shaking, I waited until she ended her terse phone

conversation. With no further movement from outside, we ventured gingerly back to where we'd come from. "But why is *he* so different?"

She sighed. "I can't give too many specifics. I don't *know* too many specifics. He has his own cover to preserve. But I can tell you his name's Emmanuel Wheatley, and he's been looking into Langer's organization for some time, based on some of the same suspicions you had. He only needed someone like Alma to help build his case."

"But what about Daddy?"

"If you tell them what you saw at the house, there's a better chance of proving he's not involved, and—"

"No. There has to be another way." If I spoke to the police, that meant confessing that I'd seen the one person I was forbidden to see. And if my father got the blame for Resi's crimes, he could very well end up paying with his money, with his reputation, or with his life. But if he learned that the slave he still owned had crossed the line in the sand he'd drawn, I had no doubt he would find a way to make him pay first, and with everything.

"He—he has a plan." *He'd better have a plan.* "*We* have a plan. We just—we need more time."

"Louisa, we don't *have* more time."

She was asking, like always, for the one thing none of us could afford. But hadn't we always managed to make time— even just a minute—when it seemed there was none to make?

"Even just a minute."

Erica let out a noise that sounded suspiciously like a groan.

I glanced around the room frantically, my wits fully about me again for the first time in many hours. Where was my phone? I thought I'd seen it on a charger on the bathroom counter. Gritting my teeth, I began peeling myself off the sofa.

"But don't you see that's what Resi's counting on? If you

talk to the police, yes, you're endangering *him* and your father. But if you don't, you're endangering *us*." Erica glanced meaningfully out to where we'd just come from. At the perimeter of the impromptu safe house that we both knew could be breached at any time. "Alma, and Maeve, and Sloane, and now, the longer we stay here, Ivy, too. And—" She flicked her eyes upstairs.

"The kids," I breathed. I'd seen what Resi and her helpers were capable of doing to adults. Putting them near children was unthinkable. "Fuck."

"Do you see that this is beyond what we're capable of doing on our own anymore? We need the police. And for that, we need Alma. But we also need *you*."

I hiccupped. I now felt like the most selfish person alive. But I still wanted more time.

"Like it or not, Louisa, you and he started something that's now bigger than both of you," Erica explained. "This may have all started when boy met girl, but now that others are involved, the calls aren't all going to be yours to make. Louisa—" Suddenly, her voice cracked. "Some people have sacrificed an awful lot for this."

Her face had suddenly gone deathly pale. She tried to recover, but she'd slipped up, and she knew it. And I knew it, too. *She'd lied.*

Milagros was not fine. And Erica was not unbreakable.

"Erica—" I started, but she waved me away, turning her head. It was surreal.

It's not that I really thought Erica couldn't be vulnerable. Couldn't be in pain. It was just that by now, I assumed she must have learned all the ways to cope that no one had ever taught me because no one had ever thought I'd go through anything hard enough to need them.

But how did anyone cope with *this*?

"I always knew," Erica said, taking off her glasses and dropping them on the delicately inlaid end table, "that she and I were on borrowed time. We were already so much luckier than we should have been, luckier than *anyone* should have been. This isn't a world where people like us get to live in peace for very long. In the end, they always come for you. They *always* make you pay the price. But I just thought—" Her voice wavered as she swiped at her eyes desperately. "I should have seen it coming. I should have—"

"Why are you *here*, Erica?" I almost leapt up from the sofa again before reminding myself how much it had hurt the last time. "You need to be with her."

Erica swallowed, fighting back control. "Milagros knows me better than anyone, and she knows—assuming she's conscious, which I can't be sure of—why I'm not with her. That has to be enough. The story of slavery is one of endless suffering, and most of it we're powerless to stop. But this, we can." She raised her head. "And that's worth everything."

"Erica."

She just blinked.

"You made a promise to Milagros, all those years ago, that you'd come back for her."

She mostly didn't move, but she raised her eyes, telling me to go on.

"I think you'd be the first to admit that she didn't have any real reason to believe it, after what the world had put her through. But she did. And you did. And—" I looked desperately around the room. "And Ivy. Those kids had no reason to expect anything but more abuse from her. She literally inherited them, and she could have done anything with them, or to them. But she chose to love them."

Slowly, Erica nodded.

"Well—I made a promise to *him*. And he promised to believe it."

Amid the veranda, silent except for crickets, I watched Erica's slim collarbone move up and down minutely as if, incredulously, it was now *her* who was struggling to breathe normally.

"You said you're going back to this guy tomorrow morning, right?"

Erica nodded.

"Then give me that long. That's all I ask. If I don't figure out something by then, I'll go with you." I went for my phone.

"But, Louisa, what—" She stopped short as if something had occurred to her. "Wait a minute. Where's Ivy?"

As if on cue, Ivy threw open the doors to the veranda and stumbled toward us, out of breath, her eyebrows, impossibly, even higher than they'd been before. "I don't mean to scare anyone," she said, panting. "But I think someone might know you're here. I need to go check on the kids."

"What? How do you know?" I asked, trying to keep my voice steady.

"After a night like this, I needed a cigarette, so I walked down to the end of the driveway," Ivy confessed, noticing the looks she was getting. "Do *not* tell the kids. Or my nursing professors. At least it's not smack, okay? Anyway, I saw a strange car parked down the street. It gave me a funny feeling, so I kept an eye on it. And then I saw someone get out and start walking toward the house. And I think he saw me."

There was no way to tell whether the noise we'd heard was related. But it wasn't necessarily *not* related.

"Ivy, where's—"

Wordlessly, Ivy handed me the burner phone, charged and ready, and with my hands as steady as they could be under the circumstances, I dialed a number I knew by heart, one I hadn't intended to call that night, or maybe ever again. I turned back to Erica while I listened to the ringtone.

"Who are you calling?"

"I think if you can involve the cops, I can involve someone even worse than that." I held up a hand when I heard the voice on the other end of my dad's phone: a female voice. The housekeeper. It wasn't unheard of for her to take messages, but given the circumstances, it sent a chill right down into my bones.

"Miss Louisa. Thank heavens. Your parents have been—"

"I need to talk to Daddy. Please," I cut her off as politely as I could. "Where is he? Why isn't he answering?"

"Sorry, miss, but he can't come to the phone right now."

"But why not? This is really important. He'll want to hear from me."

"I know he will, miss. He's been desperate to find you. But still, I'm afraid you'll have to wait. He's—he's with other people."

"Who?" I demanded, already knowing there was no possible answer that wouldn't make the situation worse.

"The police."

11

HIM

In the jungle river town, life unfolded like a dream—the dream of freedom, the one I'd never before allowed myself to have. The place was painted in emerald and sapphire. The air hung heavy, pregnant with the scent of hibiscus and orchids. In town, taco stands and handicraft shops dotted every corner as locals whizzed by on motorbikes, engines humming with the rhythmic splash of fishing boats cutting through the aquamarine river that spliced the town into two. A stroll along the dock revealed marinas adorned with boats of all sizes and colors, their masts standing tall against a backdrop of lush foliage. Monkeys and parrots shrieked and chattered from deep within. In short, it was paradise.

That is if the postcard someone had taped to a cabinet in Langer's lab was anything to go off.

I turned it around in my hand a couple of times before tossing it aside, forcing my eyes to settle on what I was supposed to be looking at, and my brain on what I was supposed to be thinking about: the chemical formula I'd written out from memory on the 3D holographic display. The device had promptly spat back a visual representation of the molecule, and I moved my finger to rearrange the atoms, watching them bounce against each other like eager little insects. But it was my own face that teased me, reflected faintly in the glass like some haggard, dusty, wind-whipped ghost.

It didn't make sense. And not just the formula.

I had to be the biggest idiot alive to trust *Max Langer*, of all people, to keep my sister safe until I could get to her. And if I *was* that much of an idiot, it went without saying that I didn't like my chances of reaching an earth-shattering scientific breakthrough in a matter of hours.

For the millionth time, I glanced out the window at the murk of the empty office park. Silence. I was alone. The helicopter was gone, the Porsche left behind. From now on, any getaway I made would be on foot.

In other words, I was doomed.

"I had a feeling you might say that," was Max's response on the helicopter, when I told him my plan—the plan I should have told him about right from the start. The plan that would, like no plan before, help *all* of us: Maeve, Louisa, her father, Max, *and* the girls.

I had neglected to mention myself. But if Max had noticed, he hadn't said anything. He'd just listened closely, nodding. Reassured me that he'd look after Maeve, no matter what.

He knew my mind was made up.

He'd also told me how to change the entry codes but also that Resi knew a hack to get around it. So when I'd arrived at the lab, I not only did that but checked the locks and even pushed furniture in front of some of the doors. That wouldn't hold forever. But hopefully, I wouldn't *need* forever.

Hopefully, in coming back, I hadn't signed my own death warrant.

But I very well might have. Which probably explained the compact Smith & Wesson 9-millimeter that now sat on the steel table next to me. I'd never touched a gun before tonight, of course. Not like I hadn't been curious, like many red-blooded males. But it had never needed to be spelled out for me that slaves handling firearms was Not Allowed.

Of course, a lot of things had changed. But *that* hadn't. Because the *world* hadn't. Yet.

Anyway, I was already so far outside the law at this point it didn't matter. Besides, Max Langer had given it to me. I wasn't sure how much credence *that* had, though, now that the former corporate wunderkind was outside the law, too.

"Were you armed this entire time?" I had demanded when Max suddenly whipped open his jacket and pulled the pistol out of a holster.

"I was not. And why are you shouting?"

"Oh. Sorry," I said, realizing that the whole point of the headset was so we wouldn't *have* to shout.

My eyes followed his manicured hands as he demonstrated deftly unloading the magazine and toggling the safety. My eyes grew wider by the second.

"Normally, I leave this stuff to my security staff, but I'm going in alone from here," Max said before chambering a round and handing the loaded pistol over to me like a stick of gum.

I stared down at it uncomprehendingly.

"Well? Give it a try. You're right-handed, right?"

"Yeah, but—"

"Then that's likely your dominant eye. But let's find out." After demonstrating, he signaled to the pilot to unlock the door and pushed it open.

Palms slick, heart hammering, my fingers curled around the cold, hard metal of the trigger, gazing down the sight with both eyes open as Max had suggested, aiming for the moon.

"Physics says it has to come down, you know," I said.

"It's bare desert below us now. Shoot."

So I aimed a single bullet at the throat of that cold purple-black horizon, the jolt it returned as deep as if the projectile had lodged itself inside *me*.

"Thanks," I said grudgingly. "I guess."

Max smiled. "I think that's the nicest thing you've ever said to me."

Back in the lab, I decided Max must have Maeve by now. They must be on the plane, my sister's golden eyes soon to reflect the promise of the horizon at first light, winging toward that postcard paradise I'd just thrown aside. And that did let me breathe a little easier, to think of Maeve safe in the clouds.

But not enough. Because I should be there. I should have *been* there. I should have been the first one she saw, the first arms she ran to when they opened the gates for her. Because even though Max understood what freedom meant to the world, I was the only one who knew what freedom meant to *her*, and to myself. And it would be my only chance, ever.

"Hey." Back on the copter, Max had recognized that same look in my eyes. "Kid. Look at me."

Max had told the pilot to touch down in an empty wash about a mile away from the lab, and as much sand as the rooftop landing had churned up, it was about a thousand times worse now. It rattled the reinforced glass windows and made chaos of everything onboard, clothes and hair included, spraying grit in our eyes and down our throats. Still, I lingered, while the pilot's annoyance practically vibrated through the engine. A bullet hole in his fuselage, and now *this*.

But Max hadn't seemed to notice. I met his icy blue eyes one last time. Blinked. Held a steady gaze, the same one that had first made him pause and look twice, all those months ago.

"I might be the one buying her, but *you're* the one who saved her," Max had said. "I know that. And so does she."

I nodded and swallowed.

He held out his hand, and here it was: that weird half-handshake, half-hug that men engaged in when they both felt emotion, knew they felt emotion, and knew neither one wanted to acknowledge it. "Don't get yourself killed, okay? It would be bad for business," he explained. "And say hi to Curly Sue for me. Maybe someday I'll get to meet her properly."

I smiled, despite myself. "Like I'd ever let her near you."

Max grinned. "See you on the other side, kid."

I threw off the headset. Closed my eyes, blinking away the desert grit, clearly the one and only reason why they suddenly felt misty. Then I leaped—gracefully enough, I liked to think, stumbling only once as I landed in the dust of the wash. As I did, I could have sworn Max shouted something else, but if so, it was lost in the chaos.

So I kept moving, out of the swirling storm made by the dragonfly wings. The ones that would have been, could have been, my ride to freedom—not like there was any point dwelling on *that*. And I made it all the way across the dry river and toward the lights of the industrial park below before pausing to turn back. But the copter was already gone.

Now an hour had passed, and I was still in the lab, jumping at every noise loud enough to cut through the rhythmic hum of machines and my own pounding heart.

The lights overhead flickered like fireflies in a jar, casting eerie shadows on the walls. I paced back and forth, my mind racing as I scrutinized the molecules, examining and manipulating them from every possible angle, and the clearer it became —I was fucked.

Theoretically, the solution I'd put on the screen *should* work. The basic hypothesis, based on what I'd read in those lab reports I wasn't supposed to see, was that the formula Resi had found, when injected, would depolymerize the chip and magnetize the components with the help of nanotechnology. At that point, it could then be drawn safely out of the body, intact, physically degraded but theoretically still transmitting, by the use of a neodymium magnet. That was the idea, anyway. The problem was, that only got you halfway. You couldn't examine or experiment on intact chips without first pinpointing exactly where they were in the body. And you couldn't do *that*—or at least Resi couldn't—without lopping off limbs and, uh, killing people.

Which—as arrogant as it sounded—must mean the formula was wrong, not me. It was missing a part, I realized. The one that could actually attract the polymer and somehow locate the chip, and prove my solution correct.

My weary mind bushwhacked back through the intricate web of chemical knowledge the old professor had long ago cracked my head open to pour inside.

I recalled the lamplit nights hunched over the desk in the professor's cluttered study, and couldn't help, for a second, but wonder what old Jurgen himself would think if his former slave were to actually pull this off. The pompous, pie-eyed old bastard wouldn't give a shit whether my discovery helped slaves. But he sure *would* give a shit that it was *right*.

Yeah, I stood by my loathing for my old master and always would, but we'd had *that* in common. That longing for that rare, curt nod of approval. The professor from his abusive stepfather, me from the abusive professor. The one that in a million years I would never admit to wanting—wouldn't admit to wanting it from Max, either. Or even *Keith*, bizarre as that seemed.

But that, I supposed, was the sad lot of all fatherless boys.

I was starting to overheat. I should have turned on the A/C, but there was no time now. Any second, Resi was going to figure out I was here. Fuck, what was I thinking, standing here lost in memories like some sentimental idiot? This kind of research took *years*, normally. And here I was, trying to do it in one night, on zero sleep, and in fear that any second some thug could burst in, grab me from behind, and slit my throat with piano wire.

Well. No less pressure than on a typical day with the professor, then.

A noise behind me came like a whip cracking against metal. I scrabbled for the gun like a paranoid madman, my slick palms fumbling with the safety.

But when I saw who had entered, I dropped the weapon and turned my back, fingertips digging violently into the metal countertop.

The petite girl in the doorway looked taller and older, somehow, in a black tank and jeans, boots clacking on the tile. Ebony hair pulled back slickly. Meticulously. Like the cold, calculating creature she was.

Lemaya said nothing. Maybe she'd just come to watch me fail.

"I—"

"Let me guess," I cut her off, the anger in my voice rising over the hum of lab equipment. "You're sorry."

"Yes," she said. "But I know there's no excuse for what I did."

Actually, there kind of was. Not that it helped.

"I know," she offered. "Go fuck myself."

"Please do."

"Deserved. Anyway, you'll never have to see me again, if that's any consolation. I'm leaving. Forever. Right now."

"Where?" I turned my head slightly, unwilling to reveal any curiosity.

"As far away from here as I can get."

"But—"

"My owner's dead, and no one else knew he had me. It won't be easy, but if I lie low, I'll be fine."

It would be half a life, at best, a pale shadow of what she'd been promised. But it would also be away from Resi, so it might be okay. And it was no consolation at all.

"What are you here for, anyway?" I growled. "A hug good-bye?" I'd rather hug a king cobra.

"No," she said, squinting at me curiously. "You wore *that* shirt to dinner?"

With a groan, I remembered Felix's contempt toward my wardrobe. "*You* told me to buy it! And not the point."

"Sorry. Anyway, I'm here because of Maeve."

"Maeve?"

"She really was my friend."

"Oh," I said. "So then it makes *total* sense that you betrayed her *and* us because you wanted to marry a millionaire."

"Okay, yes. I did want that," she blurted out. She was sounding younger by the minute. "But I loved Max, or at least, I thought I did. And Resi said he loved me, he just wouldn't admit it, and that if I gave her more time, she could *make* him admit it. And that's why I went along with her, at first. But once I realized she was lying about everything, it was too late."

"Too late? How?"

"Either I did what she told me to do, or she'd kill me."

I supposed I should have gathered that.

"Anyway, I wasn't lying about Maeve. I-I don't lie about everything." There was desperation in her voice. To be believed. To be trusted. To be looked at as more than a con artist, as more than what the world had made her be. Something I inherently sympathized with, despite everything. "She was my best friend. My only friend, probably. And if there's one thing I regret about what happened, it's that I'll never see her again."

"So what?" I said stubbornly. "You want me to take the message?"

"No, I want you to take this."

I turned completely, and she approached with a computer printout with a jumble of letters and numbers.

I scanned it rapidly. "But this is—" I snatched it out of her hand. "The formula *was* wrong." I raced to the computer, rapidly punching buttons until the molecule burst onto the holographic screen, staring at them in disbelief.

Now my solution worked, of course. Cue the professor's nod. "How did you know about this?"

"Because I'm the one who left you the formula to begin with."

"What?"

"Well, after Resi found out Corey wouldn't be coming back, she ordered me to go comb through his office and take back anything he left that looked like it might be important. And I found the tablet. And I almost took it, but I decided to leave it there. For you. I-I mean, Max told me you were good at that kind of thing."

"Well, shit," I said, jaw hanging open. "Thanks for almost getting me *and* Louisa killed before I could do anything with it."

She grimaced, then asked in a tiny voice, "Water under the bridge?"

I groaned and ran my hands through my limp hair. "We still need to synthesize a catalyst. To make the serum."

"Good thing we're in a chemistry lab, then."

"I'll need your help," I said, returning to the cabinets and removing more compounds. "What do you know about electrolysis?"

"Surprisingly? A lot."

I turned back, raising my eyebrows.

"I worked here for like a year, you know. Ammonium persulfate, right?"

I smiled. "You're almost forgiven."

I carefully measured out the ammonium sulfate solution and added the freezing-cold liquid to the beaker. Lemaya prepared the grainy precipitates and handed them over so we could immerse them in the solution. As I combined them over the burner, the mixture began to bubble and hiss, the heat of the reaction spreading through the beaker. A thick, gooey slurry formed, coated in a yellow hue whose smoke stained my fingers as I tried to stir it with a glass rod.

As the reaction continued, the air grew thicker and heavier, pressing down on my chest and throat, making it more and more difficult to choke out words. Of course, under normal circumstances, we would have been using goggles, masks, maybe even full-on protective suits. These were not normal circumstances.

I tried to breathe through it, I kept working, but it was no use. Each inhale felt like trying to pull air through a faulty oxygen mask. Next to me, I noticed with alarm, Lemaya's face was already turning purple. She gasped, her chest heaving as she tried to breathe.

"How do we ventilate this place?" I demanded. My own lungs felt weighted with lead, a slow, wheezing asphyxiation.

She rushed to a control panel, slamming one random button after another. "I-I don't know. There are supposed to be fans. Why aren't they working?"

"I don't know. I might have disabled that somehow when I disabled the codes."

She punched the wall in frustration, then turned. "Turn off the heat." She gasped. "It's the only—"

"No," I bit back, dashing to the window and throwing two

of them open, knowing I'd regret it, but that I'd regret stopping the reaction that much more.

With a final burst, the reaction was complete. I switched off the heat with relief as the fumes dispersed on the slight breeze, watching as the mixture settled into a cool, opaque texture and a calm, clear golden hue.

Lemaya and I looked at each other. For a few seconds, our grateful breaths were the only sounds. The gratitude soon morphed into dread. The dread I'd been trying to shake off since I'd arrived in the lab.

Because the serum needed to be tested. And there were only two possible guinea pigs. But really, there was only one. And I'd known that from the second I'd jumped off that helicopter.

It was why, when describing the plan to Max, I hadn't mentioned myself.

"You said I was almost forgiven," Lemaya was saying, God bless her, steeling her delicate mouth into a line. "Well, I want to be completely forgiven."

I shook my head. "Not this way." I'd been angry at her. I may have thought I hated her. But still, she was a slave, overwhelmed, like me, by a slave's desperate dreams and impossible choices, and nothing she'd done came close to warranting death.

As for me? Well, I'd done a lot wrong—recently, and just altogether. I didn't know about *deserve*. But the point was that nobody knew better than me how to take pain. And the worst pain was *worse* than death. If I had to choose between the two, logic told me to choose death.

Hell of a choice to make, but that was my life.

Robotically, I went to the computer. It only took a second to print out the formula. I went to a drawer and removed a neodymium magnet, a matte metal disc shaped like a roll of tape, and handed it to Lemaya. Then I walked purposefully over to the fire extinguisher and opened the glass case. I gripped the metal handle tightly, and with a quick twist, removed the silvery canister with its long nozzle and valve.

"Stand back." With one thrust, over the screaming of my aching shoulder muscles, I heaved the extinguisher at the computer and its holographic display, shattering it into a million luminescent smithereens.

"Just to be safe," I explained. "Here." I reached for the suit jacket I'd draped over a chair and dug into the silken inner pocket for what I'd carefully stashed there before meeting Max up on the helipad.

First, the cash I'd removed from my safe: three weeks' pay plus a "signing bonus," as Max had phrased it. Lemaya's eyes widened at the sight of the bills as I counted some out into a separate pile.

"This is yours," I said, glancing up. "For your new life."

"I can't—"

"Yes, you can." I left her share on the table and shoved the rest in a flimsy manila envelope. I added one of three flash drives I'd hidden, containing the files from Corey's tablet. And on top of that, the printout of the complete formula. "I won't need these, either," I said after a pause, slipping off my gold watch and rings and handing her those, too.

Then I paused, staring down at the envelope. Lemaya silently handed me some blank paper and a pen.

"Thanks."

I'd thought it would be tough to figure out what to write. I *wasn't* a writer. I wasn't even really a reader. I didn't understand figurative language or flowery descriptions. And I certainly wasn't so arrogant as to think—despite everything—that I understood love. Not the same way the intended recipient of the note did, anyway.

Still, when the pen hit the paper, I found I didn't have to think too hard about it.

I handed Lemaya the envelope and all of its contents. "Where you leave it is up to you."

"But will they be able to find it?"

I glanced down. "If the serum works, they will."

"Oh." Lemaya swallowed, catching on, her tawny, delicate hands turning ashy as they gripped the envelope. "But I—we won't know if it's still transmitting."

"Assume it is."

Finally, after a pause, I reached for the Smith & Wesson. Removed the magazine, inspected it, reloaded it. Removed the safety and chambered a round like some kind of tactical expert, as if I hadn't been shown the same damn thing for the first time an hour or so ago. Cleared it. And now it was Lemaya's turn to hide her shaking hands as I placed the weapon in front of her.

"But what about you?"

I took a deep breath, having hoped not to be forced to explain that when I'd entered the lab, I'd known there was a good chance I wouldn't be leaving. "What you have is more important."

"But will you see Maeve?"

"That's the plan." Well, it was the plan if everything went perfectly. And in my life, when did *anything* go perfectly?

"You *will* see her," she said. "So please tell her I'm sorry," she said fiercely, and if there was a tear in her voice, there was nothing on her face. "And—and that I really do love her. And that I hope she can forgive me someday."

Lemaya's eyes shot to the window we'd left open for ventilation. Like a shot, she rushed to close it. But she paused. Craned her neck.

"Okay, so I don't want to alarm you or anything, but—"

"Ah, fuck. It's them, isn't it?"

I quickly closed the window and locked it. "I mean, I don't know for sure if—"

"It's them."

"I didn't tell them where we were," she said in a panicky voice. "You believe me, right?"

I closed my eyes briefly. "Of course I believe you. I knew they'd be here eventually. Look, do you know another way out of here? Other than the main door?"

She nodded. "Come with me. Take the serum. We can—"

"No." I shook my head. "They're coming after me, not you. That's why you need to escape alone, with that envelope, while I hold them off."

"But how are you going to do that if—" She bit her lip as if she had an inkling.

If I'm dead, the job will be finished.

Of course *she* couldn't go until the serum kicked in because my chip, if it came out, would be going with her. That made this tricky, to say the least.

Well. I snatched up the serum. It was oddly beautiful, thick and glistening like honey inside its beaker. I pulled back a syringe needle and carefully measured out a dosage, though determining a safe amount didn't seem to matter much. The point was to see if it worked. Keeping myself alive was a secondary consideration at best. Not like I wasn't likely to be dead shortly, anyway, even *without* the serum.

The lab had grown quieter without the hum of the massive computer, and Lemaya watched me, her eyes wide under the harsh fluorescent lights. I was calm until I realized that the syringe was full. Then, suddenly, a cold fear gripped my chest, as heavy as the reaction from earlier.

Breathe.

It might be the last time.

In terms of potential places to get comfortable, there

weren't many options. I settled on a swivel desk chair and rolled it over. There were two general areas where the chips got implanted—in the forearm or between the shoulder blades. Many slaves didn't know which one they'd been given. But I had made a point, a few years ago—with the professor's permission, even—to find out, suspecting it might come in handy someday. Now I unfurled my forearm toward Lemaya, the veins snaking through my scarred tissue like rivers of blood through a bombed-out battlefield. She, of course, didn't even blink. She bore more than her share.

Trembling, I raised the plunger on the syringe. I knew what needles felt like, of course. Slave children had to get vaccinations just like everyone else. The only difference was that when we didn't cry, instead of a lollipop, our reward was one less caning that day. Compared to that, a needle prick was nothing much at all.

Odd how that wasn't very comforting.

"Oh, let me do it," she said boldly when I hesitated again, grabbing another chair and pulling it up next to me at the steel table. "I'll probably never be a vet tech now. But I've sure watched enough videos."

I handed it over immediately. And to think I'd been furious when she'd walked in. The idea of trying to do this without her was unfathomable.

The harsh lab lights seemed to get hotter by the second, increasing the sweat on my face that I was no longer trying to swipe away, making my breathing shallower. The way I jumped at every sound. She knew. She knew what this was doing to me and what it might do to her. But all she did was nod, her free hand closed around both of mine.

"Ready?"

Despite myself, I tightened my grip.

"We can wait, if—"

"No. Do it now, or we won't get to do it at all." A noise like an electronic chime sounded from somewhere in the lab.

"Shit. Does that mean they're inside?"

She bit her lip. "It might."

"Do it." I gasped. "Do it now. Don't wait."

She nodded and took a deep breath. "Don't look at it," she advised. "Okay? Keep your eyes on me."

"Okay," I managed to say. "But after you do it, just—just don't let go. Until—"

"I won't," she said. "I promise. I'm not going anywhere."

I hadn't been able to see Louisa's face when she'd said those words, facing death another time. And I'd never thought I'd see that face again.

"You can pretend I'm her," Lemaya said quietly. "If you want."

I nodded. Blinked. Tried to swallow. Tried to settle my now-blurry gaze on something, anything. A shard of light hit the one piece of jewelry she still wore—a silver crescent moon with some Arabic writing underneath. I'd read that these—and crosses and stars and other shapes, too—were very popular generations ago, when God was more than just a storybook character.

"Do you know how to pray?" I rasped. "Did they teach you that?"

She nodded. "My first mistress did, a little bit. Everyone thought she was nuts. For believing *anybody* had souls, let alone slaves."

Well. She *was* nuts. My mind hadn't changed.

I didn't think it had, anyway. I *had* tried asking "God"—whoever or whatever that was—for a favor, and it hadn't done me any good.

Or maybe it had. I'd seen Louisa again, hadn't I? Once.

And I was seeing her now. Gray eyes like the stormy North

Sea, then a smile like the sun coming out after a twenty-year tempest. And grace. Yes, amazing grace. Things I didn't deserve, but she'd offered me just the same. And what *was* a miracle, anyway?

"I prayed with Maeve." Lemaya's eyes—dark brown, almost black—stayed locked on mine.

"Will you—"

"Of course." She closed her eyes. Mumbled something that sounded like singing. Something I was so content to listen to that I didn't realize the needle was already in. Something that surely was a blessing.

A blessing, too—as the acrid taste of chemicals thronged my sinuses and raced through my every capillary, as I lost my grip on Lemaya's hand and fell away from the steel table, sending the chair spinning, and smashing the rack of test tubes behind me—that my hands, just for a second, had been warm in hers.

Because everything after that was very, very cold.

12

Home.

Let's face it: While it contained people I needed to see, it certainly contained no one I *wanted* to see.

Right now, though, I couldn't have what I wanted. But maybe by going home, I could give myself a better shot.

"Agent Wheatley is there now, and I explained the situation," Erica said as she dialed for a taxi. Meanwhile, I thanked Ivy inadequately and accepted a jar of that floral-scented aloe with a promise to reapply it (and see a real medical professional as soon as I felt safe to). Then I offered Ivy my phone number before I remembered it *wasn't* my phone number. I didn't *have* a real phone number anymore, or any other contact information.

But still, we promised to meet when it was safe, if ever. We needed to talk about Ethan. Although I had a feeling I'd soon be talking about him plenty.

After checking the perimeter again, my professor hustled me outside to a taxi. Both Erica and Ivy had insisted I get a few hours of sleep in the expansive spare bed, and as much as I'd

protested, I didn't regret the chance for some blissful uncon-
sciousness. But I was up soon enough to attack it all again,
dressed in Ivy's leggings, flip-flops, and a hooded long-sleeved
T-shirt with some floral surf brand logo, the drawstring pulled
tight around my bunched-up curls, topped off with a pair of
comically oversized movie-star sunglasses masking most of my
face.

"Talk to him and *only* him," Erica warned.

I nodded and placed my seared body gingerly into the seat,
watching weak streaks of pinkish-gray light just grace the
suburban rooftops on four sides, offering a grounding glimpse
of the distant peaks. This endless night was finally ending, and
my clothing was too warm for the weather, but the weather
wasn't the point. When I got home, I wanted people to focus on
me, not the angry, glistening, pus-filled blisters wallpapering
my body, and the where-on-earth-have-you-been questions
that would inevitably follow.

When I was finally alone, standing in front of my full-length
filigree mirror, I knew I'd have all the time in the world to see
fully what I had lost.

"But what about you and Alma?" I finally asked Erica, just
before she closed the door.

"Wheatley sent a squad car to park down the street and
keep an eye on the house," she explained. "The officers don't
know the details, only that we're under protection. He said it's
better if we stay put for now."

"Now you have to trust *three* cops instead of just one?" I
exclaimed. "And what about that guy Ivy saw, and—"

Erica closed her eyes, her ragged, deep breath revealing just
how much she was struggling, even *without* Milagros lying intu-
bated in a hospital bed somewhere. "I know, I know. But we're
getting to the point in this thing where you don't ask too many
questions." She gave me a fast, awkward, very-Erica hug,

slammed the taxi door, and signaled to the driver. And then there was no arguing because she was halfway down the block already.

Thank God Erica was still relatively calm. Because home, when I arrived, was pure chaos.

Nearly a dozen police cars were outside, jammed together in the circular drive, lights flashing, tires crushing the carefully manicured landscaping. A pair of them had even cracked one of the ocotillos nearly in two. Officers in official windbreakers, some with holstered assault weapons, marched grimly in and out of the front door, hoisting files and folders and electronic equipment. And across the front door, that yellow tape with the black lettering that always seemed to signify something horrible, at least on TV.

My breath shortened and my fight-or-flight kicked into overdrive, *again*. At this rate, I was certain I'd wind up hooked up to a heart monitor by the end of the day.

Something crunched underfoot, and I glanced down to see broken glass scattered across the lawn, glinting in the sunlight. Following the trail, I gazed up fretfully to see one of the living room windows smashed wide open.

"Daddy?" I shouted.

As I stood frozen, the front door flung open, and the housekeeper ran outside in a tizzy, disheveled silver strands flying from her usually neat hair. She was flanked by two alarmed-looking cops in windbreakers, and she caught me by the arm as I tried to duck under the tape.

"Where is he?" I demanded.

The housekeeper sighed. "Miss, please, you can't—"

"I don't care." My eyes scanned the house again, my heart slamming against my ribcage, checking for any signs of damage or injury. I marched toward the tape. "I believe federal law bans you from preventing access to my domicile." I had no idea what the fuck federal law said, but the key was to sound like I did. "And where's Agent Wheatley?" Neither of these two cops matched the description of him Erica had given.

"Miss—" the housekeeper began, a million questions frozen on her lips, even *without* a glimpse at the burns.

Not waiting to hear them, I tore away, grabbed the yellow tape, threw it aside, and ducked underneath through the front door, sprinting toward the living room, coming to a stop in the kitchen just outside it, the housekeeper following on my heels.

My father—voice raspier, face more drawn and haggard than when I'd left him—was in the midst of an explanation to yet two more agents, both wearing the same windbreakers with bold yellow lettering on the back. The place had been flipped upside down—drawers pulled out, cushions upended, papers fluttering everywhere—but to my relief, no guns had been drawn and other than the one smashed window, no signs of a struggle. That was the privilege of being an ex-millionaire CEO, I supposed. It was certainly the privilege of being *his* daughter that let me burst past the barriers without the bullets flying. But I obviously wasn't complaining.

"Mr. Wainwright-Phillips, our evidence shows that you were the primary investor in the venture," a plump, freckled female agent with spiky strawberry blond hair was saying in a flatly unsympathetic tone. "Your name is on every single piece of paperwork we've been able to recover. There's no other—"

My father interrupted, which even *I* knew he shouldn't be doing without his lawyer. But I didn't blame him for protesting. He *was* being unfairly accused.

"And I told you there *is*. The bastard defrauded me, with the help of one of my own slaves. It was all going on right in front of my eyes. God, I can't believe how blind I was."

I closed my eyes, trying to calm myself enough not to scream before I heard the rest of his outlandish theory.

"I lent him a highly valuable slave, one of my best investments, in good faith, in a deal that would benefit all of us"—I couldn't help rolling my eyes—"and he stole him right out from under me."

Stole?

"Mr. Wainwright-Phillips." This was a tall, muscular, dark-brown-skinned male agent. Wheatley. He was younger than I had pictured, and his voice was different, in a way. Not sympathetic, necessarily. But capable of grasping nuance, at least.

Talk to him and only him.

Pulling that off would be tricky. Anyway, right now, my father held the floor.

"And what's worse, the whole time, he was using him to *spy* on me."

No. That wasn't the explanation, I reminded myself. I *knew* the explanation.

"I think he even told the boy to go through my file cabinets at one point." He looked at the female agent. "I should have known they were plotting something the second they started talking to each other in *German*, of all languages. I wouldn't be surprised if they were somehow doing it *before* I bought the boy. I'll tell you what you *should* be investigating, is that slave dealership. Who knows what kinds of other scams they're running over there? That's what I get for trusting the Europeans. They're all a pack of lying, cheating, thieving—"

"He was trying to help you!" Against my best judgment, I burst into the living room.

"Loulou!" My dad rushed toward me, and I shrank away from his embrace, not only to avoid yelping in pain as my charred skin flared in protest.

"Where in God's name have you been? And why are you dressed like—"

"Sir, I told her not to come in, but—"

He held up a hand, uninterested in hearing the housekeeper's explanation. He sighed and rubbed his temples. He looked like he'd aged ten years in a day.

"Loulou, I was worried sick and I'm hugely relieved you're back, but whatever you have to say, I'm afraid I don't have time for it right now, as you can plainly see." He waved at the housekeeper, all imperious and dismissive, even with his entire life and fortune under threat. "Take her upstairs. We'll discuss everything later."

"No." My teeth clenched. I could only imagine the wild expression flashing in my eyes. The housekeeper wouldn't *dare*. "Agent Wheatley?"

Wheatley turned suddenly, and I jumped at my chance.

"He—he has a plan," I began. Somehow, that line had sounded much more convincing in my head.

"Oh, he has a plan all right," my father broke in with contempt. "*Had* a plan this whole time. To rob me blind."

The female agent looked more irritated by the second. "Miss, you're interfering with a law enforcement operation here. I'll have to ask you to sit down, be quiet, or leave the room."

But Wheatley said nothing, so I forged ahead, hoping I wasn't giving too much away.

"Langer had nothing to do with it. And if you'd just give him time—give *me* time—" Frantically, I looked from my father to the agent, then to the other agent. Three completely different expressions, all fixed on me. Hot tears were forming in the corners of my swollen eyes. Shit, I was failing at this already.

"Miss, we don't conduct our investigations based on fanciful teenage notions," the female agent snapped. "Now, for the last time, I'll have to ask you to—"

Gripped by desperation, I ripped off my hood and threw my sunglasses on the sofa behind me, tugging the long-sleeved shirt over my head to reveal the skimpy tank top underneath, and, well—

I'd at least had a night to get used to the way my body looked. No one else in the room had.

"Good heavens," whispered the housekeeper.

"Loulou, what *happened* to you?" my dad exclaimed. "We need to get you to a hospital." Without waiting for a response, he reached for his phone from where it sat on the ponderous mahogany coffee table.

"Daddy, no. I've—I've *been* to a hospital."

"And they let you out like *that*? No, Loulou. You need proper —" He was already dialing.

"Daddy, *no*." This was exactly what I'd been afraid of. But what other choice did I have?

This time it was Wheatley who quickly interrupted. "Sir, I'm a trained EMT, and it's clear to me these burns have already been treated."

Ironically, the pain, which I had been valiantly ignoring, seemed to swell up all at once. The housekeeper had already sprung into action, reappearing instantly with some cold compresses, which I accepted for some temporary relief. Enough to finish this, anyway.

"Miss Wainwright-Phillips," Wheatley was saying, having finally turned directly to me. "I completely get that you think there's more to this story. I think there is, too, and I have for some time." He flashed his partner a pointed look. She remained unsmiling. "But I'm afraid that what you were about to say is probably not going to be as helpful as you'd hoped."

Blood rushed into my ears. "Why not?"

"Because as Agent Labrecque here informed me a few minutes ago, Mr. Langer is gone."

"Gone?" My vision blurred; my already wobbly legs nearly gave out completely. The housekeeper, though, was still right there behind me, catching me as I collapsed and guiding me to the leather sofa.

Agent Labrecque, meanwhile, cleared her throat, plainly resentful that her partner was treating me as anything more than an irritant. "His private jet filed paperwork to take off this morning from Tucson."

"Was—" I gulped for air. "Was anyone else on it?"

The two cops looked at each other.

"Besides the pilot, I mean? Please," I added in a voice little more than a whisper. "I have to know."

Wheatley kept his eyes fixed intensely on Labrecque. In the end, it was the female agent who spoke. "Besides the crew, two slaves were listed on the manifest. One of them," she added, glancing down at her notepad and back up, "belongs to your father."

In a second, I could no longer feel my body, the burns, or anything else. My father's face was a blur, and the agent's voice seemed to drift up as if out of a drainpipe. My senses had collapsed into a singularity: Erica's words.

Not all slaves turn out to be heroes.

Him

Blinding sunlight. My head throbbed as my vision adjusted. The air was hot, dry, and still, bringing with it the faint scent of sunbaked sand.

I jerked in place, only to have fire rip through my muscles, my joints locked. Every movement felt like pushing through a thick fog, even the slightest twitch greeted with a chorus of aches and pains ricocheting through my body. My throat felt like I'd been trying to swallow sandpaper. One thing was for sure: Rio Dulce was sounding better and better by the second.

Moving also alerted me to a familiar sound. Chains.

All right. What kind were they *this* time?

Well, I'd been collared, for one, by a thick band of metal and leather clasped tightly around my neck, with a chain trailing off somewhere behind and upward, the perfect length to prevent me from both standing up *and* lying down. She wanted me on my knees, in other words.

A smaller chain hung from the front of the collar, linked to a bit pushed under my tongue, attached to a mesh cage that fit over the lower half of my face. No talking, then. No screaming for help.

Hands cuffed behind me, which seemed to be Resi's style.

But it was my throat that concerned me most. It had already started to constrict, thirst clawing at the edges, making swallowing difficult. The sun's position suggested early morning, which meant I had a couple of hours or so before I had to worry about being boiled to death by the noonday heat. If I could survive that, I might just last long enough to die of dehydration. Or more likely, be tortured to death by Resi, because I had a strong feeling that watching from a distance as I succumbed to the elements wouldn't be nearly entertaining enough for her.

So *this* was how I was going to go out. All in all, I would have preferred the serum.

The serum. Cold shot through my body, so much stronger than the heat. I pushed my brain to remember something, anything, from after I'd passed out. Had it worked? Was the chip out? Had Lemaya gotten away? Had Louisa, or her father...?

I'd been at peace when I'd done it. With the fact that if I died, I'd never know. Now, since I happened to still be alive—a minor victory—I *had* to know.

Just like that, adrenaline pumped through me again. I struggled against the restraints and the pain convulsing my body to try to get a glimpse of my forearm. *Fuck.* Between the collar and the position of my hands, there was no way to tell. Which I was sure was the point. Well, that and torture.

Collars, man. Some owners favored them, though they were

largely considered stodgy and old-fashioned, reserved for either punishment or decorative use, like for high-end sex slaves.

Shit.

Best not to dwell on that. Actually, I'd been chained by the neck before. In fact, it had been one of my first master's favorite punishments if, after he caned me senseless, he felt the message still hadn't sunk in. A day and night with no food, no water, no ice for my bruises, kneeling in the garden like a dog, watching his kids play football and slurp on lollipops, sure had fixed my smart mouth, though.

Oh.

Did Resi know that? Know where my mind would go? Know just how to *force* me to act and think like a slave again after I'd grown too used to the opposite?

Where was this chain attached, anyway? A rusty, horizontal cast-iron bar with a post on each side and a series of solid rings jutting out. Only one was currently occupied, by the other end of my chain.

Of course. A hitching post. For horses. That figured. It was the West, after all. The Wild West, apparently, which was *not* just a staple of old black-and-white movies, as I'd been led to believe.

Hanging off behind it was a pathetic-looking building—my best guess was a long-abandoned toolshed, though even that seemed generous. At any rate, its rusty, corrugated tin awning created, at the sun's current angle, a slight shelter. An almost completely useless one, given the length of my chain. I strained a little anyway, to see how much closer I could get.

Which brought me back to my hands. Cautiously, I tested one, then the other, only to have the muzzle stifle my even more agonized scream.

These were no regular cuffs. They seemed to be constructed of barbs of pointed, unforgiving, glass-sharp wire, wire that ate deeper into the already mortified flesh of my wrists with every futile movement, the same way the weight of the collar crushed against my windpipe, making every breath and swallow a struggle, too.

This was what happened, I supposed, when they thought you were an escape artist. They just made stronger and harsher restraints.

"Fuck you, bitch," I screamed as best I could into the muzzle bit, just to make myself feel better.

Okay, enough of that. I took a deep breath. Figuring out things was kind of my thing. Problem was, the hotter it got, my synapses would start being cooked to death along with the rest of me.

Well, let's continue to assess. Honestly, they'd kind of dropped the ball on my legs, having only looped some thin rope around my bare ankles. They'd kept the rest of my clothes on me, including the torn, dusty, unbuttoned shirt—the same stupid feather-print one Lemaya had bought me, apparently as a joke—exposing only my chest, where the sun's rays continued to sear, layer by layer, into my already-inflamed skin. That skin was mostly dry, like the air, but some sweat mingled with the dust on my face, forming a gritty layer that only got worse as I tried to swallow or move my tongue. The muzzle and collar were already hot. In an hour or so, without shelter, they'd be like aluminum pots on a stove.

Adding that to my list of things not to dwell on, I maneuvered myself enough in the collar to give me a 360-degree view. The sand was dotted by the low tufts of sage and barrel cactuses that seemed to be a thing everywhere. Except out here, they were the *only* thing. And in the distance, a line of telephone poles, or saguaros, or both. A highway? Beyond that—in the opposite direction—soaring, reddish rock formations with ledges seemingly carved out of them, along with small arches and spires of the kind I'd also only seen in cliché depictions of the Wild West. They were real, though. For some reason, I felt kind of happy about that.

It was a place—like the rest of the desert, really, though I'd never admit it—I would have liked exploring, under different circumstances. I'd prefer a Porsche to a horse, though. A beautiful girl next to me, her hair bouncing in my face as she laughed with her entire mouth open. Stopping everywhere and anywhere. Chasing the mountains. Chasing the sunset. Getting lost on purpose. Getting lost forever.

Sure, okay. Of all things to start daydreaming about now, by all means, let's make it something that boasted roughly ten million reasons why I would never, ever have it.

Back to reality, which was that this quaint Western panorama was slowly killing me. Following the sun and the mountains, all I could estimate for now was that I was somewhere south and west of the city.

Too far to be found, maybe.

Unless the serum hadn't worked and my chip was still in, in which case Louisa, or her father, or both, would track it here. Which would ostensibly mean I'd be rescued. Except it didn't because Resi would be waiting for them.

And this time, I wouldn't be talking our way out. I wouldn't be talking at all. Nobody was walking, or running, away from this one.

And then I'd really have something to feel guilty about, if I didn't have enough already. But maybe even that was better than letting Resi or her goons find and kill Louisa where she was. And if preventing *that* meant I'd be a slave forever, well. It would still be the easiest choice I'd ever made.

Bottom line, my one chance was to figure out a way out *now*. Giving up on my other senses, I strained my ears. Maybe I could catch a sound for a clue. But all I heard was the distant keening of the wind and the occasional scuttle of sand against the shack's wooden walls.

I was relieved at the breeze, until, instead of cooling me off, it blew sand into my eyes and down my throat. And worse, it didn't die down. Weakly, I curled in on myself and closed my eyelashes against it, the tiny particles hitting against my skin and skittering beneath the splintered wood behind me.

When the sand died down. That's when I'd start escaping again.

After all, someone was counting on it. One person in the world who didn't want me to die. Two, actually. Maybe even *three*.

Which, all in all, was weirder than being chained to a hitching post in the middle of the desert.

Forcing myself to swallow, grit raking my parched throat, I raised my eyes to the vast, clear dome of sky overhead. At least there would be stars tonight.

13

"Miss." The housekeeper gently patted my arm over the T-shirt fabric. "This is doing you no good. You're better off in your bedroom. Some aloe, a cup of tea, a few hours of rest—"

"No," I whispered, almost to myself. "No."

"Loulou, it's time to stop this." My father's faraway voice was gentle now, almost pitying. "You heard what I said. It was all a scam of Langer's." He paused, swallowing. "I know, because that's where I sent the boy. I suppose I might as well tell you now."

A little slow on the uptake, Daddy. "You're wrong."

"Mr. Wainwright-Phillips, I still don't see how this is relevant to the investigation, and—"

My father ignored Labrecque. "I know you think I don't understand what you're feeling right now, but I do. The fact is" —he cleared his throat in that painfully awkward way he sometimes had—"*I* wanted to think better of the boy, too."

I blinked, uncomprehending.

"This will shock you, but I liked him, Loulou. Perhaps—perhaps more than I should have, and in a way I shouldn't have. More as a person, less as a slave. And I had thought that if I started treating him accordingly—with more trust and autonomy than his previous owners gave him—he'd rise to the occasion and prove me correct. So I trusted him. I gave him a chance."

"Mr. Wainwright-Phillips!" barked Labrecque, having lost whatever patience she had. "I'm afraid we need to continue with the questioning."

"But I was wrong, and I can see that now. The fact is, they can't be trusted, and there's no use pretending they can. They don't think like us. They'll never be *able* to think like us, and in the end, it's harmful to try to treat them as if they can. Harmful for us, *and* them."

I sank further into my chair as my father's words swirled around me, most of them meaningless. My wounds coalesced into a single blazing, red-hot knot of pain.

"I know you're entertaining abolitionist thoughts yourself, and even though you won't believe it, I respect that," he continued. "So was Langer, and maybe he influenced me more than I'd like to admit. But he was wrong, Loulou, and this proves it. Can't you see how dangerous it would be for all of us to give freedom to slaves—either a single slave or millions of them—who wouldn't know what to do with it? Sweetheart, you're the smartest girl I know. You must."

You see, Louisa, no one ever bothers to teach us right from wrong.

Some of them have spent so long being oppressed and beaten down by the system that when they get a little power or freedom, they don't know what to do with it. And then they make the wrong choice.

I made a promise to him. And he promised to believe it.

You have three hours.

"Miss." A soft voice in my ear. The housekeeper again,

quietly handing me ibuprofen tablets and pressing another cold compress to my neck, careful not to interrupt the conversation. As I turned toward it, all at once, my head broke the surface. My hearing became crystal-clear, my vision no longer a blur.

And I looked. *Really* looked—into the woman's silvered hair and unadorned face, her wizened brown eyes blinking from behind wire-rimmed glasses. A face that had been around for so long, I'd come to no longer really see it, like some shabby paisley sofa I took for granted would always be sitting shoved into a corner, patiently waiting for me to collapse on it. That mentality was my inheritance from my parents.

But Ethan.

Ethan.

Memories crashed into me one by one, waves breaking on rocks. Of after school, of me and my brother both throwing open the door, tossing our bags aside, and dashing into the kitchen for homemade brownies and macaroons, but only *he* would stay. Asking the housekeeper about her day, listening to her stories, and sharing his own, trading jokes that I never would share. Because I always had a friend to gossip with, a new makeup look to try, extra credit to work on, ever something better and prettier and more important. And when Ethan relapsed again, my mother broke down and my father withdrew, mourning the loss of the perfect son they'd struggled against all odds to shape him into. Only the housekeeper, of all people, had cried openly, mourning for *him*. The *real* him. And I should have cried with her because I knew the *real* him, too. But it was too late. I couldn't. I didn't know how.

I raised my chin. "Track the chip."

Him

Movement. Out of the corner of my inflamed, dust-filled eyelids. My head jerked on the end of the chain.

A two-inch-long brown gecko blinked at me curiously from

behind a rock, opened a frill on its chin, then dove back down, somewhere under the earth where it was no doubt cool and moist and wonderful. At this point, if it meant a respite from unyielding, unwavering heat, even for a few minutes, I'd gladly grow scales and eat bugs for however many months remained in my short reptilian lifespan.

This was pathetic. *Why* was I still here, letting Resi kill me? There had to be some natural escape route, some plan I wasn't thinking of. There always was. But I'd tried many, including scanning my surroundings for possible tools, but all I'd found was a vintage bottlecap with an interesting logo, and a stone with a vivid, coppery blue vein running through it. Things that, long ago, I might have given to Maeve to add to her collection of vaguely pretty things, things she collected in place of the jewelry and other gifts that free girls took for granted. Things that were utterly useless to me now, though I'd managed to kick them into a hiding place under the shed just in case. And then, in a blind panic, I'd resorted to the embarrassingly amateurish technique of straining against my chain as hard as I could, just to see if it would give.

But that had been hours ago. If every single muscle didn't palpitate with pain, if I hadn't had a smashed wrist and a torn shoulder and zero sleep and a brain the consistency of porridge and whatever else they'd done to me, I might still be on my game. Instead, all I'd been able to do was take one finger of my good hand and bend one wire at a time, scream into the muzzle when it punctured another hole in my skin, and twist it into a better, looser direction. And hope that in a few hours, I'd be able to slide even one hand out, and from there, find a way to get out of the collar, which was now on its way to searing a fiery line around my neck, so hot it had already seemed to turn the corner into cold.

Speaking of cold, I was growing nostalgic for the six-by-six wooden box I'd once been locked in for almost an entire day in the middle of the most brutal Romanian winter on record, with only my threadbare wool uniform to cover me. Until I stopped shivering. Until my skin turned the color of an iceberg. Unwilling to render me completely useless for work, the overseer had finally let two of my friends drag me out of there, just in time to prevent my toes from falling off from frostbite, although, to this day, I still lacked feeling in most of them. But it sure had fixed my—oh.

Again with the heartwarming memories.

But really? I could bear this if it weren't for the thirst. Every breath felt like inhaling pure dry, scorching air, and my cracked lips begged for moisture. My tongue, swollen, dust-covered, immobile, clung lifelessly to the roof of my mouth over the bit they'd shoved in. I wasn't above screaming at this point, but I couldn't even do *that*.

My eyes followed the line into the distance, now, near a slight, dark rise in the landscape in front of a towering structure that seemed to have had pieces stripped out of it systematically. I was surprised to see some small outbuildings. Civilization? A mirage, more likely. Just refraction bending the light waves.

Well, at least there was still science.

By the way, were there sound mirages, too? Because if not, I was pretty sure a vehicle was approaching.

My adrenaline could still flow, too, apparently. A rumbling engine shattered the desert silence, and I squinted against the quavering but unbroken line of the horizon. As the vehicle grew closer, I cursed myself for being stupid and hopeful enough, even for a second, to think it might mean salvation.

I wasn't even sure I *deserved* salvation. If I'd failed at anything—if I'd put Louisa, or Maeve, or the girls, or anyone, in danger—then I'd failed at everything. Come to think of it, that was a saying the old professor used to use.

That "shitty little Datsun," as Max had put it, would have collapsed like a cheap tent on these roads, which was probably why Noam had switched to a light military-style SUV, one that spewed a thoughtful cloud of dust and exhaust for me to choke on as it shuddered to a stop just a few feet away. Oddly enough, there did seem to be a kind of road here, leading off the distant highway, albeit half-buried under the constantly shifting dust. My mind drifted again to the outbuildings. What was this place?

One side of the vehicle sank lower as its driver emerged, on his face a slightly irritated but unmistakably malicious smirk. His humongous lace-up boots sank into the sand, and his bald, glistening head was big enough to block out the sun, which I supposed I should be grateful for. And also, maybe, that he was alone.

The silver 9-millimeter Noam had earlier used to try to take down Langer's helicopter was still weighing in his hand, and the noontime rays seemed to hit every angle of it.

Reflection. Refraction. And maybe—*Would you just shut up about science for once in your goddamn life?* I scolded my own brain.

I'd be lying if I said the sight of it so close didn't make me shudder, but if I was sure of anything, it was that Resi's henchman wouldn't shoot me dead before *she* arrived to join the fun.

Other than that, all bets were off.

"So here's the stray," Noam announced. "All chained up, waiting for your bone."

Great, the dog analogies again. Corey had loved those. But this asshole was no Corey. For one thing, he looked like he could actually win a fight. IQ was probably about the same, though.

From the trunk, Noam produced a small plastic water bottle, dripping condensation and comically small in his hand.

Still, I desperately jerked my head toward it in an almost Pavlovian response.

With his teeth, he unscrewed the plastic cap and spat it aside, then held the bottle up to his own mouth, letting the cold water run down his sweaty cheeks and chin and dropping in dark drops on the sand. I strained against the chains almost involuntarily as if I could dive and catch them before they expired.

Noam's laughter. A sound I really didn't ever care to hear again. "Go fetch."

I gasped as I watched the strangely crystal-hued bottle arc in the sun, spraying whatever was left of its contents every which way, and feeling any pride I had left melting away in the heat as I dove for it, straining against the chain. The most I could do, though, was kick it toward myself and tilt my head down toward it, try to figure out some conveyance to get it past the muzzle and shake out even a drop. The best I could pull off, though, was poke my tongue a little bit past the bit that kept it pinned down, enough to touch the very top of the bottle, though the slight moisture I felt there could very well be my fevered imagination. In the end, I just slumped back down into the dust on my knees, limp against the chain, wishing Resi had covered my ears, too, if only to block out the sound of Noam's wheezy laughter.

Dully, I stared down at the dark spots on the dirt where the spilled water was already disappearing, slowly, hopelessly, blinking grit and detritus out of my inflamed eyes.

But no tears. Not yet.

Her

"You heard me. Track it. Now." I spoke with precision again. Like cut glass. No hesitance. No doubt.

"Loulou, you heard what the agent said," my father

protested with a sigh. "There's no point. They're gone. Even the plane is off the radar."

"Daddy, he wasn't on the plane. In fact, he's probably still somewhere very nearby, in serious danger that he put himself in at least partly on *your* behalf, and if we don't find him now, *we* might be dead soon, too. And we might not be the only ones."

"How do you know this?"

I leaped out of my chair again and gestured to the length of my burned body. "For fuck's sake, Daddy, do you think I did this to *myself*? Oh, and by the way? I know what happened to Ethan."

His face, as I'd expected, went pale. A mix of shock, horror, anger, and something I couldn't even name. Complete and utter denial, maybe. "What in God's name are you talking about? What does that have to do with—"

"Everything," I said. "It has everything to do with it."

"I don't—" He looked at the agents and then back at me. "Where? Where is he?" His eyes had gone from exhausted to wild, those of a desperate father clinging to hope.

"Track. The. Chip," I said. "And I'll tell you."

Robotically, he removed his phone from his pocket, again, and began swiping. It was a simple app, the tracker chip. Once someone bought a slave, ownership was electronically transferred and the records updated, with the new slave linked to the owner in the app. From then on, it took only seconds to pinpoint their location and summon the police if needed.

At least that was how it was *supposed* to work.

"I can't," my father said. "It isn't working." He looked bewildered. "This has never—"

"I'm afraid you no longer have that privilege, Mr. Wainwright-Phillips," Labrecque broke in, her voice booming with glee. "Your slaves—along with all your other assets—have been frozen indefinitely, pending the outcome of the investigation."

"This is bullshit!"

Every head spun toward me.

"Miss Wainwright-Phillips, you're completely out of line," Labrecque hissed, her voice dripping with condescension. "We have protocols to follow in these situations for a reason. It's for your safety *and* that of the slaves."

I scoffed audibly.

"Now, if there were some kind of emergency situation, for instance, if someone were in imminent danger—"

"Someone *is* in danger!"

"A free person?"

But I could tell by Labrecque's smug little smile that she knew damn well that it wasn't, and it was almost enough to send me lunging for her neck. "No."

"Then I'm afraid we can't help you."

"Agent Wheatley." I turned desperately to the cop Erica trusted.

To his credit, he was already on it. "Amy, we need to make an exception in this case," he told his partner. "You know we do."

Labrecque's face seemed to pinch in on itself. "Exceptions can only be handled by the field office," she recited. "And it still takes five to seven business days after the form is filed to unfreeze the chip. I'm sorry. Now, sir, if—"

"Oh, come on!" I interjected. "Do you want to get to the bottom of this or not? Do you want to track down the *actual* culprit? Do you want to prevent innocent people from dying? Do you want to finally do something meaningful for once in your rote, meaningless, laughably undistinguished career, or do you just want to sit at your goddamn desk for the next twenty years stamping papers, regurgitating statutes, and running interference for the abusive power structures that underlie every aspect of this shitty, corrupt, oppressive society we live in?"

I gasped for air, expecting my father to break in any time and *force* me upstairs. Being rude, to him or any authority figure, was the first deadly sin in his house—a worse sin, perhaps, than whatever message was being delivered. But he barely moved, just sat there, hollow-eyed and staring at nothing as if a switch had been flipped off inside him. And then:

"I knew, Loulou," he said. "About Ethan."

"What? *You* knew?"

"Well, I didn't *know*." His voice was thin, hollow, reedy. A complete absence of gravitas. "But I had my suspicions. I didn't investigate any further, or tell you or your mother because—"

"Because you were in denial. Not just about him. About everything. About—"

About his slave, too. About a sonless father who wouldn't allow himself to acknowledge the fatherless son when the boy had been kneeling right in front of him.

But that might be a conversation for later.

Now, my father just closed his eyes and sighed the sigh of a man who was watching his entire carefully constructed world blow down like a house of straw and was now standing where it had been, shivering and frightened and dying of exposure.

But hey, if that's what it took.

Wheatley broke in one more time. "I'll tell you what, Miss Wainwright-Phillips," he said. "You look like you could use some rest. When we're finished here, I'll drive you to the field office, we'll fill out that paperwork, and you can tell me anything else you feel is relevant in a relaxed, private space."

He met my eyes with an intense, pointed expression, one clearly meant for me and only me. I couldn't fully read it, but part of it was definitely, *trust me.*

Sorry, my dude. Can't do that yet. At *most*, I was starting to like him, sort of. But I trusted Erica, and *Erica* trusted him. That was enough for now.

I'd also had so little sleep that I felt my eyes growing heavy even as I stood.

The last thing I glimpsed as I let myself be led upstairs was my father sitting motionless in his chair, his head buried in his hand.

Good.

"You'll bring Master Ethan home?" the housekeeper asked softly but anxiously as she spread cooling aloe balm over my searing, weeping blisters, which drank it in like water, quelling the pain briefly.

"I will. I promise," I said through a yawn, already only half-conscious. "But I can only do one at a time, okay?"

HIM

"You done over there?"

Noam chuckled again as if he were sitting on a sofa watching some brainless streaming reality show instead of someone struggling to live. Idly, I wondered if this stupid motherfucker had ever been a slave. His tone and posture bore no traces of it, but that didn't necessarily mean anything. I'd come to understand, quite recently, that nothing about anybody necessarily meant anything.

I watched Noam warily as he stepped behind me to look at where my hands hung: numb, seared by the sun, bloody, useless, lifeless. Barely able to even interlace my fingers.

"So I'm actually here to do two things. One, to make sure this wire's still on good and tight. She made me put it on ya once and it cut me up pretty bad. I don't wanna hafta do it again."

Without warning, he raised one massive, heavy boot and brought it down hard on the wire, crushing my hands into pieces and driving what felt like a hundred shards of jagged metal into his flesh simultaneously.

"There. That oughta hold. And second," he said as I writhed silently on the end of the chain, whimpering into the muzzle, "she told me to torture you, as she put it, 'slowly, carefully, and methodically, with a thousand cuts.'"

Okay. Sure. Fine. I was praying for death now. Happy? Between *this* and *that*, instant death would be an absolute day at the goddamn beach.

"But," Noam said, "I'll level with ya. I don't know what the fuck that means. It's hot as a rattlesnake's gooch out here, and I don't got the patience for a thousand anything. Plus, I get paid either way. So I'll throw ya another bone, mutt."

He casually raised the pistol, racked the slide, and shoved its barrel under my chin.

Well, shit.

My first thought: *Of all the times to be wrong.* My second, for some reason: *Where's Obadiah?*

HER

After an hour of sleep and no more, I reluctantly opened the door to an unmarked black leather passenger seat of a brand-new, unmarked, gleaming black Ford SUV to find Wheatley—changed from the windbreaker into an expensive-looking black turtleneck under a suit jacket—behind the wheel waiting for me, his eyes behind dark, luxurious shades as shiny as the vehicle's exterior. He raised them as I got in, wondering what the cop would think of the three-inch blade shoved in the waistband of my black leggings.

"Miss Wainwright-Phillips—"

"Louisa, and save it." *The new Louisa.* The old Louisa—drilled in manners and propriety by my father—would have driven herself into a blind panic to speak to an authority figure this way. But there was kind of no going back now. "I'm thankful for everything you've done for us so far, assuming it's for the right reasons, but I'm not setting foot inside this vehicle until you tell me two things."

He paused but nodded seriously.

"One, I want to know if Erica, Ivy, Alma, and the kids are safe."

He didn't miss a beat answering. "They are. Whoever their visitor was, once he saw the squad car, he wasn't keen to come back. And if he does, we'll move them."

I nodded. "And two, I want Maeve and Sloane un-detained."

"Who?"

I rolled my eyes. Okay, so he wasn't quite all the way there yet. He was still further than I'd *ever* expected a cop to be. "The two slaves. From Resi's. Maeve was supposed to have been on the plane, but since *he* wasn't, I can only assume she wasn't either, and that both girls are still in the detention center. I understand the safety concerns," I continued. "Erica explained them to me. But I want to see the wheels in motion."

"I'll get them in motion," he said sincerely.

"Thank you," I said. "Now how far is the field office?"

"Well, that brings us to what I *was* going to tell you when you got in," he said patiently as I hoisted myself up and back down into the dealership-scented leather seat. "Don't tell Labrecque, but we're not going to the field office." He turned and caught my eye, ever so slightly. "We're going to find 773496S6."

My stomach lurched, half from shock, half from being jerked forward when he released the brake and stepped on the gas pedal, and the SUV's engine kicked up with a roar, speeding me away from my neighborhood, again. Back to the boy I'd now been ripped apart from forever, twice.

In whatever condition he was now in.

From a compartment near his seat, Wheatley handed me an unlocked phone displaying a GPS tracking app. With trembling hands, I zoomed in on coordinates in a regional park near Lake Pleasant, about half an hour north of the city, one I'd visited often as a child on picnics. And what *he* was doing there, I had no idea, but it was a good bet it wasn't a goddamn picnic.

I glanced back at Wheatley. "But Labrecque said the only way to unfreeze the chip is if you can prove a person is in immediate danger," I said, adding darkly, "A free person."

"True."

"Then how—"

He depressed the gas pedal further and guided the SUV out onto the freeway, smoothly merging us into northbound traffic.

"I lied."

Oh, I did like this guy. I liked him a lot.

14

HER

It was probably a violation of some federal law, but I grabbed Agent Wheatley's dash-mounted VHF radio anyway, frantically searching for a button to mute Agent Labrecque's shrill voice as she demanded, over and over again, for Agent Wheatley to come in and reminding him that he was violating Federal Statute 21.306F and some other bullshit legislation she was probably making up.

Even better would be a button that would let me scream that Wheatley was on the phone and that he'd pick up when he was done saving people that his partner was willing to let die, clearing the names of people *she* was happy to condemn, and putting out the flaming garbage fire *she'd* turned this case into.

Apparently, no button did that. Probably best.

I wondered if Labrecque had told my father where I was, and if so, whether it had registered. Or whether he was still sitting catatonically in his armchair, trying to calculate exactly when and where he'd started transforming into a monster. I hoped for the latter. Either way, he wouldn't be following us because according to Wheatley, now *he* was being electronically monitored. The agent had also explained that the remaining three slaves, while also technically frozen, would be allowed to stay in the house with the agents also monitoring *them*. Thank God because I'd been terrified they'd be hauled off to some ghastly detention facility—probably the same one Maeve and Sloane had been unceremoniously tossed in.

Instead, as Wheatley drove and alternately badgered, swore at, and thanked the various colleagues whose help he was trying to enlist, I tried to watch the scenery. It seemed mildly less panic-inducing than waiting for that dot on the GPS—the one that had become my entire world—to either move or disappear.

The fact was, this particular state highway, where strip malls and housing developments gradually gave way to tranquil saguaros and mesquite, had never brought me anything but nostalgia. But as the line of Lake Pleasant beckoned closer, its waters crystalline amid the aridity, my charming memories of singalongs and Twenty Questions had turned to dust, too. What an utterly naïve fool I'd been then. And *he* may have told me there was nothing to forgive, but it would take more than that to forgive myself.

Saving his life—if it came to that—might be a good start.

Still, nothing quelled the pounding in my chest or the fluttering in my stomach. How long had he been there, anyway? Was he alone? Why the hell wasn't the dot moving? Was any of this even part of his plan, or was I crazy?

How goddamn long did this quaint scenic drive take, anyway?

"Good news. They found her owners."

I snapped my head toward Wheatley, who was finally off the phone. Panic and adrenaline pulsed through my veins, blocking out Labrecque's irate voice still crackling over the frequency. "Wait, what?"

He mashed a couple of buttons on the radio as he pressed further on the gas. The scenery outside was flying by at high speed now, the sun glinting off the sluggish surface of the 300-mile-long aqueduct that followed this stretch of highway, diverting murky water from the Colorado River into the lake and points farther south. We were close enough to see the hydroelectric dam and power facility that had always been a welcome sign that arrival was nigh. But the road stretched on still.

"*Former* owners," he explained. "Erica's people were working on tracking them down using her network."

Erica's ability to *still* work for the cause with her wife in critical condition and goons stalking her—not to mention being technically *dead*—made me dizzy.

"Turns out they bought her freedom over a year ago," he went on. "Paid the fees and everything, but it was never recorded due to some filing snafu. So I told them to release her as soon as it's safe."

"Which one?" I asked tentatively. "Maeve?"

"No, the other one. Sloane. Say." He adjusted the mirror, peering at something I couldn't see. "Do you know anyone who drives a blue Datsun?"

"No," I responded, annoyed at his derailment. "And what about Maeve?"

Wheatley paused. "Not so good news. She's about to be sold."

"*Sold*?! How is that even possible?" Was there no end to this nightmare this poor girl was trapped in? She must be beside herself by now, and the language barrier would make it worse. She'd have no idea what was even happening to her. "To *who*?"

"I don't know. And neither do they."

"How could you not *know*?"

"Because it's someone with an offshore shell company and good lawyers who clearly has no interest in *being* known."

"That shouldn't even be legal!"

"It isn't. And they're supposed to know that. But given the glorified dog catchers they have working down there, it doesn't surprise me," he finished darkly.

"Well, we have to stop this!" I was upright in my seat now.

The sun glinted off the metal guardrails of the canal overpass as the car hurtled toward it. The park entrance was just beyond it, a sign displaying its name in bold letters. Wheatley's quick glance behind us showed a clear road, allowing him to pick up even more speed.

"If we find *him*, what am I going to tell him?" I admired the endurance of the agent's eardrums, given all the shrieking into them I was doing. "That we lost his sister, *again*?"

"Oh, fuck no." Though it answered my question, I suspected it was actually Wheatley's response to the sudden sound of sirens.

"Game over, Manny," said Labrecque over the radio. "Turn around and head back to the field office PDQ and I'll consider telling the director to put you on mental health leave for a week or so. If not..."

My knuckles turned white on the edges of the seat. "Maybe this is a weird time to ask, but why are you doing this?" I shouted over the sirens. "Why are you risking your job for us?"

"Would you believe it's because of a university course I took?"

"But—"

Swearing again, he slammed on the brakes. The SUV skidded to a stop nearly sideways, sending me hurling into the dash, restrained only by my seat belt, which I quickly unbuckled. I could see now why he'd stopped: Two police cars with angry, swirling blue lights blocked the road ahead, trapping us on the overpass. In the rear, two more had appeared out of nowhere.

This was over. After we'd come so far, Labrecque would never allow us to bridge the distance. And she and the other officers would never listen to me. I'd be lucky if I didn't get thrown in a cell myself, and despite his protests, my father, too.

And meanwhile, that blinking dot would disappear forever.

A rush of wind lifted me as I robotically opened the SUV's door, only struggling for a second to work the handle. In the dry heat, I still shivered at the sight of the inky depths of the canal, but the guardrail wasn't even waist-high. A faint fishy scent emanated from the black, sludgy, barely-moving water as I leaned over it.

Was this for real?

From behind me came the sharp clang of metal against metal as car doors slammed. The sounds reverberated off the concrete walls of the overpass, and my heart raced faster amid the distant sound of more approaching sirens. Reinforcements. The voices grew increasingly insistent. There was no escape.

But now that I'd started running, I couldn't stop. Not now.

And besides, *he'd* done his part. He'd planned. It was *my* turn to execute. And yes, maybe this particular execution was more idiotic than usual.

But hey, I'd never claimed to be the smart one.

I assessed the length of the drop, but my horrible spatial reasoning could only conclude that it was somewhere between twenty feet and snapping my spine like a potato chip.

But first things first. I lifted the still-blinking phone. From the middle of the overpass, it would be an easy toss to the other side of the canal, but once it left my hand, there was no going back. I closed my eyes, took a deep breath, and wound up.

Over on the driver's side, Wheatley despairingly slammed

the door of the SUV. "Fucking Labrecque. Look, we've got to think of something else. She's not immune to reason, even though it seems like it. Maybe if we can explain—*holy shit*."

That was the last thing I heard before I jumped.

HIM

Noam did not pull the trigger. Instead, he raised the pistol and sent the butt end careening into my head, blowing part of it open like a ripe piece of fruit.

Was it too late to hope he'd change his mind and shoot me?

Noam laughed, and even though there was nothing for it to bounce off, it echoed—off the cactus, the tin roof, the sky, until at last, he dropped the gun and stepped away.

By then, I'd dropped as low as my chains would let him. Blood and torn flesh were trailing down my eyes and pooling in the desert sand. They were all I could see as I gasped for air through the red cloud that choked off my other senses. For a few seconds, there was almost silence, except for the distant cry of a vulture. Of course.

I wasn't surprised when Noam returned, but I was by his weapon: A pickaxe. The exact same kind they used to give me in the winter to work in the quarry two villages over, when there was nothing to do at the farm. But it also made a fantastic improvised weapon, against a fellow slave if you wanted forty lashes, or an overseer if you wanted death. I'd witnessed both, but nobody had ever successfully turned it on *me*.

Until now. It connected with my ribs, shattering what felt like at least two of them with a nauseating crunch. My body jerked and twisted under the impact, sure I could feel the splintered edges of my own bones tearing into my organs, not to mention what remained of my clothes, blood soaking into the fabric. Still, the thug aimed for one of my kneecaps and shattered that, too, adding a few kicks for good measure.

My breaths were coming out in shallow gasps now, each one more excruciating than the last. I tried to push myself away, to twist or duck, but all my strength had left me. I had no choice but to hang there, weak and unresponsive, limbs heavy and numb. This was what death felt like, I was pretty sure.

Noam lifted the ax, aiming for my head, again.

But the blow didn't come. Of course I wouldn't be so stupid this time to expect that it never would.

But it didn't.

And not only that, a second later, it was *all* gone—the noise, the weapons, the vehicle, and Noam's gargantuan shadow.

Instead, there was a pair of slender hands tenderly cradling my bloody, savaged body, their graceful fingers carding through my matted, blood-soaked hair, wiping away trails of bloody tissue from my face. Wavy tendrils fell around my rescuer's cheeks, traces of her own tears framed in a glistening halo of light.

Resi's lips were as cool and soft as a satin pillow against my skin. "I'm so sorry, baby. I didn't tell him to *kill* you."

15

On land again, I ran. I'd done it before. Wet, muddy, freezing. The ratty leggings and old sneakers I'd thrown on in haste were waterlogged and squelching. The remains of the canal's contents were probably injecting bacteria into every blister on my body. But still I ran across the bare desert and into the scrim of palo verde and mesquite that shrouded the entrance to the park.

For now, I didn't look at the phone. I'd look at it once I got inside and could slip into the trees and disappear from the cops, which were all that remained between me and him. And answers, and time, and peace, and everything else I dreamed of but wouldn't take the time to torture myself right now by pausing to think about.

Back in the canal, for a few terrifying seconds, I'd thought I'd drown. The banks had been steeper than they'd looked, and I hadn't counted on there being no good way to pull myself out. Plus, my body didn't have the strength to tread water for long. I'd groped and kicked violently along the artificial banks, gasping to hold my head up and prevent black liquid from flooding into my eyes and ears until my flailing limbs at last hit a ladder and I could hoist myself gasping onto the sand like a hooked fish. Another run back toward the overpass, a few more moments of panic when I couldn't spot the phone I'd thrown. Finally snatching it up, I was back on track. I didn't look back to see if the cops were on my tail. I'd find out soon enough.

The park entrance, though late in the day, wasn't exactly empty, and I got more than a few shocked looks from hikers and picnickers as I passed, my phone's blinking blue light bobbing in my hand, my burn-ravaged face no doubt a frightening mask of panic and resolve. In the distance, the sirens still wailed, sirens some of them could no doubt guess had something to do with me. I didn't care. I needed him, needed answers, and I wasn't stopping to keep up appearances.

Gazing frantically around the parking lot, my eyes settled on a tiny, rusty car parked in the corner near a clutch of cholla, clearly trying to go unnoticed but all the more conspicuous for that.

A blue Datsun. Fuck. Wheatley *had* been onto something, and I hadn't even bothered to hear him out.

And now he wasn't here to help me.

I swallowed, heart pounding. Around me were ramadas and picnic tables and an oversized, glass-enclosed map set on a rustic wooden display stand, one I wouldn't have time to look at even if I *hadn't* been terrible at reading maps, which I was. I turned in a circle. Around the bend, I saw the sign for a nature trail, arrows pointing every which way. Desperation surged through me as I looked down at my phone, the blinking light dancing erratically in the sunlight that had already evaporated most of the dampness of my clothing.

I took a deep breath and picked a trail I thought might lead toward his location, though it also might not. I'd find out when

I and the dot grew farther apart, and I had to come back and start all over again. Thankfully, the trail was empty and so silent that my panting echoed off the trees. I now couldn't shake the feeling that I was being watched, or that someone was following me. Someone besides the police.

But what could I do?

Keep running.

HIM

"It worked, you know, sweetie," Resi whispered, gently brushing a single lock of hair away from my temple with one manicured vanilla nail, her breath soft and cool in my ear. "The serum. Much as I hate him for it, I guess Max was right to choose you over me. You really *are* a genius."

Despite it all—despite my entire world having been reduced to pain, humiliation, and imminent death—my heart leaped a little. But my brain wasn't working well enough anymore to decide whether she was lying, or, if not, what she thought telling the truth would gain her. And even if she *was* telling the truth, it didn't mean Lemaya had gotten away clean, or that *any* part of my insane plan had worked the way I'd prayed it would.

And Resi had no intention of telling me. *That* was the real torture. *That* was what she was here to do.

Well, that, and torture me in every other way. Pain shot through every inch of my body as I hung limp and helpless from the chain. One side of my brain felt like pulp. Likely multiple ribs were broken. Some part of my leg was shattered. Arms and hands? I couldn't see or use them. Maybe I never would again.

"Too bad I like you so much better as a slave."

Frankly, I was expecting Resi to continue the torture in some more diabolical form. But to my surprise, she didn't. Not yet, anyway. Her thick, brand-new cowhide gloves were smooth and supple against my skin—the nicest thing I'd felt all day—as she carefully and methodically began to unravel the barbed wire wrapped tightly around my wrists. Each movement was precise and deliberate, the metal scraping against her gloves as it fell to the ground in a series of dull thuds.

"I was giddy as a little girl on Christmas Eve last night, thinking of how pretty you'd look in these chains," she whispered as she worked. "Ah, but that was my fault for letting you go last time. Turns out I was a little bit charmed by you. I guess I wouldn't be the first one, huh?" Was she talking to herself now or what? "Couldn't do much about your legs, though. Although I don't expect you'll be walking anywhere anytime soon."

Her gloved fingers continued moving expertly, carefully unfastening the barbed wire cuffs wound around my clotted, rust-covered, inflamed, infected wrists. The sharp edges grazed against my skin, but as the metal fell to the sand, I couldn't help but feel a glimmer of relief. A relief I felt even though I knew I would regret it later, and even though I couldn't move my arms more than a few inches. Didn't mean I wouldn't try.

Two soft thumps in the sand revealed she'd removed the gloves. "No, no," she said with a pealing laugh, knowing just from my squirming that I expected her to undo the collar next. "You'd try to get away, and we can't have that."

Well. I knew I shouldn't have gotten my hopes up. But the muzzle?

"I've always thought someone should lock up that silver tongue of yours," she said, reading my mind. "After all, I don't want you biting. Or worse, have you talk me into letting you go."

Well, there went plans A and B.

"Of course we all know who ended up with the muzzle last time, not like I want to bring *her* up. Anyway, I saw *this* one online and I couldn't stop thinking about it, and they always say that's how you know you should buy it. So I can still see your pretty face, but you'll only speak *what* I want and *when* I want. It's win-win, don't you think?"

Yeah. Resi got to win twice.

"Now be a good boy and greet me properly."

Wait, did that mean the muzzle was coming off? *Yes.* She unbuckled the contraption and let it clatter to the dust alongside the cuffs. Immediately, the dry, sandy air hit the weeping sores all over my mouth, my lips so weak and cracked I could barely move them.

And now, through the red, crusty film that blocked much of my vision, I could clearly see a clear gallon container dangling daintily from a plastic handle between her long fingernails.

She had *water.* And on the ground beside her, a first-aid kit. Gauze. Antiseptic. Painkillers. Aloe.

"I know they taught you how to do *that*, at least. It was the first thing they taught *me*."

Mistress Hahn. Ma'am. That's what she wanted to hear. And if it got me even a sip of water, so what? Not like I hadn't said it a million times before to women who didn't deserve it any more than she did.

"Well?" she asked.

Live. Don't die before you're killed.

I tasted the word on my lips even before I spat it out.

"Bitch."

"Okay," she said brightly, rebuckling the muzzle. "I guess we'll try this again later."

Worth it.

The sun had begun to set, the sky tinged pink and orange, whispering of an eerily beautiful desert twilight. I could feel the temperature dropping as the night approached, and despite myself, I shivered in my useless shirt.

And Resi seemed to feel it too, since she dropped down in

the dust, drawing her knees up to her chest and hugging them to herself excitedly, like we were about to play Spin the Bottle.

But wait. She was leaving now, right? She had to be leaving.

Instead, she beckoned to Noam, who looked none too pleased.

Oh, right. The cuffs.

The metallic scent of my blood mingled with rust, sweat, and fear in the acrid air, and my hands started to shake as Noam used his own bandaged hands—Resi didn't have any gloves that fit him, evidently—to grumblingly redo his work from earlier. The goon lazily moved one wire, then another, back into position around my wrists, each sharp thorn digging deeper into my already tormented flesh. Every twist and turn of the wire contained a thousand claws shredding a thousand bloody trails down my skin. Tears formed, but I didn't cry. I held my breath instead.

It's like trying to die.

"Yeah, I stopped crying, too, after a while," she said, eagerly watching me silently keen. "But I learned to let it out again. And I can teach *you* to let it out. Oh, honey, I can teach you so many things, you have no idea."

Every breath was ragged and shallow until even *that* felt like torture. And finally, as the wire tightened, it constricted my circulation until I swore I felt my own blood pulsing right up against the hot, rusty metal. And still, Noam kept ratcheting and squeezing. *No more. Please.* Until:

"Stop," she said.

Noam did. He stepped back, glaring at me as if it were somehow *my* fault. And Resi, at last, rose in one graceful, fluid motion. But she paused to drink me in, pleased.

"I read your file, you know," she remarked. "And I think all your owners were wrong. You *can* be good." She leaned in and rubbed her clean, manicured thumb against my bloody, macerated one and kissed the top of my head. Her clothes were the same monochrome color as the sand: leggings, a complicated leather belt, and a flowing blouse, which blended into the pink-tinged sky and swirled in clouds of dust as she strode back to the SUV in her heeled, lace-up boots.

"You just need what *I* got too late," she said. "Someone to give you a chance."

HER

My heart pounded against my ribs with every step. Each time the trail split off into different directions, I quickly chose again and kept going. The trees offered little shade, and the desert sun beat down, quickly coating the residue from the inky canal water in dust and sweat.

The trail wound uphill, deeper into the desert. My lungs screamed for mercy, but everything else screamed louder. I stumbled over rocks and roots, tripping but never going down, closing in on the blinking dot, losing ground as my trail broke off in a different direction, panicking, but always regaining it.

I knew where I was headed now. I'd been there before, this place on the hill. At the top was a pyramid-shaped monument, a cenotaph for a territorial governor from centuries ago, and the best place in the park to A) inspire children to learn about history or B) teenagers to get high and chug beer. Had *he* picked this place, this blast from my past? Or had someone else?

It didn't matter. My spirits buoyed and I picked up my pace. But as the monument rose before me, concealed by another clutch of palo verde and marked by an escarpment on one side, I let my guard down and slipped, tumbling to my knees in the red dust, my phone flying from my hand and bouncing away into the scrub. I reached out, fingers splayed, and just managed to catch it before it skipped away into the rocky canyon. I nearly retched at the thought of losing my only connection to him *now* but forced myself to stand.

Breathing still ragged, hands trembling, I closed the phone's map app. It lit up the screen, the glowing blue dot indicating my location, a larger one indicating his. I looked at the memorial, and then back at the map. I saw nothing and no one at the top, but this had to be it. This had to be him. The GPS wouldn't, *couldn't* lie.

Could it?

Smoothing my shirt and running my fingers through my bedraggled mess of curls, I took a deep breath and set off again, still stumbling across the uneven terrain, my shoes kicking up plumes of dust with each step.

The going was strenuous, but eventually, I reached the cenotaph base. The monument loomed over me, its stone structure rising tall and imposing against the sky. I gulped some air and began climbing up the sandstone steps carved out of the hillside, each footstep echoing hollowly in the stillness.

Finally, I made it to the summit, gasping, legs trembling. The panorama seemed to suck the air from my lungs as I turned in a desperate circle, surveying the vast expanse of desert and lake. My phone screen was empty, reflecting the empty horizon, already purpling. The end of *another* day.

"Hello?" I called weakly.

My fingers shook with weakness as I opened the map app again, staring at the two dots.

One for me.

One for him.

The dots were practically on top of each other now. It was here. *I* was here.

And it was official. He wasn't.

After all that.

I dropped like a ragdoll on the stone. The temperature kept

dropping, reminding me that my clothes were still damp. I hadn't cried in almost three hours. Probably a record. But right now, I didn't have the strength to do anything else.

Through my tears, my eyes settled on the plaque at the base of the cenotaph, glinting in the waning sun, its brass text rubbed smooth by blowing sand.

"Though we may stand alone, we are never alone in spirit. May the path of justice and truth guide us through the darkness."

A bit melodramatic, all in all, and not the sort of words I'd ever paused to meditate on during a school picnic, or a little later, chugging a cheap beer. But I did now. And also because there was an envelope lodged at the base of the plaque. I dove for it.

But instead of reaching it, *I* and the envelope were wrenched violently backward.

In my ear, a hot, throaty chuckle and a toothless, goaty grimace. An arm squeezing the breath out of me, and the tip of a knife at my throat.

Of all the—

"Don't cry, princess. Yeah, it's not the reunion you wanted," said the voice. "But it's a reunion."

16

S tars.
　　Antares. Almach. Aldebaran.
Andromeda. Cassiopeia. Perseus. Gemini.
Sternenflüsterin.

"Where'd she go?" Maeve had asked, popping open the skylight of our attic room and clambering carefully up beside me in her hand-me-down nightgown. The cold black slate of the eaves was rough and uneven beneath our hands and feet, and the hazy golden light of Luxembourg City did its best to ruin the stars for two kids who'd been waiting all day to see them. But tonight, it hadn't succeeded. Not completely. "Where's Sternenflüsterin?"

I sighed and kicked the eaves, watching rotting roof tile and moss tumble down onto our master's manicured lawn. I'd be raking that up tomorrow.

She's not real, you ridiculous kid. You made her up like Frankenstein, from half of Scorpius and a little bit of Libra. There aren't any pink unicorns with diamond hooves and rainbow manes, in the stars or anywhere else. And if they ever do find one, they sure as hell aren't going to give it to *you*.

"Well," I said instead of any of that, "we're always facing away from the sun at night, so we see different constellations as we orbit around it. It's like... a big game of hide-and-seek."

"So what does that mean?"

"She'll come back," I told her. Maeve yawned and nuzzled my shoulder. Like me, like always, she'd worked a twelve-hour day, and now her fine but tangled blond hair fell across my oversized hoodie, her fingers digging into the fabric, helpless against sleep. "She'll always come back."

I jerked awake, rattling my chain, surprised I'd fallen asleep at all. Yes, I was exhausted, but I'd also be dead soon, so all in all, it didn't make a ton of sense.

The stars, though. This was no Luxembourg City. It wasn't even fully dark yet, but already, they were all arrayed for me in this utterly overwhelming violet sky. Every single one.

In Rio Dulce, too, Maeve would be able to see Sternenflüsterin. She'd be able to see every constellation she'd ever made up, and that far south, maybe a few new ones, too.

Meanwhile, I'd be dead, but I'd always suspected that was probably what it would take to save her. Frankly, it hadn't seemed like that big of a deal, back when there'd been nobody but Maeve that I cared about leaving behind, and nobody who cared about *me*. But now?

"It worked, you know." If Resi, for whatever reason, was telling the truth, and my plan had somehow succeeded despite the laughably terrible odds, then I knew I'd never see Louisa again. Ever. There'd be no way for her to find me.

I *hoped* there wouldn't be because that was the best chance for her, and her family, and the other girls, to be safe. And it was the only hope I had left.

Some water sure would be nice, though. My thirst had

become a fire, a craving that drove me to inhale the harsh, dry air as if it could somehow condense into liquid in my mouth. But only blood lingered, a metallic tang that intensified with every sand-raked swallow.

Worse, the cuts on my legs and hands had festered with sores, rashes, and cavities. With each movement, grains of sand grated against them. My whole body was burning from the inside out. Or maybe the outside in. In any case, from everywhere.

And it was cold. It was fucking *cold*. I shivered and cursed the desert, and my luck to have wound up in a place whose weather made the least goddamn sense of any biome on earth.

And now an exhaust-spewing SUV was sputtering up the road. Noam.

A growl formed deep in my throat. It seemed my transformation into an actual dog had begun.

As Noam approached, only my eyes moved. As the goon raised the pickaxe, I squeezed in on myself like a frightened snail. But I couldn't wriggle, couldn't squirm, couldn't even move. All I could be was a target. This time, at least, everything went black early.

Much to my dismay, I woke up alive. I didn't think my pain could get worse, but, well, I'd been wrong a lot recently. Hell, *that* was torture in itself.

Cry, you bastard. You're going to die here, and no one's going to ever fucking see, so let it all go. Do it. Cry.

But I couldn't. Maybe I'd forgotten how.

"I told you, baby, let the tears fall," whispered Resi in the moonlight.

I went rigid. Where the hell did this motherfucking bitch keep jumping out from?

"You'll feel better."

I growled into the bit again. It wasn't a threat, really, or a plea for help. It was a plea for death.

Kill me. End this. I don't care.

Like before, I wasn't sure if I meant it. But I also wasn't sure that I didn't.

Resi smoothed the hair on the crown of my head, the few strands untouched by blood, and planted a light kiss that, if I didn't know whose lips they were, I might have leaned into. Just because it was something that wasn't pain.

Instead, I managed to jerk away by a centimeter. For Resi's sake, I could accomplish *that*.

"Still defiant, huh? Oh, honey. I tried."

A crumpling noise, and I blinked to see her hold up a manila envelope. My heart lurched, somewhere deep inside. When her hand emerged, set delicately in the ridges between her thumb and finger, glinting triumphantly in the moonlight, was a microchip. *My* microchip, because who else's would it be? She hadn't ever successfully removed any others, as far as I knew.

"It came out," she said. "Still transmitting. It just didn't travel as far as you'd hoped."

I squeezed my eyes shut, and it all came back. The envelope. The formula. Lemaya.

It was over. Resi would destroy the formula, of course. And instead of helping free slaves, I'd only managed to get one—Lemaya—killed. And soon enough Louisa, myself, and probably a hell of a lot of other people, too.

"Your bro Corey didn't think you'd seen enough of that for one lifetime," Resi said, though I could barely hear her anymore. Was it too late to choose death? If I couldn't do anything to stop this, I probably should. "But luckily, I do, so I have a little deal for you."

She reached down delicately, opening the case she had been

carrying from the start, revealing a vial of sulfuric acid. Because she *would* have a vial of sulfuric acid.

"Anyway, up to you." She shrugged. "Oh, and yeah, obviously I *might* be lying about everything. But none of that matters because you love her too much to risk it."

Through my shock and sickness and grief came the crumpling of the plastic water jug.

"Well?"

The words fell dejectedly out of my atrophied tongue. "Yes, ma'am."

Satisfied, she grabbed my throat, tilted my head back, and tipped it all down. And because there was no longer any reason not to, I closed my eyes and opened my mouth, whimpering as I gulped cold liquid silver, the life she alone could give and take away, like the mistress she'd been waiting her whole life to transform into. Like the slave it seemed I was always destined to be, no matter how strong, no matter how smart, no matter how capable.

But at least Louisa would never see me this way.

I changed my mind again. I wouldn't cry after all.

That was the one thing I wouldn't give Resi.

"Good boy."

My head collapsed onto my shoulder again, eyes staring dully and obediently at the dirt.

Resi's hand curled slowly and tenderly around my neck, cool as ice. My eyelashes fluttered. Like I liked it. Like I was already hers.

"You'll learn to love that phrase."

HER

I knew now that the man outside Ivy's house hadn't even been after Alma and Erica. He may not have even known they were there.

It was *me* he'd been stalking. For hours. For *years*.

Obadiah's clammy hand clapped onto my face before I could speak, scream, or attempt to fight back. As if I could anyway. It was a miracle I'd even made it up the steps.

Figured. Last time, I could have fought but chose not to. This time, I wanted to but couldn't.

He wrenched my phone away easily, then dug into the envelope and reached into it savagely, pulling out a fistful of bills, a wad of papers with scientific notation, and a note in handwriting that made my stomach leap. Unfolding the note, the former gardener grinned in what could pass for recognition, though I knew he couldn't read what it said. In any case, he let it flutter down the rocky escarpment in the breeze, so now I never would, either.

"Ya know, Miss Loulou, I always heard there was nothing in the world better than freedom." He sloppily folded up the remains of the envelope and jammed it into his pocket. His rotting mouth contorted, and his grimy-as-ever fingers burrowed excruciatingly into my wounds as we descended the stone steps, the rising moon already casting eerie yellow shadows.

My senses clouded over with panic, and the chill again highlighted the dampness of my clothes. I'd hoped to be alone up here, but not anymore. Where were the stoners? Where was Wheatley? Where were the police? Where was *anybody*? And most importantly, where was the boy I thought I'd find? I was supposed to *save* him, and now here I went again, needing saving. Pathetic, stupid, useless girl. And now, a dead one.

Because there was no one. We were alone. The predator, at long last, had trapped his prey.

"But the truth is, it ain't much different than being a slave,"

Obadiah was rambling. "Long hours, hard work, rich assholes telling ya what to do all the time. Sure, having money is nice and all, but now I gotta pay for food and beer and rent, so at the end of the month, it don't add up to much. And if that weren't bad enough, I finally get the chance, after all this time watching from a distance, to touch you, *really* touch you, and what happens? My new mistress—uh, boss—tells me I can't. Even worse, she orders me to burn off all that pretty skin of yours before I get the chance to enjoy it. No," he continued, "freedom ain't been all it's cracked up to be."

Dragging me off the main path and into some low trees, he released his hand from my mouth. But I didn't even get to scream before he jerked me around and rammed me by the throat up against the trunk of a palo verde, the bark raining down on my hair and face as I wheezed. Even in the weakening light, his few remaining teeth glowed yellow as they neared.

"That is, until now."

17

HER

The old gardener seemed hypnotized by his own knife—the same serrated one he'd apparently taken when he left our house, for sentimental reasons. Now its tip traced a cold, meticulous line under my chin, up my jaw to my ear, its path seemingly too precise for a lummox like him. Then again, he'd had years to rehearse it in his head.

I pawed uselessly at my waistband, where Erica's knife should have been. Gone. I must have lost it in the canal when I jumped.

Useless. Pathetic. Stupid—

"That white throat deserves a pretty red necklace, I think," he said, not realizing what I had lost. Then he dropped the hand with the blade. "But if I kill ya first, ya wouldn't feel nothing, and that just wouldn't be fair to either of us."

His hot, decaying breath was close enough to land on my face. I tried to jerk away, clawing at the bark, trying desperately to find some purchase to fling myself at him, or away from him, or at least to buy myself a little time to figure out how to stay alive for even a little more time.

High above, a huge goshawk screeched in fury at having a rival snap some hapless prey from its maw. Automatically, we both peered up, transfixed by the plummeting black speck. My chance. I brought my knee up with all the strength I could collect, crying out as the knife nicked the side of my neck. He was ready for me, though, and instead of the higher target, I connected with his shin.

Obadiah stumbled, the knife flying in a cinematically perfect arc over the steps of the cenotaph and toward the edge of the escarpment. I lunged for it, my fingers closing weakly around the hilt. The keyword being weakly. He reached me in seconds, twisting my wrist back like a screw. It was gone. That had been my one try. Pathetic.

He shoved me back against the tree trunk, angry now, one hand pinching my throat shut, and his other hand moved on to my shirt and the top of my leggings, pawing and tearing at the fabric. I gasped for air, clawing desperately at his arms, but my strength was gone. It all faded, and soon I couldn't see his rotting, stubbly, wrinkled face anymore, which maybe was a blessing of some kind, especially when I managed to replace it with something much nicer.

I couldn't change what I would feel, though.

But one second passed, then another, and to my surprise, I felt nothing. And gradually, from behind my captor, I recognized the sound of a round being chambered. A hammer being cocked. And finally, silence, as Obadiah stopped slowly killing me.

"Hey, asshole, you can talk shit about my company all you want, but you weren't exactly in the running for any service and devotion plaques, either."

Obadiah snapped his head around. "Langley? Aren't you s'posed to be on a plane?"

"It's Langer, you dumbfuck. Remember me? The guy who bought you, freed you, and hired you at the top of the pay scale plus benefits, just to watch you spend half the day sitting around drunk off your ass? And I'm in a really shitty mood, given that I gave up my chance to sip top-shelf reposado on a tropical beach to stare at your ugly fucking face. So if you don't want to test me, drop the girl."

His fat fingers left my throat long enough for me to get a glimpse of my rescuer.

Max Langer Action Edition held a sleek, compact pistol that stylishly matched his leather moto jacket, T-shirt, and jeans, his normally sculpted hair hanging loose around a face with the kind of hunted look it certainly had not had when I'd last seen him, making suave *bon mots* around my home swimming pool.

Come to think of it, that's where he'd first met Obadiah, too. And here they faced each other down once again. One holding a gun, the other holding me.

"What are ya gonna do, kill me?" Obadiah demanded.

"Yeah," Max replied. "But first, I'm gonna fire you."

I tried to reach up and pry the grubby digits off my throat, desperate—grateful as I was for the help—to do something except stand there waiting to be rescued like a goddamn damsel in distress, not to mention gambling on Max's aim.

Max kept the pistol aimed steadily. "Last chance."

Obadiah bared his grotesque teeth. "I hear they're already on you for kidnapping and murder. If I was you, I wouldn't wanna be burying a body when the cops show up."

"What cops? Last I saw, every squad nearby was headed back south."

Wheatley. I suspected he'd done what he could to help me by leading Labrecque and the others down the wrong trail. But he'd seen the blue Datsun, and he must have also known there was a chance he'd left me to die.

In other words, Max was saving my life, and it wasn't everyone who could say that about a billionaire tech mogul.

Obadiah's grip tightened around my throat, his breath hot and rancid against my cheek. "You could just walk away and pretend ya never saw nothing," he said to Max. "What do you care? You didn't have no problem fucking over her daddy, and she's just a younger version with tits."

Max huffed a sigh and closed his eyes. "Because we aren't all doomed to become our parents." He glanced pointedly at me. "And I like to think I haven't completely failed at proving it, yet."

"Wanna bet?" Obadiah squeezed me like a squeaky dog toy. I gasped and clawed at his hands, sinking into the earth.

And still Max, my one hope, kept the gun aimed steadily. "Listen, man. I get it. You've had a rough time. You want better. We all do. Better than a shallow grave in the desert, anyway. And that's all you'll get if you don't drop her."

"You don't got a clue what I've been through, ya spoiled rich fuck."

"Granted, no, I don't. I don't spend a lot of time researching the life histories of my low-level security staff, although maybe I should take this as my cue to start." He met Obadiah's increasingly wild eyes steadily. "But nevertheless, let's end this little woodland frolic and I'll get you what you're owed."

Obadiah hesitated as if he were—of all things—thinking, and I writhed, unable to even gasp, my vision starting to go spotty. How was my entire life suddenly depending on an expert at hiding his better nature figuring out how to appeal to someone who didn't have one?

"You're bluffing," my captor rasped.

Max took another step forward, gun aimed unwaveringly at

Obadiah's chest. "Maybe. I've been known to. But I've also been known to kill people, so it's up to you to decide what side of me you think you're getting."

For a long moment, nobody moved. The desert held its breath, the setting sun casting long, gloomy shadows as I hung there, dying. But a second later, I hit the ground with several thuds, coughing and heaving and fruitlessly gulping air.

Who would have thought that being burned half to death, followed by nearly drowning in a grimy canal, followed by a two-mile sprint up a small mountain, followed by struggling against being raped and murdered would leave me with nothing in reserve?

In any case, Obadiah took another reluctant step back, raising his hands slightly as his eyes darted between Max and the gun.

I flinched as Max approached before looking up at him with watery eyes as he gave my shoulder a hesitant squeeze, rummaging inside his leather jacket.

"Shit, I forgot to bring water. Sorry, I usually have people for everything," he said apologetically as he helped me into a semi-reclined position. "By the way, I'll take that envelope, too," he said to Obadiah, who handed it over sullenly. Max turned back to me. "I think this was intended for you."

Not that it mattered when the note was lost to the wind. What else could be in there that I could possibly need? Even money was no help now. The only thing that could help was the law on my side. But I didn't have that anymore, and neither did Max. And neither did Wheatley, most likely, so there was no point in counting on him. I just prayed that wouldn't leave Erica and the others sheltering at Ivy's house totally exposed.

"Can you walk? Okay, that's a no," Max said after I remained motionless. He kneeled down, his gun hand still pointed toward

Obadiah. The other gently curled around the backs of my knees. "Do you mind? Your boy might, but I won't tell if you don't."

I paused. "Can't trust you."

"No, really, I won't—"

"Not about *that*."

He looked perplexed. "But I thought you knew that Resi—"

"I know," I sputtered. "But I also have it on good authority that you don't do *anything* without an ulterior motive."

Max sighed and ran a hand through his uncharacteristically tangled hair. "Your boy taught you well. Look, while I figure out the best way to prove myself—other than saving your life, that is—will you at least trust me to get you somewhere where nobody will kill you? After that, it's all negotiable."

I nodded. Good enough. At least good enough to melt into the smooth, fragrant, buttery leather of Max's jacket and bury my head on his shoulder as we descended the steep sandstone steps. And if my boy had a problem with it in principle, well, I knew he'd understand in practice. We were doing it to help *him*, after all.

"How'd you get here?" I murmured.

"The Datsun followed you. I followed the Datsun."

"What the hell are you yapping about over there?" the old gardener growled as he followed along. "I don't got all day."

"Oh, I'm sorry, how inconsiderate of me. Is this throwing off your entire rape and murder schedule?" Max demanded. "No? Then shut your goddamn piehole. I told you I'd give you what you want, and I will, but only after you take us where we want to go, which is to Resi and the kid, because they sure as hell aren't here. Sorry," he stage-whispered to me. "Didn't mean to get you stuck in Fuckface's company even longer. I wanted to kill him, too. Really."

"But—" I looked frantically behind me as he carried me

down. "We can't leave. He's somewhere in this park. The chip can't lie. Can it?"

"No," said Max gravely. "It can't. Not by itself. But your boy can make it lie for him."

"Then that means—"

I dug deep into the envelope, heart racing, and after a few seconds of rummaging, emerged with an object. An object that sat between the dirt-caked ridges of my torn-up fingers. For a second, Max and I just stared at it.

"The kid did it," he said quietly. "He goddamn did it. And I suspect something in that envelope tells us how."

Mind-boggling that something so small was the key to keeping millions of people enslaved.

Or possibly, freeing them.

"Is it too late, though?" I asked. A grave question for a man whose entire fortune and life had been wrapped up in this thing. "For Project White Cedar? For—" For him? For my father? For all of us?

Max took a deep breath and surveyed the vast coolness of the lake spread out below in the fading twilight. I followed his gaze. "I don't know. All I know is that we have to get that envelope somewhere safe, and then find *him*. I have an idea how, but until we do that, everything else can wait. I only wish we could take the helicopter."

"No?"

"No." He turned away from the vista resolutely, and I relaxed further into his arms. "Now that I'm a fugitive, it's time to switch to something less conspicuous." He turned to Obadiah. "Where'd you park that Datsun?"

18

HIM

Resi hummed as she delicately cleansed each grain of grit and daubed on antiseptic and bandages, working in a semicircle of stark white light. I idly wondered where it was coming from until my gaze drifted dully over to the tall metal lantern covered in mesh, its electric flame casting long, wavering shadows. I'd seen lanterns like it somewhere before. Remembering where might help me. But I couldn't remember much at the moment, other than that Resi had given Noam the microchip and vial of acid and dismissed him to whatever spider hole they were camped out in.

A hole I needed to find a way to get *myself* into as soon as I could.

In the meantime, somehow, she'd loosened my chain enough to allow me to finally collapse prone on the sand. Its blissful softness enfolded me like an enemy I'd forgotten had tried to kill me, and I drew in a shaky breath, the pain flaring up every few seconds as she wound bandages around my broken metacarpals.

"Would you like me to?" I asked gently, meeting her eyes once more, expecting to be scolded.

Instead, her fingers dug into my arm as she helped me up off the ground like a newborn foal, my broken knee crumbling almost immediately. And, yes. There went my chain, released from the post with a silky metallic sound, and I tried to desperately shove down my elation.

"Stay close, Starling," she ordered.

Starling?

She was naming me, I realized. Just as she'd threatened.

After twenty years of resisting, I'd reached the one situation where I couldn't.

So I nodded and limped on as Starling, Resi's leashed pet, dragging one useless leg behind me.

The desert air hung heavy, a blanket of stillness only broken by our breaths. Every so often, a slight breeze tugged at Resi's hair, carrying the raw scents of sand and sagebrush, wending between silvered rocks and the occasional patch of sparse mesquite.

My muscles ached with every labored non-step, but I masked the pain before it showed all over my face. There would be no escaping here. My mangled body had no strength, speed, endurance, or reflexes to speak of, and Noam was still lurking nearby, waiting to pound me into a smoking crater if I got out of line.

But I had to keep moving because the farther we went, the better sense I'd get for the lay of the land, and that could only help me. It would especially help if I could figure out where Noam was, and even better, where he had stashed that chip and the vial of sulfuric acid. Because whatever else I did, I had to destroy *that* first.

There was nothing scientific about what I was about to do.

Besides, Resi knew as much as I did about science, so facts were useless here. To get her under my spell, I'd have to do the unthinkable.

I'd have to get them wrong.

"No, Maeve. Don't apologize, ever. You were brave. Just like your brother."

"Don't worry, Louisa," Maeve replied in English, much to my surprise. "It's just another part of the story," she continued in French. "And it isn't always one we want. But—you can make up your own story, one that's much happier. And then no one can take it away from you."

"If it's up to me, you won't have to make up your happy ending, Maeve. You'll have a real one."

When the call ended, Max peered at me through the rearview mirror, and I removed the crumpled envelope from inside my hoodie. I'd made a cursory glimpse into the rest of its contents, which, aside from the chip and the money, I didn't fully understand. But if he'd gone through this much effort to get them to me, they were undoubtedly important. "I can confidently say I think you're the only one besides me that he'd trust with this," I said, handing it to my professor, who tucked it safely in the backpack she carried and instructed us to let Obadiah back in, then let her off at a gas station down the block.

"Wait. What about everyone at Ivy's? Wheatley—"

"He's managed to keep a protective unit at Ivy's, with the help of a friend on the city police. But to no one's surprise, the director suspended him," said Erica, holding up the envelope. "But if my suspicions are correct, whatever's in here may help undo that. And I don't want to make any guarantees, but it might help your father, too."

I nodded. That's what I'd hoped all along was part of his plan.

"And as for the person who *left* me that envelope? Has he earned your trust?" I asked, remembering what Erica had insinuated earlier.

Erica smiled.

But before she could respond, Max broke in. "Much as I'd like to, I'm afraid I won't be sticking around to wait for the cops to figure out just who they're going to arrest. Which is why I'll be headed south of the border as soon as we finish this job. Assuming I can find a plane to borrow, since mine's indisposed."

I gasped. "But what about us? You can't just—"

"Hold *on* a second. Fuck me, you really are his girl, aren't you? What I was going to say is that it's an open invitation. There'll be four of us."

"Four of us?"

"Me. And Maeve," he said. "And once we find him, your boy... *our* boy." He paused and looked at me seriously from behind those glacier-colored eyes, every trace of irreverence out of his voice. "And you."

What he was proposing, of course, to me, was everything. My heart soared, then dropped as if someone had replaced a feather with a cold, heavy stone. "I'd never be able to come back."

"Well, not until slavery's abolished, probably. But you'd be with him. And he'd be with his sister. And I'd be there to take care of all of you. Don't worry, not all the time," he clarified. "I mean, you are adults and all."

Seize it, my instincts said. *Seize it while you can.*

But what about *my* dreams? What about my parents, and med school, and my career, and Erica and Milagros, and Ethan? I might never see him again.

You didn't get a choice, any more than I did.

My boy had been right about that. Those *weren't* my dreams, and that wasn't my life. Until recently, the only dreams I'd ever chosen were the ones already on offer in my gilded cage, and that wasn't a choice at all. In fact, the only *real* choice I'd *ever* made was to break out. He'd shown me the path. It was the

20

HER

It had all happened in one single, terrifying blur.

One minute, the Datsun was jouncing and jolting across an increasingly hostile-looking desert, the engine letting out ever-angrier growls of protest. I was verging on carsick and officially giving up on ever getting comfortable in the hot, cramped back seat, slathering more salve on my burns for the fortieth time and darting my eyes back and forth between my dwindling supply of water bottles to a fuel gauge needle tilting dangerously close to "E." From the front seat, Max, for the past half-hour having gotten nothing but pained moans from me in response to his never-ending string of witticisms, fiddled with the radio knobs, alternating between static and some kind of weird religious broadcast from a backwater border town, seemingly the only place in New North America where religion was still a thing.

This truly was the end of the world.

The next minute, the engine gave one final, resentful

shudder before silence fell, leaving only the desert's chilly stillness and the call of a lone buzzard circling above.

I peeked out the window, where sand, fine and relentless, had swallowed the road—assuming there had ever been a road—whole, leaving the pathetic old car and three thoroughly fucked people marooned on the waves of a blue-black sea of earth. Even the mesquite seemed to have given up on growing here.

"Get out and see what's wrong," Max said, jabbing his gun at the old gardener with as much menace as he could believably muster after three hours of pretending to be just a second away from shooting him.

But I could only watch from the back seat, my breath shallow, as Obadiah threw open the door and emerged into the night, the weak headlights illuminating about half of his form in eerie white phosphorescence. Max followed, gun still aimed at Obadiah's back.

Obadiah crouched by the front of the car but glanced up again quickly. "Hey, Wallace," he said, "an extra pair of hands might help. Maybe ya drop that thing and—"

"Nice try, asshole. Quit trying to be clever because we both know you're anything but." Max shifted his weight from one foot to the other, the gun never wavering, stifling a yawn. It had to be late. I hadn't looked at my phone. No clue what time it was. We'd lost any decent reception hours ago.

Obadiah, muttering his usual under-the-breath curses, made a big show of slowly getting on his knees to peer at the car's undercarriage, his hands moving quickly to loosen a small, obscured panel, pulling out a fistful of wires. "Might be the problem," he mumbled to Max. "Heat must've fucked it."

As Max took a half step closer, squinting at the wires, Obadiah sprang up, hurling a handful of sand into Max's eyes, then darted past him and toward the next rise.

she probably should have blindfolded me somehow anyway. There weren't many signs—it wasn't as if the workers had been able to read them—but there were corners, changes in elevation, differently surfaced walls where the raw copper ore clung, and where countless grimy hands had once felt their way through the pit that had become their home and their tomb. Paths to find my way.

Water dripped in the distance, cascading down the torn tiers and pooling in deeper auxiliary pits, its muted roar marking places where moisture gathered in abundance.

When I could, I paused to inhale deeply, trying to separate the aromatic layers—the mustiness of damp earth, the acrid hint of copper and other even rarer earth metals, and beneath it all, the faint, forgotten scent of something else I recognized. Something I'd encountered in one of my old professor's experiments.

Quietly, my heart fluttered. I stomped it back down before it could show.

"I know what you're doing, you know," whispered Resi.

Did she? If so, I was impressed because even *I* wasn't sure yet. Not like I didn't have ideas. But like always, it was speed chess, calculating and recalculating with every new piece of data. I pulled my senses back from the vast, empty cavern to focus once again on the structure she was leading me to.

I should have known.

A mausoleum carved into the earthen walls. A patchwork of weathered stone and corroded metal blended into jagged contours. Dim, flickering lights cast shadows on the rusted metal door, once impenetrable, now askew, groaning with every gust of wind that flew through. Beside it, a crude sign bore the same logo as the one on the fence by which we'd entered, unreadable under a layer of pulverized tailings and dirt. Above, wooden scaffolding clung precariously to the rock, frozen in the act of expansion, as if the owners had aimed to destroy even more lives but thanks to some economic downturn had never got the chance.

Around the structure, old mining equipment lay half-swallowed, while faint trails pounded out by countless feet led past them into darkness or winding up toward the distant rim. The air hung heavy with the scent of earth and sweat, mingling with the acrid tangs of metal, blood, and fear. But as she threw open the door, none of those were the scents I cared about.

Roughly half of the fluorescent lights hadn't burned out or fallen to the floor and still survived to irradiate the pile of harsh metal bedsteads stacked haphazardly on top of each other, stained with years' worth of blood and agony. Oh, for fuck's sake, the rusty, bloody chains, shackles, and collars the slaves had worn on their ankles and wherever else their overseers had found it convenient to put them were still heaped in lazy, careless piles around the room—the chain I wore now almost certainly had originated here. It may not be ironic, but Resi had one hell of a sense of humor.

Meanwhile, she pirouetted inside like a newlywed into her brand-new dream home. Evidently, the place, when the mine closed down, had been used for storage after the remaining slaves had either been worked to death or sent elsewhere. Because the smell I'd recognized was coming from the corner, under the pile of chains, leaking out of an old, battered box. Acetylene. Used for cutting and welding metals, no doubt. But thanks to my old professor and certain experiments he'd forced his slave to help conduct, I knew it could be made to serve another purpose. Two purposes, actually. And if Resi knew what those were, she would never have brought me here.

The question was, would she find out? And how could I get to it? She was already fingering my chain, glancing around curi-

I stood, alternately shivering and sweating in the desert night, the barbed wire casting twisted shadows on both our faces as Max's fingers moved over the aged keypad, the beeps punctuating the stillness. A green light flickered, and with a groan of protest, the massive metal doors rumbled to life.

"How did you know the code?"

"Because I set it. It was just a guess that Resi didn't change it. But it makes sense since she's never had any reason to keep *me* out before."

Before we went any further, Max offered me a sheathed knife, then reached down and unstrapped the holster from his leg, complete with pistol—larger and thicker-barreled than the one he'd been using, probably a Colt .45—and handed it to me.

"Ever fired one of these?" he asked.

"Surprisingly, yes."

"Oh, thank fuck," he said, turning away in relief. "I was getting tired of being the only one with any tactical knowledge around here."

"My grandfather thought I should learn. I hated it, of course. At first, I was crying so hard I couldn't even see the target."

"But you did learn."

"I did learn."

"Here. Have fun."

I checked the safety and strapped it around my waist without another thought. It felt solid. Weird, but solid.

I shuddered as the gates slammed shut behind me, knowing that sound didn't mean half as much to me as it did to Max, and it didn't mean half as much to Max as it did to *him*, trapped down below.

I'd been wondering this whole time why Resi would choose to bring him here, and now I knew. It was because she wanted to remind him that no matter what he did, he was still a slave.

Her slave now, even though he wasn't. He was my father's, I realized with the kind of surreal revelation I hadn't had since high school, smoking a bowl and looking at my own hands as if for the first time.

My father owned the boy who had just disrupted slavery in a way no one ever had before or since, and it was likely that neither of them knew it yet.

It seemed like the brighter he shone, the more darkness it took to extinguish him.

Was he hatching some new plan, even now? Trying to escape? To fight his way out? And why imagine what he was doing now, what he was thinking now, or what his face would look like when, and if, he finally saw me again? Did it matter? I couldn't fathom it, anyway. I'd take him. In any way, in any shape, in any form he cared to take, I'd take him.

And to do that, I would do whatever it took. Just like he would do for me.

Whatever it took.

HIM

I kept tugging. Maybe I couldn't feign the desire to do it, but I thought I was doing okay at feigning the desire to get it over with. Breathlessly, subtly, I guided her toward one of the metal cots nearest the chains, its stained mattress torn into by about a thousand generations of rats. For a moment, my heart hammered, a faint drumbeat urging me to resist, to turn back, to let her kill me, if that was what it took. I couldn't *act* my way out of this. I couldn't play a role in my own mind.

But I had to keep playing it. Sucking in a whimper, I watched as she attached the end of my chain to a solid leaden ring on the wall, checked it twice, three times, securing it with enough give so I could just settle myself on the narrow metal cot.

She reached for the hem of the stupid shirt that was getting exactly what it deserved, revealing the defaced wreck of the body my old masters had started and Noam had helped along.

My trousers were next, the once-luxurious suit material I'd been so impressed with sliding down my legs, a mere blood-soaked rag. I stepped out, laid bare. I quaked, trying to keep my face impassive, while she bounced on her heels, eyes glinting with delight as she stepped away.

I drew in a sharp breath as she kicked some of the chains aside with her tall boot, the sound echoing like the moans of those who had worn them. But her attention, to my relief, was elsewhere.

I sat, the mattress creaking under my weight. The room was still, save for our breathing. Hers excited and uneven. Mine measured. I hoped.

Her hand pressed against my bad shoulder. I lay back, heart hammering, spine rigid against the thin fabric as her hands explored curiously across my chest, fingertips forming depressions in my scarred skin and tracing the contours of my muscles. They dug deeper, nails grazing the wounds on my face and collarbone, the ones Noam had ripped open and she had carefully treated. Maybe I could do this. Maybe if it only got this far.

No chance of that. She'd take everything. And until I could get out, I'd have to let her. In the meantime, since I couldn't act, I'd have to leave. My mind would, anyway. Maybe if I closed—

"Oh, and keep your eyes open, Starling." She smiled.

"Why, ma'am?" I breathed. "So I don't think of her?"

"No." She sighed delicately into my ear. "I know you will anyway." She leaned even closer, her tongue delicately flicking the outer corner of my eye. "I've just always wanted to see what golden tears look like."

Then, like the strike of a match, she raised her head and threw one leg over my waist to straddle me, painfully grabbing my mostly useless arms and pinning my limp wrists above my head on the metal bedframe as she shimmied silkily out of her flowing blouse, revealing a half-moon of pale skin, lightning flashes of white scars.

"Eyes open, remember."

I was already squeezing them shut, but I popped them open again as she gripped my wrists tighter, lifted herself, and mashed herself down again on my face, squeezing our bodies together, nearly gagging me on the salty dew that had formed between her legs.

Of course the last thing I wanted was to profane Louisa by taking her here. Putting her here, even theoretically, would be a sacrilege. *I* had been made for this place. Louisa hadn't. Louisa was citrus perfume and pink velvet chairs and Paris art prints and soft golden lighting, and all the things they hadn't allowed me to touch then, and I wouldn't allow myself to touch now. But my breath hitched and I closed my eyes tightly, thinking maybe if I could reduce her to elements—a flyaway curl, a bare shoulder, a tiny mole, an outline of a girl I no longer dared to fill in completely—I could selfishly have her with me, still. Because I'd never needed her more.

Resi's weight ground more heavily down on me, her breath hot and ragged. Meanwhile, she twisted behind her to latch her fingers onto my dick, which was betraying me. Fucking weak, the way all men were weak, and it stood rigid, a faithless column of straight-up fuck-you to my heart. Resi curled her long fingers around it, her laughter muffled in my neck as she rocked hard, roping her fingers in my bloody, coagulated strands of hair and shoving me still further up, sending some kind of sickly lavender scent up my nostrils in place of the equally horrid stench of the mine.

"Good boy." The tendons in her neck stood out like cords as she strained against me, unaware or uncaring that I wasn't moving of my own accord. The rattling of chains and the slapping of our bodies filled the room and echoed in the empty spaces of our tawdry crypt.

Her vanilla nails etched the vaguest traces along the curves and lines of my muscles, just enough to make my nerves twitch, to break past the numbing effect of the opioids, which I suspected would wear off in a matter of minutes.

All I could see were the shadows along the ceiling, on the flickers of light from the greasy yellow tubes overhead. On darkness. On nothing.

Look, even while being used and exploited, I'd always prided myself on finding ways to enjoy sex. But now she was even fucking stealing that, breaking it down into a pile of rotting, twisted trash, like everything else in my life she'd ever got her hands on.

My muscles trembled, trying so hard to remain still and impassive, to feel nothing. Her hand slid down my chest, fingers tracing the V of my abdomen before dipping lower. I gasped, gulping for the toxic, chemical air of the mine. Because at least it wasn't her.

Resi chuckled darkly. "Thinking of her yet?"

I swallowed and blinked, vision a wet blur, focusing my face on the moldy ceiling, and let out a mewl, all the more pathetic for how I tried to shove it down.

"Still so quiet. Okay, how about this? Let me tell *you* a story. A story of a brave girl out in the desert, fighting her way back to you. No food, little water. The dust gathers in her hair and eyes, digging agonizingly into the raw burns covering her body. Thirst grips her throat, hinting at death. A girl who grew up in luxury, who wasn't made to endure such things. But she presses on, for you."

Where the fuck was she going with this?

"And what does she think *you're* doing right now?" Resi continued, sliding wetly up my thigh again to straddle my midsection fully, leaning down until our noses touched in a parody of cuteness. "She's thinking you're fighting for her. That all those cute little gears in your head are turning. That you've got a plan. A plan to get back to her." She hummed and giggled. "Come on now, help me out. Keep it going. What do you think she'd say if she saw what you're really doing? Saw you like *this*?" She giggled ecstatically, wriggling her hips on my dick. "If she saw how hard you are for me? Would her heart break? Would she scream? Would she *cry*?" Her voice grew more and more excited, relishing as my whimpers grew more and more strangled, desperately trying to suck in every emotion I'd ever felt. But it was no use. "No shit. She always cries. The question is, *will*. *You*?" She punctuated each word by scraping her sopping pussy violently up and down my shaft, that for all its wetness felt hard and abrasive as any wound.

From my eye and down my cheek, it slipped. Then another and another. Fuck me, after all that, I was *crying* because of her, just like she wanted, and hungrily, she lapped them all up like a kitten with her little pink poison pill of a tongue.

"*Are* you?"

A groan ripped from deep within my chest—pain, pleasure. Who cared?

"*Are* you?" she repeated. "Speak, now."

It was all worthless now.

I vomited out the words. "Yes, ma'am."

Holy fuck, this bitch deserved to die. Why didn't I just fucking kill her already? My hands were free, after all, though broken, and surely I could summon enough strength to hurl her off the bed and onto the concrete floor using only my body weight, use my one functioning leg to smash that smirk on her face and pound it into a bloody death grin, leave her bleeding out onto the pile of chains where she belonged.

But oh, she'd fucking love that. Because it would mean she'd turned me into *her*. And then Noam would arrive, and see to it that my body was soon lying broken and twisted on top of hers, just one more rotting corpse in the charnel house.

Yeah, I was already turning into her, and I was going to die anyway. But if my only choice left was how I would go, it sure wouldn't be like that.

So my mind reached out into the dark, groping toward memories untainted, for places I had been that *weren't* torture chambers. Goddammit, there'd been so few. And they weren't places. They were people. Louisa. Maeve. My mother.

That was it. And I couldn't bear to bring any of them here.

Blocking out my eyes from the starved shape her lips made and my ears from the series of moans escaping her mouth as she whetted her nails on my chest, gouging my skin past the scarred white, into the red, where it hurt, it fucking *hurt*, and all I could do in that moment was bite back my moan and pull a thin, dark veil of nothing clumsily over my mind as I shuddered and spasmed into her—hating every fucking second of it.

A few seconds later, *she* finished with a cry like a strangled songbird, collapsing onto my chest, heart pounding as if our arteries had been cut and spliced. She inhaled deeply as if she could sense more tears forming even now behind my squeezed-shut eyelids.

Yes, but no. No more for her tonight. Please. She'd taken enough.

She left a sticky slick of moisture between us as her weight shifted and she propped herself up on her elbows and pulled away from our locked hips. For a few seconds, she just lay there with her cheek propped on her hand, staring at me in my horror, like an infatuated teenager on a lacy pink pillow.

And I lay still, afraid to move. Unable to move.

"Starling." Her tongue purred around the made-up "name" she'd decided was mine. "So bright. So lofty. So pure, while you're lying there in chains. Thing is, you still"—she giggled—"you *still* think you're made for something better than this. For something purer. For *her*. And I just—I can't help but think—shouldn't someone have beaten that out of you long ago? Oh, God, you poor, sweet, vain, *delusional* little slave boy. What are we going to do with you?" She jabbed a manicured nail toward the area between my legs where she had just been, eyes like blue-hot blazes in the greasy yellow light. "I suppose it doesn't matter because I know better. *You* know better. You aren't above me. You *are* me. After all," she said as she rolled off me, her long finger delicately trailing a streak of blood- and pus-tinged tears down my cheek, thieving another kiss. "You chose this."

I wept for Louisa, but it was Resi who had lapped up my tears. How fucking unfair was that?

At last, she pulled away, a single arm still draped across my chest like yet another shackle. She nestled into the curve of my body, and there we lay, mistress and slave, a lovers' travesty, two bloody angels on a metal slab.

What had I done? What was there to do *now*?

Well, die, probably. It was what I deserved.

But instead, as Resi's breathing slowly but surely evened out, I began to look around. The lamp sat on the floor near the bed, near the pile of chains, just out of reach of my hands. But I didn't need my hands. Once more, I glanced at Resi, her hair spilling over the bed like hay, each rise and fall of her chest beating away the time. I let out a slow exhale. Otherwise, the room was silent, the air hung thick with the musk of a place where everything was a waste: Spent tailings. Spilled seed. Crushed bones. Shattered lives.

Resi's arm draped over me, heavy for a woman so light. Her fingers twitched in her sleep, which was as restless as one might expect given the living spectral horror she was.

The opioids would wear off soon. I could already feel my full capacity for reason coming back, flowing through me, and I welcomed it back like an old friend. My pain, however, was an old enemy. But I couldn't stop because I'd led Resi to this slab—endured *that*—for a reason. I screamed at myself, wishing I had a prod to electrocute myself into moving.

Get up, you pathetic, weak bastard. You can die after you kill her.

I stirred a finger, then an arm, pawing weakly to get the bottlecap—the same one I'd found in the sand earlier that day—loose from where I'd awkwardly palmed it under my bandages while Resi had been gazing up at the stars. Using the last two fingers of my right hand—the only ones even half-functional, I'd discovered after a methodical test of all of them—I scraped the jagged edge against the cinderblock wall a few times, then managed to push it against the rusty valve of the canister of acetylene gas that had been propped behind the pile of chains. The cap levered the valve open just enough to leak the gas—and maybe, if I was lucky, undo the lock on my collar, or the other end of the chain. But that would be the hard part.

All in all, there were two outcomes. One was that it would slowly infuse the chamber, killing Resi and hopefully Noam, too, whenever he came to check on her. But only if my theory was correct and they couldn't smell it under the acrid, coppery aroma that infused the mine. In the meantime, it would give me a sliver of time to get myself free somehow. Or, if I *couldn't* get myself free—far likelier—it would kill me, too. Just like every other plan I'd enacted recently.

Anyway, staying alive wasn't the point. The point was making sure Louisa couldn't get here, or at least ensuring there would be no one here to greet her when she did.

The gas set, and I edged gingerly back over to the bed. But the rusty springs I lay on creaked like a gunshot in a tomb, and Resi's eyelashes fluttered. I went rigid, stilling my breath, and her hand retreated.

I had only seconds. Heart pounding, I used my good leg to kick the chains over the canister, then camouflage them with the dirt and debris littering the floor. Ripping a few strips of filthy fabric off the bedding with my teeth, I settled myself back down on the cot, clumsily wrapping myself in as many layers as I could to filter the air for as long as I could while I worked on my collar and chain.

Preparing to die. It seemed like I'd been doing that a lot lately.

Ah, who was I kidding? I'd been fucked since the day I was born.

Case in point, before I could position myself to start looking for tools to work on the chain, the door swung open, followed by Resi's eyes. Alighting on the new arrival, she practically pushed me, naked, off the bed.

"Mistress—I mean boss," Obadiah stammered, eyes darting from one nude form to the other.

Fuck. This must feel like Christmas morning for the old perv.

"We got—"

"What are you doing?" Resi demanded.

I might have been tempted to say the old gardener looked like shit, but that would be redundant. His security uniform was rumpled and ragged, coated in sweat and dust, but characteristically, he just stood in the door, leering and cackling at Resi as she angrily dove for her clothes and threw them on in a fluster. She clearly hadn't planned for this, having become far too accustomed to humiliating others and forgetting what it felt like to *be* humiliated.

If it was the last thing I ever saw, maybe the prayer had worked after all.

"Where the hell have you been, looking like that? I thought I told you to—"

"It's the girl."

"What?" Resi's eyes flashed, surprise and annoyance she couldn't hide. Just like that, the tables were turning. "What about her? You were supposed to—"

"I tried."

Fuck. I should have known all along. Resi had lied to me, of course, but it was worse. She hadn't even considered Louisa *worth* luring here. Instead, all along, she'd planned to send this motherfucker to rape her, slit her throat, and dump her body in a canal or something before she ever got close. For some reason, this made me want to murder Resi more than anything she'd done to *me*.

"Maybe try calling off your batshit brother who's been waving his goddamned gun in my fucking face for the past three hours."

Brother? That didn't make sense at all. Because Max Langer was gone. He was in Rio Dulce, with Maeve, and—

"They're on their way here, aren't they?" Resi demanded. "Max and the girl?"

To my surprise, for the first time since we'd met, her deceptively angelic blue eyes looked slightly feral. This clearly wasn't part of *her* plan, either. Problem was, if she ended up with Louisa on her hands despite her best attempts to dispose of her, I had no doubt she wouldn't hesitate to lie in wait and give the girl who'd just leveled up to serious thorn-in-side status everything she'd threatened and more. And *I* would have a front-row seat.

And Obadiah's face gave away the answer. I jerked against my chains, eyes flying frantically to the rigged gas valve.

Because there was also a *third* outcome, one I'd really hoped I wouldn't have to use. But since I hadn't figured out the microchips and we were all as good as dead anyway, I could at least do the world one favor and bury this fucking place under ten tons of rubble, so that not only Louisa but *no one* would ever have to look at it.

Meanwhile, Obadiah had dropped all pretensions of respect for Resi. His frustration with her was popping out all over his bloated purple grotesquerie of a face.

"Will ya shut your big yap, woman?" he demanded, just as I went for it. I made one last desperate leap forward, my good leg poised to kick over the lamp whose spark, when it reacted with the acetylene, would blow this whole goddamn mine to kingdom come.

"That's what I've been trying to say. *They're already inside.*"

22

HIM

W*hat?* Max and Louisa, here? *Inside?* I wasn't sure how or why. Only that I'd been milliseconds away from killing the one person I'd spent the past twelve hours killing *myself* trying to save.

In that fleeting moment of chaos, I aborted the kick. It became a fall instead, the chain on my neck jerking me down and back to collapse in a naked, mutilated heap at Resi's feet. Smooth.

At the sound, still facing Obadiah, she froze and started to turn.

Prey. Predator. Play dead. Make yourself small. After all, there was still a tiny sliver of a chance she hadn't noticed what I'd been trying to do.

Yeah, right. Like any predator, her instincts were razor-sharp. Her eyes locked onto my shift in focus, and in two swift strides, her hand latched onto my battered, broken, bandaged wrist.

"Watcha doing there, Starling?"

"Nothing, ma'am," I lied, pulse thrumming. Look, if Louisa was doomed to end up here no matter what, I was sure as hell going to selfishly try to live long enough to see her again, even if I had to watch her beautiful eyes as she inevitably found out what had just happened between me and Resi. And then watch whatever Resi and the goons chose to do to her after that.

Some reunion. I was going to try for it anyway.

"Yeah? Nothing?"

"Yes, ma'am." I swallowed. "Nothing."

Over her shoulder, Obadiah was just standing there lumpily, watching the scene play out and waiting for the cue to burst into his wheezing laugh, as if the fact that we'd all been just seconds away from total annihilation were just too funny for words. If even *that* blithering idiot had figured out what was going on, what were the chances that Resi hadn't?

Zero, as it turned out.

With one quick, livid motion, she gouged the bottlecap off its notch on the gas valve angrily, shutting it down, and threw it across the room. Apparently, it had been a rhetorical question.

She spoke in a voice as light and hollow as synthetic jade. "You. Hurt. My. Feelings."

What? Wait, was she serious? I almost *laughed*. In any case, her benevolent mistress act was officially curtains. Which meant my obedient slave act was, too, thank *fucking* God.

"Starling," she said, stepping closer to where I, for lack of any other immediate options, still kneeled on the filth-covered floor. With one swift motion, she grabbed a lock of my hair and yanked it up by the roots, twisting my head up as I hissed sharply.

Then she exploded, kicking aside the metal bed we'd been lying on, clawing and ripping away the bandages on my hands and my bruised and bloodied torso and the wounds on the side of my head, her vanilla nails shredding to bits the delicate scabs and hooking into the weeping gashes, undoing in seconds the hours of care she'd spent on me out in the desert. "Or should I say, *boy. Slave. Dog. Pup. 77—*"

"—34966," I finished for her, gasping. "That's right. Keep 'em coming."

Man, defiance felt good again. Even if it *was* about to get me killed.

"So you figured out the truth about the chip," she said haughtily. "Between that and the bracelet, you probably think you've freed yourself."

Huh? But the serum hadn't worked. My chip was still in. That's why—unless—my mind was off to the races again.

"But you're not even close."

"Well, I'm a hell of a lot closer," I choked out.

"Shut up. You haven't even earned the privilege of a name if you were about to do what I think you were about to do to me."

"*And* everybody else, remember," I said.

She grabbed the chain from my neck and jerked it toward herself with more strength than I'd thought she had. "*Fuck* everybody else."

Whoa. The pain. The pain, old friend, as I became more and more unmoored from the life raft of the opioids, was raw and glaring and unadorned as she dug those vicious vanilla nails deeper into my hair and skin, sinking into my wounds like razor blades, revealing my crushed, bloody, impaled hands and wrists, hanging down like scraggly trees.

With a deep scratch across my cheekbone, she released me. I gritted my teeth to hold back a scream, sinking lower in my chains.

"Get me the grinder," she said.

What?

Obadiah lumbered over to the shelf and pulled out a tool,

one that indeed appeared to be an electric angle grinder with a spinning cutting disc, glinting in the wan fluorescence. She fired it up, the blade giving off a high-pitched whine. Then in one motion, she plunged it into my scalp like an ax, her perfect pink tongue poking out in a deranged smirk as she turned my world yet again on its axis. Turned it into a blur of pain and vibration, of my barely stifled bleats of agony as chunks of my hair and flesh flew off and back onto Resi, leaving behind red trails dripping down my scalp and into my eyes, mixing with multicolored fluids from the old, shredded wounds.

Finally, the tool switched off, the whine still vibrating in my ears. Resi set it aside. I could still feel it, though nothing sounded in the room other than my slow, labored breathing—and hers.

Reaching to the floor, she bunched one of my severed, bloody golden locks between her fingers. Her blue eyes were feral now, a rabid white wolf coated in the remains of the kill. She stood there, blinking away the blown-back flecks of my blood and flesh, holding a hand to her face, watching the scarlet trails dripping down her fingers and pooling in her nailbeds.

We watched each other, shoulders heaving.

Blood, too, trickled down my forehead and chest, staining the dust on the concrete floor. Hands crushed, wrists impaled, remnants of torn bandages dangling forlornly off them. I trembled, and a chasm of pain rose up to engulf me. Pain that I just fell into because what could I do? Resi couldn't just *kill* me right now, could she?

"We could have—" she began and didn't finish. Just stood there, her voice impossibly small. "Why aren't you—Why aren't you like—"

Oh. I could have kicked myself for not realizing it before. "You wanted to believe it, didn't you?" I wheezed out through my blood-filled sinuses.

"What?"

Yep. I was right.

Without even knowing it, I'd drilled all the way down. Down to fear. Fear for the power of the one thing she couldn't twist, couldn't mock, couldn't crucify. She'd tried. She'd tried with Max, she'd tried with the girls, and now she'd tried with *me*. And somewhere along the line, she'd lost them all because she couldn't destroy what she couldn't understand.

"Deep down, somewhere," I remarked thoughtfully, "you wanted to believe it."

"Stop it," she whined, almost to herself, her knees bending minutely. But that slight bend revealed a universe.

She was in pain. But not the same kind *I* was in. The bad kind of pain. And it was almost enough to make me feel sorry for her.

Almost.

Mostly, I just wished I'd realized it earlier. "It's all right, Resi," I continued.

"Stop." Her shoulders moved up and down.

I even tried to force a twisted smile. Showmanship, you know. "We all want something to believe in."

"Muzzle him," she screeched to Obadiah. "And get the acid."

HER

"It should be here," Max muttered, shoving aside a long-empty water cooler and a broken swivel chair, and kicked an old desk nameplate reading *Gerald Langer* into the wall with a certain amount of pent-up aggression. We searched the cramped space, raising little clouds of dust that floated in the slivers of fluorescent light piercing the gloom.

Once the slumbering beast of the mine elevator had groaned to a halt at the bottom of the shaft with a cacophony of

creaks and clunks, Max had immediately led me to a dilapi-
dated shed at the mine's base, its door hanging off one rusted
hinge. Inside, old office equipment lay corroded and scattered,
file cabinets vomiting their moldy contents over the floor. All
the while, the smell of oxidizing copper coated my throat,
hampering my breathing.

Yeah, I was definitely going to die down here. *But God, just
let me find him first.* That was all I asked.

"What should be here?" I asked, resting my exhausted body
against a warped desk chair, my voice echoing in the claustrophobic space. I was about to collapse, and I also knew every
minute we wasted here was a minute we couldn't waste. And
that *he* couldn't spare.

Max sensed it, undoubtedly. "Well, let me put it this way.
Resi isn't keeping your boy here through the subtle art of
persuasion. She's got him locked down somehow. So I was
thinking—"

"A master key."

He nodded.

"And your dad told you that he kept it *here*?"

He rifled through a pile of yellowed architectural render-
ings. "Well, that would have required him not to have been an
unimaginable prick, so no, he did not. I was kind of just
hoping."

I sighed.

"Anyway, we don't need it. We're armed. What I do suspect
is that our boy is likely in one of two places."

"Go on."

"One, the slave barracks, but I don't know where they are."

"What? But they're right here on the blueprints," I
protested.

"These are the old blueprints."

I groaned.

"Sorry. Two, my dad kept a safe room somewhere, in case the slaves ever rioted. He called it his 'whisper room.' But he didn't tell me where *that* was, either, and for obvious reasons, he kept it off the blueprints. You know, in case *they* ever got a hold of them."

"Did he ever have to use it?"

"He was starting to worry," Max said with a heavy sigh. "There was an economic slowdown and he was cutting corners everywhere. The slaves were basically being starved to death. They had nothing to lose, and at that point, some of them had managed to survive here long enough that they knew the layout of the mine intimately and taught the others. The plan got pretty far along. Until somebody tipped him off."

"Oh, God."

Max looked a little pale. I wouldn't blame him if he hadn't talked about this much. "He sold about two-thirds of the slaves to another mine, the ones perceived as less culpable. The other third—the ones he decided were the ringleaders—well, never left." He coughed. "So. Uh, are you gonna be warm enough in that, or do you want my jacket?"

I just stood there, mouth hanging open. Fucking hell, how long had my boy been here? No doubt enough time to be haunted by the vengeful specters of all those dead slaves *and* tortured—twice.

I felt ill. Except he'd seen just as bad, if not worse. Had it done to him. It was *me* who'd seen nothing. Done nothing. Experienced nothing.

I was the liability, I reminded myself, as if that helped anything.

"And, oh yeah, one more thing," Max added. "We're splitting up."

I moaned. "Do you *want* to die? Have you *seen* a movie?"

Max grinned a little as he stepped back into the surreal

moonscape of the open pit, and I, after only a moment's hesitation, followed. "I won't die and neither will he, nor you. I promise."

"You can't promise that."

"Sure I can," he replied. "I'm in business. Underpromise and overdeliver."

"How exactly do you overdeliver on keeping us alive?"

"You'll find out when it happens. Anyway, you've got a knife, a gun, and this." He dug into the inner pocket of his leather jacket once again and pulled out a silver whistle on a cord.

I looked at it. "Rape whistle?"

"Your term, not mine. I have one, too. Three short blows if you get into trouble. Of course a gunshot will probably be another key indicator."

My stomach flip-flopped.

"But in any case, we'll meet back here in fifteen," he concluded.

"But how? Max, I get lost in my own neighborhood sometimes. There are no signs or maps or—"

"The way the slaves did it."

"And that would be...?"

"By the stars. You can almost always see Polaris." He pointed up, then down, kicking aside some more rubble. Curiously, I followed with my eyes. "And by the sound. The way the wind changes direction, picks up in some places, goes still in others. And by these pilings of ore they made. See? They used more of this yellow-green pyrite on the north side, more of the silver molybdenite on the south, and gradually replaced the colors as they went in either direction. Sometimes they'd arrange it in patterns and use other colors. Blue veins for a safe place, or red veins for a danger zone. To the overseers, it was the perfect camouflage."

"How do you know all this?"

Max paused, his eyes flickering with a memory quickly extinguished. "An old friend."

I nodded.

"Took me a long, long time to earn his trust. And before you ask what exactly happened to him... don't."

I shivered. Max handed me his jacket without another word and his flashlight, too, before producing another one and clicking it on. The beam of light cut through the darkness but faded after a few yards.

"That reminds me."

He turned again, and I bit my lip.

"Did... did he ever thank you? You-know-who, I mean." I looked down, scratching a line in the dirt with my shoe. "He's kind of bad at that."

"He is, and he did. Not that he owes me a thank you for the act of *not* being a scumbag. You don't, either."

I looked up again and smiled. "Well, thank you, anyway. For, you know, it all." I bit my lip again, then went for it. "And, Max?"

"Yeah?"

"If we get out of here—if we get out of here, I... I need your help with something else. *Someone* else. My brother. He—"

He held up a hand. "Don't worry. I know where he is."

I gaped. "You do? *How*?"

He shrugged. "Same reason I know everything else I know. I find out."

"Where is he?" I asked in the smallest voice I could muster.

"He—"

"No," I blurted out. "I changed my mind. I don't want to know. Not yet. I'm barely keeping my anxiety in check long enough to do *this*."

"Fine," he said with a half-smile. "One at a time, right?"

I tried to give him a half-smile back. "One at a time."

He nodded and turned. The implication was, *this isn't goodbye.* I didn't believe him, but even if it was, I'd come to understand that goodbyes weren't always the end.

Max started down one of the paths leading up to one of the terraces. I watched until his light disappeared, then took a deep breath and started down another narrow path angled downward, trying to catalog every marker I saw. The first marker had about 90 percent pyrite veins. The next one had about 80 percent. If I kept following, maybe I could find my way back, at least... but these things were twenty years old. How much could I really trust them?

Meanwhile, the disconcertingly cool air carried the scent of copper, earth, blood, greed, and of the lives lost to all of them. It was hard not to sense a lingering presence here. Something *worse* than thugs with high-powered rifles aimed directly at my hippocampus. Something that seemed to stain the very molecules I breathed in and out and make the shadows cling to me so tightly I couldn't shake them.

I didn't believe in ghosts, though—well, no, that was a lie. I absolutely did.

I was still shivering, but a drop of sweat trickled from my brow, stinging my eye, blurring my vision. I blinked it away, wishing the temperature would make up its mind. Not to mention, I should have set a timer on my phone. How was I supposed to keep track of when to turn back, and—well, shit. I was failing at this spectacularly already, and I wasn't even dead yet.

I won't die and neither will he, nor you.

Really? I was relying on Max, someone I'd only definitively decided wasn't evil a couple of days ago, to ensure that?

Not like I had a choice.

A glint of metal caught my eye. A rusted cart, its wheels

locked eternally. Beside it, a pickaxe, handle splintered, head tarnished. I ran a finger along the edge. Had some slave once picked up this thing and turned it on their overseers? Made a run for it only to die because, as had been repeatedly impressed upon me, none of them *ever* made it out of the mines alive?

A crossroads veered downward, below a rise. I hesitated, then chose the left route, where the air grew heavier, striving to pay attention to how the wind and the markers changed. Up here, though, half of them appeared to have been kicked or blown aside. Even more troublingly, the light seemed to be dimming. My mind was working overtime now, spinning scenarios straight out of a campy horror flick. Discarded corpses, husks of souls? Faceless, undead monsters, flesh rotting and peeling, out for revenge? *It was your fault too,* they'd screech, dragging me off to hell, and they'd be right.

In the face of *that,* a bullet to the head sounded downright charitable.

Besides, as grim as all my cartoonish, imaginary horrors were, chances are whatever real threat Resi had dreamed up was even worse. And that *definitely* made me feel better.

A sudden clatter and a rush of air, and I whirled around, heart pounding.

Nothing.

Trying to distract myself, I swept my flashlight along the rough-hewn walls, tracing faded markings. Symbols of warning, of depth, of danger. A couple of blue copper agates caught my eye, arranged in a carved-out section of the wall. On the other side, a red deposit. An arrow, maybe, if I squinted. Warning or direction? And to what?

A flicker of movement drew my gaze upward. Something swooped down from a far-up perch, screeching. I flinched back with a gasp, nearly dropping my gun, my weak, sweat-slicked fingers fumbling buffoonishly on the trigger. As my heart raced, another dark shape emerged, then another, tiny little black missiles seemingly aiming at my head.

Bats. Harmless bats.

I stumbled on farther, heart hammering against my ribs. A sharp stone jabbed into my palm as I caught myself on the wall, but I barely noticed the sting. I had to keep moving, to remember the dizzying array of ores and deposits and arrows and indicators, of everything that might mean something. My eyes darted frantically around the bifurcated passage I'd landed in—not so much a tunnel, more of a ledge shooting off in two different directions. *Choose,* the ghosts whispered.

From the left passage, a sudden rush of cool air clawed at me, and I crept forward onto the narrow ledge, the echoes of the bats' screeching still ringing in my ears.

And when it finally stopped, I heard footsteps. Not ghosts. Real, human footsteps. *Real* danger.

I couldn't turn back, so I had to choose.

And a minute later, I found myself greeted, predictably, by a body like a wall and a bag over my head.

Not *again*.

But this time, I had a good grip on the gun.

23

HIM

It didn't surprise me that whatever sicko architect had happily accepted a check to design this place had done it with torture in mind. And given that, it also didn't surprise me when Obadiah dragged me like a bloody ragdoll toward some previously unseen shadowy recess of the barracks, where no doubt Resi kept the control center of her ghastly little funhouse.

At least I wasn't naked anymore. At some point, she'd ordered a whining Obadiah to button me into what may have been an old slave uniform before it became a tattered, filthy rag.

Okay, so the rape part was over, then? Come on, I had to take comfort in *something*.

And as much as I *wanted* that thing to be Louisa's imminent arrival, I was more concerned now with what she'd find when she arrived. Chains, guns, monsters waiting to rape and/or torture her—and a bloody, maimed boy kneeling on the floor with another woman's sickly lavender perfume all over him.

Obadiah was approaching, his every step jolting through my frame, muscles tensing and flexing, the pain rolling back in thick, unbearable waves. The cold metal bit into my wrist once more as he immobilized it on another slab jutting from the wall. I could barely move my hand anyway, but for this operation, even *barely* was too much.

"You know, for maximum efficiency, you probably want to secure the other wrist," I managed to spit out without retching. "Come to think of it, I don't think you have the qualifications to be a lab assist—"

A blow to the skull cut me off, the long-suffering wall behind me rewarded with another splatter of my blood to add to its collection.

I decided to stop talking.

But sure enough, here was another old friend, bit strapped tight over my raw lips and tongue, the metal cage pressing into the flesh of my cheeks. My blood smeared against my teeth, warm and coppery, flowing down over my blackened, bruised chest and mangled hands and enlarging the pool already beneath me on the floor. I gagged on the taste, my world blurring once more, the edges of my vision beginning to darken.

Obadiah snorted and joined Resi, who stood by a table cluttered with instruments and substances gleaming in the buzzing fluorescent light. I cataloged all of it, watching as her fingers twirled artfully over a row of glassware.

She rolled a vial back and forth, the liquid inside catching the sparse light. I was proud of my ability not to flinch when she uncapped the sulfuric acid, though its inimitable tang was so instantly overwhelming that it left my nasal passages watering and my throat constricting.

My body knew what was coming. I'd *seen* it. An accident, in the university lab in Heidelberg, with a postgraduate researcher —sadly, involving one of the ones who had treated me like something resembling a colleague and not one of the countless pompous dipshits who couldn't stand the fact that I was even there. But all that guy got in return for his tiny bit of compassion was a melted, hardened yellow-black crater where one side of his face had been, just another horror the young slave working next to him couldn't ever unsee.

Because this shit wasn't fire. It didn't stop when you took the source away. It had to be chemically neutralized, and until it was, it was a slobbering, gluttonous beast, consuming your flesh from the outside in.

So. Now sure would be a good time to figure out a way out of these chains. However, having mostly concentrated so far on blowing everyone to bits, I hadn't had much time to brainstorm anything else.

And it was too late, anyway. Resi's hands now moved in careful, deliberate strokes as she used baking soda to apply a chemical-resistant stencil on my broken wrist, just below the bandages—pretty ingenious, really, and oddly fascinating to the nerdiest part of my brain, even knowing the carnage in store for me.

I didn't have to look. As my heart pumped blood, despite all my attempts to slow it down, I could feel the distinct serifs of each digit being carefully traced, one after another. Digits I used to wear. Digits I wasn't allowed to forget. Hell, I used to have to *recite* them every goddamn morning.

And Resi, chillingly, was gentle.

Sweat rolled down my body now, turning my skin into a hot, bloody slurry, and my heart kept pounding in my ears. Meanwhile, her damp, sticky halo of blond hair had turned piebald, reddened by flecks of flesh and blood, yellowed by the bulbs' sickly film. I swallowed, one last time, and the last thing I saw before she tipped the vial was my own blood delicately colonizing all the grooves in her fingers.

"You thought you could free yourself, boy," she hissed angrily in my ear. "Like *any* of us will ever be free."

HER

I jolted.

"Did you just fucking *shoot* me?" Noam roared in my ear, grabbing the gun from my hands before I could react.

"How the hell am I supposed to know with a bag over my head?" I bit back, despite the fabric muffling my words. "Do you have a bullet-shaped hole in your body with blood gushing out of it? There's your answer."

I went for the whistle, trying in vain to latch onto it with my teeth from inside the bag, but he tore it painfully off my neck. "Little brat, how are you still alive, anyway?" he snarled.

"Good question."

He grabbed my arms and wrenched them unnaturally behind my back, and I screamed. Loud. High-pitched. Because why not? I had no reason to stay quiet anymore. He scooped me up and started loping away, not nearly as fast as he probably would have liked.

I *had* shot him. A shivery little thrill passed through me. Probably grazed his leg, if I had to guess.

And it hadn't helped me at all. I was no doubt on my way to Resi, anyway, for further torture.

Which could be useful. But my options for mounting a rescue were dwindling by the second. The gun and whistle were gone. The knife? Undetermined. I couldn't feel its weight, but I also hadn't felt him take it. At any rate, my hands were useless, though not, as far as I could tell, restrained with anything besides his hulking arms.

But he *had* been shot. That had to be worth something. I jerked against his welded grip, testing it out as he, moaning painfully to himself, dragged me somewhere far from anywhere I'd seen or had time to examine. The stale air from the nylon bag filled my nostrils, tainted with metallic copper and musty earth and gunpowder.

I squeezed my fists, resisting the urge to thrash wildly. What would he do? What would he tell me if he could?

Wait. Plan. Don't die.

Well, I hadn't yet. My record was perfect.

I wriggled, stretching my fingertips, feeling for the knife. It had to still be there. I sighed, breath catching against the inside of the bag, and focused on Noam's labored breathing and slow, limping steps. The wound was slowing him down; he wouldn't be able to keep this pace for long.

He grumbled something under his breath as we rounded a bend, my shoulder scraping roughly against the cavern wall. I clenched my jaw against the pain, swallowing down a yelp. *No. Keep quiet. Wait.*

Suddenly, he paused. Were we here? I sensed him shift, then grunt as he eased me down. My back hit first, then my head, and a little cry of pain escaped before I could stop it.

All at once, the bag ripped open, stale air rushing out, replaced by an acrid coppery tang that stung my dry eyes. Copper. Blood. Fear.

"Oh hey, Louisa," Resi's voice cooed, lazy and dripping in mockery. "Good timing."

I squinted, adjusting to the sudden flood of greasy light. To Resi—her sickly sweet giggle echoing off the cavern walls. To Obadiah, hunched over something—*someone*—near the wall.

My heart seized.

I'd seen him a mess before. No doubt. But *was* that really him? Muzzled and cuffed to a slab of stone, his bare, pulverized scalp coated with dirt and blood, his skin as pale as a corpse where it wasn't blackened and yellowed and daubed with fresh splatters of red? Blood that Resi *also* wore. Blood that meant she wasn't done hurting him. And she hadn't even *started* hurting me.

He was breathing. I was breathing. That was a good start.

"Where's Max?" Resi asked.

"No clue," I said. Come to think of it, this would be a *really* good time for him to show up.

Resi nodded to Noam, who seemed to understand the gesture. "I suppose you're thinking," she said, "that now that I've got you both here, I'm going to give you some long, grandiose speech about why I'm like this and why I'm doing what I'm about to do, et cetera, et cetera. But I think we kinda covered all that already, so..."

She flicked the acid onto his wrist.

I screamed. Because he couldn't.

Horror swallowed me whole as his wrist—scarred but till now unbroken—transformed into a grotesque, twisted mass. The acid devoured it, relentless, eating through flesh and muscle, bubbling, blistering, consuming. The air's coppery musk was replaced with the effluvium of burnt flesh and hair.

And the worst part was, despite the muzzle, I could *hear* him scream.

Something hot and terrible and profound surged in me. My grip on the knife tightened as I rose, blinking through the pain radiating from my shoulder. But I couldn't lose myself. Not now. If I ran at Resi with the knife, the goons would pounce on me in seconds, and he'd still be there in chains. Dying.

Wait. Plan. Breathe. Keep acting. Don't die.

If I couldn't hear his voice, I'd just have to keep imagining it.

The numbers were seared onto his skin forever already. It had taken seconds. It was over. Resi had done what she wanted. She could stop.

Why wasn't she stopping?

"Oh," she mused. "I guess you expected me to stop, huh?"

"Please," I choked out. "I'll do anything."

"Anything? Why? Tell me."

"Because—because I love him," I said. "And because he saved me. And now it's my turn to save him. I know he—he thinks I'm not ready for it. That my life hasn't prepared me. But," I said louder, just in *case*, "it has now. Here."

I stepped forward and tossed the knife from my inner jacket pocket down to clatter on the stained stone. My heart raced. My breath hitched. And I said:

"I'll—I'll be your slave instead."

Resi looked from Noam to Obadiah, incredulous. "Uh, honey?" she said. "I'm not really sure you understand what slavery really means."

"No," I said. "Thanks to him, I understand perfectly."

He was struggling in the muzzle, thrashing, gasping, screaming noiselessly now like a hooked fish, the acid still eating through him. In a minute or so, give or take, he wouldn't just be tattooed. He'd lose the hand. Maybe the arm. Maybe more.

And, fuck. What could be worse than being unable to touch him when he was just centimeters away?

Well, nothing.

But we'd been there before.

Keep acting. Keep breathing.

"Burn me. Rape me. Or have them do it. I don't care."

Resi laughed. High, warbling, deceptively pleasant. Like the high school mean girls whose cruelty had been almost *beautiful*, glittering diamonds.

But even diamonds could shatter if struck in the right place. Chemistry told me so.

"Well, come on," she said. Before she could beckon Noam to drag me forward, I darted toward them myself, hands outstretched to accept the set of chains Noam produced from the seemingly bottomless pile. I even lowered myself to my knees without being ordered to, inhaling sharply as he locked my wrists in the cold iron cuffs.

Noam yanked on a lock of my hair, forcing me to look up at my new *mistress*, at the red harlequin smile painted in flecks of blood and tissue across her face.

I was inches away from him now. Right where I wanted to be. Because just as Noam hadn't thought to check me for the knife, he'd forgotten to check me for the master key, too. Which was good because I'd had it in my hand the entire time, having found it in Gerald Langer's own *whisper room*, after following the red-veined arrow. Sure, the mining slaves had never gotten the chance to use it, and most of them had paid for it with their lives, but they sure had given it their best shot. Left it, I liked to think, for the one person smart enough to give them credit for it.

My only regret was that I'd needed Noam to take me here. Otherwise, I would have shot him in the head.

"Your boy fucked me, you know."

What? My heart turned a traitorous little somersault, but I shoved it down as I slipped the key into the tiny lock, breathing only when I heard the tumblers move once, then again. "I don't believe you. I mean"—my face flushed—"ma'am."

"Show her."

The bald goon grabbed a cell phone, an app cued up to a video feed from a camera mounted somewhere on the ceiling, and shoved the screen in front of my face. I looked away and shoved down my gag reflex as if the thing were emitting some kind of toxic miasma.

But I turned back. Because I couldn't look away from what she'd done to him.

"God, see how fucking huge and hard he was?" she purred dementedly as I stared, nauseated, at the pixelated images.

"When you were trekking through that goddamn desert trying to save him, he was moaning for me, begging to taste me, begging to come inside me."

My stomach churned, but I kept working the lock. Fucking hell. How could this pathetic, perverted woman possibly think any of this meant anything to me, other than proving it was actually possible to hate her even more than I already did?

"So, Louisa—oops," she taunted, creeping nearer. "I forgot. *Slave*. Any regrets yet about your noble sacrifice? I mean, besides the fact that I'm still going to kill both of you, but I figured that went without saying."

My eyes flicked to him. He writhed, barely conscious. Could he hear her? Could he hear *anything*?

Like it mattered. I'd feel the same, say the same. In silence, in noise, in darkness, in light, in night, in day. Whether anyone could hear or whether *everyone* could hear.

And that was exactly what Resi would never be able to understand. Because I did love him. And he *had* saved me.

But that was so, so far from all he'd done.

"Regrets? No." I kept going on the lock, applying minute pressure on the cuffs, whispering an escape artist's prayer for it to yield. "I'd make it again."

"What?" She blinked once.

"Luckily," I said with a smile—showmanship—as the lock clicked open and my chains fell away. "I don't *have* to make it at all."

"Oh, fuck," she said. "*Obadiah!*"

At her desperate screech for backup, the reluctant goon sprang forward, his overgrown frame a cannonball hurtling toward me, bent on rage to collect the payment he'd been promised and denied over and over again.

His timing: perfect.

Because Resi, in her outrage at being outsmarted by *me*, of all people, had lost hers. In a frenzy, she grabbed the remaining acid in the vial. I lunged for it, managing to veer it off course by barely a centimeter.

Which was enough. The vial hit its target dead-on, shattering in Obadiah's face. He shrieked like a demon, clawing at the flesh of his eyes as it bubbled and melted, the acrid stench of smoldering skin seizing my nostrils as he collapsed in a writhing pile of contorted limbs and incinerated tissue.

The world around me seemed to stop dead as Obadiah's screams echoed and his body convulsed on the floor, hands blindly grasping at nothing.

In the chaos, I dove toward Resi's metal shelf full of fun, pure adrenaline buoying me now, greeted with a series of unlabeled vials and beakers. Ones a chemist would know. Ones *he* would know, not that he was in any shape to tell me. *Breathe. Think. Don't cry.*

What neutralizes acid?

Tsk. *Slow learner.* A base, of course. But where?

My gaze settled on an unlabeled container of white powder. I snatched it up, fumbled with the lid, wailed in frustration as it resisted in only the way an inanimate object could. But at last, it popped open, and I stuck in a finger and tasted it. No mere powder was going to kill me *or* him more dead than we were being killed now.

But before I could open it, a pair of small, cold fingers closed onto the box, trying to wrench it away. I clenched my teeth and growled, pulling it back. But robbed of her hired muscle, Resi was smaller than me and weaponless. I grunted and kicked her away, in the process letting what I was reasonably sure was baking soda loose all over the room in an enormous frosty cloud, eliciting a blissful fizzing sound as it at last overpowered and neutralized the acid melting him piece by piece.

He slumped in his collar, his once-shimmering eyes dulled

and glassy with pain, barely able to focus. The chains rattled weakly as he gasped, gulping air as best as he could around the muzzle.

I kneeled, my fingers curling around the cool metal cuff around his withered inner arm, the jagged numbers seared into his skin in gruesome greenish-yellow cavities. The lock, though, blessedly yielded to the key. With a sharp twist, it snapped open. The collar came undone just as fast, clattering to the ground with finality.

Immediately, he wilted against me, eyes glazed but astonished, his still-muzzled breath warm against my neck. I slipped an arm around his waist, propping him up with what little strength I had left. And finally, I undid the muzzle's buckle, unpeeled the straps, and flung it away.

"Lou," he said before it was all the way off, and for a second —but only a second—I dared to fret about what he would say first.

I really needn't have.

"I love you."

"What?"

Despite imminent danger, despite certain death, I froze, trembling in sheer amazement. At hearing the words, at hearing them *now*, at the fact that he was actually *clinging* to me and maybe even smiling, and delivering a series of half-blind, chaotic, bloody kisses to my lips, my forehead, my nose, my eyelids. And at the fact that I was probably putting both our lives in further danger by pausing to kiss him *back*, because of course I was.

"Am I not getting through to you, slow learner? I love you, I love you, I love you, I love you. And—"

But in the degraded gold of his irises, for a split second, reflected back, I saw Resi catapulting toward us from behind, wielding the knife I'd theatrically tossed away. On instinct, I whirled, snaked out with my arm, and scooped up a discarded piece of ore. Even weakened, my aim was good enough to connect with Resi's temple with a satisfying *thwack*. She physically jerked and crumpled, the knife clattering out of her grip. She hauled herself up almost immediately, of course, but before she could counterattack, a series of frantic, shrill noises cut through the chaos.

Rape whistle.

"It's Max," I breathed.

"Right on time, I see," he muttered sarcastically against my lips, filling me with bizarre delight. But then his body went taut, head turning, eyes searching, mind calculating.

I knew that look.

"Wait. Where's Noam?"

Before I could say another word, the mine—that vast, barren tomb in which we had all forgotten we were buried alive —answered for me. A blast rocked the ground. Dust rained down. The world blurred.

And I clung—like the last time, like the first—to all his weight, to all his heat, to the miraculous unbroken circle of his arms on my waist.

Closed my eyes and fell.

24

HIM

I'd been nearly buried alive once before. Four years old, baby limbs twisted back against their range of motion and jammed in a locked wooden trunk half my size. Fingers raking off bloody shards of wood, screams buried in my throat, gasping for just one last chance to breathe. It lasted barely a minute, probably, but felt like hours.

And I was there again. In the darkness, in the void. Dying, helpless, breathless, voiceless in a tiny box.

Until, from beside me, a light.

When the box had popped open again and the sunlight came pouring in and the sparrows started chirping, when I was weeping and gulping air and giving thanks for the piece of shit life I'd been so generously given back, the first thing I glimpsed was Master Jhemp, two years older, eating a chocolate bar with his mouth open, crumbs gathering in the corners of his pale, doughy lips and tumbling down onto the lush, manicured lawn.

O jee, I was just kidding. What, did you really think you were gonna die? It's true what Papa said. Slaves really are pathetic cowards. Wouldn't last a day without us around telling you what to do.

But when the light came this time, it wasn't Master Jhemp's voice I heard.

"Are you okay?"

What?

"Remember when I asked you what a miracle was, Lou?" I murmured weakly. "Well now, finally, I know the answer."

"What?" She coughed, her lungs rattling with a sickening hollowness.

"A miracle is having reached twenty years old, having made it out of every hellhole they ever tried to toss me in, and having *you* here, asking *that*. Here I am, a bloody, broken-limbed, mutilated slave slowly suffocating to death at the bottom of a mine, and I'm *still* the luckiest son of a bitch in the goddamn world."

Her fingers curled lightly around my wrist, where they held on and didn't let go.

As I spoke, I slowly realized I wasn't suffocating. That I *could* breathe. We *weren't* buried alive. There was still air and—though the electricity was out, the fluorescent glow gone—distantly, more light. We were still in the slave barracks, and the building was even still partially standing.

Forcing words out was painful, through gritted teeth, ignoring the hot streaks of pain, sharp and dull then sharp again, shooting through every nerve. Dust swirled as my lashes struggled to open under layers of toxic detritus. Head pounding, limbs once again twisted at bad angles under a stack of rock and plaster and metal and barbed wire. Sizable but not so large I couldn't throw it off.

Good. Because for more than a few reasons, we *really* needed to throw it off.

Louisa lay curled up under me, mostly in shadow, hair dressed in a thick coating of snowy, undoubtedly highly toxic dust. Her fingers seemed impossibly small and delicate, and now she turned to nuzzle me, one hand on the flashlight, the fingernails of the other digging further into my skin through the ragged fabric of my shirt. It killed me that I couldn't really hold her. When we'd fallen—after she'd saved me, speaking of miracles—the only thing I could do was lightly drape my arms around her. Now I couldn't even do *that*. And God, she deserved so much *more* than that. "You deserve to be out of this nightmare I sucked you into," I murmured into her ear, "and to rest, to sleep. To be safe. And I'll give you that if it kills me, which it very well might."

It already *was*.

"Lou." Had she heard anything I'd just said?

She stirred and tried to raise herself up, but her wet cough interrupted the effort. The heat from her burning lungs seemed to radiate out at me.

My own chest tightened, the realization of the cause hitting me like yet another blow. No wonder I'd felt nauseated, dizzy, hallucinatory. And every second we stayed here, it would get worse.

And I needed to tell her. But I also had to get her out of here, so not yet. I didn't know all of her anxiety triggers, but now was *not* the time to start compiling a list.

I glanced up in a panic as another beam of light flickered over the rubble. Whose? A whistle sounded, the same one from just before the explosion, and beside me, Louisa stirred again, kicking weakly at a piece of rubble pinning down her leg.

Through a hole in the debris, I could make out Max scrambling toward us, furiously throwing aside everything in his path. About time. But he clearly couldn't see us—in fact, he was already heading off in another direction.

I opened my mouth, but only a raspy croak emerged. I tried again, desperately. "Max."

"Max!" Louisa's voice was more robust.

"Louisa?" Max's head snapped back.

"I'm here."

Max hurtled over to us, but his face paled when he laid eyes on me, struggling to raise the upper half of my body. "Fucking hell, kid. I guess she always did have a weird thing for hair. But never mind how you look. Can you walk? That's the question."

"Never mind if I can," I managed to say. "I will. We have to get out of here, now."

"Well, the main exit's blocked off," Max began. "Elevator's fucked. And all the outdoor pathways leading out of the pit are now rubble." He brushed some dust off his shoulders. "But hey, on the bright side, Obadiah's dead."

"What about Noam?" I asked warily.

"Long story. Look, there's still a chance. My father built at least one secondary exit."

"You know where?"

"I know *not* where."

"Good enough. Lead on."

Max helped Louisa to her feet first. She had a sprained ankle and bruises that were quickly darkening, obscuring the burns just now starting to helpfully scab over. Her face was grim with pain, but she didn't complain. My own injuries seared hot and cold, but the pain felt secondary at this point. We had to move.

Max helped me up next, slinging one of my stiff arms over his shoulders. For now, I could hobble, which was enough. Louisa slid under my other arm with her slight weight.

I blinked into the gloom, scanning for an exit in the tangle of fallen beams and rocks, but another wave of nausea hit me, the room briefly spinning on its axis. We were already running out of time.

A metallic glint caught my eye and I squinted through the haze. There—a narrow opening in the rubble leading farther into the mine, back the way Resi had dragged me before. Max nodded, starting toward it without words. It was our best shot.

"Thanks for coming back, Max," I said quickly, only to have Louisa and Max exchange one quick, knowing glance.

"What?"

"Don't think I've forgotten about our agreement, slave."

Resi was not quite there, in more ways than one. She looked almost ethereal in the dim light, round eyes vacant. She wasn't coated in asbestos or copper dust like the rest of us, and her hair sparkled under Louisa's weak flashlight, now rolling around on the ground. She still looked clean—except for the blood and mascara smeared across her face like some kind of neo-expressionist mural.

Then it hit me. She'd *planned* this. She hadn't gone crazy on me for trying to blow up the place. She'd gone crazy on me for trying to do it before *she* got the chance.

But the knife at Louisa's throat—the very knife Louisa herself had dropped earlier—was real as fuck. And of *course* she'd gone for Louisa, the only one of us she was strong enough to physically restrain.

"You know, Obadiah tried this already—" Louisa's voice cut off with a sickening gurgle, and my stomach dropped as blood cascaded down her throat like a trail of rubies. Not an artery. Maybe a vein.

"Did Obadiah do *that*?" Resi sneered. "Stupid dead toothless fuck. Good riddance."

"You fucking—" I bit my tongue so hard I tasted copper, choking on my helplessness, as trapped as when I'd been locked in that goddamn trunk.

Louisa wasn't looking at me. She hissed through clenched teeth, her breaths rhythmic, controlled, like she was forcing herself to stay calm because she knew panic wouldn't help. *God, she is brave.* And what was I doing? *Standing* here. Barely. Body broken. Mind foggy. Useless. No plan.

"Let her go," I said, hoping it didn't sound like a pathetic plea, even though it was. "Look at this place, Resi. This is *over*."

"Resi," Max broke in calmly. "I know I should have asked you this a long, long time ago, but just what the fuck is your problem? Do you seriously not understand that we're *all* about to die if we don't find a way out of here right now?"

"There *is* no way out of here."

My heart pounded. She was lying. Wasn't she? How had she planned on getting out otherwise?

"And you won't shoot me."

"No, I won't," Max replied.

Really? He wouldn't? Seemed like a perfect way to deal with this to me.

"I'll die the way *I* want to die—and that's by killing them first. How *you* die is up to you."

Louisa whimpered and shifted. Resi twisted her arms back violently, wringing out another stifled cry. She was as sick of being used as a bargaining chip as I was of watching her *be* used.

Resi was Max's monster to handle. I *knew* that. And I trusted that Max knew what he was doing. But it was Louisa's voice that had let me *out* of that box. And *she* needed *me*. It was time for another plan. If only my entire body and brain weren't as much rubble as the mine now was.

"You aren't this person, Resi," Max said.

I almost laughed.

"Oh, for fuck's sake. I'm exactly this person. And so are *you*. We're the children of a monster. The only difference is that I *know* what I am, and you've been running from it your whole life. Well, surprise!" She threw one hand up in demented glee. "Look where we both ended up! And the saddest part is that you had a *chance*. You had *millions*. You had everything you needed to give this whole fucked-up world exactly what it deserves. But instead, you thought you could *save* it, like the stupid, pathetic, naive bastard you always were."

"Someone had to," Max said quietly. "Someone had to *try*. Look, contrary to popular belief, I'm not so arrogant as to think I know what the meaning of life is. But I do know there has to be more to it than just fucking over everybody who fucked *you*. Because if it is, we'll *all* be slaves for the rest of our lives." He exchanged glances with me. "Whether we started that way or not."

"Did *he* teach you that? Did *she* teach you that?"

"No," Max said. "You did."

His voice was calm, eerily so, as he stepped toward Resi and Louisa. "When we played outside in the evenings. After chores. After homework. You would start running," he said, breathing deep. "Out into the desert, as far as your legs could carry you, your hair flowing behind, until it just blended in with the sand. And every time, I chased you. I'd scream at you, beg you over and over again to stop. That he'd track you down no matter how far you got. That you'd just make it worse for yourself. And I was right. He always did. And then he'd make *me* watch him punish you. As if it were my fault. Which in a way I guess it was." He swallowed thickly. "Because I couldn't stop you."

"So you talked," Resi said quietly, voice echoing oddly in a space now utterly silent except for the beating of our hearts.

I tried again to catch Louisa's eye, but it was like she wasn't even aware of me. *Why?*

"I talked," Max continued. "I figured if he wouldn't let me leave, the least I could do was talk you through it so you could hear my voice. So you could have something to listen to that wasn't—that wasn't—anyway." He coughed. "He muzzled me next time because no son of his could be allowed to talk to a slave girl like that. Like she was anything more than a hole to be fucked."

Resi's expression twisted minutely. Because if she was skilled at anything, it was tricking you into thinking she could stop being a monster if you just pressed her buttons right.

Don't fall for it, Max.

The silence shattered. A low rumble from deep within the mine. Dust rained down; the ground beneath us shifted. Louisa whimpered again. *What the fuck was that?* We might be dead sooner than even *I* thought.

Enough of this. I slid into a slight crouch, muscles screaming in protest. Resi didn't even turn. She hadn't looked at me once, in fact. From where I stood in darkness, with the angle of the one light shining up from the ground, she couldn't even see me.

Perfect. I could use that.

"But I still talked," Max continued. "Even if you couldn't hear my voice."

"I didn't *ask* you for that, Max." Resi seethed, her nails digging into Louisa's neck like she was some kind of living stress ball. "I didn't *fucking ask* for some idiot boy to make me into something different than what I was. Than what I *knew* I was."

"I know you didn't. I did it because I *wanted* to do it. Because I love you. I love you as my sister, and I loved you even *before* that. It's why I gave you everything. And I would have given you more, so much more. I would have given you my entire fortune if you'd only asked. I would have fucking bankrupted myself just to take away one single second of your pain, and I—Fuck, *Schatzi*, why was it not enough? Why was—" He stopped, on the edge of some emotion so large and terrible he couldn't voice it.

"Anything, huh?" Resi demanded. "What about *her*?" She grabbed one of Louisa's damp, dusty curls and yanked her farther into the light. "Would you give me her? Would you give me *him*? Would you let me torture them to death, slowly and painfully, if that were the only thing in the world that would make me happy?"

Max shook his head. "That wouldn't make you happy, *Schatzi*."

"Of course it wouldn't. But who cares?" Resi screeched. "As you keep telling me, we're all going to die anyway!"

"We're not." I forced myself to hold her gaze. "We can walk out of here together. It's not too late."

She raised the knife. "Yes, it—"

I didn't let her finish. Pushing off with my good leg—*good* being a laughable term at this point—I lunged, straight at Louisa, knocking her out of Resi's grasp. One short, sharp cry escaped her lips as we tumbled down together. She rolled away with whatever strength she had left, swallowed up by the darkness.

But Resi had strength and speed too. And I had nothing.

"I didn't want it to be you first," she whispered. Her knife plunged toward my throat—an artery.

A gunshot shattered the silence, the echo ricocheting wildly through the chamber's collapsing rings. With a meager little cry, she crumpled, knife spinning from her fingers in a perfect, symmetrical spiral.

I whipped around. Max stood there, lowering his pistol, face drained of blood. He took two steps forward and sank to his knees.

Trembling, I crawled immediately toward Louisa, who was shaking even harder. Clumsy elbows, useless fingers—I clawed for anything to stop the bleeding at her neck, finally grabbing a rough wool blanket and balling it up against the thin red line along her jaw. She rested her head on my shoulder, pressing into me closer than she had after the blast, if that was even possible. There were tear tracks on her cheeks. Old or new, what did it matter? She'd cried enough. She'd cried *fucking* enough on my behalf.

God, she just looked so *tired*.

It's over, I wanted to tell her, just whisper it in her ear and cradle her against me. But I didn't. Because it wasn't.

I tried to take a deep breath and only coughed. "Guys," I rasped. "I don't want to alarm you, but I figure you're already alarmed enough." They turned toward me, Louisa's breath still hitching, Max still staring at something I couldn't see. "The air. It's, uh, highly toxic."

They stared.

"And, well, we've all been breathing it in since the collapse."

Louisa didn't say anything at first. Then, fingers trembling, she reached for her flashlight, its weak beam sweeping toward our intended escape route. The tunnel—our only way out—was choked with debris and shattered rock. An impassable wall. She gasped, shrinking back, her shoulders rising and falling with each quick, sharp breath. I didn't even have to look at her to know exactly what she was feeling—stomach twisted into knots, lungs working too hard, panic creeping up her throat.

This was what I'd been trying to hold off as long as I could. It was inevitable, but she'd been doing so *well*.

"There's another way out," I coughed, my lungs tightening with each word. "Max"—I barely swallowed the next hacking fit—"Max said so."

She clung to me as we struggled to our feet, both of us staggering. The key now was just to buy enough time before we lost consciousness.

"Max, what—"

But he wasn't listening. He wasn't even looking.

Dark hair obscured his face like a shroud as he knelt over Resi, blood seeping through his fingers as he pressed them to her gushing wound. His other hand brushed back her hair from her face. Her strange, glassy, angelic face, still twisted in something almost divine in its ancient anguish. Max laid her down delicately, like a bouquet of white nightshade—precious, poisonous, already dead. When he bent to kiss her brow, amid the dust streaking his cheek, I saw a single tear track. A mark he, like all of us, would wear forever.

Louisa stared at them.

"You don't need me anymore, kid," Max said. "You're practically free already."

Apparently, he hadn't noticed the number burned into my arm.

"Max!" Louisa bit her lip, her body wracked with sobs trying to break free.

But there was nothing else to say. Ten tons of rock buried us, and *this* weighed more.

She just stood there, rigid, eyes staring at nothing. "We can't." She gasped. "We can't go."

"What?"

"Without Max, how can we—"

Removing someone's chip doesn't make them not a slave. It just makes them a slave who's breaking the law.

Without Max—without the offshore accounts, the private jets, the forged documents—what could I do? Run?

And I *couldn't* run. Physically or any other way. Louisa, albeit hysterical, was right. What the hell were we escaping *to*?

"We have to try, Lou. I—"

"But Maeve—and Daddy still—and you're still—we can't go back. We—" She gasped for air, eyes wide and unfocused.

And something in me snapped. I might have failed at everything else, but I had *one* job, one job I couldn't fail at no matter what: saving her. And *she*—the girl who had done everything to save me—was stopping me from doing it.

"Lou, I love you and I'm sorry, but *shut up*," I rasped. "And for the last time, *quit holding your breath*. What have I told you? If you stop breathing, I guarantee you, *you will die*. You will *not* make it out of here."

"But what about—"

"Let me finish. You are not allowed to think about *any* of that."

"But—"

"No. Shut up. I don't care. Don't think about Maeve, or Max, or your dad, or"—I swallowed hard—"or about me. The only thing you're allowed to think about right now is getting yourself out of this goddamn mine alive. That's the *only* thing that matters. The one and only thing. Do you understand me?"

"No," she whispered, shaking her head. "No, I can't. What about—"

"Goddammit, Lou. I'd say don't make me shake you, but I *can't* shake you. Answer me. *Do you understand?*"

At last, she nodded, tears spilling freely.

"I need a yes. Say yes."

"YES," she screamed. "Yes."

"Good. Now I need you to find us some water, yeah? Just *find some water*. Don't think about anything else."

She didn't move.

I almost groaned.

"Don't leave me," she whispered. "I've lost you enough already."

"I won't leave you, *mäi léift*," I murmured, pressing a kiss to the side of her sweat, dirt, and tear-streaked face. *That* I could do. "I'll be right here. Now water, yeah? You can do that. I believe in you."

She still didn't move, and for a second, my own panic started to build. But then, she dove into the rubble, after a few seconds emerging with a half-filled plastic jug among the remains of the chemistry supplies. Calmly as I could, I indicated for her to rip another strip off the blanket she was pressing against her wound. "Soak it with water and hold it over your mouth and nose. Breathe slowly. It'll help filter out some of the gas."

She placed the cloth to her face, pressing it flat like a shroud. She tried to do the same for me, though my arms were too weak to hold it on properly, and I gave up in frustration, flinging it aside.

"But—"

"Never mind. Remember what I said? We're going to move, yeah?" I said. "Just keep moving. Don't think about anything else. Keep moving. That's *all* you have to do right now."

So we did. And for a few seconds, there was silence at last. The sound of our labored breathing was all that echoed in the dark.

But out of the tunnel to become her tomb, Resi's voice drifted. "I still heard your voice, Max," she whispered. "I always heard it."

25

HER

We made slow, steady progress. He leaned on me more than he wanted as we waded through debris and rubble, dust choking me as it gathered on my makeshift gas mask until I couldn't brush it away anymore and stopped trying. Somewhere ahead of us, rock grated against rock. I knew it was killing him that he couldn't grab me or do anything but press me against a craggy mine wall, hearts pounding, as a pile of rocks tumbled down to bury the place where we'd just been walking, sending up a cloud of dust so thick we lost each other again, for just one single, terrifying second. And I screamed for him again, only to catch on to his bloody, dusty arm in relief a second later.

I won't leave you, mäi léift.

He couldn't promise that, of course, just as Max couldn't promise what *he* had promised, and I'd been an utter fool to believe even for a second that either of them could.

But believing, being a fool, was the only chance left to me. Perhaps it was the only chance I'd *ever* had. So I took it.

And anyway, he wouldn't allow me to do anything else.

A moment later, the dust settled, and we continued, our progress dwindling to a slow crawl. As we reached the final bend, another cascade of rocks blocked our path. We picked our way through the rubble, my flashlight beam flickering over piles of twisted metal, broken tools, ore, and rock. My head pounded, and my limbs felt less like they were moving and more like they were oozing through some thick, sticky, viscous matter. For the millionth time, I reminded myself to just keep breathing and not to worry about *what* I was breathing. Because what I was breathing was killing me.

"We have to move faster," he said from behind me, choking out the words so painfully it made me wince. "Move as fast as you can without getting out of breath. Can you do that?"

I nodded, despite the growing pit in my stomach.

Because something was wrong. I *knew* it was.

But since I couldn't explain what, we quickened our pace. I dragged him along as best I could amid my own flagging strength, half-running, half-stumbling through narrow scrims of rock. My chest burned with every breath, and black spots danced at the edge of my vision as I tried to make out what remained of the copper ore symbols the slaves had placed to guide their way—now scattered everywhere—while the pit in my stomach spoke louder and louder, telling me that the some-where we thought we were going—the same direction Max had been going—was about to turn out to be nowhere at all. And when that happened, it would be too late.

I stopped.

"What's wrong, Lou? We—"

"We have to turn back. This was the wrong way."

"What? But Max said—"

"The whisper room," I cut him off. "*Whisper.* Don't you see?"

Clearly, he did not. "But Max—"

"Max didn't know everything about the mine because his dad didn't *tell* him everything. And one of the things he didn't tell him was that his panic room was also a breathing room," I said. "And, if needed—"

"An escape room," he finished.

"They built it with an air shaft. I felt it. That's how the bats were getting in and out. And the slaves knew where it was. I think part of their plan was to destroy it before Max's dad could get there. Either that, or use it to escape themselves."

"Shit. If they'd only held out for a few more days, they would have killed him."

"Yup. Shame, isn't it?"

"Do you remember the way?"

"This way." I tugged his wrist, only about 25 percent certain I was right. But soon, things started to look familiar, and I dared to let my heart lift as the passage opened into the dug-out chamber I remembered from before, following the red arrow to the chamber with stalactites dripping from the ceiling like stone icicles. His eyes widened. I knew it now. I was right.

But we almost stumbled into a heap of rubble.

The whisper room was gone.

"We—" The fabric clung to my mouth, gagging me, damp and useless with dirt and dust and tears and sheer terror, my voice hoarse from the gas and smoke from the blast. I was dying already. I'd breathed. I'd held on. I'd believed. I tried. I'd tried so hard for him. "We… we can't get out…"

"Listen to me," he cut in sharply, his eyes locked onto mine. "This isn't the end, not yet. Stay with me, Lou," he urged. "Yeah? Just keep breathing. Don't stop." His eyes darted around us. "Grab that pickaxe."

We clung to each other, gasping and coughing as we began to claw at the debris. I dug the ax into the rubble, ignoring the rocks falling down, slicing and tearing into my skin like blades. He joined me, helping as best as he could, which truthfully wasn't much. Together, we heaved chunks of rock aside to create an opening barely wide enough.

"You first."

"I can't—"

"You can. You're stronger. Follow the air. It'll guide you."

My heart pounded like a death knell in my chest as I pictured the ten tons of stone overhead that could collapse and bury us alive at any moment. But still, I forced myself to breathe, squaring my shoulders. I dropped to my knees and clawed my way through the tunnel. Rocks scraped my skin raw, and dust rushed into my makeshift gas mask, choking me anew. Tempted for the hundredth time to rip the damn thing off, I resisted, knowing it would make it *harder* to breathe, not easier.

"Lou!" he croaked behind me, his labored breathing bouncing off every rock. The shaft sloped upward, barely wide enough for us to slide through on our bellies. I turned to see him dragging forward, face contorted in pain. The rocks had reopened his wounds, and blood now dripped from his head and torso, leaving a gruesome trail behind him.

"I—I can't breathe," I cried. "It's—it's too—"

"Yes, you can."

"I'm tired," I said, slumping against the stone, and all at once, I felt it. Knew it was true. I was more tired than I'd ever been in my entire life.

"Me too, but I'm not letting you give up. Not yet. I promise. Just keep breathing. We're almost there, Lou."

"How do you know?" I demanded between gasps.

"Because I can feel it. I can feel the air. Can't you?"

I closed my eyes, concentrating. He was right. "You're—"

"Dig, Lou!" The words escaped him as pained gasps. "Stop fucking talking to me and dig!"

Tears and sweat clung to my lashes and eyelids, gluing them nearly closed. My hands clenched the handle of the pickaxe. Rocks bit into my knuckles, blood staining every stone beneath me. Every breath stung like a thousand wasps. Every movement screamed for release.

But I moved. Stone by stone, rock by rock, we inched forward. The tunnel grew smaller, more constrictive—a serpentine passage into the belly of the earth. But soon, it stopped.

His labored wheezing echoed around the rocks, merging with the mine's distant groan.

"There's no opening," I coughed. "The rocks won't move anymore. We—we went the wrong way," I moaned desperately.

"No." He gasped. "Oh, fuck no. Drop the pick. Use your hands." He coughed violently, the sound muffled by the thick air and stone.

I plunged back into darkness, hands blindly scraping against the rough surface of a boulder. The skin of my knuckles had ripped away, grime mixing with blood. Desperate sobs hitched in my chest with every inhale of muck and dirt and worms and stone. His own ragged breaths echoed in my ears, still doing his damnedest to help me along, though his voice was no more than a rasp. At last, though, my fingertips brushed against a thin line of cold air leaking from above, and I could barely believe it. I dared to *hope.*

Until a large, cold hand closed around my ankle.

I shrieked, heart pounding wildly as I was yanked backward.

Zombies. Oh God, they were real, and they were—

"Noam?" I stuttered, recoiling at the sight of him, which was barely him anymore, his massive body as much of a smoking, blown-open crater as the mine itself. His face was tissue and bone, one eye missing, though his gaze was still somehow, unerringly focused on me.

"What—what are you—"

"I'm—I'm doing what I came to do." His voice rattled. He was delirious. Closer to dead than I was.

But that wouldn't stop him from killing me.

His grip, still iron, tightened on my ankle again, then let go. I scrambled forward, pulling away from his hand, but he wrestled me back as his lip curled into a bitter rictus, and his reanimated corpse coughed again, a violent, throttling sound.

From behind me, his breath hitched with pain as he turned his body, aiming a weak kick at Noam, who lunged wildly, throwing his arms up.

My scream was cut short as the earth made its complaint again. I could only watch in horror as three boulders, one after another, crashed down, swallowing Noam—and the path we'd been on.

Coughs racked my lungs as I struggled to draw air, waiting for the dust to settle. The silence was broken only by the faint groans of the mine as the earth shifted around us. And then even that faded, replaced by our wheezing.

I turned to him in disbelief. "What—"

"No time." He gasped, pushing me forward with the weight of his dirt-covered, bloodied shoulder. "Go."

I needed no further urging. Acridity had my throat in a vise. I was asphyxiating.

My fingertips scrabbled against the rock, discovering a thin crack. I wedged my fingers into it, digging my nails into the stone until they broke and bled, and blood ran down my arms in rivers. Sweat trickled down my brow, flooding and stinging my eyes. Every breath was a battle, every movement a bloody war.

I gritted my teeth, using every ounce of my remaining strength to heave the rock aside. It budged, revealing another narrow crevice. The groaning sound of the earth intensified as we widened the opening just enough for us to pass through. The air grew thinner, the passage steeper. His coughs and moans of pain filled the darkness, each one driving a stake through my heart. And then all at once, he stopped.

"I—"

I cut him off, reaching back to grip his wrist tightly. "Shut up. Yup, now it's my turn. *Move*, dammit."

With Herculean effort, we edged our way through the crevice, clothes snagging, skin scraping so deep I could swear it was bone on bone.

Behind me, he tried to speak but could only cough again, a rasp that tore at my heart.

"Can you see it?" But the echo of my voice, bouncing off the passage's walls, was the only answer.

"I..." My head whipped around just as a heavy thump reverberated through the narrow tunnel as he collapsed onto his knees, his head dropping forward.

I screamed, scrambling back toward him.

"Go, Lou. Go," he forced out. *"Do not fucking die here."*

"But it's *here*," I sobbed. "It's here. It's right here. See?"

Screaming as I pushed my body beyond all human endurance, I shoved back what I thought was the last stone.

Only to reveal more stone. Cold, dead stone.

I collapsed. Gasping, I turned around, hoping to see any trace of hope left in his eyes.

But his eyes were turned away, unable to focus on me. He was clinging to consciousness by a thread only. "Lou," he rasped. "I'm... I'm so sorry..."

"Don't," I choked out. "Don't you *dare* apologize."

I turned to him, vision blurring as I cupped his face between my hands, marred beyond comprehension as it was.

The eyes were the same, though. Even in darkness were his eyes that had once been light, light to astound and baffle and transform me, even as they wore amber-gold rings of sorrow. Eyes that deserved so much more than *this*.

"Freedom." He choked out the word. "What's that, anyway?"

Ordinarily, I might have laughed at his casual brushing off of one of the fundamental pillars of being human. But now I could only choke and weakly suck more poison into my lungs.

"I already almost died a dozen times this week," he said. "And if—if the only reason I survived any of that is just so I could die here with you—then I'm glad—I'm glad I survived."

"What's your name?" I asked him, gently brushing my bloody fingertips over the place where his hair should be.

"What?"

"Your name. Please. I've never once asked, ever. It's not for me to ask. But I want to call you by it. I want to *know* you. Just once, before—Tell me."

His eyelashes fluttered weakly before his eyelids came to rest. I didn't expect them to reopen.

"What—what do you want it to be?"

"You—you can't be serious."

"I am." He gasped. "You—you made me a person, Lou."

"You were *always* a person."

"You know what I mean. Just—"

"I couldn't. You—"

But of course I knew. I'd known the moment it came to me, long ago, when I lay in his arms, trembling and ecstatic, a billion years before now. When he'd first given me an orgasm in that stupid, frilly pink princess bed that symbolized everything that didn't fucking matter—and somehow, everything that did.

And he knew I knew. He'd known it all along.

"Whisper it."

He was so close, yet I could barely hear him now.

"Whisper it, and—and maybe—"

"Yeah?" A tear slid down my cheek. Then another. The fact that I could still cry at all was a miracle in itself, but the idea that I'd ever *not* cry for him was more preposterous still.

"Yeah."

Like many times before, I curled my body in the empty space beside his. Silly girl, I'd once dared to hope I'd have all the time in the world to do this. That we'd be able to drink each other in, in silence, in peace. But if *this* was the only peace we would ever know—well. I could forge us an altar of stone.

And as softly as anyone could, my lips brushed his ear, and I released the name into it.

As for that name? I'd never planned on telling him.

But I'd never planned on a lot of things.

He didn't respond. His eyes had closed, his chest rising and falling more shallowly with every breath. I counted the seconds, wondering on which one it would stop.

Time.

But like freedom, what was time?

I closed my eyes and joined our hands, though he couldn't entwine or squeeze anymore. But it didn't matter. I had strength enough.

So far, all of his worst moments he'd suffered alone. And even though I couldn't change anything else, now I could change that.

So I whispered it again—over and over, a thousand times—though I couldn't even be sure what he really heard, or really felt, in the seconds before his hand went limp and fell away.

And after that, I couldn't even whisper anymore.

Only breathe.

In breath, my existence coalesced. No other sound, no other sensation. Darkness. Silence.

Breath. In and—

Wait a minute. What was I breathing, anyway?

And just like that, each lost sensation returned. The grit under my back. The burning in my lungs. The distant wail of— yes—sirens.

And *light*. Not a bulb. *Light*.

I opened my eyes. I could barely see, the haze still swallowing even the faintest outlines of our surroundings.

With a weak burst of energy, I scrambled toward the light, which filtered in through a pinprick gap in the stone. To my astonishment, a light tap was all it took to topple it away, a weak wave all it took to get attention.

Then I turned.

His hand still lay next to mine, limp and lifeless.

I brushed my fingers against his face. His skin was cool.

Blind, numb, I could only think to shake him and say it again: the name he'd asked me to choose. And then again. First a whisper, then louder, a raw, keening incantation. As if that would make any goddamn difference in the face of—

But he'd *said*. He'd *said*. Maybe—

The crunch of boots on rocks yanked me back into an even sharper reality, loud and painful. Voices shouted orders I couldn't understand. I just clutched him tighter until other hands descended, pulling me away, hoisting my arms, prying up my fingers.

"Check the boy."

I understood *that*.

One of two female EMTs, brown hair pulled back in a stiff bun, brushed aside a layer of filth off him and bent down, examining him.

"He's still breathing. Get—"

Suddenly, she stopped, and her expression turned hard. She glanced up at her colleague, who followed her gaze back down. To the number burned into his arm.

26

HIM

The university hospital in Heidelberg didn't treat slaves, so the first-year surgical resident the old professor had bribed to stitch my arm up all those years ago had shoved me in a storage closet to do the job. I'd never properly seen a hospital ward, whether for slaves or free people, but when my swollen eyelids finally struggled open, I knew immediately which one *this* was.

No curtains. No windows. No art. No TVs. No flowers. No *clocks*. Just one big room groaning under the assault of fluorescent lights and harsh antiseptic and buzzing machines, packed with flat, narrow beds filled by patients who were no doubt *grateful* to be here because it meant they weren't doing whatever miserable, thankless chores they normally did.

And all solidly, expertly cuffed to their bedrails. Even the ones who, like me, could barely move their wrists.

I had an additional gift: a plastic ID bracelet bearing my slave number. A metal bracelet was soon to follow, no doubt, though it seemed unnecessary given that the same digits were neatly, permanently printed across the same spot. But then, slavery had never been anything but one huge, rigid, rule-obsessed bureaucracy.

And here I was, back in it, forever.

I flexed my fingers, grimacing at the rattle of the chain and the ache that shot up my arm. They'd put me on *something* for the pain, but it didn't feel like an opioid, thank fuck. Surgery must have set some of the broken metacarpals, though my motor skills were still shit. My shattered leg had been operated on, too, and I weakly attempted to lift it. I wouldn't know for sure, I supposed, until I tried to walk. I vaguely remembered a surgeon grumbling that she'd done what she could for me. After that, I remembered nothing. Including whether they'd used the anesthesia as an opportunity to insert another microchip in my arm.

But I had to assume they had.

How long had I been here? Days? Weeks? The room offered no clues, just beeps, whirs, and the occasional pained whimper or rattle of a chain.

I tried to sit up and look around, but a jerk back and a wave of nausea was my only reward, so I threw myself back down.

Ridiculously, one question came to mind: Who the hell was *paying* for this? Slaves didn't get treated unless their owners wanted them treated, and last I'd checked, Keith could barely afford to feed himself, let alone surgeries and medication for a slave he couldn't stand the sight of. And Max—

Max.

The mine, every horrific, suffocating second of it, came back like ten tons of rock crashing down, and I closed my eyes against the images I couldn't unsee, the pain I couldn't unfeel. Blood. Acid. Chains. Melted flesh and shattered bone. Rock upon rock upon rock. Even thinking of it, my lungs struggled, my throat closed up.

Noam. Obadiah. Resi. And *her*.

Crying my name.

The name I didn't actually have and never would. Not that I really cared. I'd gotten along just fine so far without one.

What I did care about was that she wasn't here, and I didn't know if she was okay.

I tried to sit up again, but it was just as futile this time. *Fuck* this place.

And then I thought I had my answer. A hand—a female hand—placed itself over my wrist, over the chains. A hand missing half its fingers.

"*Schwesterchen*," I gasped as the girl I'd known most of her life by that endearment alone nuzzled against me, weeping tears like crystal prisms all down her lightly freckled cheeks, exactly like the last time I'd seen her, seven years ago.

Only this time, with no bars between us.

"*Brudderhäerz*," she wept, brushing over the bandage and covering my cheeks with kisses as my hands snapped back against the chains again, keeping me from holding her, keeping me from the moment I'd envisioned for all that time. But I wouldn't complain.

"*I told them all you'd come for me*," she continued in Luxembourgish. "*I made up the story. And finally, it came true.*"

"*Bass du ok?*[1] How did you get—" I demanded in our native language, my throat scratchy and rough as I forced it to spit out the words.

"Shhh," she said. "*We found a way. And I'm more than okay.*" She kissed my forehead again, stroking the bandages that must have covered my head with her delicate but undeniably work-roughened hand. One I remembered feeling exactly like this when I held them, only... smaller.

---

1. Are you okay?

"And so is Louisa."

I melted back into the bed in relief. And yeah, a little hope.

Idiot. My sister and Louisa were both alive and apparently safe, and so was I, which was already a far better outcome than I'd ever expected. Good enough to pay for with a lifetime of slavery, or a lifetime without Louisa, or, in all likelihood, both. How could I possibly be so greedy and stupid as to hope for anything else?

Maeve paused again. *"I was right about her, yeah?"* she whispered with a smug little wink.

"A, Frechdachs[2]," I said with a throaty laugh. *"Nondikass,"* I hissed as the door of the ward flew open and a middle-aged nurse with severe silver hair marched toward us, having zeroed in on the visitor instantly.

"Can I see some ID, please?"

Shit. I'd come here to *save* Maeve, and now I was putting her in danger all over again for my stupid fucking—

"Yes." To my surprise, Maeve's voice was calm and confident, even speaking English.

And suddenly, I realized that something about her was... different. And no, it wasn't the lack of a metal chain on her wrist—I'd figured, like the other girls, she'd shed that long ago. And no, it *wasn't* her severed fingers, even with my shiver of revulsion at the realization of who and what must have done that. Maybe, instead, it was her golden pixie bob haircut, geometric-patterned athletic-style dress, or the mini backpack she jauntily carried, both of which looked new and chosen with care.

Or the way she didn't tremble, didn't use a title, and didn't immediately cast her eyes down—not for more than a split second, anyway.

---

2. "Naughty badger," an endearment similar to "cheeky monkey."

But the biggest surprise of all came next. She reached into the backpack she was carrying and took out—yes—an ID card.

Before she handed it over, I glimpsed the whole thing: Her photo. Her birthdate. *Her name*, printed right on the laminate in indelible ink.

In other words, this was no con—and Maeve couldn't con to save her life, anyway. She wasn't like me. She was as honest and sincere as a pink unicorn with a rainbow mane, and that was what I loved about her.

Which left me with one word. One question, encompassing a thousand others.

How?

"I'm sorry, Miss," said the nurse, matching up the photo on the card with the girl in front of her, "van Someren."

What?

"But in this ward, the only visitors allowed are the slaves' owners. I'm afraid you'll have to leave."

Maeve drew herself up with a dignity she'd always had but had never—in all the time *I'd* known her anyway—been allowed to use.

"Oh," she said in slow, careful, perfect English. "I'll go."

And then my sister, Miss Maeve van Someren, gave one last tear-streaked look at me and swept out of the room, the heels of her chunky sandals tapping on the linoleum.

When she'd left, the nurse, silently and with little enthusiasm, began to check my vitals.

"How long have I been here?" I ventured to ask. "Ma'am," I added with a sigh when she didn't answer right away and instead kept passive-aggressively tightening the blood pressure monitor.

"Given your head injuries, Dr. Perez put you in an induced coma for a week to reduce the chance of brain swelling," she responded, clearly annoyed by the fact that a mouth was suddenly attached to the body she was manhandling. "Now that you're awake, she said we can free up your bed."

I sank down again, closing my eyes briefly. I hated how servile and defeated my voice sounded when I spoke again. But if I wanted to know, I had to get her to answer. "So I'm going back to my master, then, ma'am?"

My master, whose house I'd been assured I'd never again be allowed into. Only the mines remained, but if that were the case, shouldn't Keith have just let me die where they'd found me, cut out the middleman, and saved himself thousands of dollars in hospital bills?

"Guess again."

Oh.

HER

Two weeks ago, I'd crawled out of the rubble of a collapsed copper mine, and still, *this* was the hardest place I'd ever been in.

Iron gates ushered us into a vast, labyrinthine government facility seemingly more suited to holding animals than the humans it contained, detained behind layer after layer of chain link and steel bars like some kind of sadistic wedding cake.

After five minutes here, I already knew I'd never A) Feel clean again and B) Find my way out, at least alone. And still, a short, humorless, uniformed government slave handler named Deare led us deeper, each gate obediently clanging closed behind us with a sound that echoed off the vaulted ceiling.

Breathe.

I did, only to be rewarded with the scent of acrid disinfectant filling my lungs, which itself masked a more pungent odor. The bare, colorless cinderblock walls muffled distant shouting, the scuffling and clinking of shackled limbs. It all made me feel tiny and vulnerable, though I knew the inmates here, for the most part, weren't dangerous. Just very, very unlucky.

We walked on. Through seemingly infinite passages and corridors, our footsteps echoing on the linoleum, beneath the flickering yellow fluorescent lights I'd come to associate, now, indelibly, with slavery. Occasionally, I caught a glimpse, in the distance, of a shackled figure in a gray scrub uniform being led by a handler, and my stomach churned hard enough for me to worry that I wouldn't be able to keep my lunch down. I tightly clutched my handbag—searched thoroughly by the guard at the gate—my bare fingernails digging hard into the leather.

But perhaps the strangest thing of all was that the shoulder I leaned into for comfort—the arm that drew me close—was my *father's*.

In the days and weeks since the mine, I hadn't dared say it —dared to *think* it—but eventually, I'd had to face the truth: Keith Wainwright-Phillips was different.

Getting me back alive was certainly part of it, given that his second-to-last call from Agent Labrecque had been to inform him that the Cebolla Canyon mine had collapsed with me in it. I'd at one point thought I'd hated my father, but he still didn't deserve to think the worst, even for a second. And once I realized *that*, it wasn't much of a stretch to realize that I still *loved* him. And that I was *glad* I still loved him.

Accepting the truth about Ethan, of course, was part of what had changed him, too. And if he couldn't have him back— if there was nothing he could change, for the arm of the law that had enslaved his son appeared long indeed—well, it made sense that he'd turn his attention elsewhere.

And the last ingredient, undoubtedly, was that they'd dropped the investigation into his involvement in the White Cedar debacle.

"New evidence has surfaced exonerating you from any

wrongdoing, financial or otherwise," Labrecque had informed him nasally over the speakerphone in his study earlier that week. Her disappointment was almost tangible. I'd listened from the other side of the door, breathing the way I was supposed to—three seconds in, five seconds out.

I knew exactly where the evidence had come from, of course: the flash drive in the envelope I'd given Erica, and that Erica had handed over to the police. But *only* the flash drive— nothing else. The note, sadly, was gone. His chip had been destroyed, and the scientific formula that had removed it, for now, would remain carefully concealed. As much as I wanted to shout to the rooftops about my boy genius and what he had discovered, I knew Erica was right to want to keep it all under wraps. In the hands of the wrong person, the formula could be a dangerous cudgel—they'd seen that already. Besides, the only people who could be trusted to do anything with it were currently, well, indisposed. And lastly, the money, as it turned out, had already been spoken for.

"I used it to free Maeve," Erica had explained immediately upon her arrival in my hospital room earlier in the week. For a few seconds, the room had gone silent but for the dull hum of machines. "I think it's safe to assume it's what he intended it for," Erica had gone on calmly as if this were the kind of revelation she divulged all the time. "Don't you think?"

"Wait, *what*?"

Erica frowned. "I told you, I—"

"No, no, I get it, I just—*how*?"

I couldn't believe it and didn't understand it, but it was true. Maeve was free. Her brother, through his genius—in many ways—had done exactly what he came here to do.

And wherever he was, he probably had absolutely no idea.

During my three days in the hospital, I'd clung to a ridiculous hope that things would somehow turn out okay, even after the EMTs had spotted the number on his wrist, ripped us apart, whisked us off in different medevac helicopters, and in general made it abundantly clear that they wouldn't turn out okay at all.

Fact was, we'd never even had a chance. I'd known that from the start. I'd panicked over it, and he'd talked me down, and that was the one and only reason I was alive. But now I was stunned to realize that *he'd* known it, too. He'd fought his way through the belly of hell itself knowing that if he got out alive, slavery would be his only reward. He'd fought for a life that wasn't one.

But mostly, he'd fought for me.

And that was why, while the nurses in my private room in my well-appointed hospital had treated my wounds like clock-makers, humming and sponging and rubbing me down with a rosy-smelling salve, pumping oxygen into my lungs and taping and retaping bandages to my throat, I had to fight the urge to beat them all off and demand to know where he was. What kind of treatment he was getting, if any. And if, now, anybody had even bothered to tell him that his sister was free.

Which I still had to get to the bottom of. "I thought Max—"

"Max transferred ownership of her to me for a dollar, electronically, just before you drove to the mine," Erica had replied patiently. "Good thing, too, because if he hadn't, she might have been detained indefinitely."

"Why?"

"Because he's been declared dead, and there are going to be years of legal wrangling over his money as part of the White Cedar fallout. All of his accounts are frozen, and they'll stay that way for a long time."

Dead? I didn't believe it. Not for a minute. Not for a *second*. And I suspected Erica didn't, either, given how she glossed right over it.

"Will you miss him?" I asked her.

"The abolitionist community will miss him," Erica said primly. "What *I* think is immaterial. And by the way, if you're wondering why we still had to pay the manumission fee for Maeve when her last sale price was a dollar, the government caught onto that little trick some time ago, unfortunately. I tried it with Milagros, too, with no luck."

Milagros. "Oh, shit, Erica. How—"

On the professor's face *now* appeared the biggest smile I'd ever seen on it. "She's fine, Louisa. I left her room five minutes ago, where she was planning out where she'll put her 'woke up like this' tattoo."

So Milagros had survived. Maeve had survived. *We'd* survived. But Max Langer, the man who'd confidently under-promised, had not yet overdelivered.

Technically.

Look, yes, we'd left him in the mine. Yes, we hadn't seen him make it out. But if there was one thing I knew about Max Langer—if there was one thing *I'd* been *taught* by someone who knew him even better than I did—it was that that man didn't do *anything* without an ulterior motive. Even die.

But fuck, that private jet sure would have been nice. The offshore accounts, too. Because without those, my boy and I were right back where we'd started.

Unable to touch.

"We'll find your boy," was all Erica had said before she left, though not before encountering my father in the doorway and exchanging a long glance. I had no idea what it meant, but given everything else, it fell near the bottom of my list of things to investigate.

And that brought me to my father, who, for a change, had said nothing at all. He'd just sat quietly beside my bed, clutching a disposable cup of terrible coffee, studying my face as if I were some stranger he vaguely remembered from long, long ago.

Instead, during the day, he'd *read*. Out loud. The way he used to before bedtime, every night, without fail, despite having a million other things he could have been doing. But this time around, instead of fairy tales, he read from my favorite novel, *Les Misérables*—in English, of course—and from *his* favorite novel, *War and Peace*, a book he'd been recommending I read for years, though I'd never gotten around to it because, come on. And after a while, he'd given up. But now, his rich voice rolling over the words, both familiar and unfamiliar, was warmer and thicker than any blanket they could drape over me, especially when I would awaken to the sound of someone screaming and realize it was me. And realize I could still breathe. And realize my boy's hand had not gone limp in mine all over again. It simply wasn't there at all.

But my father's was.

In the greatest confusion, there is still an open channel to the soul.

Each evening, as the hospital lights dimmed, he would close the book and just look at me. And every evening, I expected the interrogation—the one I'd spent the past few weeks dodging, even *before* the mine—to start, but it never did. And the minute I realized he was *never* going to demand that I speak was the minute I decided I would.

I told him a lot about some things and a little about everything. About Erica, about Ivy, about Max, but most of all, about *him*. And ultimately, of the escape. *Our* escape.

And he listened, silently, a range of emotions flickering— shock, anger, relief—but he never interrupted. He never invalidated or objected or presumed I felt or thought anything different than what I told him I did. For the first time, perhaps, he was seeing his daughter as a person. Just as he now—ironically and too late—saw his son. And just as he saw—

Well, I wasn't pushing my luck. My dad was different, at any rate.

"You nearly died in that mine, Loulou," he finally stated, voice raw and overcome. "Trying to save *him*." A slave, was what he was thinking but didn't say.

"Yes," I said. "I did, Daddy. Because he saved me first. More than once and in more than one way. And what's more, with the evidence in that flash drive, he saved *you*."

My father's eyes were as glassy and far away as the distant mountains, and he said nothing more, just looked down at the cup in his hand, then back up, away from the drop of liquid that had suddenly appeared on its top. One that definitely wasn't coffee and one that prompted me to propose something that left even *me* aghast.

"Find him."

He looked up in surprise.

"Maybe you can't find Ethan yet," I said. "But you can find *him*."

I said nothing about what might happen after that. I knew it might not be what I hoped for. I knew I might regret it altogether. I knew my father could change his mind, or change it *back*. But I also knew we had to try.

And that's exactly what he began trying to do, the next day, right after driving me home from the hospital. But the bureaucracy would tell him nothing, and with my boy's microchip gone—and apparently no new chip inserted—the slave database was useless.

It took another full week, just before Christmas and my final exams, which for his sake I was determined to pass, though my concentration was shot and the idea of going back to psychology or English or *o-chem*—after all that—seemed frankly absurd.

Not to mention that I was starting to wonder when I would have to face the fact that he might, in fact, be dead after all.

At any rate, that's when Ivy's nursing school contact in a different hospital across town had tipped us off that he was there, with his treatment being paid for by—of all things—the government.

But it was already too late. Immediately upon learning the news, according to Ivy, Maeve had rushed there to *finally* see him with her own eyes. But she'd gotten all of five minutes with him before he'd been moved again—to my despondence, into the same detention center Maeve had been freed from. On orders of the government. Indefinitely. With no explanation. Even Labrecque couldn't offer us an explanation because she didn't *know* the explanation.

Well, shit. There was no question about involving my father, now. Whatever he planned to do with his slave when he got him back, it couldn't be worse than being *there*.

Daddy, once he learned *that*, had thrown himself into the task of getting him returned to him as zealously as he'd once worked to get *rid* of him. Of course, with Max Langer out of the picture, he was also now back to not having a job, so he didn't exactly lack time. Mostly ignoring the other slaves—though I doubted they were complaining—he had sat slouched in his study for hours upon hours, unshowered, unshaven, guzzling coffee, having to be reminded to eat, dialing number after number, making demands over the phone as aggressively as I remembered him working during his early days in the corporate world, when creating the largest buffer possible between his family and poverty had been his one and only ambition. When he had motivation. When he had a *goal*.

My father, when he wanted to be, was good with goals.

And that's when Agent Wheatley had called.

He was back on the job, apologetic, and invited Daddy and me to come to the detention center the following day, where he'd explain everything.

"Explain everything?!" my father had thundered. "There *is* no justifiable explanation for why you've wrongfully detained my slave for over two weeks and—"

"Daddy," I'd interrupted softly, from just on the other side of the door.

"We'll be there." He'd hung up.

We. And here we were, at the end of our journey into this human kennel, Deare pausing to usher us into a tiny, windowless cinderblock room where another uniformed handler named Tarrant—like most of them, lumpy and buzzcut, with a bit of an extra chin—waited, along with three stiff-backed chairs arrayed in a row.

For me, Daddy, and Wheatley.

And then, the door on the other side of the room flung open, and here *he* was, being tugged roughly through it on the end of a short chain lead linked to his cuffs and held by yet another handler. Muzzled, shackled, the restraints all joined together with enough chains to restrain a rabid tiger—albeit one who was stiff-jointed, limping, and obviously in pain just about everywhere. I stifled a cry. God, this place really was for animals.

And when his lead chain had been attached to the ring in the floor, he dared to flick his eyes up.

And when he saw me—*oh*.

Fuck it all. I ran toward him, swallowing the name I had the nearly uncontrollable urge to cry out. I hadn't spoken it aloud to anyone yet, not even Maeve. After all, it wasn't mine to give away anymore. It was his, provided he even remembered it.

And if he didn't? Maybe, technically, it had never existed.

Maybe it never would. Not like it mattered. All that mattered was that he was here.

He jerked on the chain, trying to reach out to me. Before I could touch him, however, a flash of lightning struck me blind.

"Stand back," Tarrant barked, having fired up the sizzling prod as if he meant to use it on *me*.

I screamed and froze to the spot, immediately back in that white mausoleum of a room, where the leather and the cold marble walls had swallowed the echo of my screams. My father reached out and pulled me back into a fierce bear hug.

And then, as I tried to steady my breath, as I forced myself to look at my boy again, as the weight of everything that had happened crashed over me—I heard his voice.

"The fuck?"

I turned, stunned.

"Arlo?"

27

HIM

Institutional life had its rhythms, ones I'd never really forgotten, ones I could have easily readjusted to under most circumstances. Sleep, eat, work, eat, sleep. Simple. But most institutions—mines, farms, factories—also had certainty. They owned you, and unless a miracle occurred, you weren't getting out. You accepted that, or you died.

Here, there was no certainty. I didn't know anything. How long I'd be in this place, why, or what had to happen for me to get the fuck out of it. And *that* was what was killing me.

They'd given me pain meds at the hospital the morning of my arrival, but they'd long since worn off and nobody seemed interested in giving me more. Besides, I figured it was around eight, and I'd probably missed pill distribution—if they even had one. At any rate, they dragged me limping into processing, where, like usual, I was stripped naked, scrubbed raw, thrown into a starched gray scrub uniform, and led to the chain-link enclosure I'd be sharing with sixty other guys, most of whom were already snoring. I stuck out my hands lazily through a hole in the link so the handler could remove my chains, then collapsed on an empty metal bunk with a sigh, wishing I could run my hands over my scalp just to see if my hair was growing back yet, like the stupid, vain bastard I was, even in here. But I didn't yet have enough range of motion to put my hands behind my head, so all I could do was tuck them in close to my chest. I blinked against the lurid lighting, which dug crude patterns into my retinas. All in all, I'd prefer the darkness of the mine.

I blinked. What a place to cry. *That* wasn't happening.

Maeve had spent time in a place like this, I reminded myself. Thanks to me, she was out. And that was enough to let me sleep. A little bit.

"Hey."

What now?

The guy next to me poked me on my bad shoulder, just as my eyelids were falling shut, causing me to jerk in pain. "You the one who blew up the mine?"

I turned toward my bunkmate, likely a farm laborer only a bit older than me, though his leathery face made him look about ten years beyond that.

"Well, I didn't actually—"

"My father got sent there when I was six. Never saw him again."

"Yeah," I said with the trace of a smile. "Yeah, I blew it up."

The guy nodded with satisfaction and turned his face away. "Nice."

Just wait till he found out about the chips.

I woke up from a nightmare about two hours later, gasping, coated in a sheen of sweat. My heart pounded desperately against my ribcage as I clawed at the cold metal of my bunk and pressed my forehead to it, grounding myself with the chill. It seemed to be more or less a variant on the same theme—a girl's hand. But the wrong girl's hand. The wrong girl with wispy blond hair, blue eyes, and a hand that proceeded to put a collar on my neck and jerk me toward her so fast it stole my breath, giggling at me until I woke up.

"Bad dream?" the guy asked from the adjacent bunk, not unkindly.

"Yeah," I admitted, massaging my shoulder weakly against the bedframe for some kind of relief from the physical pain, if not the mental kind. They were both getting worse.

"Dreams in here..." My bunkmate trailed off, running a rough hand over his even rougher face. "They grip you like reality never could."

I wasn't sure yet which I preferred—the dreams I knew, or the reality I didn't. Right now, frankly, I wished I could be like Maeve and just make up my own.

The next day, I still didn't get any pain pills. But I did get a work assignment: the laundry room, probably because they thought it would be less taxing on my injuries, though it wasn't. It was like all other institutional slave labor: a cacophony of clattering machines, wet sloshing, and overseers screaming at me to work faster or else. And as the rhythms washed away grime, they also washed away most of my thoughts. Good thing, too, because I was sick of my thoughts. They were all about either the past or the future—the past was tragic, and the future was just one huge, terrifying blank.

And that was when one of the more sadistic handlers approached me, toting enough chains to bind an elephant, all dangling down from his arm. "Your master's here, slave," he said, grinning. "Hands."

I closed my eyes as the cold metal closed around my wrists and more chains snaked around me, almost grateful for it. At least it meant answers. Even if they weren't the ones I wanted.

Besides, at least in the visiting room, it was the right girl.

Louisa. Alive, whole, a raindrop on scorched earth. A long

scar snaking in and out of the burn scars on her neck, her gray eyes forced to cry for me again as I kneeled in chains. And if this was the last time she'd ever see me—which I had to consider, despite the cautious optimism I was desperately trying to kill— I should have died in the mine. Free, or as close to it as I'd probably ever get.

And then a *real* blast from my past appeared.

"Good to see you too, man," said Orbital Dynamics Marketing Manager Arlo Callwood—or whatever his name and title really was—with a small smile, crossing his arms. He shrugged off his tailored jacket, revealing the muscles underneath, though he didn't take the proffered chair. Instead, he looked at the handler, gesturing to my chains. "This necessary?"

"We tried," broke in Keith, who'd seemingly undergone a brain transplant, not that I was going to question it.

"It's protocol, sir."

"Protocols can be flexible," replied Arlo. "You'll realize that when you move up the ranks."

The handler sputtered. "But my commanding officer—"

Enough with the arguing over this. "All things being equal, *sir*," I dared to interrupt with an exaggerated clearing of my throat, "I'd rather stay in chains if it means I can get an explanation sooner."

"Fair enough," said Arlo. "First off, as you probably guessed, my name isn't really Arlo. It's Emmanuel. Agent Emmanuel Wheatley, of the federal white collar fraud division. I've been undercover at Orbital Dynamics for the past year and a half. Initially, at least, I was investigating reports of financial anomalies. But I'd suspected for some time that the anomalies were more than financial."

"Wait." I would have said something clever, but in this case,

I was actually speechless. "Hold on. Did you *know*? About me, I mean? The whole *night*?"

Arlo—Emmanuel—shook his head. "Yes. And no."

"I don't—" I stole a glance at the dagger-glaring Tarrant, then stared at the floor again quickly. I'd have to fall into the old habits again, if it was between getting the whole story and another zap to the neck.

"It was me who first proposed the trip to Phoenix to Corey, actually," the agent continued. "Who's dead, by the way. They pulled the plug." He coughed. Nobody blinked. "It seemed clear to me that if there was something weird going on, it wouldn't be in San Francisco but operating much closer to Langer himself. The trip seemed like a prime opportunity to get into Langer HQ and see things from the inside. Corey, of course, didn't know who I really was. But I sure did my homework on Corey, and when I got there, I knew immediately that *you* weren't him."

"Ah, fuck. Well, I hope you had fun watching me make an idiot out of myself. Congratulations. *Sir*," I tacked on with audible irritation.

"No, I didn't."

I raised my head curiously, though not without another sidelong glance at the handler.

"Because even though I knew who you *weren't*, I didn't know who you *were*. It was clear to me you really did work for Langer, but other than that, you didn't seem to exist. I went so far as to think you might be in witseg, a fugitive, a competitor's plant, or even doing the same thing I was, as an operative for a foreign intelligence agency. The accent, you know."

My hands clenched involuntarily in the chains. Wait, so had I fucked up, or hadn't I?

"I didn't want or need to blow your cover," Wheatley went on, "so I didn't."

I bit my lip and looked at my hands again. "But did you—"

"No. The answer is no. Never, not once, did it ever occur to me you might be a slave."

Really? I let out a short laugh. "No offense, sir, but you should probably turn in your badge."

"Damn right I should. You fucked everything up pretty much from beginning to end. Now, looking back, *I* feel like the idiot. Anyway, shoddy police work on my part or a good con on yours, I'm impressed."

"Thanks," I said. "I'll take it, if you insist. Just one question, though... What about Felix?"

"Felix, sadly for him, is just Felix."

Somehow, despite everything, we both laughed.

"Even doing what I do, I've never seen a slave successfully try to pass for a free man—for that long, anyway. Something always gives them away." He paused. "You know what you did is a crime in itself, right?"

I scoffed. "So what are you gonna do? Arrest me?"

"No. Punishment is for your master to decide. But in the eyes of the law, you do belong in a mine."

"I know. But I had my reasons." My voice was quiet. One of the reasons I'd done it sat in the chair across from me now, and I couldn't look at her if I wanted to keep this conversation going.

"I know you did. And what you did took balls. Helping those girls—"

"Like you care," I grumbled. "They're slaves."

"They're people."

My head snapped up.

"Things are changing in the feds, you know. I'm one of the ones trying to change them."

"You told me you took a university course," Louisa broke in.

She'd been listening as closely as I had, while Keith just stared at the whole thing like we were speaking in tongues.

"I did," Wheatley said. "From one of Erica Muller's associates, in fact—a former fugitive, one my own father tried to put away back when *he* was at the agency. But beyond that, I've seen evidence with my own eyes that the system is broken, that the line between free and slave is an accident of fate. You're living proof, man. That evidence you gathered—without it, we'd be investigating and probably charging the wrong man." He looked at Keith.

"Yeah, and look where it got me," I muttered.

"Look, I'm under no illusions that it was easy for you. But you saved their lives, your master's reputation and future, and probably Langer's conglomerate, or most of it. White Cedar is fucked, of course, but Orbital Dynamics will live on. Langer's shares will eventually go to his lenders, and the board will appoint somebody else as CEO."

"Yeah," Louisa cut in. "Making billions for everyone at the top, while he kneels here in chains. How is that justice?"

"Loulou, what *are* they teaching you at that school?" Keith muttered.

"That said," Wheatley continued, ignoring them both, "I know it's your own future you're thinking about now, and I don't blame you. Did you know Mr. Wainwright-Phillips has been fighting nonstop around the clock since you got thrown in here to get you back?"

I blinked. "He—he has?"

"Yes," Louisa said, her hand on her father's arm. "I couldn't believe it either. But he has."

"And now, it's my turn to apologize because it was me and my colleagues who were preventing that from happening. I couldn't risk anything happening to you while I bought myself time to get back on the job. It's also why you haven't been re-chipped. Oh, and by the way, whatever happened to your chip is none of my business," he added pointedly.

Louisa looked as relieved as I felt. Whatever Wheatley knew or suspected about the breakthrough, it would remain safe—for now. Idly, I wondered if Louisa had told her father about it. In any case, he'd invested in White Cedar, so he had to at least suspect. Not like it mattered with me in chains, and Langer—for all intents and purposes, anyway—dead.

"But now," Wheatley said, shifting his focus back to Keith but still addressing me, reaching for some papers and a pen folded inside his suit jacket. "Your master can sign some paperwork right now and you're fr—well, you're out of here, at least."

"Nice catch," I muttered, watching Keith accept the papers and sign.

So that was it, then. I had my answer. I was going back. To be sold, almost certainly. Keith desperately needed the money, after all. Maybe not to a mine—he didn't seem to hate me *that* much anymore. After all, he could have just left me to rot. But somewhere quiet and out of the way. An office? Maybe somewhere I could still do science, if I kept on being lucky and good. In other words, back to business as usual. Before my mission to find Maeve. Before—

"Stop," Louisa said.

Keith did, pen poised melodramatically in the air.

"I want an answer now, Daddy. *He* wants an answer." She met my eyes. "So give it to him. What happens after this?"

"I—" Keith sputtered as if he hadn't known this was coming.

"You already lost Ethan, Daddy," she said softly. "Don't lose me. And you will if you don't do the right thing."

Keith took a huge breath, and the pen dropped out of his hand. "If things were different—" he began.

"If things were different, what?" Louisa prompted, not unkindly. "What would you tell him, Daddy?"

A long pause.

And then, to my utter disbelief, he answered.

"I'd—I'd look him in the eye and tell him to stand up," he said.

We all gaped. And Keith was gasping, perspiring, like he was struggling to breathe. A religious epiphany could do that to someone, I'd heard. And if I were being honest, the moment was doing something similar to me.

"I'd tell them to take those chains off him once and for all. And—and I'd tell him that he never has to bow his head to anyone, ever again."

The room went silent.

Even the handler looked stunned.

"Do it," Wheatley commanded Tarrant.

Tarrant hesitated. But with me no longer in his custody, he had no choice.

Dazed, I held out my hands—for the last time?—as he went to work on no fewer than three different padlocks. One by one, they clattered to the cold concrete.

I rose from my knees, my joints screaming after being frozen like that for an hour.

And then, before I had time to process it, Louisa crossed the floor in a stride.

I watched as Keith shakily capped the pen and closed his eyes, like the scene before him was physically painful to watch. And for him, it probably was—Louisa's silky hand gently entwined with mine, her curves yielding to a body encased in the plain gray clothing of servitude. And then, as if things weren't bad enough for Keith, I kissed his only daughter, and it was *not* a chaste kiss. After all this time? Oh, fuck, no. I gave her my open mouth with two weeks—make that twenty years—of deep, insatiable, pent-up need, and she returned it like the starving warrior she was.

"It's okay, don't mind us," Wheatley remarked, arms folded.

"So then—" Louisa prompted, flushed and out of breath, her grip still firm and solid in mine, waiting for her father to regain his voice and sanity.

"I can't afford it," said Keith. "I'm sorry."

I felt my body crumple along with hers, our shared swoop of hope crushed like a snowdrop under a truck tire.

Keith swallowed again, looking stricken. "Loulou, the debts haven't gone anywhere. The legal costs from the White Cedar investigation only piled onto them. His sale price was considerable, as you know, and there are administrative fees on top of that. I can't just make the money appear. Quite honestly, I can't afford to keep him now and still keep the house, too. I—I'm going to have to sell him."

Yup, there it was.

"The bracelet needs to be replaced within thirty days," said Tarrant, who seemed weirdly gleeful now that things were no longer deviating from the routine. "And you'll need to make an appointment at the regional slavery bureau to have him re-chipped. We don't handle that here."

In my arms, I felt Louisa's shoulders start to rack. I just squeezed her, as weak as *I* felt. It wasn't supposed to be this way, I thought, all while mentally beating the fuck out of myself for ever daring to hope it *wouldn't*.

"It's okay, *mäi léift*," I whispered rapidly, desperately brushing her long curls back from her ear, not sure she could even hear me and definitely sure I didn't believe it. "I'll be okay. We'll figure it out. We always do."

"Look, man," Wheatley spoke up, "you deserve better than this. You really do. Botched con aside, you obviously have a gift —maybe a few gifts."

Keith broke in, clearly tired of being the bad guy when, for once, he was trying *not* to be. "I *told* you if I—"

"I understand, Mr. Wainwright-Phillips. Really," Wheatley said, holding up a hand and addressing me again. "Actually, I suspected all along this would be the situation, which brings me to the whole reason I'm here."

"Which is?" I asked. *Please*, no more reversals. Peace was all I prayed for as I clung to Louisa, the peace to keep my arms wrapped as protectively around her as I could get them, for as long as I could keep them there. As if I'd never get another chance. Which I might not.

"The truth is that your case has gained some attention," Arlo—no, Agent Wheatley—said carefully. "There were... interested parties at the federal level."

I stared at him. "*Interested parties?*"

He hesitated. "Your involvement in the mine collapse has raised a lot of questions. Not just about you, but about how you managed to slip through the cracks. The lack of a chip. Your intelligence. Your connections. And, well," he said after a long pause, "partially to get them to quit asking questions, I suggested we repurpose you. Well, 'hire' was the word I used. 'Repurpose' was theirs."

"What?" I looked at Louisa, then her father, but they looked as confused as I was. "Paid?"

"Well, a stipend. Your real payment will be your freedom, once your contract is up," said Wheatley.

The words didn't hit the way he probably thought they would. *Freedom.* The idea was so foreign, so distant, it may as well have been another language. One of the ones I didn't speak.

"Mr. Wainwright-Phillips, rest assured you'll be compensated by the government for our use of the boy," he continued. "And I should mention that this is a one-time offer, one that not everyone gets. Frankly, it was a pretty hard sell on my part to get the top brass to let me offer it to you at all, given your... well, history."

My head was spinning. No more reversals, I'd said, but this... "So I'd be a cop?"

"Not a cop. Regulations prevent us from accepting slaves or former slaves as cops. You'd be a consultant. On forensics, foreign intelligence, that kind of thing. Maybe even some undercover work, eventually. And after some training, naturally. In any case, I promise we'd find a way to use you that takes advantage of your gifts. However." Wheatley paused, and even before he said the next part, my stomach fluttered. "You'd have to agree to have no contact with your owners, former owners and their families, or anyone from your past life, as long as you're in this job. For security purposes, we need to ensure that you're loyal to no one but us. It's nonnegotiable. Break the rules, the deal is off, and then God knows where you end up. Simple as that."

Louisa's face, unsurprisingly, went sheet-white.

"And *my* family?" I asked weakly as the understanding that this wasn't a joke started to sink in, little by little.

"Your family, too."

I blinked. Maybe I was even shaking a little, too, because I hadn't felt like this since Max Langer had sauntered into the garden past a herd of ravenous javelinas. A group of free people —authority figures—my *master*—were talking *to* me, not about me. About choice. About freedom *itself*. And I didn't have the first goddamn clue how to respond.

All I knew was that when this was over, fuck. Could I please relax with some bourbon and a good research paper on molecular orbital theory?

In the end, I did the only thing I could think of. I looked at Louisa.

"We'll—we'll take care of Maeve," she said, her voice somehow both shaky and full of conviction, though she must have known that she might be helping kiss goodbye the very thing she'd been hoping for. "Between me and Erica and Milagros and Ivy, she'll have the best support system anyone could possibly ask for.

"It'll be dangerous," Louisa said. It wasn't a question.

Wheatley swallowed. He wasn't fooling anyone. I'd heard stories. I knew what "repurposing" meant. It meant I'd be sent to places where my "skills" could be put to better use. Places I might not come back from.

A tool by another name.

"So what?" My voice was hoarse, like I'd been shouting for hours when I hadn't said much of anything at all. "I get handed a mission and sent off to do the dirty work nobody else wants to do? Disposable as ever, just with a new uniform?"

Wheatley didn't deny it. "You'd be given proper training," he said instead as if that changed anything. "You'd be protected. I'll personally ensure you'll be just another member of the team and treated as free to the extent the law allows. You'll live in approved housing owned by us. You can come and go as you please, within certain limits."

Briefly, I gazed down at the chains he'd shed. "So from slavery to jail to a... nicer jail?"

Louisa elbowed me, right in my bad arm—well, my worse arm.

"For how—how long?" I asked Wheatley. My heart was pounding again, and the goddamn room, of course, was utterly silent. I was convinced everyone could hear it.

"Three years." Wheatley coughed. "But after that, you're free. Completely and permanently."

"If he's still alive," spoke up Louisa.

He hesitated. "In the interests of complete transparency,

some of the missions will be dangerous, and I can't guarantee his safety. But that's also part of being on the team. There are no certainties in this job, for any of us."

"And can he refuse?" Louisa asked, voice barely a whisper. She had to know that even if I were sold—or if they ever let me leave this detention center, which wasn't certain—there was a chance, albeit a small one, that we could still see each other. But with the feds, zero. Hell of a choice, as usual.

"Of course," said Wheatley. "And so can your father."

I took one last deep breath. "Lou, look at me. Yeah?" I held her trembling shoulders as best I could as she, bless her soul, tried to focus as best *she* could. "I won't do it. If you want me to, I'll—" I looked frantically at Keith, of all people, though he looked just about as baffled as I felt.

Then, to his shock, he stepped forward and lightly touched my shoulder. "It's up to you, son," he said, totally awkwardly and unhelpfully. But kind of nice just the same. "But I... I think it's a good offer. Better than your other options."

My other options.

Chains. Muzzles. A number on my wrist. Being sold off to some rich bastard who at best would stick me in the corner of a drafty office taking dictation, at worst would put me in a cage. Forever.

I swallowed hard and turned back to Louisa.

Her face was pale, her lips pressed together so tightly they almost disappeared. But she met my gaze head-on.

"It's your choice," she whispered. "But if you take it, I won't make you wait for me."

That hit worse than anything else. Worse than the mine, worse than the beatings, worse than the fear I'd lived with my whole life.

"I don't—" I stopped because I didn't fucking *know*.

Did I want this? Did I *want* anything, now that my one and only mission for the past three years was complete?

"I'll stay," I said firmly.

"Goddammit, you stupid fucking idiot, do you *still* not know me at all?" Louisa growled and actually *shoved* me. Really. I almost fell. "How the fuck do you think I could possibly ever live with myself if I made you stay in slavery indefinitely for *me*?"

Okay, wrong answer. But we'd *had* this conversation, long ago, on the night the clouds had covered the stars. As if we'd always known that it would somehow come down to this. But *why*?

Because, dumb fuck, for the hundredth time, freedom isn't free. And the world seems determined to teach you that if it kills you.

I swallowed, throat dry, and tried again. "Three years, Lou. No contact. You wouldn't be free, either, waiting for me. And I would never make you do it."

She shook her head helplessly. "So——" She never finished. Just melted into my arms, sobbing, tears slowly soaking through the rough fabric of my uniform shirt.

And then I started memorizing. The exact achromatic gray of her eyes, the radius and angle of the Archimedean spirals her curls made as they fell over her shoulder, the acute angle of the curve of her cheekbones, the kinetic energy present when she flushed from the anger and fear and grief of it all. I chronicled it all like a lab report: the elasticity of her skin in my arms, the weight and volume of her body, the oxygen she consumed when her breath drew in sharply when I kissed her. And I filed it all away in the same vast archives of my brain that had once been reserved only for theories and equations and formulas and chess openings.

Because it was all that mattered now.

I turned back to Wheatley. "When do we start?"

Her grip faltered.

"Tomorrow," he replied. "You'll be transferred to a secure location, and your training will begin immediately." His voice softened, just slightly. "This is a good deal, man. You're lucky."

Lucky. Like the sevens that began the number burned into my arm.

Keith just exhaled, rubbing his temples. "That's it, then?" he asked Wheatley.

Louisa's nails dug into my skin, but I barely felt it. And she was barely breathing. "No," she whispered. "Not yet."

I turned back to her just in time for her to throw herself against me, her arms around my neck, her whole body pressing in.

"You think if you hold me tight enough, the world won't tear us apart?" I whispered.

She pulled back just enough to look at me. "I—I'm—"

"Because when you hold me like that ... it's enough for me to believe that maybe you could. Enough for me to believe in you, in me, in souls, in God, in anything at all. In other words, woman," I said, "You just made a miracle."

The brave little smile she gave was everything. "I love you, you know," she whispered fiercely. "I love you, I love you, I love you, and I don't care who hears it."

I closed my eyes and swallowed the lump in my throat. My arms locked around her on instinct, my face buried in her hair, breathing her in, memorizing every single thing about her because after this, there would be *nothing*. "I love you, too."

And over her head, I met my master's eyes dead-on. Kept them there. So Keith knew what I was asking—no, not asking.

Ordering.

Take care of her.

28

EIGHT MONTHS LATER

Every slave dealer on both sides of the Atlantic knew that I, Sébastien Pomerleau, accepted only the best. However, the girl I had just bought, sight unseen, was far from that.

But the dealer had no choice but to sell her if he wanted to stay in business. If word got out that Arnold Flamm had refused me—even once—Aurum Luxury Slaves risked never again making a sale to any member of my elite circles. Spoiled Euro-trash brats like me had that kind of pull, and everyone knew it.

So when my personal assistant called Aurum with the request for the French girl, only freshly added to the listings, Flamm quoted an outrageous price, clearly hoping I'd change my mind. But when I got on the line myself, even the dealer, with his oily superciliousness, folded.

"Let me be the judge of what's inferior and what's not, Monsieur Flamm," I said with a light laugh. "I put my trust in a fine establishment like Aurum to ensure she's at her best by the time I receive her. After all, when it comes to slaves, this isn't, as they say on this continent, my first rodeo."

Who could argue with that? Not Flamm, especially after I wired the obscene dollar amount he'd quoted into escrow within the hour, pending inspection of the girl at a cocktail party I was throwing that Friday afternoon. And, I added, I wanted her delivered. By the dealer. *Personally.*

None of this was exactly normal, but it wasn't Arnold Flamm's place to question the eccentric tastes of the rich.

And that's exactly what I was counting on.

Now, as the sleek black transport van with its discreet logo pulled up next to the other luxury vehicles parked in my manicured, circular drive, there was no way Flamm didn't know that the scrawny, scowling French girl in the back—complete with scoliosis and rickets and the tendency to bite—wasn't up to my standards. He must have been ruing his inability to convince me to opt for one of the curvy, peachy, eager-to-please specimens he'd imported from Belgium last month. But I had told him I wouldn't hear of buying any other slave. I wanted *this* one, 974312, and that's all there was to it.

So it was no surprise to me that Flamm—a short, stout, overly tanned man in a gold-crested suit jacket and too much product in his black hair—was sweating like he'd just run a marathon as he stood in the drive, motioning to the uniformed handler who'd accompanied him. To my dismay, I was sweating, too—recently relocated, I wasn't yet used to all this goddamn humidity—but I hoped the swipe of patchy but artfully tousled golden hair off my face looked at least semi-effortless as, hiding a slight limp, I emerged in a crisp white linen suit on the marble steps above the manicured lawn of my brand-new Greek Revival home in a gated community on the outskirts of D.C., with a glass of bourbon one of my uniformed slaves had handed me. Behind the house, in the sprawling back gardens, a live jazz combo played as chic guests sipped mint juleps beside the marble fountain or snapped selfies under the trellis.

We'd better make this quick. My ice was melting.

Partially so no one would examine it too closely, I stuck my other hand casually in my pocket, watching impassively as the rear doors of the van swung open. A female handler stuffed into tight black uniform trousers tugged the girl down by a chain lead, wearing a muzzle and the standard khaki clothing of the Aurum dealership slaves, its plainness meant to imply neutrality, a blank slate, a slave who could serve in any way her master might require.

The scrawny, hollow-cheeked girl twisting at the end of the chain might disagree. Which was unsurprising, considering that as recently as two years ago—if my theory proved correct —she'd been French supermarket heiress Delphine Bisset, living with her parents in a house outside Paris about the size of this one, with slaves of her own. Her life had been a powder-pink whirl of pool parties and shopping sprees and Riviera holidays.

But I knew about all of that, of course. *We* were one and the same, she and I.

Did *she* know it? Maybe. She watched me out of the corner of her large brown eyes, exhausted but still unmistakably engaged as she blinked against the bright sunlight, even as the handler tugged her forward with such a violent jerk that she almost face-planted on the lawn.

I drew in a sharp breath, louder than I'd meant to. "Go easy on the girl, please, yeah?" I said lightly. "I have guests, monsieur. I can't bring in a filthy, grass-stained *gamine* to greet them."

The female handler looked at me askance. I eyed her back,

lazily savoring the rich caramel bouquet of my drink, the remaining ice clinking against the crystal.

I wasn't concerned. We both knew who had the power here, after all.

The handler wrangled the girl the rest of the way through the portico and shoved her to her knees on the rock-hard, polished floor before the marble columns, in front of *me. Her new owner.*

"If she'd just comply, it would go easier for her," the handler remarked.

That's what they always said. They lied.

Now it was Arnold Flamm's turn to bound up the steps, smile strained, palms visibly sweating. "Mr. Pomerleau. It's a pleasure."

I glanced briefly at the outstretched hand but kept my own in my pocket because Sébastien Pomerleau didn't have to shake any hands he didn't feel like shaking. This, like the bourbon, was a perk of the position.

I did look the dealer straight in his dark, predictably soulless eyes, though, for the same reason I made it a point to look all men like Flamm in the eyes.

Because I could.

Next, I studied my soon-to-be slave openly, while she studied me right back, not so openly. Then I frowned, trying to ignore the sweat trickling uncomfortably down my back.

Something was wrong. Despite myself—despite my preparation—my heart rate picked up slightly.

Fuck.

I'd made my opening in the chess game, but it was time to change up the strategy. *No plan survives contact with the enemy,* they'd told me in training. I knew that already, but it was nice to hear it acknowledged. And for once, given the resources to do something about it.

"Take the muzzle off," I ordered the handler. "I want to see her face."

"But—"

"She wouldn't bite me," I said in English, looking at the girl, whose scabbed-over lips twitched when the muzzle was unbuckled, obviously thinking about it. Then I repeated myself in French. "*N'est-ce pas, fille?*"

She froze, having clearly understood the French, which was a good sign. But not good enough.

Flamm stepped forward, ignoring the handler, and jerked the girl up by her hair. "Rest assured, we've already addressed that," he hissed at her in English as, for the first time, an unshed tear appeared in the corner of her eye. "It took some of our most creative methods, but we've addressed it."

I closed my eyes briefly. Fucking hell. "Allow me, monsieur." With my free hand, I reached for her now-bare chin and held it lightly between my fingers, my gold watch glinting beneath the long sleeve of my jacket. She gnashed her teeth briefly but didn't try to sink them into my fingers.

Instead, a look of surprise crossed her face. Surprised, too, was the handler, going by her suspicious glance, though thankfully, Flamm wasn't.

Working the lines on my father's yacht was my rehearsed explanation for the condition of my hands, which I would only need if the girl were stupid and brazen enough to say anything. Luckily, she was far from that. Her face had actually softened a little as she sized me up, even as she kept her eyes turned away.

She knew.

Well, shit. This kid was smart.

"I know that trick, girl," I said in French. "Look at me so I can see your eyes."

Not only was she smart, but she knew where her bread was

buttered. Without even a glance back at Flamm or her handler, she obeyed, raising her chestnut irises to meet mine.

Well. She was the right age and coloring to be Delphine Bisset, though it was hard to connect the pale, hollow-cheeked moppet in front of me to the girl with the silky brown tresses and professionally whitened smile grinning in the hundreds of snapshots I'd spent the past few months examining. There were millions of skinny, brown-haired, brown-eyed fifteen-year-old slave girls at dealerships all over the country. Normally, nobody gave a shit about any of them. Only her birthmark—if it were indeed concealed by the metal chain on her wrist, as I hoped—would make her of particular interest to me.

It was a cruel and heinous crime, you see, to kidnap free-born children and sell them into slavery.

Flamm cleared his throat nervously, obviously afraid I was about to change my mind.

I had no plan to disabuse him of the notion. "Do you know anything about her background other than what was in the file?"

"Raised in the household of an excellent French family who sold her off quickly when they fell on hard times," he said, trying to play up the girl's minimal credentials. "She ended up on a farm in Moldova until one of our agents found her."

"Former farm slave, huh?" I said, eyeing the girl with mild disinterest. "I like some spirit, make no mistake, but those places aren't exactly charm schools."

"Of course, monsieur," Flamm said desperately. "But they break them under the lash."

I smiled. "Not always."

She refused to flinch as I raised one of her arms as much as the chains would allow. Counting the old bruises and scars mottling them, my stomach sank lower and lower. They weren't the kind of scars you got guzzling champagne on a yacht in Cannes.

Not to mention, the way she kneeled in shackles was—well, she wasn't comfortable, exactly, but she also clearly knew flopping around like a fish would get her nowhere.

Heart still pounding, I picked up one of her hands, under the guise of examining the tag attached to the chain, looking for the distinctive mark, a blurry photo of which had begun this whole operation. But I didn't even need to spot the shape of Florida instead of Massachusetts to know that this waif, trembling in her drab garb, was no pampered society princess. The dealer, loathsome as he was, had been telling the truth about that. She was a born slave, most likely, whether in France or somewhere else. It didn't matter. What did matter was that we'd just spent two months on this for nothing, and—

"You're not going to keep me, monsieur?" she asked in English.

"Quiet, slave," said the panicky Flamm, reaching past the handler and kneeing her square in the back. She tried in vain to steady herself on the marble, but she couldn't in her tight cuffs, and this time, she really did face-plant. As she lay there, a tear delicately slipped out of her eye, rolled down her cheek, and onto the floor.

The job will try to get to you, they'd told me. Don't let it. Well, no shit. Here I was, once again, standing here looking at my goddamn sister. Looking at *myself*. And what was I thinking about? All the late nights in the field office I'd wasted working on this case when I could have been in my one-bedroom Arlington apartment, listening to moody old jazz records, browsing dense scientific journals, and scouring the internet for any mention of microchip technology, Max Langer, Maeve van Someren, Keith Wainwright-Phillips, or—

"Mr. Pomerleau?"

The girl was staring at me openly now. *Everyone* was staring at me. Sébastien Pomerleau, international playboy, was standing hunched in his own marble foyer, speechless, condensation dripping down the back of his hand and beneath his sleeve, over the numbers seared forever into his wrist. And which—story of my life—were preventing me from touching, speaking to, or even looking at the only ones who mattered to me. And which were netting me a few hundred bucks a month while some anonymous corporate entity—as I'd lately discovered—quietly formed an LLC, patented *my* scientific discovery, and applied for millions of dollars' worth of venture capital funding to get it running under the guise of using it on pets. *Animal* pets.

None of it made sense. I'd thought that formula was safe. But what the hell was I going to do, sue? The government still didn't officially consider me a person, even though I *worked* for them.

Okay, so maybe I was under a bit of stress, as suggested by a fellow consultant in a peer-support session they'd made me attend, and not just because of the job. A job that, at this rate, I wasn't even sure I'd be in much longer.

I looked down at my glass of sad, brownish water. Well, my bourbon was fucked. *Everything* was fucked. Back to field training for Sébastien Pomerleau, federal lapdog.

And then I looked down at the girl, whose head had dropped so low I could see the nerves flexing above her crooked spine. Above the collar of her uniform glistened the tops of fresh, untreated lash wounds. No wonder she was helplessly swiping her teary eyes on the shoulder of her uniform. This "luxury slave dealership" was no less of a nest of horrors than all the rest, as if I'd ever doubted that.

Well, shit. There was nothing I could do to help myself, but that didn't mean there was nothing I could do to help *her*. That was another perk of the job—for as long as I could keep getting away with it, anyway.

"Shall we complete the transaction, sir?" asked Flamm.

"I don't think so."

Flamm coughed and sputtered, wiping his brow, barely keeping a handle on his oily, practiced sycophancy. "Excuse me? Why ever not?"

"Because it's the wrong girl," I said, heart hammering as I veered further and further off script. Why did these things always seem to end up as one-man nights at the improv?

Meanwhile, any bravado the girl had was gone. She was shaking. I grabbed her again and tipped her up to face me. *"Joue le jeu, gamine,"* I told her, knowing Flamm wouldn't understand. *Play along, kid. Wrong girl or not, I'm getting you out of here.*

She watched me as I turned back to Flamm. "Just as I thought. You're trying to pass off some cheap American housemaid for the French girl I requested. How stupid do you think I am?" I demanded, continuing to shake her. "The minx doesn't understand a word I've been saying. *Tu ne comprends pas, hein?*"

She shook her head, pretending to be utterly baffled.

"See?" I snapped, swatting her as hard as I dared on the ear. *Good girl.* "I'd almost expect this kind of chicanery from some bargain-basement operation, but not from Aurum, which I *had* planned on *highly* recommending to several close personal friends of mine who are in the market for trained luxury slaves." I could practically see Flamm gulping as a few party guests poked their heads in at the commotion. "And furthermore, I'll have you note, forging a slave's identity is a federal offense."

This was true—at least, I was pretty sure it was—but it was also more or less impossible. However, maybe I could scare the dealer into forgetting that. A badge and a gun might help, but consultants, sadly, didn't get those. I spoke louder, praying I'd be heard by the guy on the other end of the tiny wire I was wearing pinned inside my shirt.

Where are you, Manny? Put down your goddamn martini and come back me up.

"I assure you, Mr. Pomerleau," Flamm stammered, his voice rising an octave, "there's been no mistake. This is the merchandise you ordered. Perhaps she's a bit confused, but I'm certain that once you scan the microchip, she—"

"Enough." I held up a hand. Just what I needed: for this asshole to pull out a portable chip reader and prove just how entirely full of shit I was. "I know precisely what I ordered. And this"—I let go of the girl dismissively—"is not it. I have *guests* here, Monsieur Flamm, clamoring to see this girl. And now you've left me with the utterly mortifying task of going in and informing them that our evening has been *ruined*."

Flamm blanched, tugging at his damp shirt collar. "There— there must be some misunderstanding..."

"No. The only misunderstanding," I continued coolly, hoping now just to keep this slimeball talking while Manny got into place, "is you thinking you could cheat me and get away with it."

"But I—"

"I'm afraid Mr. Pomerleau is correct," came a deep voice from farther inside the house.

Thank fuck. I stepped aside to make way for a muscular man in a flashy dark suit and an even flashier badge, who exchanged only a slight, knowing, slightly exasperated glance with me. "Forging the identity of a slave to pass her off as another is indeed a federal crime under statute 107.31A. You're under arrest for—"

"Arrest?!" Flamm sputtered pathetically. "I haven't done anything!"

Which was true. But it also wasn't.

"This is outrageous!" he continued, his face turning purple as Manny whipped out the cuffs, which we both knew were for show. Not like I wouldn't fucking *love* to see this asshole chained up as much as *he* loved chaining up slaves. "He hasn't even paid for her. She's still *my* merchandise, merchandise I paid good money for, and I refuse to be strong-armed by some jumped-up Eurotrash..."

"You want to say that again, maybe?"

The dealer's words died in his throat as I stepped into his space. It seemed to spark in the slightly built dealer a realization that he was at the mercy of two larger, younger, fitter guys, one of whom had his hand resting on what was probably a gun. For good measure, I grabbed the lapel of the dealer's crested jacket. Not gonna lie, it felt good, as manhandling these spineless, bullying sons of bitches always did. I tried not to revel too much in it, though. I'd seen where that led.

"I thought not. I'll tell you what, Monsieur Flamm. We'll let you off with a warning this time," I said, feeling the weight of Manny's gaze over my shoulder. *I've got your back, man, as always. Just don't fuck it up.* "If you give me the girl. No charge. Consider it fair compensation for the distress and inconvenience you've caused me tonight."

Flamm gaped at me, eyes bulging. "You can't be serious! She's worth—"

"I'm dead serious. The girl stays here. You avoid federal charges," I said, even though nobody deserved federal charges *more* than this scumbag. "That's the deal. Take it or leave it."

The remaining color drained from Flamm's too-tan face as he realized I wasn't bluffing. His gaze darted over our shoulders, where he found only a handful of other guests sipping mint juleps and happily enjoying his squirming.

After another long moment, Flamm slumped where he stood, sweat rolling in waves off his forehead. "Fine," he ground out between clenched teeth. The genteel mask had dropped to the ground, revealing him for the violent thug he really was. That they *all* really were. "Take the little bitch. She's more trouble than she's worth, anyway."

The handler, fed up, shoved the whipped, chained, tearful, incredulous girl forward into her new life, her shoulders still shaking. But when I—after a satisfied down-low fist bump with Manny—rested one rough, scarred hand comfortingly on her shoulder, she relaxed into it. And I allowed myself a small smile and a sigh.

But Flamm wasn't finished. "Expect to hear from my attorney," he said as he turned back to his vehicle, pausing to stare me down with a mix of hatred and bafflement. "This isn't over, Mr.—well, whoever the fuck you really are."

But I wasn't entirely sure myself.

—◆—

"Man, why do you keep doing this? You know we can't free her," Manny told me later that evening, unwinding over pints in a cool, dimly lit, wood-paneled pub in Arlington called O'Winsbury's, highly frequented by the feds and the handful of slave consultants working with them. Since one of those former consultants now owned the establishment, it wasn't hard to put in place an unspoken agreement that we were allowed to socialize normally as long as we remained discreet about our status in public.

A year ago, I would have laughed to imagine the very government responsible for having instituted slavery and keeping it running all these years might be willing to throw out their entire rulebook for someone like me—someone who'd *broken* the rules more consistently and enthusiastically than just about anyone else I knew. But when it came to the government, I'd been surprised to discover, virtually every single page of that book was highly negotiable, as long as you were providing them with something they wanted. And in return, they'd provide you with something *you* wanted. As a result, I had all the European streaming TV, takeout tacos, and moderately priced bourbon I could consume.

Of course, what I *really* wanted was something they couldn't provide.

What I really wanted was not to be tortured every goddamn minute of every goddamn night, agonizing over everything I was missing.

Over whether anyone was standing there beside her in the place I wanted to be, just *watching* her—watching her smart, watch her be moral, watch her be brave. Not, for once, because she had to be but because she *was*. And whether this same faceless replacement douchebag's hand was currently lost in perpetual curls, manicured fingers claiming timeless curves my own rough ones had claimed first, whether some disembodied magic dick was plunging into her, causing her to joyfully vibrate as the amorphously repugnant asshole it was attached to taught her all the filthy and divine things I'd dreamed of teaching her, of teaching both of us, but had never had either the time or the permission to do it. Whether she'd found someone who could actually make her feel *safe* to finally let go, to breathe, to open her eyes and say, *hey, life and love don't have to be twenty-four seven torture!* Someone to make her feel as safe as she deserved to feel, the kind of safety I'd never, not once, been able to give her. And someone who could actually spend *time* with her in something other than secrecy and fear, and remind her of the bliss she could have *right now* instead of yet another dose of endless, excruciating waiting for someone who'd have nothing to offer her even if by some miracle she *did* wait.

Someone who'd given her permission *not* to wait. Because as much as I couldn't, I couldn't not.

But if I paused too long to think about everything I really wanted, I was certain I'd snap the blinds of my apartment shut and either collapse onto the sofa in grief or start kicking doors off their hinges with rage. And then my chances of ever getting any of it would go from slim to none.

On the bright side, the electronic ankle monitor they'd strapped on me—which gave me nearly a 100-mile radius, far enough to drive through the night most weekends in the disgustingly sensible but decently fast Ford sedan they'd given me, chasing the sunrise over the long bridge over Chesapeake Bay and walking for hours in the cold flume of the Delaware coast—was a hell of a lot more comfortable to walk in than shackles. And was concealed fairly well by a pair of jeans or one of the more practical suits I wore when I wasn't playing Sébastien Pomerleau, suits my stipend had just barely enabled me to afford. And that I'd had to pick out *myself*, not that I minded.

That aside, the best thing about the monitor was that it wasn't a metal bracelet or a microchip.

Which was the only reason I hadn't ripped it off.

Yet.

Besides, I'd been assured I wouldn't be given either a chip or a bracelet, as long as I behaved myself. Which was getting harder and harder, especially as the monitor's clunky dead weight constantly reminded me that I: A) was still a slave and B) that, providing I *did* behave myself, I had exactly two years, four months, and three days to go before I was free. And that there was no guarantee that anything, or anyone, would be waiting for me when I was.

If I was. Because even though they'd promised it, I also had perfect faith in my ability to find ways to fuck it up. Hell, I'd already found some. And after the discovery I'd made on the Delaware corporate registry, I was about to find more.

It kept me awake at night, but even before that, I hadn't been sleeping much. That's why I spent my nights driving. At home, it was all that *time* to fill—no sinks full of dishes to wash or blazing-hot fields to hoe, no hours to be counted down until my body was too exhausted to fight sleep—and my dim, silent, sterile, empty apartment, and the nightmares, and the pain, even though the agency was sending me to physical therapy so my body could actually function in the field, and giving me effective meds so my brain could function, too.

I tried not to complain. I really did, even though there were so many better places I could be. But there were so many worse ones, too. In this job, I saw them all the time.

Manny tapped his pint glass against mine, a sharp *clink* snapping me out of my thoughts. "You gonna answer me, or just sit there brooding into your beer all night?"

I smirked. "I *do* love a good brood."

"Yeah, I noticed." He took a sip, watching me. "But seriously. This is what, the third one you've saved this year?"

"The fourth," I corrected him.

"Jesus." He exhaled through his nose. "Look, man. I get it. I really do. I know what you're trying to do, and hell, I *respect* it. You know how I feel. That's why you're here. But you're on thin ice."

Thin ice. As if I didn't know. As if I didn't feel it cracking beneath me every second of every day.

I feigned a nonchalant shrug. "Flamm was a greedy, sadistic little prick. He deserved to get played."

"You were one step away from getting *yourself* played, Monsieur Pomerleau."

At that, I just smiled and tipped back my glass. "Wouldn't be the first time."

Manny groaned, rubbing a hand down his face. "Goddamn it, man. Didn't you learn *anything* in training? It's dangerous to let your personal experiences affect your decisions in the field."

"Look, I know we can't free her," I admitted. "We can't free any of them. But that job Nanette found for her in the federal budget office is cushy as fuck, and she can feed us intel while she's there. She's really smart," he added. "And you have to admit, on *my* part, it was a good save."

"A better save than when the congressman's daughter caught you hacking into her dad's computer and you told her it just broke your heart to think of her using a network without a properly-installed firewall," said Manny, grabbing two more pints of Guinness from the bartender and handing one to me. I'd recently discovered that a stout—though it didn't compare to bourbon—was a good social drink. Which I'd never needed, since I'd never been *allowed* to socialize over anything except a bowl of gruel in however much time I'd been allotted to eat it.

"Hey, identity theft *is* heartbreaking."

"What about *my* heartbreak when Lindeman strangles you to death and I have no consultant? Ever think of that?" He paused. "Look, I'm not trying to imply this transition has been easy for you, but—"

"Fucking hell, Manny, you think it's about easy? I wouldn't even know what to *do* with easy." I took a breath, trying to steady myself. "Look, we'll still find the heiress," I promised. "There's still a particular lead I want to follow, the one we got from that freed guy in New York." I didn't mention that after tomorrow, the only leads I might be following were my own. "In the meantime, you know there are plenty of girls *and* boys who deserve to be saved just as much as she does."

"Of course. You know how I feel, man. And Lindeman was impressed with what you did for those kids last month in Balti-more. Actually, I think he's impressed with you in general when he doesn't want to toss you out a tenth-story window. And remember, this is a guy who used to be the head of an entire *division* set up to find abolitionist fugitives."

Around us, the bar was starting to fill up with our colleagues and friends, who greeted us before finding seats. Manny raised his voice. "But the bottom line is that we're a law enforcement agency, not a shelter for abused slaves."

"Wait, we aren't?" I asked with a wry sip. "Then how do you explain me?"

Manny laughed. "Dude, I *can't* explain you. Nobody told me working with a slave would be like this. For some reason, I pictured a lot more bowing and scraping and less, well, going rogue."

I set my glass down incredulously. "Dude, did you do *any* homework on me at all?"

"Clearly, not enough. At this point, I'd be happy just to get you to respond to your goddamn name at least *once*," he said. "All in all, I think I've had better luck getting you to answer to Sébastien Pomerleau."

I couldn't help but laugh because he was right. I'd finally coughed up the name—her name—*my* name—because they'd threatened to send me back if I didn't, but the fact was, I had always found it far easier to be Sébastien or Corey or Starling or Lucky Sevens or Rocket Boy or even boy or kid or man or mutt or whatever anybody else deigned to call me, than take on an actual identity. My *own* identity, one that couldn't be ignored, brushed off, or shed in an instant. One I would answer to and answer for. One I could keep.

As absurd as it was, I wasn't ready for that yet. And I didn't yet know what the last step might be on the journey. Although I knew the *first* step had been hearing it from the right mouth. And I could only hope that that mouth would still care to say it.

I stared down into my glass, then looked up again to see that Manny's face had turned serious.

"Bruh, you're lucky and you're good, and that gets you ninety percent of the way. But your problem, the way I see it, is that you still don't know how to be a person. And most of the time, I don't think you even *want* to."

Well, ouch. I turned my glass in circles on the table. "I-I think you're right. I don't. Or maybe I still don't know the person I want to be."

"Well, I hate to break this to you, man, but you're gonna have to bite the bullet, like every other human being on the planet, and figure it out. Because I know you *do* want your freedom, and I don't want to see you put it in jeopardy."

Freedom, which, as I had been frequently informed, wasn't free. Look, I wasn't *that* humble, but I was humble enough to know that the world was far from finished teaching me that lesson. Maybe it never would be.

And my stomach swooped as I thought about the burner phone I'd bought that morning and the call I'd made up my mind—right this second—to make that very night.

Because yes, I did want my freedom. Not with half of me anymore. With all of me. And despite it all, I wanted to be a person, too. I really did. But I also knew that it wasn't freedom —at least, not *just* freedom—that was going to make me one.

A few more of our colleagues grabbed seats at the bar then —one of them being Daniela, one of the other slave consultants, a leggy brunette whose suffocatingly tight pencil skirt drew the eye to the pillowy space between said legs, one of which she hooked around my wooden swivel chair, propping her chin in her hand with goopy anticipation as she asked about my day. Over her head, Manny raised his eyebrows, but I just ran a hand through my hair before hastily executing my escape from the air-conditioned pub and into the sultry heart of a southeastern night in late August, into the empty, moonless streets of a world where nobody knew or cared what my name was, or if I had one at all. A world that, as a kid, was all the promise freedom ever held. A world with a million more Danielas waiting for me, who would pulse and moan and call me anything I told them to call me, but never by my name. A world that in the end would just be another cage.

I had a phone call to make.

By the time I got to work the next morning, I had five missed calls from Manny already. He met me just inside the door to our department, and for a moment, he just stood there frozen, his face as ashen as when he failed at something. Federal agents weren't used to failing.

"Lindeman's office," he said, pointing. "I'm sorry."

29

Let's face it, my track record with coffee had never been great.

And yet here I was, red-faced and frantic, mashing buttons and spinning dials on a humongous, gurgling copper espresso machine at what I was optimistically calling my new job, all while juggling the wand that was supposed to froth the milk to the perfect microfoam consistency but was actually just dripping warm, milky liquid all over the tile.

"Excuse me, ma'am."

Ma'am? Ugh. That was almost worse than *miss.* "Call me Lou," I told the customer without looking over, but he only rapped his knuckles loudly on the counter.

"I don't care what your name is. I've been waiting for my double-shot soy latte for ten minutes! Do you even know how to work that thing?"

"Yes, sorry, I'm new here. Just trying to figure out how to—" I yelped as steam shot out, scalding my hand. Frantically, I dashed to the sink and held it under the cold running water.

Fucking hell, was there any spare inch of my skin that wasn't destined to be cooked to death?

Another woman spoke up loudly. "This is ridiculous. The slaves at The Copper Leaf across the street work at three times this speed."

"That's because they're beaten if they don't," I shouted back.

"Excuse me?"

I sighed and finally glanced their way, gathering from their tailored power suits that they were Financial District lawyers who had wandered in without realizing they were in a slave-labor-free establishment and that great patience had to be exercised. Not that I wasn't trying to be a good employee. I'd never had a service job before and had for a long time assumed I'd never need one. But I was on my own now, with books and subway fares and phone bills to pay for, and the choice had come down to which of two things—coffee or cooking—seemed less menacing. Coffee had won. I only wished I'd buckled down and finally figured out how to use that espresso machine my dad had bought last year.

I'd meant to. I really had. I'd also, shortly after he'd bought it, become very, very distracted.

Speaking of being distracted, I'd completely forgotten which drink I was supposed to be working on. With mounting panic, I scanned the names attached to the orders on the screen in front of me, hoping they'd offer some clues.

Double shot soy latte, he'd said. Right? I glanced at one of the names. "Are you... Michael?"

"No."

"Shit." I stood there helplessly, my face collapsing into that familiar about-to-ugly-cry crumple I'd once made the mistake of looking at in the mirror and now couldn't unsee. Idiot. Had I learned nothing? I'd fought my way out of certain death in a collapsed mine, but it seemed making a macchiato was simply too advanced for the feeble abilities of Louisa Wainwright-Phillips, Hothouse Flower. Well, that and grocery shopping, taking a trip on the subway without riding ten stops in the wrong direction, and finding a cheap apartment within fifty miles of my new university that didn't smell like an entire family of rats up and died in the walls.

The woman lawyer scoffed in irritation. "Let's just get out of here," she told her colleague. When they left and I had stopped unhygienically snorting and sniffling all over the glass bakery case, I grabbed my phone, feeling obligated to call the girl who'd gotten me the job in the first place and offer to resign in disgrace.

"I can't do this, Bex."

"You what?" The girl on the other end sounded like she was walking, which she usually was when she wasn't in this very coffee shop. "Why the hell are you there alone on your first day? Didn't anyone train you?"

"Basia started to, but she left early."

"Figures. She's probably out picketing outside that slave dealership that just opened across the river. God forbid a coffee shop owner would be concerned with whether anyone actually gets their coffee."

I tried to smile but only hiccupped. "I just feel so useless. There were these lawyers in here and—"

"Lawyers? Fuck 'em. I'd like to see them try to work that thing. Besides, if they want slaves waiting on them hand and foot, it's not like they don't have plenty of other places they can go."

"Oh, they already have."

Rebekah chuckled. "You know I referred you for that job for a reason."

"Because you thought I'd be good at it?"

"Bless your heart, no. Because you were brave enough to want to try. Anyway, I'll call Laken and tell him to come over there and help you. Just sit tight, okay?"

It took Basia's partner twenty minutes to come over and save my ass, but save it he did. Luckily, the only customer to arrive in the meantime ordered an iced tea, which even I couldn't fuck up, and thanks to Laken, it only took another two hours before I was successfully pulling espresso shots. Of course I still hadn't memorized any of the drink combinations and didn't even know what half the terms meant. But I'd like to think I had a chance. After all, I'd passed o-chem for two straight semesters—the second one without my tutor, even.

It was funny, I thought later as I finally threw my apron down and started trudging the three blocks to the subway station, desperately hoping to avoid another side trip halfway to Cape Cod. Although an ocean view would be a hell of a lot nicer than the one from the room I was currently renting below a takeout chicken restaurant, whose price was still a stretch for my paltry savings. The only time anyone ever seemed to think I was brave was when I was forced to be. But then again, maybe that's what bravery was.

I wondered if Rebekah felt the same way. Yes, *that* Rebekah.

At first, I'd thought I was hallucinating when, a few weeks earlier, I'd spotted the name "Rebekah Roth" in the university directory, right there in black and white like any ordinary student. I shouldn't have been shocked, really. My childhood friend wasn't dead, after all. She and her family had just fled to the other side of the country after she'd let a slave boy kiss her and touch her boobs in her childhood treehouse. Or at least, that was the story my classmates and I had all spread around in hushed horror at the time, with Rebekah's presence eventually lingering among us only as a kind of ghostly morality tale. Either way, I hadn't ever expected to see her again, let alone as a business student at one of the largest, most esteemed universities on the East Coast.

But to my astonishment, here were my shaky hands dialing the number, quickly before my anxiety had a chance to devour my nerve. I wasn't exactly sure why I was calling. Maybe because after everything that had happened—to us both—it seemed like a sign. I might even call it fate.

Which should have given me hope, but all it really did was make me think about how if *he* were here, he would tease me for believing in it. And then, as usual, sort of start believing in it himself and never admit it.

Shut up. How the hell do you ever expect to function if you're constantly lost in the memory of someone you might not ever—

"Hello?" inquired the voice on the other end.

I went suddenly shy. "Rebekah? Bex?"

Silence.

"This is Louisa. Louisa Wainwright-Phillips. Lou. Remember—"

Remember? Remember how I scrolled past all those evil memes about you without calling them out? How I just watched open-mouthed across the hall while someone scrawled "whore for slaves" in permanent ink across your locker? How I just walked by like you were invisible when I saw you crying on the stairwell?

Fuck. What was I thinking? I didn't deserve sympathy. I deserved to be shoved under an oncoming Green Line train.

So it didn't surprise me when Rebekah immediately hung up.

It did surprise me a second later, however, when another call came in—from a different number. I answered it immediately, and this time, I had an idea.

"Ericamuller," I blurted out.

"Huh?"

"Erica," I repeated, enunciating more clearly. "Muller."

A long pause as my heart battered my ribcage.

"I think we should talk," said Rebekah finally. "Meet me at Café Jennet in an hour?"

And that was how I first stumbled over the threshold of my future workplace on a breathtakingly crystalline autumn day in September, shivering and drawing my cute but totally inadequate gray cashmere cardigan around my shoulders. I knew the wardrobe of a lifelong desert girl wasn't going to fly in New England, but given my finances, a shopping trip was out of the question. Right now, everything but survival was out of the question.

I'd agonized for weeks about when, where, and how to drop my decision to transfer to a new school on my father, who was scarcely leaving his study these days, even to golf. It wasn't like before, though. I genuinely did think he was working. He even said he was working. But I was afraid to ask what he was working on, and he'd been volunteering nothing, at least not since we'd hit a wall in the search for Ethan. The database had been no help. Free people who became slaves—either via debt or a felony conviction—were completely disassociated from their former identities, for exactly this reason. Besides, even if my dad somehow found Ethan and could afford to buy and free him, which he couldn't, he'd be legally barred from doing so—again, for exactly this reason.

Given that blow, it was a miracle that whatever my dad had turned his attention to now was even getting him out of bed in the morning. In any case, I thought it wiser to leave him to it. In the meantime, we would just have to accept that my brother had been enslaved forever and then vanished off the face of the earth, and only a dead man—or at least a man who preferred to be thought dead—knew where he was.

No wonder I was haunted. Day and night. By everything. By Max's fate, by Resi's tomb, by electricity, and by having been buried alive beneath the layers and layers of rock that often had me jerking awake in the darkness with a scream and a name—the name—dying in my throat as if it would remain trapped below unless and until I was addressing the boy it belonged to. And haunted by the faded, reddish-yellow half-moons all over my body, so many that I had to flip my gold-rimmed cheval mirror so I wouldn't stand for an hour obsessing over them every time I got undressed. Haunted, in full, by the bombed-out bunker I'd once called my life. It had been a good life, too, for a while, at least with the privilege of ignorance on my side. But a person with scars like mine could never live that life again. And I didn't want to.

In the end, I'd kept it simple, breaking the news at a casual Sunday breakfast by the pool with my father, right after the housekeeper—the only one of the slaves still working—cleared the plates. The old valet was convalescing after a fall, and my father was now valiantly footing his medical bills. As for the maid, I had been saddened but not particularly shocked when my father had announced plans to sell her. At the last minute, though, he'd found an alternate solution: renting her out to a friend from the country club to fill in for their cook, who was also having health problems. To his credit, he'd promised the maid he'd put away a percentage of the money she brought in to eventually free her. But we all knew—like my promise to take her to the ocean, which finally happened thanks to five hours in the Cadillac each way, one night in a kooky hostel in Pacific Beach, and a lot of awkwardness and eye rolling—there were no guarantees. He'd promised something similar to the house-keeper, too, and even finally put the house on the market to raise cash. I was convinced his heart was (finally) in the right place. It was just his wallet that wasn't.

And neither was his daughter.

"I need to be somewhere else right now, Daddy," I said. "I need to be someone else. I already am someone else."

Mourning doves cooed in the palo verdes as my father stared into the depths of his coffee cup for what felt like an hour before responding. "You know I can't spare a cent right now, Loulou. You'll be on your own for everything your scholarship doesn't cover, and Boston is far from the cheapest city these days. And with most of the service roles filled by slaves, a job won't be easy to find."

"But, Daddy—"

"Hold on, Loulou. I'm telling you this just to inform you, not to dissuade you. If you think this is the right choice for you, then—well, I have no doubt that it is."

"Really?" I asked, blinking in surprise. "You're not going to try to talk me out of it?"

A smile played on his lips. "I've noticed that trying to talk you out of things hasn't been very effective lately. In fact," he added, "I'm starting to think that betting on your determination is the safest investment I could ever make."

Well, shit. I didn't even have that amount of confidence in myself.

It was settled. But as I packed up my inadequate wardrobe, booked a ticket using my father's miles, and anxiously prepared to take my seat on the plane, one question kept tugging at me.

Will you be able to find me?

Yes, he'd told me not to wait, and I loved him for that. For setting me free, for giving me the only gift he had left to give me. Even if it felt more like a curse than a gift to have to grapple with the possibility that some hateful bitch, right this second, was filling the space in the hollow of that magnificent body that I had foolishly thought I would be the only one to ever fill. And worst of all, was doing it openly. Was sharing coffee dates. Was making dinner and streaming shows and walking with him side by side down an ordinary street like two ordinary people, the same way I had longed to do every goddamn day since we met but couldn't, not to mention being the one holding his hand when he finally, finally got to enter a world he'd been in but never part of. And that was when this hypothetical trollop was not teaming up with him to mount elaborate undercover capers at glamorous DC political galas wearing one of those slinky black catsuits, after which she would slowly and sensually peel it off, arch her long, flexible back, and—well, I could continue this ridiculous and unproductive train of thought, but that was the gist of it.

Look, I knew that in his mind, regardless of what he wanted —even with his colossal jealous streak that I'd never, ever get him to admit to—he'd had no other choice. It would kill him to imagine me wasting even a second of my life—let alone three whole years—waiting for him. Waiting for a ghost.

But if he was a ghost, why could I still feel him?

Ghosts were incorporeal. They were cold. Ghosts haunted. They didn't—when you were lying wide awake in a frozen, barren bed, shivering and haunted by everything else—hold you. They didn't make you feel loved and warm and safe. They didn't, night after night, murmur, *it's okay, mäi léift, we'll figure it out, we always do* in your ear and make you believe it, enough to finally get you to close your eyes, even out your breathing, and sleep.

Well, maybe really clever, charming ghosts could figure out a way.

In any case, how could I—in the face of one trollop or a thousand—ever let go of that? How?

In the end, that's what I told Milagros. After a goodbye dinner of homemade pozole with my other family, under that August dry heat that swelled unbearably during the day before dropping to perfection and lingering into the night. And I was delighted to find that the crystal-blue phosphorescence emanating up from the bottom of the pool—that light that had once adored him—made his sister's face shimmer just as brightly. She lay in the hammock next to me, her remaining fingers curled and resting lightly on the sleeve of my white lace coverup. Between the cannabis smoke and the peace of Maeve's soft, sage-scented breath, I felt more relaxed here than anywhere else, even though in mere days, I would fly into the void.

"No one's asking you to let go, you know," Milagros said, resting the cane she was using these days on the side of her chair and settling herself back into it. She relit the joint Ivy had passed her.

"They're not?" I asked from the hammock, genuinely surprised, twisting the stem of my glass of Spanish wine, its bouquet alone a pineapple-scented headrush of memory. "It sort of seems like everyone is. Or at least the world is."

"Well, if I'd let go of Erica, I wouldn't be here," Milagros pointed out, inhaling deeply. "Of course sometimes you should let go, too. And before you put this thing out in my eye for suggesting that, I mean on your own timeline, no one else's. And in the meantime, whatever you do—I can't stress this enough—take care of yourself. Which is something I really wish someone would tell Erica. Someone other than me so she'll listen." She exhaled slowly.

"Where is Erica?" asked Ivy, her long, languid legs draped over the lounger, her black crochet coverup elegant as ever. An afternoon of splashing in the pool—not to mention being talked to, given treats, and treated like people by someone other than Ivy—had worn the kids right out. They had both passed out on the guest bed, which was both cute and mortifying given my own memories of that bed and that pool. Meanwhile, my professor had slipped into the house soon after dinner, not to reappear.

"Working," Milagros said with another puff. "Don't ask. Since she was reinstated by the department, her hyperfocus has been through the roof. But it's something that will benefit all of us. So she says. Then again, she says that about all her work."

"It's true, though," Ivy said.

"I know. How convenient that it also makes it impossible for anyone to argue with her about it, especially me. But hey," Milagros shrugged, blowing out an indolent cloud of smoke, "I knew what I was getting into with her."

"But what if I don't want to?" I asked suddenly. "What if I —" *What if I can't let him go, ever? What if I can't let this die? Let us die?*

"You know," she said, seeming to read my thoughts, "maybe this is a stoner thought, but light is never lost."

"Huh?"

"Photons travel until they're absorbed, bent, scattered. Even when we think it's gone—it's somewhere, doing something. Warming a surface. Feeding a leaf. Lighting up dust in the air."

Her gaze traced the arc of Orion rising above the coconut palms. "I always thought it was comforting, in a way. Back when I was scrubbing office toilets for ten hours a day, back when I never thought I'd see Erica again, never thought I'd get to use my mind, never thought I'd be free. Back when I only had the *memories* of joy to comfort me. I even sometimes thought it was a waste. That none of it mattered. That it might as well not have happened. But," she said, "every bit of light we put into the world ends up somewhere. Even if it's small. Even if we never see where it lands."

"Why do I feel like this is something he'd be explaining to me, if he were here?" I remarked.

Her gaze slid to the door, toward the children sleeping in

peace behind it. "We don't get to fix everything, Louisa. We want to. We try. We almost always fail. But that doesn't mean what we do doesn't matter. A single act. A single feeling. A choice. You never know what it might become, years from now, in someone else's hands."

Then, lightly, she added, "Even falling in love with someone they told you not to. That's light, too. Maybe the kind that travels the farthest."

She passed the joint to Maeve, who inhaled inexpertly, coughing a little with good humor. She had her knees pulled up into her chest, head partially resting on my shoulder, watching the moon waver on the surface of the pool in the peculiar reverie of someone inventing new worlds in her head pretty much all the time.

Honestly, in freedom, Maeve was killing it. She was improving her English and studying furiously to get her high school equivalency degree so she could apply to university. She was going for long hikes in the Saguaro National Park and boldly reading her vivid, fanciful poetry at open-mic nights, where I was her biggest fan. Jobs for someone like her were hard to come by, but she was looking hard and cozying up in one of Ivy's many spare rooms in the meantime.

Maeve was like a solar eclipse—it hurt for me to look at her, and yet I couldn't not look. It was hard to believe that after seven years apart, brother and sister could still have so many of the same quirks, but they did, starting with that cute little way *ah* sounded like *ach* in their accent. Their habit of reaching for their hair when things got awkward. The gears in their heads that never stopped turning, even for a second. But most of all, it was the eyes—that sudden bold stare that always knocked me flat.

"He told me you used to make up your own constellations," I said to Maeve, raising my head to the galaxies.

"Ah," she said, though of course it came out like *ach*, complete with that adorable, guttural little noise at the end. "You mean *Sternenflüsterin?*" Maeve said, shifting in the hammock, resting on her elbow, golden irises sly and glimmering in the moonlight. She pointed up to a cluster just above the horizon. "She wasn't made up. She was real. She's right over there."

I laughed, but Maeve sobered. "That was part of my ending, too, you know. He was in it," she said sadly, nuzzling her touch-starved cheek lightly against my shoulder. "But maybe he'll be the... the epilogue," she finished, proud to have come up with the right word.

I just stared up at the entire sky as if I could take it in all at once. "He will be."

For Maeve, this was true. Siblings would always be siblings. They were for life.

But a love formed in secrecy, in darkness, amid torture and pain, held no such promises.

And maybe that was why it felt so much like fate to find—upon my arrival in Boston—Rebekah, who understood that more than anyone.

Before entering Café Jennet to meet my old friend, I stopped and stared for a minute at the stylized galloping horse over the door, two boxes for its head and body, four crooked lines for legs, and another line for the tail.

Freedom was what it symbolized. Rebekah told me that immediately, turning a tiny espresso cup around in her manicured hand. At first, I was stunned by her black blazer and business-school-confidential auburn hair, styled straight and held back with a pearl clip. Not in and of itself, but just because in this coffee shop, with its jumble of avant-garde art, anarchist newspapers, and fliers for offbeat music shows stuck haphazardly to corkboards, it was an anomaly. There had to be an explanation. I was right, and upon my arrival, Rebekah launched right into it—with no prompting, no hugs, and to my shock, no demands for an apology.

"Everyone always wondered why my parents didn't just wash their hands of me and sell me into slavery," Rebekah said. "The truth is, they threatened to. The only reason they didn't is because they found this boarding school on the Maine coast designed for 'cases' like mine. Rich girls who got in trouble with slave boys, basically, which explains why it felt more like prison. Some of them told me they had even been pregnant, and well, there sure weren't any babies around."

"This was all legal?"

Rebekah shrugged contemptuously.

"How?"

"They had our parents' permission. And our parents were rich."

I didn't ask more. There was no need.

"Two years in that place and girls like me were declared 'reformed.' I got the college to accept me, though I had to fill out the dreaded 'please explain' section on the application. But I still had my parents to worry about. The only way I could get them to pay for my degree was by convincing them that I'd repented of my slatternly ways, declare that slavery is an effective, valuable, and necessary institution and that I would never again look at a slave boy as anything other than a particularly attractive and sturdy piece of furniture."

"But—" I leaned forward.

"It was all lies, of course. In reality, between classes, I hang out here with Basia and Laken, working behind the scenes with the Freedom Alliance and plotting to overthrow the government."

I practically spat up my hazelnut latte all over the table.

"Relax, I'm kidding," said Rebekah. "Sort of." For the first time, her old smile crinkled the corners of her eyes in a wistfully familiar way, the kind that reminded me how, as children, we used to explore the wash near the country club, searching for jackrabbits and lost balls while pretending, just for the afternoon, to outrun our privilege and become plucky orphans of the storm.

Rebekah was the same person she had been then, really. It was just that now she'd been through hell and had her social consciousness completely and utterly transformed.

So relatable.

"But your parents must suspect—"

"Nothing. They suspect nothing, and I plan to keep it that way. My family name and Mom's connections at the business school make it easy to keep it on the down-low. Hell, I've even converted some of the people I've met over there. Solicited some donations." She put down her coffee and turned to me. "How are you financing your education, by the way?"

I told her.

"Seriously? And you have no extra money other than the scholarship? Where are you even living?"

My response made Rebekah's expression take on the consistency of sour soy milk. "All right, you're coming with me," she said, throwing on an elegant light fall coat and herding me toward the nearest subway stop. "I have a spare room. My parents pay for the apartment, so I don't need the rent money, but I'd like the company. It's just that the company needs to be someone who won't report me for sedition. I have a good feeling about you. I suppose you're looking for a job, too?"

I nodded pathetically, the unexpected kindness making my eyes well up already.

"I think I might have something for you. How are you at espresso?"

I nodded again quickly, hoping there would be absolutely

no follow-up questions. "Why are you helping me, even after... everything?" I asked softly as I tried to follow Rebekah through the gate, fumbling inelegantly with my fare card. "I didn't even get a chance to apologize for being a spineless, complacent wimp back then. Or tell you what I—" I swallowed. I knew I'd have to share my story, too, even though I wished I had Maeve's gift for weaving narratives so it wouldn't feel like extracting two rows of teeth with no anesthetic.

"You don't have to," Rebekah said, turning back and expertly swiping me through the turnstile with an extra card from her wallet.

"Huh? So then you know what happened—"

"Oh, I don't know the details, don't worry. But things get around fast in our community. Basia keeps her ear to the ground. She knows Erica Muller and had a passing familiarity with Max Langer. He and the mine made the news, of course, but we filled in the rest from her. That's why I knew I could trust you."

Amid the bustle of the station, I slumped on the hard wooden seat, unconvinced. "But I didn't even—why did you—"

"Because people can change, Lou," Rebekah said over the roar of the approaching Green Line train and the mellifluous voice ushering us onto it. "I did, so it's fair to assume you did, too. Isn't that wild?"

"It is kind of wild."

"Right?"

"What... What happened to him?" I asked against my better judgment, crowding onto the half-full car and sliding onto the hard plastic seat next to Rebekah. I clutched the pole as the train jerked into motion, taking us closer to Rebekah's town-house in Brighton. I glanced warily at the passengers on either side of me, hoping they couldn't overhear. "I mean, we all knew he went to the mines. But did he—"

"You don't have to look so nervous," Rebekah said. "I don't mind talking about it. These things should be talked about."

These things. Like they were a case study out of a sociology textbook instead of a love story. But maybe that's how she had to train herself to look at it in order to move on.

Move on. Move on. Move on. Even the very train wheels beneath me seemed to be murmuring it as they spirited me away down the tracks.

"I didn't even look," Rebekah confessed. "I didn't want to know, and what could I do, anyway? If my parents found out I was searching for him, we could lose what little we still had to cling to. Plus, I had my sisters to think about."

"But——" I closed my eyes.

"The mines are a death sentence, Lou. You know that."

Of course I knew. And I knew that with just one less stroke of luck—without Max Langer—that was how my own story—*our* story—would have ended, too. Good God, we owed that man a lot. And I hoped that wherever he was—on earth or otherwise—he had some good tequila.

"Did you love him?" I finally asked because let's face it, that's what I really wanted to know.

Rebekah answered with conviction. She'd thought about this. A lot. After all, she'd had time. "I was only sixteen, Lou. I didn't know what love was. And neither did he."

Did you not? "But did you——"

"What do you want me to say?" Rebekah cut me off. "I think of it, and of him, every single goddamn day. I'll never forgive myself for what happened. I wanted to die for a long time afterward. I came close to making it happen, and at that school, I wasn't the only one." She leaned forward, resting her elbows on her knees as if she were speaking directly to the cosmetic dentistry ad plastered above the seat on the other side. "I still spend a lot of nights lying awake racking my brain for just one thing I could have done differently, one thing that could have saved him and me. But that's pointless because this isn't the past anymore. It's the present. And we can only take it all—all of our anger, all of our regret, and all of our compassion—and give it to the ones we can help right now. Because they're the ones who need it."

I clamped down on my lip, hard, as if a sob might escape if I didn't. I knew Rebekah was talking about her own story, and she was right, but—

"Tell you what," Rebekah said, green eyes suddenly alive again as if the prospect of action were the only thing that could drag her out of the dark depths of memory. "I have an idea."

—◆—

"Is there anything you'd like me to call you?" I asked the teen boy slumped in the upholstered chair in the dusty, repurposed church basement, because one of the first things I'd learned here was that you didn't ever ask a slave their name. Too much of a potential trigger. You only gave them the option to use one.

"No, miss." The typical answer.

When I first saw him, crumpled near the clinic's back entrance like discarded laundry, I had to gently push back the sleeve of his filthy jacket to see that the arm beneath it ended just below the elbow. The skin was rough and puckered where the limb had been severed, recent, not fully healed either. Whoever had patched him up had done it in a hurry, and not in a hospital. It was amazing they'd even bothered to fix it instead of disposing of him right away.

In other words, he'd been lucky. Or good. Or both.

"Call me Lou. I'm going to touch you now, but this is a safe space and I'm a trained medical volunteer, so there's nothing to worry about. Okay?" He nodded, and I gently smoothed back the sandy curls bloodily matted to the gash across his face to get a better look. Now it was my turn to bite my tongue.

After all, stories were some of my favorite things in the world. But this was a don't-ask-don't-tell clinic, where such stories—including mine—went untold. Like what this boy's owners were like, or how he'd managed to evade them. After all, the chips hadn't come out yet, much as I prayed for the day they would. Much as I prayed for—

Well. Back to the task at hand: inspecting the slave boy's wounds. The whip gash across his cheek and nose looked fresh, as if the overseer had decided to try looking him in the eye for once while doing it. But more urgent were the untreated burns cratered on his palm and verging on infection, maybe from being forced to pick up scorching tools or chemicals bare-handed. Burns not unlike my own.

Fuck this world.

He flinched but said nothing as I applied a rose-scented salve—the same one Ivy had given me way back when—to the worst of the burns, then bandaged them the right way, mentally cataloging the steps, determined to get a gold star, or at least not fuck up completely. Rebekah and I had bet each other a pedicure on what I'd become first: a competent medical professional or a competent barista. The verdict was still out.

The slave boy whimpered, clamping down on his lip as if he'd expected to be punished for that small noise.

"Hey, hey," I said. "Let it out. You can cry here. You can scream. You can tell me to go fuck myself if you want. I don't care."

"But the rest got it worse, miss. Lou." He bit back another whimper.

"The rest?" I froze as it hit me: he wasn't just any runaway.

I remembered the viral clip I'd seen—shaky footage from someone's phone on campus, smoke rising thick from the hills behind the mining compound, police with helmets and rifles pushing slaves in chains down the slope like cattle. The words *Terrorist Slave Uprising* flashed across the screen in red, followed by a thinkpiece from some sanctimonious columnist in thick glasses entitled "Polls Say People Aren't Worried About the Pennsylvania Slave Uprising. Here's Why They Should Be." Beside me, Rebekah had muttered something about "media manipulation" and turned away, but I just sat there, my blood cold.

Now I understood why. This boy—burnt, bleeding, mangled—must have been one of the ones they reported escaped. One of three.

The rest hadn't been so lucky, or so good.

I looked down at his bandaged arm, the stump where a hand should've been, and it clicked. When that accident had mangled his arm, the chip had gone with it. It was the only reason he hadn't been tracked down and dragged back. And ironically, the only reason he now had a chance.

"They said they'll start with the ringleader, miss—Lou. Garotte him in front of everyone."

They're afraid, I thought, but didn't say it. That was good. Dangerous, but good.

"Ringleader?"

"This guy—this guy who planned the whole thing." He swallowed thickly. "He wasn't much older than me. He could read, though, and knew all kinds of things. Helped me learn, helped me make quota. Gave up his rations so I could eat, at the start. And—he saved my life. Took forty lashes for me without blinking. But—" he swallowed. "Now they're calling him dangerous."

"Did *he* have a name?" I asked, not exactly sure why, just knowing it mattered.

"Someone gave him the name Riven."

I squeezed the roll of bandages tighter.

"His old master, or someone. And we found out. So that's what we called him, even though he told us not to." He clamped down hard on his lip, the memory apparently too strong to bear.

"It's okay," I told him again, trying to breathe and focus on the matter at hand. This wasn't about me, or the way that name dislodged something about Rebekah's past. "Cry. It doesn't make you any less brave."

The kid jerked. "Brave?"

"Yeah."

When they met mine, his blue eyes were wide. "No one's ever called me that before."

30

HER

W ell, it was late November again, and this was college now. Forget the frat parties and coordinated pink dorm furniture I'd imagined at a simpler, sillier time. When I wasn't poring over my notes for biochemistry or behavioral psychology, it was now clandestine abolitionist meetings, long hours in the science library, and aprons sodden with spilled vanilla milk. But also late nights in the apartment guzzling bubbly, attempting to learn to cook (Rebekah wasn't much better, to my relief), and watching movies—not all of them intellectually deep—with Rebekah. Three mornings a week, I took the Red Line to the South End, where I learned to wash away blood, dry tears, and never ask. Most of the time, I left feeling powerless in the face of the kind of injustice it felt impossible to ever move the needle on, but to be fair, so did everyone else there, and when I went home on the subway, I felt both supremely alone and profoundly tuned in. And I didn't regret a thing.

One night in November, we watched a live news feed on

Rebekah's laptop while curled on the sofa, one in which her mother, all poise and polish and pantsuits, declared:

"Struggling families deserve support as much as the rich. A home helper, a caregiver, a strong set of hands. And slaves deserve to live stable, calm, industrious lives. Lives that prevent tragedies like the one in the mine in Pennsylvania. My plan ensures dignity, security, and order—for everyone." Bunched on a set of bleachers behind her, a crowd of faces, adults and children, hanging on her every word, jiggling signs reading: *Vote Elizabeth Roth for Senate — A Slave for Every Family!*

Rebekah watched in silence, her expression unreadable.

"You okay?"

She didn't look away from the screen. "You ever feel like you're a ghost in your own life?"

Later that same night, out on the balcony, I passed her the joint. She passed me her sweater. We didn't talk about the speech, but it hung between us anyway, just like the cold, and the smoke curling into the dark.

"I didn't think this was how it would be, either," I said. Rebekah closed her laptop and passed back the joint—which, unashamedly, really did help my anxiety more than anything else I'd tried—and we both watched Brighton, its lights bouncing off the weathered brownstone, hidden lanes and alleys twisting away toward the river, hiding its murky secrets and revealing its ceaseless brilliance.

Rebekah exhaled, and I nudged her shoulder with mine. "Hey. You're right where you're supposed to be. We both are. Maybe it's not perfect, but you said so yourself. What we're doing—it matters."

It was a lie. Because Rebekah and I, we were just the same. I'd thought *he* was the ghost.

But maybe I was. Because here I was, reaching for something I couldn't touch, haunting a life that wasn't mine anymore. Because whenever I had a blank, a field, a void—whether on an electronic device or in my own mind—I entered it in: my eternal question. My god particle, my universal story. Sought it, dreamed about it, ached for it, closed my eyes and grew toward it. While drawing a clumsy heart on top of a cappuccino or while jerking my lolling head off the open pages of my textbooks. In every empty moment of the day, and in all the hollow spaces of the night.

Where are you?

"That reminds me," said Rebekah, and I raised my head with a start. "Rowan from the clinic asked about you the other day."

"The med student?" During breaks while volunteering, I'd chatted with him a bit, mostly about the clinic. Mostly.

"Yeah," said Rebekah. "He's cute. And he cares. He's not just virtue signaling, like some of them."

"Yeah," I agreed. "You're right. But—"

"It's okay," said Rebekah, handing back the joint. "I know. Believe me, I know."

And we both turned back to the view.

The front door was stuck again. I shouldered it open, juggling two iced lattes and a bag of dry noodles, the kind Rebekah pretended to turn up her nose at but always slurped up anyway when we were too tired or lazy to cook, which was often, even though we both said we had to learn.

"Bex?" I called, kicking off my shoes.

No answer.

Then I saw the chain on the table.

Heavy, scuffed metal. Thick links. The kind you attach to a slave's restraints to drag them along.

I froze, one hand on the coffees, the other on the bag, and just... stared.

"Lou."

Her voice came from the sofa. Low, steady. The way she sounded when she was trying not to lose it.

I turned.

Rebekah sat ramrod straight, fists clenched on her knees. Beside her was a boy.

No, not a boy.

A young man.

As a teen, I'd only seen him from a distance a couple of times. But here he was, still in gray detention scrubs, larger and stronger and taller than I'd pictured, muscles tauter from years of hard labor, his hair longer, thick and dark and tangled. His face ashen and bruised, his expression thunderous. The kind of furious that comes from being pushed past breaking again and again. From expecting to be dead long ago and half-resenting that he wasn't. His ankles were chained, the cuffs clearly tight enough to bite into his raw skin. He had red marks on his neck and face, ones I recognized now—they'd collared and muzzled him at one point, too. He was still breathing raggedly from whatever ordeal he'd just been through. All in all, he resembled a rabid animal about to be put down, except—his eyes.

In fact, it was only his eyes that I'd had right. Golden green, like dappled leaves in summer sunlight. Bex had described them perfectly.

The bag of noodles hit the floor.

No one moved.

"I had to," she explained. "They were going to terminate him. Publicly. As an example after the uprising in the mine."

"Does your mom know about —"

"She gave me the money," she said. *Money?*

Then I remembered watching Rebekah get ready that morning, more conservative than usual in her tweed jacket and tortoiseshell hair clip, saying she had to attend an economics lab downtown on "corporate procurement models," which I realized now was her euphemism for a discount slave auction at the detention center. But bored already and rushing off to class myself, I'd thought little of it.

"But how—"

"After I fed her some bullshit about how executions are barbaric and that showing mercy to the ringleader of the uprising would boost her progressive image." She took a deep breath.

"And?"

"And that I could reform him. Turn him into a good slave. One who can be given to a family in need."

A slave for every family. It seemed that in the two of them, I was looking at the pilot program. But for some reason, when I looked at them, none of the words that came to mind were *dignity, security,* or *order.*

More like *chaos.*

Meanwhile, his lip curled. "She bought me." His voice was low, but not quiet. "That's what you people do, right? Throw money at a problem to make it go away?"

"I *saved* you," she snapped. "The least you could do is—"

"Be grateful," he finished, jerking his chains dramatically. "Right. Although I can't help but think gratitude might come a little easier if you weren't the one who got me *thrown in there to begin with?*"

I swallowed hard and glanced again at the shackles she hadn't taken off him.

She followed my gaze. "I don't have the key," she said apologetically.

"She doesn't *want* the key," he said, as a slow, sardonic,

almost satisfied grin spread across his face. "She's afraid of me. Afraid I'll *take my revenge*."

"Shut up," she seethed at him.

"Yes, miss," he growled at her.

With that, she rose and stepped between us. "Louisa," she said with a resigned flourish. "Meet Riven."

He nodded at me. "Charmed," he said. "And don't call me that."

Much as the idea of forcing them to share one bed their first night delighted me, in the end, I let Riven have my room. Most nights, I didn't sleep there anyway, because going to bed felt like giving up. Instead, I lay on the wicker balcony sofa, furry blanket draped over me, got high, and watched the stars go blue.

Maeve was right. You were supposed to be here, at the end. And in the beginning. And in every line in between.

If Rebekah's had returned, against all odds, even vengeful, even as her enemy—then so could mine.

So could all of them.

I recited it again. My litany. My paean. My matin and my evensong. My list. My lost.

Max Langer.

Ethan Wainwright-Phillips.

And—

31

HER

November's ice combed through my hair as I approached Café Jennet for my afternoon shift. In the frosty window, I caught sight of myself and stole a glance at the person staring back: a frivolous West Coast sun bunny doing her best to pose as a serious working Bostonian, my hands shoved deep into the pockets of my new white wool coat with the high collar, which, given the coming deep freeze, I didn't exactly *regret* buying— only spending as much as I had. The pink-and-black plaid cashmere scarf, meanwhile, had been a nineteenth birthday gift from Rebekah. About that, I regretted *nothing*. I regretted nothing about my new persona at all, even if I wasn't quite nailing the part yet.

I did, however, regret that my biochem final was less than a month away, my panic was already surging, and I had to resort to studying in snatches between orders. My fingers curled protectively around the solid shape of my textbook where it lay nestled in my leather bag. *Today.*

Before throwing open the door with its handmade

Christmas wreath, I paused to inhale the cold, relishing the pleasant sting in my lungs as I exhaled a plume. To my desert-born heart's delight, the snow had started sooner than forecasted, its tiny, delicate flakes kissing the ground and adding a layer of silence to the streets. There might come a time when I'd hate winter as most longtime New Englanders seemed to, but that time wasn't now.

Once inside, enveloped in a blanket of roasty warmth, I cleared a pile of anarchist fliers and a gaudy pine garland off the counter and extricated my biochem textbook from my bag. Then I grabbed a mug and a packet of Earl Grey, my fingers sliding against the damp surface before filling it with hot water. Tea only, this afternoon. Staying awake was important, but too much caffeine would just goose my anxiety, and I couldn't afford to lose time on *that*.

Over at the register, Malin, a freed slave girl Basia had hired to work with us until she could figure out what to do next, stood chewing on her ragged nails as she gaped at the computer display.

Basia put a hand on her shoulder. "It's okay, Malin," she said with a wink at me. "Take your time."

"But they want a decaf, and there's no button," Malin said. "This is madness."

Malin, tall, freckled, and curvy, had apparently spent most of her life as a personal maid and close companion for the teenage daughter of her master. It sounded okay generally and explained her peculiar personality, except that, according to Basia, the master's son had used Malin for another purpose. In other words, she was another reminder that with slaves, it was never okay, ever.

Basia just laughed, threw a clean apron on the counter for me, and disappeared into the back.

"Put in regular, and I'll give them decaf. If I remember," I finally told Malin, tying the apron over the thick, fuzzy sky-blue sweater I'd borrowed from Rebekah when the weather first turned cold, and so far had managed to avoid giving back. Speaking of Rebekah, the Freedom Alliance had its meeting in the back office today, and I'd have to break it to Malin that we likely wouldn't see our boss again all afternoon, even if the espresso machine spontaneously achieved sentience and began spewing scalding shots of coffee at everyone in an attempt at world domination.

"Hey, is that my sweater?" It was Rebekah, having just breezed in in her pearls, heading immediately for the back to meet Basia and Laken.

"No," I said innocently, opening my textbook and ducking sheepishly as I realized I had not, in fact, remembered to give them decaf. "Also, your mom was on TV again this morning. I turned the sound off, but the closed captions are calling her 'A Fighter for Responsible Servitude.' So, congrats?"

She groaned. "Please just burn the television."

"I would, but it's the only thing distracting me from the fact that the third member of our household—he who refuses to be named—spent the entire morning fixing the sink shirtless and muttering insults under his breath."

"I told him to wear a shirt."

"Well, he *had* one. It was just slung dramatically over his shoulder like some enslaved thirst trap."

She exhaled through her teeth. "He knows exactly what he's doing."

"Oh, I'm aware," I said. "You're the one who took off his restraints."

"Because I needed to know if I could trust him. And he needed to know he could trust *me*."

"And?"

She didn't answer right away. Just adjusted the strap of her bag and stared at the floor for a second too long. "Let's just say he hasn't hurt anyone or stolen anything yet," she said, "except maybe my last functioning nerve. At least he's not one of the ones still out there," she said, lowering her voice, as if this weren't the one place in Boston where you *could* talk about such things without getting side-eyed or worse.

"The escaped slaves from the mine?" I'd never mentioned that I'd met one of them, though we'd kept in touch when he went underground again.

"The police think he's helping them, though. Which is *super* helpful for my mom's new platform."

"Uh-huh. And is that why he's also learning to bake bread?"

"Whole wheat. From scratch. To 'contribute to the household.'"

"And totally not to fuck with you."

"He asked me if I preferred my loaves 'warm, soft, and obedient.'"

I nearly choked on my tea. "Oh my God."

"Yeah," she muttered, turning toward the back room. "Pray for me."

The door chimed again and again as the afternoon caffeine rush began, people shivering and stamping fresh snow melt all over the wood floor. With Malin at the counter, I took a position in my little nook by the espresso machine, my view of the door blocked by its massive copper piping and the stacks of cups, bracing myself for whatever today's crisis would be. Invariably, just when I thought I'd reached equilibrium, pulling shots and steaming milk like I'd done it for years, some nutcase would demand a quadruple extra-strong iced mocha latte served in an espresso cup, and it would all come crashing down again. But I'd just remind myself that, like the rest of me, my barista skills were still gestating, like a beautiful caffeine-soaked butterfly trapped in an inept cocoon. Also, Basia didn't really care, given the point of this place was just to make enough money to destroy capitalism.

"See that man who just walked in?" Malin asked suddenly, spraying crumbs from a mouthful of giant chocolate-chip cookie from the bakery case. Despite my better judgment, I both accepted her offer of a morsel and craned my neck to catch a glimpse. "The one with the curly dark hair, deep-set eyes, and biceps that could crack a walnut?"

I folded my arms, letting the sweetness melt decadently in my mouth and toying with the idea of grabbing an entire cookie for myself. It was the most hazardous part of this job. "What about him?"

Malin swallowed quickly. "He's running from the feds for sure."

Malin was absolutely convinced that one of the countless mafia scions, international assassins, or incognito billionaires constantly entering the shop would finally whisk her away to Bali, or at least to the back seat of their car to *finally* give her the orgasm she so richly deserved. Come to think of it, she actually had a lot in common with Maeve, if Maeve had chosen to take refuge in erotica instead of high fantasy.

"Oh, really?" I replied, feigning interest as I steamed milk for a latte. "What did he do?"

"He hacked into the defense department's mainframe, of course," Malin whispered dramatically. "And stole plans for a secret mind-control project."

I suppressed a snort, but the customer at the counter must have overheard, given that he paid in cash and left a generous tip, those soulful eyes lingering on Malin's breasts for a beat too long as he exited the shop.

"Better watch out," I said. "He knows you have the inside scoop."

"Oh, I'll give him the inside scoop, all right," Malin gloated with a bold little twist of her hips.

The shadows outside grew longer. The rimey haze shifted from blue to pink to lavender, punctuated by gusts of cold air, rosy cheeks, the hiss of espresso, and bells announcing customer after customer. Malin and I swapped stories with the usual cast: the wired would-be screenwriter reimagining another fairy tale as a post-apocalyptic film noir. The befuddled tourist demanding directions to Fenway Park in broken English. And, inevitably, the green-haired young slave, as much punk rock as servile, balancing a teetering tray for the office workers he toiled for. A future Milagros, maybe, dreaming of the stars.

Meanwhile, I kept juggling orders, chasing that equilibrium, squinting at my biochem notes splayed on the counter, snatching glances at the complex pathways of glycolysis and Krebs cycles between tamping grounds and steaming milk.

An hour later, despite the growing queue of orders on the screen, Malin sidled up beside me. I knew that look.

"Undercover royalty alert."

"Oh yeah?" I quirked an eyebrow, never breaking my rhythm. "I'm sure this one is absolutely, *one hundred percent* on a top-secret mission to marry a good-hearted commoner who loves him for who he really is." I managed to shift my attention once more back to my notes, blinking hard, trying to refocus and become the marvel of multitasking I knew I could be.

Just then, however, my phone vibrated from the pocket of my apron. Tempted to ignore it, I fished it out anyway, curiosity nagging at the back of my brain.

DADDY

> Loulou, call me when you get off work.
> Everything's fine. Love you.

It was rare to get a message like this from him. Our regular Sunday calls were chatty but not particularly enlightening: the weather, his golf game, the dismal state of the real estate market, and whatever business tome or espionage thriller he'd just read. I still wasn't great at feigning interest in any of it, but still, I treasured these calls, having never expected to be in a good enough place with my father to even have them. He knew and approved of my job at Café Jennet and had only commented, when I'd confessed to volunteering at the slave clinic, that it would be "tremendously valuable career experience."

Idly, I wondered whether the message meant the house had finally sold, sending a little jolt of anxiety through me. I felt unmoored already at the thought of losing my home of ten years. Then again, I'd recently reevaluated my concept of "home" quite a bit.

If it weren't so busy right now, I might have just called. But a familiar grumbling emanated from the customers bunched near the pickup counter, so I just tapped out a quick reply—

> K love you

—and dropped the phone back in my apron pocket. Turning to the next order, I grabbed a cup. *Focus.* Only three hours to go. Then:

"His Highness happens to be a total thirst trap, in case you're curious."

I rolled my eyes. "Are we seriously *still* talking about this dude?"

"Tall, expensive clothes, regal presence, looks like he's packing some serious heat."

"What, a gun?"

"Yeah, maybe that, too." Malin poked her tongue out lasciviously.

"Look, Malin, I'm so happy for you that you're finally experiencing life with its rich tapestry of dicks, but I have to actually finish making this drink, pass this class, and avoid being shipped back home in disgrace. Wherever home may be by then," I added warily, sliding the drink I had been working on across the counter.

Instead of grabbing it, Malin leaned in closer, her voice dropping to a whisper. "Wait. I haven't told you about his accent yet."

I cocked my head. "What kind of accent?"

Malin tapped a finger against her chin. "Imagine if a Frenchman and a German woman moved to California and had a baby. And that baby swallowed a frog."

I laughed. "All right. So maybe this guy is a wandering princeling." I snapped the portafilter into place carefully. "Or maybe—hear me out—he's just some Eurotrash nepo baby who thinks he's saving humanity by paying an extra dollar for a latte that wasn't made by a slave." But for some reason—even as I spoke—I risked another peek around the side of the machine. And, once again, saw nothing unusual, just some wannabe radical with a lip piercing tapping on a ridiculously expensive phone and a business-suited woman as thin as her penciled-in eyebrows, who eyed the slaves in front of her resentfully, apparently not keen that here, everyone was entitled to use the same line.

I shook my head, scolding myself. What, precisely, was I expecting to see? This was just another one of Malin's sex-crazed delusions. Taking a deep breath, I squared my shoulders as I glanced at the next order, reaching for an oversized hand-made cappuccino cup from the shelf.

"And then of course there's his name."

For the third time, her voice cut through my concentration. *Ignore it.*

"It's awfully unusual. Exotic, even."

"Mmhmm." I barely looked up, hands moving on autopilot as I measured out the ingredients.

"Shy," Malin said, drawing out the vowel sound. "Isn't that interesting?"

I furrowed my brow. "Shy? I thought you said he was confident."

Malin giggled. "No, *that's* his name. *S-H-A—*"

I never even heard the *I*. The cup slipped from my grasp, hit the counter, and shattered into a zillion pieces. Hot liquid splattered everywhere, dripping down the counter and scalding my arms and hands, probably, even though I didn't feel a goddamn thing.

Malin froze, understandably stunned by the sight of me standing helpless, arms raised halfway, eyes fixed unseeingly on the scene. "What happened? Are you okay?"

Stupid, stupid, STUPID fucking girl. Like there aren't thousands of them out there. Millions. Well, maybe not millions, but you can't possibly be stupid enough to think that—

"Honey, you're shaking," said Basia as she, Rebekah, and Laken dashed out of the back office, startled by the noise. Basia drew her arms around me tightly. "Malin, grab a towel, honey."

Malin blinked and nodded, ducking under the counter.

Rebekah turned on the faucet at the same second Malin reappeared with a clean rag.

"And you're scalded," Basia exclaimed, grabbing my arm and holding it under the running water. "We need to get—"

"It's fine," I cut her off. "I'm fine. I'm sorry, Basia. I'm so sorry. I'll clean this up, I promise. I'll—I'll—I'll—" But I was stuck, stammering, trembling, helpless. All I could do was take it in: the smithereens of earthenware, the exploded cappuccino, the foamy mess trailing down the machine and the floor. And the blurry reflection in the refrigerator, a splash of molten gold across gunmetal gray.

"Oh, shit. Lou. I'm sorry! Are you okay?"

The heads of all five people behind the counter spun around instantly.

And there, of course, was Malin's prince.

The prince I had last seen in a rough gray slave uniform, standing amid the chains he had shed. And who had now exchanged those for a luxe wool peacoat, a cashmere scarf, and chunky gold rings on his scarred hands, which he was currently running through his snow-dusted golden hair in chagrin as he leaned far, far over to rest his elbows on the glass bakery case.

"I'm sorry, I didn't mean to do that," Shai said to Basia. "I'll pay for it, don't worry."

But Basia didn't move, and neither did Rebekah or Laken or Malin, and neither did I, though the tap was still running, raining water down on my scalded arm. I couldn't. *Nothing* about what was happening right now made sense, unless I'd either fallen into a time warp where three years had gone by already, or there was a phalanx of armed federal agents outside ready to smash in the windows.

"I really fucked this up, yeah?" Shai said with a sheepish little laugh. "You look so *scared*, Lou. I promise, it's okay. You're okay. It's just me. Come." He beckoned me forward.

But I didn't move, so to set me in motion, my boss lightly swatted me on the bottom, which she could get away with because she was Basia and she once let a slave girl give birth in her freezer and then hid the baby.

Well. I couldn't feel my body as I floated incorporeally

over to the bakery case, my eyes fixed on the hands and the wrists underneath those rich wool sleeves with their brass buttons.

"He *is* a prince, right?" I vaguely heard Malin remarking to no one in particular. "Definitely a prince. I totally called it."

"Lou. Listen." As I stared, those same hands traced nervous star shapes on the glass case, and—though they were just inches away from my own—went no farther. "I did rehearse an elaborate speech, I promise, but I forgot it all a second ago, so here's the gist of it: your dad patented the microchip formula on my behalf. With Erica's help."

When I didn't move or respond, he took a deep breath and forged ahead.

"They found some decent engineers, developed a prototype, and pitched it to some venture capitalists who only invest in paid-labor startups. Behind my back, of course, but he was banned from contacting me, so I can't be too angry about it, and now we've got seed funding in the high seven figures and we—"

"Wait." I'd only heard about half of what he'd said and understood even less. "We?"

"Well, yeah." He blinked. "I own fifty-one percent of the company."

"But—" I shook my head. This wasn't helping, and none of it would unless he explained just how in the fucking hell he was *here*.

"Just let me finish, yeah?" He was half-smiling. A good sign, and also, confirmation that nobody in tactical gear was about to bust down the door.

Okay. Breathe.

"When the field director called me into his office last week, Manny—Agent Wheatley, that is—was a wreck because he thought they'd caught me trying to break the rules. I was, too.

But we were wrong. They never caught me," he said, and the first twinges of a smile pulled at my lips, too.

"Anyway, the director told me your dad had convinced the VCs that it would be bad optics to have a de facto slave as founder and chairman, so they agreed to let him use part of the seed funding to buy out the rest of my contract with the feds. So I just flew in from Phoenix, where I hired Maeve as our first employee, convened our first corporate board meeting, and appointed your dad CEO to handle the day-to-day, in consultation with me."

Still half-smiling, he paused to take a deep breath and blow some hair out of his face. "And as for the board, Erica was the first member appointed, so needless to say, we won't be getting away with *anything*."

If I'd been shaking before, I was vibrating now. *Now* it was becoming clear. "You're—"

"That's right." He swallowed. Nodded. "The F-word. The good one."

"Foamy espresso?" But I was already laughing, watching his slow smile spread, and then *he* was laughing, and it was done. My tears were flowing already, replacing the shock. "One hundred percent?"

"One hundred percent. Forever. Rest of my life."

My heart pounded in my ears with a rhythm I knew already —from my dreams. Because this *was* a dream. I'd dreamed it a hundred times, in different settings, different circumstances, different words, but always spent the entire next day in that strange liminal space between the dream's perfect happiness and the sadness that it wasn't real. But in none of them had it ever actually gotten far enough to—

"Can I kiss you?" I blurted out. "Here? Without anybody being beaten, electrocuted, or thrown in a cage?"

He laughed. "Even if you couldn't, would it stop you?"

"Hell no. But it's good to know." I grabbed the back of my apron, fumbling with the ties. "Wait. I don't want anything separating us. Not even a bakery case. I'm going around."

"Well, go around then!" Still laughing, he waved me off impatiently.

Still, I kept jerking desperately to unknot the ties until finally Rebekah reached out, grabbed the apron, and yanked it the rest of the way off. She shoved me forward, and as I stepped around the glass case amid the weight of a dozen gazes, my eyes didn't leave his because they didn't have to. His coat was still cold, but I felt nothing but warmth as Shai reached out, pulled me to him, and kissed me. And there we joined, bodies melded, curves yielding to angles. An answer given. A puzzle solved. A dream come—once again—to life.

"Wait, should we clap?" I heard Malin ask the others. "Is this a clapping moment?"

"Yeah, I think it is," replied Rebekah.

I turned back to my friends, tears cascading down my cheeks, and nodded. And they clapped, joined in by the bewildered customers standing in line.

"Oh, thanks, Malin," said Shai suddenly, reaching past me to accept the small cup across the bakery case, while my eyes followed the trajectory.

"Since when do you drink macchiato?" I asked.

"I don't. It's for you." He thrust it toward me.

"What?" I stared into the cup, at Malin's off-center but earnest dot of foam.

"Because I didn't get you one. The night we met. Not that I didn't try."

I folded my arms. "You didn't try very hard."

"No, I didn't," he admitted with a laugh. "But I'm trying now."

"Thank you," I whispered in his ear with another ghost of a

kiss. And then, coffee in hand, I stood at arm's length and took a moment to really *look*.

To my infinite relief, his hair had grown back beautifully, not a patch to be seen, and he still wore it swept carelessly to one side, though a bit shorter and darker blond; the sunny streaks muted by indoor work, maybe. He'd let a bit of facial hair grow out, too—a strange but shockingly appealing look on him. Dark wash jeans, short leather boots, and a clearly very expensive watch. Everything tasteful, classic, understated, made to last.

This wasn't his slave castoffs and institutional uniforms. This wasn't the flashy suits and gaudy bling of the Langer days.

This was *him*.

"Shai." I tested the name—not for the first time, but the first time in the world.

He smiled, swallowed, and nodded. "It's still taking some getting used to."

No shit. I shook my head, hot tears still blurring my vision. I blinked them back, suddenly angry that they were marring this magnificent view. "You didn't tell me. And neither did Daddy. Why?"

He took a deep breath and reached for my waist again to pull me close. Some people were looking, but most people weren't. We were in the middle of a crowded public coffee shop and no one *cared*.

Talk about a dream come to life.

"Your dad wasn't sure it would happen, and he didn't want to break your heart if it didn't. And once we knew it *would* happen, I told him I wanted to be the one to tell you," he said, tracing rhythmic circles on my hip, as much to comfort himself as me. "In person. And he respected me enough to let me."

The message. *That* was why my dad had asked me to call. He'd known Shai was on his way here, or maybe had already arrived. Astonishingly, my dad had *made it happen*. And he didn't want to spoil the surprise.

"Wait. My dad? You? *Respect*?"

"I know. Historically, those three things haven't really gone together, but you should *see* him, Lou. I know science, but I don't know business, and he does, and he's already taught me a lot, and well... shit, he's *trying*. He really is. Come to think of it," he said, his awkwardness filling me with sympathy for the countless *other* awkward moments he and my father must have endured in the past week, "in his own way, I think he always *was* trying."

"You know," I said slowly, "I think he was, too."

"Want to go for a walk?" Shai asked. "I know you're working, but—"

"It's all good, Louisa!" called Basia with a wink. "Consider this working for the cause."

Over by the register, Malin piped up, "What cause? Public indecency awareness? You know that by 'walk,' he means—"

Rebekah shushed her, but Basia just laughed.

"You and Malin would get along famously, I think," I remarked to Shai. "Also, it's snowing." *No shit.* He'd just come in from outside. Clearly, my brain had switched off, but I wasn't sure it would ever fully switch on again. Not as long as I had *this* to look at.

"It's okay. I lived in the desert for a while, you know." He pushed open the door with a rapid, nearly undetectable glance at me, something about its slyness bringing on memories so strong they almost knocked me over before the brisk rush of air even had a chance. And then there we were, as public as public gets, emerging right out onto the sidewalk, into the rush of traffic and the orange glow of the streetlamps just lit. In front of cars. In front of people. In front of the world that was about to be ours.

"So I kind of like the snow," he explained. "It's more like home. Only problem is I'm in a Porsche convertible."

"Excuse me?"

He laughed, brushing a few stray flakes from my hair playfully. "Don't worry, it's just a rental. A really fucking stupid rental, given the forecast," he said sheepishly. "But it's smarter than a motorcycle, which I was also considering. Although at least with that, it would have been easier to find parking."

We strolled to the end of the block, boots crunching. I nestled closer into him, shielding myself against the chill.

"You have a driver's license already?"

"Let me put it this way: Until you have friends in the feds, you don't realize how much you need them."

We paused at the edge of the common, taking in the serenity.

"And the money—"

"I'm getting a salary. A modest one. But the majority of it, for right now, will go right back into the business, to help us scale. Your dad's getting some extra to go toward freeing the other slaves. The board considered that a business expense, too. Optics, you know."

When we got to the first light, he pulled me closer, our bodies pressed together as the snow fell gently over us, the rapid beat of his heart right up against my own chest. I gazed up at him in shock. "Wait, are you serious?"

"Dead serious. The valet, of course, said he'd rather stay, and your dad's promised him a home for life, in any case."

"But Aveline—" I asked, thinking of the maid who had finally confessed her birth name to me in San Diego after one too many passionfruit margaritas. It was probably the one thing that had actually gone *right* during that bizarre little jaunt, but I didn't regret any of it, and I hoped she didn't, either.

"She's headed up north with the housekeeper—Samantha,

that is. Newfoundland, I think? Sam wants to try to see her kids, and Aveline says she has no interest in tracking down her parents, so they decided to stick together for a while."

I leaned into him, resting my head on his shoulder as we walked, the snow muffling the distant sounds of the city surrounding us. There would be time enough for all of that now.

"Are they okay? Also, how have my parents not starved to death under a pile of dirt?"

"Your dad can cook and clean, as it turns out. It's been twenty years since he's had to, but he can." He continued in a quieter voice as we waited for the next light to change, the weight of his arm resting perfectly around my waist. He raised my hand, thumb on the back of my palm, fingers mingling with mine. "And as for them... Well, it's not easy, Lou. For any of us."

And it's not something you'll ever fully understand was implied.

But there was so much about slavery I'd never fully understand. Its enormity was so unfathomable that most people didn't even try. But I did try, and I was going to keep trying. The only reason I had this life, and this man, was because a long time ago, I had made the decision to try. And that had changed the entire game.

"So about the startup," I said as we crossed the next street. "If slavery is still legal..."

He took a deep breath, his chest rising and falling against me. "It's complicated, Lou. But if we can get this distributed and on the market—even if it's not legal for slaves to possess—it will still do a lot of good. For one thing, there will be fewer people like Resi stealing, hurting, and terrorizing them because they're afraid of being caught if they run. And more will run, at least until the pro-slavery lobby gets harsher laws passed to prevent it, and don't get me wrong—they will. In the meantime, we're getting it past the regulators by convincing them that it's for pets. Dogs and cats. That was your dad's idea. Which was genius, actually."

In astonishment, I reached up and brushed away a few stray snowflakes that had landed on his lashes. "Did... did you just say something nice about Daddy?"

He caught my hand and squeezed it. "Funny, it became a lot easier once he didn't own me," he said. "And showed me my stock certificate. Look, it's going to be a hard fight, Lou. It may not happen in our lifetime."

My heart sank into my knees. It wasn't as if I thought we could abolish slavery overnight, but—

I stopped walking, turning to face him. Snowflakes clung to my lashes in the fading light, melting into my eyes along with the tears. "But it will happen. Right?"

"It will happen. And it will get easier in time, as more and more people like your dad realize that they want to be on the right side of history."

"And more people like you convince them."

"I didn't convince him. You did."

Amid a sudden gust of snow, he reached for one of my curls and gently tucked it behind my ear, talking over the noise of the wind.

I swallowed, throat tight.

"Do you understand that *none* of this would exist without you?" he said. "Our company wouldn't be here. I wouldn't be here. Your dad wouldn't be here. And *we* wouldn't be here," he added, still puzzling with my curl as if it were much more than a curl. "It was you, Lou. You changed everything. For all of us."

Tears blurred my vision again as I gazed up at him, hardly able to believe he was real. That any of what he was saying was real. Not me. Not Loulou, not privileged, naive, spoiled, ignorant— "I was just trying to do the right thing."

"And I'm no expert, but I think that's what bravery is." He

drew me closer, enveloping me. I inhaled him—I wasn't sure whether it was my memory or his stop in Phoenix, but I could swear he still wore the trace of desert sage on his hair and clothes and lips.

After a long moment, he pulled back slightly, and as we walked, my head swirled, and I kept glancing over at him, drinking in the sight of that expensive coat hugging those broad shoulders.

He caught me looking and grinned. "I know. It's surreal, isn't it? No chains."

I poked him. "*Not* what I was thinking." It was, actually, although maybe not quite in the same way.

He stared at the ground for a long second. "I wake up and feel them on me," he said softly. "Most nights, in fact. And I still feel—" He swallowed. "Well, a lot of things I wish I didn't. And that I'm afraid I'll never *un*feel. And that it'll never be easy."

"Me too." I bit my lip, looking away as he quickly rolled back his coat sleeve to reveal the number that used to be his name. Softly, I closed each one of my fingertips over it and squeezed. "You and I wouldn't know what to do with easy."

"Damn. *That's* where I got that line. I knew it sounded familiar."

A handful of snow flew past my face, and up ahead in the streetlight's glow, I spotted a small group of children giggling and flinging handfuls of loose snow at each other—probably slaves, judging by the way they muffled their laughs and averted their eyes when they saw us coming, then darted into an alley without another word as if they hadn't meant to be seen enjoying themselves.

"Milagros told me light is never lost," I said. "So even when things feel useless, and impossible to ever fix," I said softly, "Every single little thing we do is helping fix it for them. Someday."

"Someday soon," he said. "Thanks to you and your dad."

"And Ethan," I added, my throat tightening. "I hope. Someday soon."

Shai's eyes widened at the sound of the name. "Did you—"

"Not yet." I shook my head. "Still looking. Erica and Rebekah and Basia are all helping."

"You'll have my help, too, you know. We'll find him," he said, a statement of fact.

I swallowed and nodded. "Only Max knew for sure. And now—"

"Ah, of course he did," Shai said, shaking his head with a rueful laugh. "We still owe that man more than we can ever repay. *I* owe him more." He looked up toward the sky. "And, Max, if you're listening, I hope you enjoyed that because it's the last time you'll ever hear me say it."

"Well?" I asked. "What are the chances he *was* listening?"

"From the sky? Unless he's tailing us with a surveillance drone, almost zero, I'd say. I expect we'll hear from him when he makes *another* fortune down in Rio Dulce. Or loses one. Or dies for real in a shootout with guerillas. It's wide open."

We continued our languid stroll, arms wrapped around each other, glows of headlights cutting through the falling snow as we crossed into the park, our footprints the only disturbance in the path stretching away into a tessellation of naked maples. "So now what?"

"Well," he said, taking a deep, rattling breath. "Now that I'm in Boston, I have a few things on my list. Look for a place to rent. Enroll in university and start working on an actual degree. I just applied, and I'll start in the spring. I think I could probably finish by *next* spring, but you know," he added wryly. "They have their own timelines."

"And the tuition?"

"Also the VC funding, at least for the first year. The university said I would qualify for a scholarship, but I told them to give the money to a former slave who *doesn't* own a company."

"Which school?" I wondered.

"One of the ones across the river. You've probably heard of it," he said modestly.

"Any particular reason?"

"Well," he said, "that brings me to the rest of my list." He tugged me to a stop under a lamp, its soft yellow glow illuminating the funneling snow. "See, there's this girl I've been thinking about a lot in the past year. Like, every goddamn day as it turns out." He seemed to alternate between gazing into my eyes and running his thumb against the fabric of my white wool coat as if to anchor himself to me. "Whose dad, the day he picked me up from the airport in Phoenix, happened to casually mention that she goes to another school right down the road from here."

I anxiously worked my hands inside his coat, finding warmth against the solid planes of his chest, that inverted V-shape of which I could see all the luscious contours in my mind's eye. My heart pounded, anticipation rising in my throat. "And what are your plans for this girl?"

"Well, for one, I want to take her out on a date. The ridiculously clichéd kind where I pick her up at her door and bring her flowers. Where we go to dinner and I pull out her chair. Someplace in public where I can stare into her beautiful eyes for as long as I want and not give a fuck about who sees. Where I kiss her good night at her door and text her the next day. The kind I've always heard about."

I blushed, ducking my head. He tipped my chin back up with a gentle finger. Tears pricked my eyes. "That sounds perfect," I whispered, practically vibrating.

"And then," he continued, pulling me closer, "I want to spend every moment I can with her. Making up for all the ones we weren't allowed. Helping her study and bringing her coffee, not because I was ordered to but because I want to," he added. "Taking her on adventures where we don't have to lie and scheme and dodge death. Unless, of course, she *wants* that kind of adventure, because we can have those, too," he added with a troublesome gleam. "And then," he continued, his voice dropping low in my ear, "I want to make love to her. Slowly, tenderly, worshiping every inch of her gorgeous body the way it deserves to be worshiped. No more counting clocks or banging on intercoms. I want to take hours, *days* even, to teach her things she's never even *thought* of and learn everything that makes her gasp and moan and come undone in my arms."

"Shai—"

"I know, but wait. Let me get this out, yeah?" He forged ahead. "I know she's changed a lot, too, in the past year. So before any of that, I want to meet *that* girl and get to know her, too, and maybe—maybe, while I do that, she can see if she likes this version of me."

I cocked my head. "What do you mean, *this* version of you?"

He blinked, and now it was his turn to be tongue-tied. "Well, I just thought that—well—"

"Fucking hell, Shai, this *is* you," I exclaimed. "This is the first time I've ever really *met* you. The *you* that I met over a year ago, well, it wasn't really *you*. I mean, it was, but—well, you know what I mean."

"Manny said I didn't know how to be a person," he blurted out, all of his silver-tongued romantic composure melting away in an instant. "And he was right. I didn't. Or at least, I didn't know the kind of person I wanted to be. And maybe that's still true."

"Why?"

"Because—" he stopped, shaking some hair out of his face in frustration. "I know it's ironic, but because there was freedom in that, Lou. The only freedom I ever had. They told me I wasn't a person, so I said, fine. If I didn't have a name, I'd never have to answer to anything, or anyone—except for my family, and once my sister was safe, I figured I never would again."

"But why did you *want* that?"

He sighed dolorously. "Maybe because—because—I've done a lot wrong. I've lied. I've stolen. I've fucked up and fucked over. I've hurt people. All for what I thought were the right reasons, but, well... we know that's what everyone thinks, yeah? And so maybe I was afraid that if I chose to be a person, nobody would *like* that person. Maybe even that *I* wouldn't like him." He looked down helplessly and kicked a thin, snow-dusted branch out of the way in torment. He'd made biochemical breakthroughs, mounted reckless gambits and bold rescues, endured sadistic abuse, torture, and rape—and *this* was what the poor guy was struggling with: talking about himself. "Or that—"

His voice was raw, breaking open like an old wound.

"Or that what?"

"That *you* wouldn't like him."

This actually stopped me dead. "What?"

"That if you—if you said my name, if you made me a person—that you wouldn't like the person you made."

"But—"

"Look, let me try to explain. You were the only person who ever made me feel like I was worth more than just my brains, more than just my schemes, more than just surviving." He raced on ahead. "And I was terrified of what that meant—that if I let myself love you, I'd have to learn how to be more than that. I'd have to be someone who knew how to love, how to *be* loved. I was afraid of what that would make me. What it would take from me. What it would demand of me. I was afraid of *you*."

His breath hitched, his fists curling like he was trying to hold himself together by will alone. "I was afraid of how much I wanted you. How much I needed you. I was afraid that if I let myself have you, I wouldn't know how to keep you. I had so little to begin with, and if I lost you"—he swallowed hard, shaking his head—"there'd be nothing left of me."

His hands trembled at his sides. In fact, his entire body was shaking. "And that's why I couldn't say it. When we said good-bye, the first time. I used to be afraid of what you made me feel. Of the way you looked at me like I was someone worth saving, worth—fuck, worth loving—when they told me my whole life I wasn't."

I opened my mouth.

"But I'm not afraid anymore."

Our eyes locked. The tips of his fingers entwined with the tips of mine, desperate but certain. "I love you, Lou. I love you, and nobody ever taught me how to do it, but if you let me, I swear to fucking God I will try."

"Shai."

"Yeah?" he said, answering to his name immediately as if he were desperate to let me take over.

"Come here." I swept his snow-dusted lock of golden hair, cupping his face as he lowered his lashes and leaned forward into my touch with the most exhausted sigh I'd ever heard. His cheek was frigid on the surface but warm beneath, and the warmth transferred to my fingertips as I held them there.

"I can't speak for the world, but I can speak for me."

He raised his eyes.

"And I know there isn't any version of you, in any lifetime, in any universe, that I would ever not like. That I would ever not want. That I would ever not love."

His sigh of relief seemed to shake him to his core. "I was *really* hoping you would say that," he confessed. "And I know I have some catching up to do, so I promise you'll be hearing *I love you* again, every day, for the rest of my life. And if I miss a day, which I won't, call me out on it, yeah?"

"Oh, I will." I pressed myself against him again, winding my arms around his waist under his coat, poking his hip with mine. And like that, we kept walking farther into the silent park, crunching leaves, kicking snow, toward a wall of elms and along a row of maples with not a single crimson leaf left to fall.

But his eyes were fixed on something even farther away. Across the icy river, beyond the iron-gray bay, over an ocean. "And—since you asked, there's one more thing. I have to go back," he said, turning to me suddenly. "With Maeve. To where the Alzette meets the Petrusse. That's where—well. To put a marker up."

Slowly, he raised our clasped hands, scientifically examining the way our fingers interlocked, before earnestly meeting my eyes. "Will you come with us? This summer," he said, adding, "Luxembourg will be beautiful then."

As if he thought he had to sell me on it. On seeing his homeland. His real homeland, where he'd been abused as cruelly as he had been everywhere else, but that he loved all the same.

"I'd go anywhere with you, Shai. You know that." I kissed that intricate, interlocking bed of scars—a kiss that revealed, to my surprise, his initials etched in stacked script on the gold signet ring: *S-v-S.*

"I bought one for Maeve, too," he explained. "She traced the genealogy. Van Someren was our family name, from generations ago. Before the hard times."

"'Van?'"

"They say it signifies nobility." The trace of a smile, keen for my reaction.

"*Nobility?* Malin was right? You *are* a prince?" I bounced a little on his arm.

"No," he admitted, shaking his head. "Although my third great-grandfather *was* a grand duke, apparently. But don't get too excited. I didn't inherit anything. We looked into it, believe me."

"Great-grandson of a grand duke," I repeated. "Okay. Well, not every girl can say *that* about her boyfriend. Or that she named him," I added slyly.

"All right, young lady, let's clear one thing up right now: it was a *suggestion*," he said as I laughed mischievously. "Which I *chose* to accept. Probably because it just sounded so damn sexy on your lips."

"Sexy?! You were *dying*!"

"Yeah, I know. A guy can't die happy? And where'd you come up with it, anyway? Do you speak Hebrew?"

"Not a word, but my grandmother did. And it means 'gift.' Which you are."

"Gift?" He arched an eyebrow. "I think you mean 'gifted.'"

"I mean both. Now kiss me, Shai. Oh, shit, wow, that *does* sound sexy."

"Told you," he said, obliging me immediately in a pattern I remembered—forehead, eyelids, both cheeks, nose, and lips. "Let's do some more testing. Say 'touch me, Shai.'"

"Touch me, Shai."

His hands were there in an instant, up my open coat and under Rebekah's stolen sweater and the thin camisole beneath, his rough, scarred thumbs stroking the skin just above my waistband, under my navel, and above that mound of flesh and nerve as he lifted me effortlessly by the hips, pressing my body flush against his. Polar November closed in on all sides, but I only had *him*—his power, his warmth, his solidity, his realness —no longer the ghost of a touch forbidden, the dream of a life beyond reach.

Shai's mouth found mine again, his kiss bold, urgent,

demanding, *commanding*. Huge and open, ravenous as an inferno, claiming, consuming, immolating every bare, icy patch on my ears and collarbone and neck, right down to my décolletage. And oh yes, I yielded for him, molded myself in his shape, one leg up around his waist and wrapping the other, cattishly arching and fisting the lapels of his lush coat until we broke and just breathed heat for a few seconds in dewy, exquisite synergy, brows pressed together. And then I thought he would stop, but he just kept *kissing*, kissing while the flakes fell silently down on our hair and shoulders and eyelashes, kissing while our hearts lashed against our shivering chests, kissing until he cradled his head on my shoulder, gasping for air, kissing until he lowered his glistening lashes and just *inhaled*, drank me in, fuller and fuller, more and more, as if I, Louisa Wainwright-Phillips, were sweeter than liberty, indeed the sweetest nectar this boy, this free man, had ever tasted.

So what if he would always scan a room before entering to see what he could get away with? Or that he might always be polite to strangers and keep things close to the vest? Or that he might always have the knack of looking at people without *really* looking?

It all had its uses.

Now he let my boots tumble and crunch lightly on the snow. He stood there, broad shoulders heaving from what I'd done to him. But we weren't done. He grinned. "Now say, f—"

I swatted him. "We're in *public*."

"Oh, that's right, my mistake." He lifted his gaze, expression softening slightly as if just now seeing he was in this park in all its antique solitude, the snow falling more swiftly now, diagonally blanketing the oaks and planes, sentinel trees planted in the early days of the last century for the dream of freedom that had not died here, just slept a while. Then he remembered *why*. "We should probably do something about that, yeah?" He paused. "Not that you'll *ever* hear me complain about kissing you in public."

"You know what? I think you knew you would be, someday."

"I *hoped*," he replied, laughing. "I didn't know." He paused. "Okay, yeah, maybe I did know."

And now we were *both* laughing.

"Let's stay here," I proclaimed. "We're not doing anything we have to hide. Well." Now in his ear, my whisper. Soft. Hot. Cunning. Bold. A promise kept, a promise coming. "Not yet."

⸻

Oh, wait, you were expecting an epilogue? Whoops!

Just kidding, I gotchu. When you visit everlyclaire.-com/storm-tested or scan the QR code, you can subscribe to my newsletter and get a link to download *Storm Tested: An Unchained Story,* an entire 31,000-word epilogue NOVELLA, which sees Lou and Shai (doesn't that feel good to say?) off on a brand new adventure. And this is not your standard feel-good epilogue: just because they're technically on vacation doesn't mean there won't be angst, trauma, captivity, and chains! But there are spicy and sweet moments, too, of course.

I'll also take this opportunity to remind you that I have signed paperbacks of *Never Lost* (and all the other books in the series, plus additional merch) for sale on my Etsy shop at etsy.com/shop/everlyclaireauthor. For the same price as Amazon, you can get a signed bookplate and a beautiful vellum overlay with character art with your book. Now that you trust me to (finally!) give you a happily ever after, why not buy direct and complete (or start!) your collection?

And lastly, while Lou and Shai's story may have come to an end, The Unchained series will continue. Subscribe to my newsletter or follow me on social to learn the details before anyone else, along with behind the scenes peeks, beta and ARC opportunities, giveaways, and the knowledge that you're a member of the Internet's biggest community (as far as I know!) for readers who love their book boyfriends wounded, protective, and chained.

Prost,

Everly

ABOUT THE AUTHOR

Everly Claire is a full-time writer living on a palm-fringed, white-sand beach on a Caribbean island (really, you should try it!) with her partner and a couple of cats. When she's not writing, she spends her time on a boat or a beach (always with a fruity cocktail in hand), getting nerdy (and kicking ass!) at trivia night, and/or dreaming up more hot scenarios and dark twists involving protective, wounded, witty men you aren't allowed to touch (but we all know you will, anyway).

If you liked this book, a review is the single most powerful thing you can do to support me, whether it's on Amazon, Goodreads, or your social media platform of choice. You can find all my links by scanning the QR code or by visiting linktr.ee/everlyclaire. I love to chat, so don't be shy to connect!

instagram.com/everlyclaireauthor
facebook.com/everly.claire.author
tiktok.com/@everly_claire

ACKNOWLEDGMENTS

Well, it's really over, y'all. What a ride.

First, if you're reading this, thank you. You're the reason why this book exists. I am so honored and thrilled you chose to go on this journey with me, Lou, and Shai. I could not do this without you. You've carried me through self-doubt, dark nights of the soul, and the decision to rebrand, and you're the reason these characters and this world still lives. And I'm looking forward to creating stories for you for a long time to come.

Nigel, my partner in so many things. I'll be home soon. Can't wait to start our life together. Love you lots.

My PA and proofreader, Bri. Where do I start? Thank you for giving me an extra hand, an extra brain, and more hours in the day.

My content creator, Gia. You're amazing and it's been so fun to grow with you.

My Book 3 beta team, Abby, Adele, Annie, Bex, Crystal, Ember, Jamie, Jessica, Luna, Lyndsay, Ritika, Sara, and Shelby, were willing to jump right in, critique where it was needed, and provide me with enough encouragement and feral reactions to give me the confidence to take this last dark, emotionally intense chapter to the wider world.

My talented editor, Emily A. Lawrence, who spent way too much time fixing em dashes, preserved my voice perfectly, and got invested in the story even though it wasn't part of her job description.

My gifted cover designers, Najla Qamber and Nada Qamber.

My marketing team: Jane at Torchlit Ink, Layla at Bound to Love, and Shannon at R&R.

My Rule Breakers street team, now a hundred strong, who have become great friends and never hesitate to hype me up everywhere they can.

My ARC team—hundreds of you, too many to name, both new and those who've been with me from the start.

Mom, Dad, David, Rachel, and Nora. I love you and I'll see you soon. Happy 70th, Mom!

www.ingramcontent.com/pod-product-compliance
Lightning Source LLC
Chambersburg PA
CBHW030333120726
47901CB00007B/1781